The RPG Apocalypse 2

Jeremy Chambless

Published by Level Up in the United Kingdom in 2022

Cover illustration by Sippakorn Upama
Cover by Claire Wood

ISBN: 978-1-83919-390-3

www.levelup.pub

Jeremy Chambless was born in Deerfield Beach, Florida and studied Psychology at Florida Atlantic University. Gaming has always been a part of his household: as far back as he can remember, he was holding a NES controller. His own gaming passion has been focused on MMOs and RPGs. Jeremy is an avid LitRPG reader turned writer. A love for RPGs sparked his desire to create *The RPG Apocalypse*.

Chapter 1: The 'Expert'

"Shall we take a look around?" Aaron, my friend and oldest companion in this world, asked this question. Beside me, in her white healer's gown, Isabelle nodded like a happy child and I'm sure I did the same.

My friends and I were strangers in North Maledith. For all the conversations I'd had about the city, the practical information available to me was next to nil. This was a completely foreign land to the three of us. I knew the circumstances were different, but this felt almost the same as when I had been thrown into Elesham.

With surprising confidence, Aaron led us through the bustling crowds and into a narrow alleyway. Both sides of the alleyway were filled with merchant stalls. There wasn't enough walking space for more than a few people at a time to squeeze through the groups gathered around them. I felt claustrophobic while Isabelle and I followed Aaron in single file.

The difference between Egestor and Cape Tou was like night and day. Here, every stall was manned by an Adventurer wearing flashy clothing and equipment. The goods on their countertops were flowing with mana. The mana in the air was so thick I could feel it streaming past me.

My excitement tapered off, however, as I managed to get glimpses of price cards. Nothing was cheap. Even the lowest priced item was going to cost me 20,000 Zeny. I pushed the thought of buying anything to the back of my mind and simply enjoyed the scenery.

Aaron continued to peer back and forth from stall to stall. It seemed as though he was searching for something in particular. I wanted to ask him what he was looking for, but decided against it. I would have to force my way past Isabelle or shout at the top of my lungs for him to hear me.

We eventually stopped at an inconspicuous stall. There was a chubby gentleman sitting on a dirty rug behind it. Nothing about him looked extraordinary: his hair was brown and disheveled; his once expensive clothing was now mostly worn through. It didn't seem like he was an experienced Adventurer at all. In front of him were a few shabby-looking items.

"I need some information, maybe you can help me?" Aaron asked.

The man widened his eyes and sized up Aaron, "Maybe, it depends on what you need." There was something alluring, even mysterious about the way he spoke.

"I need a map of the local area, as detailed as possible."

The man pulled something from his coat and started to unfold it. He held it out towards Aaron before jerking it quickly back. "Zeny first."

I marveled at Aaron's ability to pick out such a reclusive expert in this back-alley mess.

"How much?"

The man held up two fingers and then calmly closed his eyes, as if the entire world was in his grasp. Aaron didn't respond. He chose to stare at the merchant in silence instead of arguing. Was there a mental battle going on between them I couldn't see? I made a note to try this silent technique myself someday.

The chubby man coughed and opened one eye to peer at Aaron. He held out his hand again and then showed one finger instead.

"Ten thousand Zeny?" Aaron asked.

"Yes."

Aaron started to rub his chin in deep thought. His attitude made you wonder whether buying this map was a life-altering decision. The silence between the two was starting to make me feel uncomfortable. I noticed the chubby man started to fidget. There was a growing crease along his forehead.

"Alright, eight thousand Zeny," the stall owner blurted out.

"We'll take it!" said Aaron with enthusiasm.

"Ha… ha, I was feeling generous today." Chubby wiped the sweat off his brow and then reluctantly handed over the map.

Aaron quickly stored his purchase in his shirt and then dragged us out of the alleyway into a wider street. I was amazed that he'd identified someone whose goods we could afford.

I was now able to stand side by side with Aaron. "How did you manage to pick that guy out of all the stalls we passed?" I asked excitedly.

"What do you mean?"

"We walked by at least twenty stalls. Yet you spotted someone with the information we needed and even managed to get the upper hand in a deal with an expert mapmaker." I had no reservations in praising my friend.

Aaron started to grin. He put one hand on my shoulder while the other covered his mouth to hide the smile. "That man was not an expert mapmaker."

"Then why did you pick him out?"

"Everyone else was rich, that man… was poor. I figured we might be able to afford whatever he had. Simple as that."

I thought back to the stall owner's dirty looking rug and the treasures that lacked mana. My face started to feel hot. I heard Isabelle's snickering and turned in her direction.

I must have been frowning, because she froze like a deer in headlights. She also put her hand against her mouth and then turned away from me. She was still amused by my thinking Aaron had mystical powers in the marketplace and that the vendor was an expert rather than simply desperately poor. I heard her cackling softly.

I gave a loud cough before turning back to Aaron. "Let's take a look at the map." I nudged him with my elbow.

He sobered up at once and then started to unfurl the soft leather. Isabelle joined us. She was still grinning and gave me a wink.

The map was surprisingly useful for only being 8,000 Zeny. All of the leveling areas and dungeons around Cape Tou were clearly marked. There was even a small amount of detailed information about the types of monsters that were found in each area and their level range.

The entire infrastructure of Cape Tou was recorded there as well. There was a building called the 'Party Hall'. It was something I had never seen or heard of before though Aaron reckoned the purpose of the room was easy to infer.

"Let's head there first and see if we can find a tank and another DPS. After that we can find lodging for the night and go from there." Aaron had a solid plan.

The Party Hall was the only professional looking building in all of Cape Tou. While the rest were built of timber and clay and looked like beach huts and sandcastles, the Party Hall was a solid stone. We squeezed our way inside a busy entrance and found a clerk.

To my surprise, the clerk was also an Adventurer. I thought about what Lady Briele said and wondered if the clerk was stuck here after getting in way over his head. He passed us a book, "All the tanks we currently have registered are on pages ten to twelve. Melee damage can be found on pages three to six."

Aaron took the book and started to flip pages. "How does this work exactly?" he asked while scanning each entry.

"Adventurers who register with us typically come daily to see if anyone has requested to work with them. We're too small to chase them around."

Aaron kept his face buried in the book. He flipped page after page before holding it up and showing us. "What do you think?"

The page described a tank, a level twenty Swordsman who had registered a few days ago. There was a chance he was a new arrival to Cape Tou, just like we were. We were similar in level and circumstance. I thought it was a good pick.

"Sounds good," said Isabelle and I agreed.

"Can you get in touch with this person?" Aaron asked.

The clerk pulled out a notepad and wrote the name down, "Got it." We also picked out two possible melee DPS. "Come back tomorrow around mid-day. If they come in before then I'll let them know and hopefully you can meet them tomorrow."

"Do you know where we can find lodging?" Aaron asked. This place was similar to Elesham. It was small but packed with people and we didn't want to end up on the streets.

"I didn't want to assume but, you all are new to Cape Tou?" the clerk asked.

"Yes, arrived early this morning."

"You shouldn't have any trouble finding a room. Most Adventurers don't come back once they head out."

"They don't come back?"

"Sorry, that sounded terrible. Most Adventurers don't stay here long. They typically move towards the bigger cities." He paused. "If you're still worried about finding a place then head two blocks over and look for an inn called Broken Sword. My buddy Xander runs it. Tell him Guillaume sent you and maybe he'll give you a discount."

We ended up doing just that. In fact, Xander was incredibly happy to see us. There wasn't a single customer besides us interested in a room. We called it a day and decided to relax till morning. Our conversation was desultory; it was pointless discussing future plans just before recruiting two new party members.

The following day, we ended up returning to the Party Hall just after a late lunch. Guillame greeted us and let us know he had managed to get into contact with the tank and one of the melee DPS. He suggested we hang out for a bit, as they were planning to show up within the hour.

He sat us off to the side at our own separate table and allowed us to wait there.

"I'm excited," I said. I couldn't lie. I was still having weird dreams from our encounter with the Female Thief Bug. I wanted a tank in the party more than anyone.

I had started to daydream when I heard Aaron's voice, "It's you?"

"Not you?" The voice was familiar. I turned my head and saw the chubby stall owner standing over us. He looked back over his shoulder at Guillame before coming to a realization. "Don't tell me…" His face soured.

Isabelle, on the far side of the man, leaned her head around his large body so as to catch my eye, "Is Mr. Expert Mapmaker the tank?" she asked sweetly. I nearly started choking. She was a demon in human clothing.

"Uhh…" Guillame asked from his desk. He had no idea what was going on. "Have you met before?" He scratched his head awkwardly.

"Yeah, this is fine." Aaron turned his attention back to the prospective tank. "Come sit down." Aaron had thick skin. And the former merchant didn't even seem embarrassed that we were mocking him.

"I'll leave you guys to it then." Guillame skillfully excused himself.

Chubby came around the table then sat down, although reluctantly. There was a hint of annoyance on his face. I could see he was definitely tempted to just turn around and walk away. Probably though, he desperately needed Zeny and this was his first chance to group.

"Did you like the map?" he sounded scornful.

"I have to say it's a very good map. It was a very good price too," Aaron responded.

For a moment, Chubby didn't have a retort. "I'm willing to look past the fact you took advantage of my desperate situation." Chubby forced out a broken smile.

"That's good. I'm Aaron, an archer. This is Isabelle, our acolyte. This is Joseph, our mage." He introduced each of us.

"Steven. You already know I'm a tank." The smile on his face was still twitching. He was obviously trying his best to keep his voice friendly and calm.

"Do you mind if we see your equipment before we make a decision?" I asked. Gear was incredibly important for a tank, arguably more important than for any other class.

Steven began pulling items from his inventory and before long the tabletop was full of gear. He gained a bit of confidence back after seeing our stunned reactions.

Aaron started passing item after item to each of us until we had looked over everything. My attention shifted towards the most important pieces for any tank: chest, weapon, and shield.

> ### STURDY CHAINMAIL*: STR +2, VIT +5
> A CHAINMAIL OF FINE CRAFTSMANSHIP. ITS LINKS HOLD STRONG UNDER ANY ATTACK.

> ### DUELIST'S BLADE*: STR +3, VIT+1, AGI +3
> YOUR OPPONENT WILL ALWAYS FEEL YOUR OPPOSITION.

> ### BLADE BARRIER**: STR +1, VIT +6, AGI -2
> ITS WEIGHT ENCUMBERS YOU; ITS STRENGTH PROTECTS YOU.

"Is this why you're so poor?" our archer asked. I was curious as well. Steven's gear was quite good. I had absolutely nothing to complain about, especially the most important pieces. Isabelle agreed with her eyes.

Steven nodded. "Yes, I'm poor because I recently obtained new equipment. The Zeppelin ride also took a chunk of my savings."

"You came from Eastrath?" I asked.

"Yeah, I've been in Cape Tou for about two weeks. But no one wants to take me as a tank because I'm large."

It certainly was unusual for an Adventurer to be overweight. It wasn't a good look when you were forced to move and battle so much. It meant Steven was inactive and probably therefore inexperienced.

"I don't see a problem with it. You're well geared at the very least." Aaron paused for a moment before turning to us, "What do you all think?"

"I think it's a good idea." I couldn't be sure if my desire for a new tank was clouding my judgment, but I went with the evidence of the gear.

"Me too," Isabelle said.

"Welcome to the team," Aaron said. The smile on Steven's face was no longer forced or broken. He was genuinely happy. He started to scoop up his equipment back up from the table. "Can you stick around a bit longer? We're meeting with a melee DPS. Since they'll be fighting alongside you; I think you should have a say in who we recruit." Aaron interrupted Steven's departure.

"Oh?" Steven seemed surprised to be getting so much consideration. There was a new expression on his face as he regarded Aaron: friendliness. "Sure, I don't have anything planned."

Chapter 2: The Thief

We sat around the table for what felt like thirty minutes. The topic slowly evolved towards Egester and eventually to Steven's origins.

"I'm from a small city called Shamont. It's way north in the mountains of Eastrath."

"Was it snowy all the time?" Isabelle asked.

"Mostly yeah, I still can't get used to how hot it is here." He wiped his brow. His whole body was drenched in a thick layer of sweat. His weight definitely didn't help him there.

"Did you live there your whole life?" Aaron asked.

"Yeah, my first cousin married into the royal family so I got some decent gear, made it a good place to live and level up."

I looked across at Aaron and he nodded his head. I had been under the impression that residents of Yetera weren't able to level. It was an unsubstantiated assumption though. And I couldn't pursue it, as we never revealed the fact we came from another world.

I wasn't sure why I had been under that impression. Maybe because I couldn't fathom anyone who had the alternative of leveling choosing to be poor, or living as a merchant, or just being a regular citizen: leveling was fun and battles gave me intense experiences like nothing I'd ever felt on Earth.

Steven was born here. A natural resident who could also level up and acquire skills. What were we though? What was the purpose of sending us here? There was no way to answer without revealing our own origins. It was impossible to know what reaction we would receive if that information was revealed.

The hostility Steven had previously shown towards Aaron swiftly disappeared. His royal background was the reason for his ego and 'elusive' attitude. I told myself that his aloof manner might also have been the reason I mistook him for someone important when I first saw him in the alleyway.

"Excuse me," Guillaume interrupted our conversation. "Your other appointment has arrived. Shall I send them in?"

"Yes, thank you," I answered.

The official returned a moment later with a figure following behind him. I couldn't make them out until he moved out of the way.

It was a woman around our age. She cupped her hands in front of her and tilted her head downwards. Her eyes darted everywhere around the room but refused to look directly at us.

Her hair was golden blonde and a bit more than shoulder length. She was small, even for a girl. She looked fragile, like a gust of wind would cause her to fall over and be blown across the floor.

"Hello, why don't you come and sit down?" Aaron said.

"Ah, uhm." The woman mumbled and looked around as if asking approval from an authority. Guillaume simply nodded at her and then disappeared.

"Nice to meet you. I'm Aaron, the group's archer. This is Isabelle our acolyte. This is Joseph our mage, and this is Steven our tank," Aaron pointed each of us out.

"Nice to meet you. My name is… Kimmi." She was soft spoken. "Oh, I'm a thief."

"Can we see your equipment?" Aaron asked.

Apologetically and hesitantly, she started to put her gear on the table. I glanced over everything briefly but focused my attention on what I considered the most important for a melee damage dealer.

> ### SERPENT'S FANG: AGI +3, VIT +3
> #### THE FANG OF A VENOMOUS SNAKE. ITS SHARP TIP DRIPS A POISONOUS LIQUID.

> ### SCALPEL: AGI +5, STR +2
> #### THE BLADE IS INCREDIBLY SHARP. GOOD FOR MAKING PRECISE CUTS.

I noticed Steven looking at her with big, star-struck eyes. I shook my head and realized that if it was up to him, this was probably going to be our new thief. I wasn't sure what people found interesting about this type of overly demure behavior, but it just wasn't for me.

"This is all of it," she muttered. She was definitely missing some miscellaneous magic items, like potions, and the overall quality wasn't as good as Steven's, but she did have two nice weapons. It was passable.

"What does everyone think?" asked Aaron.

"Definitely, very definitely," Steven blurted out.

Isabelle nodded. "I'm okay with it."

I hesitated for a moment, "I guess."

"Alright, that's settled. Welcome to the party," Aaron announced.

It seemed I was the only one having doubts about Kimmi joining. I was worried she would run away from monsters and cause problems. She was level twenty-one though, so if we chose our encounters carefully, it shouldn't get to that point.

"Since everyone is here we should talk about our next steps." Aaron unfurled Steven's map over the table and we bunched up. "We should decide on our next destination."

"Arturii is the place to be… but..." Steven paused.

"Why Arturii?" Aaron asked.

"It's basically the central hub of North Maledith. All the biggest guilds' main bases are there."

We all took a minute to look at the map.

"If it's the central hub then shouldn't it actually be more around the middle of the continent?" I asked.

Steven looked at us like we were aliens. "The monster levels start to climb really quickly when you head west. Arturii has a great balance." He spun the map around and took control. "Look right here," he pointed. "This is Tanyros." It was a small city, south west of us in the opposite direction to Arturii. "Look at the average level range of monsters there, and then look at Cape Tou."

The level range of mobs around Cape Tou was mostly 18-23. Tanyros was just a bit west and the level range went from 26-32. The distance was probably only a day or two of traveling.

"And now compare that to Arturii." Arturii was north and a bit more west. "The west exit of Arturii has the level range of monsters at thirty-seven to forty-six. If you walk only another day west that jumps to almost sixty-five."

He was right. The west side of Arturii was 37 to 46 and the east side was just 25 to 36. The level ranges were incredibly accommodating for new and mid-level Adventurers.

"So what's the issue?" Isabelle asked. "Can't we just make Arturii our destination then?"

13

Everyone turned to Steven for the answer.

"Well, that's what I originally wanted to bring up." he paused, "the Adventurers' Guild has been sending out notices for over a month now."

"Notices about what?"

"Missing parties. Whenever a party takes a mission and departs, the Adventurers' Guild keeps track. If you fail the mission; if you complete the mission; or if you just don't return—that sort of thing. They keep it for ranks."

"So what exactly is going on then?" I asked.

"Parties have been taking missions out of Arturii and disappearing. It's not uncommon for parties to wander too far or get lost and end up wiped out. The issue is that it's happening a lot—way too much. Even worse is the Adventurers' Guild hasn't given a reason. The fact they don't know says a lot about it."

I knew Aaron, Isabelle and I were all thinking the same thing, so I asked, "What's the Adventurers' Guild?"

"Are you from a different planet or something?" Steven asked. "The Adventurers' Guild is run by all the top guilds jointly." He paused. "Wait… are you not registered?"

I looked at Aaron and Isabelle for an answer but they had none, "No, we're not registered."

"We should get you registered then. Cape Tou is too small for them to have a building here but they'll have at least a single representative we can get you recorded at."

"Any special requirements?" Aaron asked.

"You just have to pay five thousand Zeny and provide all your details."

"And what are the benefits?" Isabelle asked. She liked holding onto her Zeny.

"The Adventurers' Guild runs pretty much everything…" Steven paused. "Eastrath doesn't have enough Adventurers to warrant something with full continental presence like the Adventurers' Guild. Most cities run their own mission halls and that's it. The Adventurers' Guild… is like a mission hall for all of North Maledith. Does that make sense?"

It actually did make sense. It was called the Adventurers' Guild but it sounded more like the ruling council of North Maledith. If all the top guilds had members seated on an organization that ran all the Adventurers, who else could hope to rule?

Steven was proving himself to be incredibly knowledgeable.

"So how do you know all of this? You just arrived here recently," I asked.

"Mostly from retired Adventurers. When they move back to Eastrath they always find a royal family to attach themselves to. It's a mutual relationship. They enjoy luxury while the royal family borrows their influence and abilities." I nodded and he continued. "I heard stories as a kid up until my late teens."

"Let's talk about registration tomorrow. We should go back to discussing our route and destination." Aaron steered us back on track. "What do you think our options are?" He looked to Steven. This is why I liked Aaron as a leader. It didn't hurt his pride to take advice from anyone, especially when he was the less knowledgeable one.

"We can head south and travel to Tanyros. There's a famous area called the Elysian Fields on the way. We can travel through there and then work out of Tanyros for the time being."

"…I heard that place is bad news." Kimmi mumbled out while twiddling her thumbs.

"What's wrong with it?"

"The enemies aren't... they aren't always the same." Her timidity was hindering her from communicating effectively. I was getting a tad bit annoyed.

"Ahem, it's only a little weird," Steven said. We all looked at him suspiciously. "Alright, it's very weird. People gave the Elysian Fields a nickname—"

"—the Land of Fallen Heroes," Kimmi said.

"Yes, the Land of Fallen Heroes. There are no monsters there to fight, but there's a peculiar phenomenon that happens sometimes. No one knows why, but occasionally you run into the ghosts of Adventurers."

"Like real ghosts?" I felt Isabelle grab the hem of my robe.

"Yeah... the issue is that every encounter is... random." He paused. "The Elysian Fields have been around for hundreds of years already. The amount of people that have perished there are uncountable. Most are lower level than us, but there have been outliers."

"Like?"

"There have been reports of level seventy-plus ghosts appearing."

"So you just die then? NEXXXTTTT." Isabelle blurted out. Clearly, she wanted nothing to do with it.

"No, no, no, that's what's so peculiar about the Elysian Fields. Each ghost has a different temperament. Some will fight you to the death. Some will just ignore your existence. There have been reports of ghosts asking for favors and even giving massive rewards."

"Okay, scratch that for now. What about a route directly to Arturii?" Aaron asked.

"Well, we can visit the Magma Caves and the Marsh Pond on the way to Arturii if we go that way. The only issue is we aren't quite high enough level yet."

"What level are they?"

"Twenty-five minimum. We MIGHT be able to handle it but it wouldn't be easy by any means. Also, if the little lady doesn't wish to visit the Elysian Fields we can take a detour around it to get to Tanyros."

Shaking her head, Isabelle made a face at Steven in response to that 'little lady' comment.

"How many days?" Aaron asked.

"Only a day detour to avoid it. Oh, I forgot to mention one thing. Tanyros is a great starting location. It will delay our travel to Arturii but it isn't without benefits."

"Are you suggesting something else is there besides levels?" I asked.

"Tanyros is popular among lower level Adventurers because good Zeny can be made there. There's a gem mine located south of the city. The majority of what you find is cosmetic but you can also find valuable gems for crafting."

I couldn't help but think about the glowing gem that dropped off the Golden Thief Bug, "Like rainbow colored ones?" I asked.

"No—wait. You've seen a Rainbow Facet?" Steven asked excitedly.

"Uhh, maybe." I couldn't be sure if that was what it was called. "What is it?"

"You can add sockets to gear and place Rainbow Facets in them. Depending on their properties they give benefits to all sorts of classes. They are extremely rare, and expensive."

"Can we find them in the Tanyros mines?" Aaron asked.

"Absolutely not." He shook his head. "Rainbow Facets only drop from boss monsters. The rare gems you find in the Tanyros mines are simply for enchanting or gemcutting. I say that, but even enchanting gear can be expensive and not a tradeskill every Adventurer can enjoy."

Isabelle seemed to warm up to the idea once Zeny was on the table, "So about how much can you make in these mines? I'm not saying I want to go… just hypothetically."

"Well… it's all based on luck but… The cosmetic gems range from five hundred to five thousand Zeny depending on how good they look."

"And what about the enchanting and gemcutting materials?"

"Ten thousand to a hundred thousand Zeny."

"Such a large variance?"

"Yeah, the stone determines the potential enchantment. Obviously, not every enchantment is as valuable as the top ones," Steven answered. I could see that.

It seemed to me that delaying our visit to Arturii for a detour to the mines was a good idea. "What do we need to if we want to visit the Tanyros mines?"

"We can do the mining ourselves, but I recommend we hire helpers. Despite it being relatively safe you don't want to go down alone. Those that can't find a party to go with typically sell their labor."

"Hired workers?"

"Yeah, we pay them a flat amount per day or a cut of the profits, depending on what we negotiate. They carry the supplies and do the work. All we need to do is protect them while they do so."

"So there are monsters in the mines," Aaron observed.

"Well, yeah. It's called the Tanyros mines but it's still a dungeon."

The prospect of making money and leveling at the same time was too exciting to pass up. It seemed from their faces that everyone else welcomed the idea.

"Let's take a vote," Aaron said. "Raise your hand if you want to go." Steven, Isabelle and I raised our hands immediately. There was some hesitation from Kimmi before she raised her hand. Aaron was the last one. Not because he wasn't decided but probably because he had reserved his judgment until the rest of us voted.

"Seems we're all in favor," Aaron said. "What gear do you think we need to prioritize?" He looked at Steven.

"Most of what we need can be bought in Tanyros. For now we should secure some camping equipment and the necessary food. It's around four days from here if we skirt around the Elysian Fields."

Guillaume suddenly came back and interrupted us, "I'm sorry but the next group needs to use the room. Is it possible you can take your business elsewhere?"

"Oh, sorry," I apologized. We weren't exactly using it for Party Hall matters anymore. Our party was now organized and full.

"Thanks for your help, Guillaume," Aaron said. We all got up and took to the streets.

"Let's talk while we head to the Adventurer's Hall representative. I think he's at the north entrance. Do you each have five thousand Zeny?" Steven asked. I nodded my head in response and the others did too. The free trip provided by Lady Briele had really saved our time and wallets.

"How soon do you think we can leave?" Aaron asked.

"We can leave by tomorrow. It shouldn't be hard to find what we need in the remaining daylight hours."

"We haven't been here long," Aaron said.

Steven was a different man to the desperate one we had met. He was full of confidence now. "I know some people. As long as we have the Zeny I can secure our food and equipment."

Cape Tou wasn't large by any means. It was a short, five-minute walk to the hall.

"Hi there, I'd like to get my three friends registered," Steven introduced us.

"I need your names, level, and class." The guy at the desk inside the guild entrance was curt in his response. Aaron approached first followed by Isabelle and then me. It seemed Kimmi had already taken care of her membership before now.

Even after providing our details, we weren't registered. The clerk needed to send the information to Adventurer's headquarters in Arturii. Only after that would there be some record of us. That information would be sent out and then all the cities on North Maledith would have our information. It was one big network that connected the majority of the continent.

After leaving the building, Steven counted off the gear we'd need on his fingers. "I know where to get it all," he said.

"Do you need us to go with you?" Aaron asked.

"No need. Give me five thousand Zeny each and I'll gather what we need. Pay for another night at the Broken Sword for me. I'll be a few hours."

We each passed Steven the Zeny and he disappeared into the crowds.

On the way back to Broken Sword we passed an absolutely bustling tavern, "Shall we have dinner?" Aaron asked.

"I'm a bit hungry," I answered. It seemed everyone else felt the same. We were placed at a small little table off in the corner. Inside, the tavern was so loud it was hard to hear our own thoughts. There must have been over a hundred rowdy Adventurers present, drinking and laughing.

"Kimmi, where are you from?" Isabelle yelled through the noise.

"Ah, uhm… from a little place called Cury on Eastrath." She paused. "You've probably never heard of it before…"

"What's it like?" Aaron asked.

"It was a fishing village." She used the word 'was' instead of 'is'. Isabelle didn't seem to notice.

"So you were a fisherwoman growing up?" Isabelle asked. She seemed interested in that aspect.

"Well… no, I wasn't. My pops was a fisherman. I just helped my mom around the house."

"Do you have any sibli—"

"How come you used the word 'was' for Cury?" I cut Isabelle off, feeling there was a lot more to the story that wasn't going to get asked if I didn't speak up.

Kimmi first answered Isabelle, "I was an only child." Then she turned to me, "My hometown doesn't exist anymore."

"What happened?"

"When I was thirteen bandits raided the entire village before burning it down." She talked as if there was no emotional aspect to the story. It was a sort of cold speech that made me think she was repressing her feelings about the situation. As if the village being raided and burned down was a fact that had nothing to do with her.

"I was playing in one of the nearby fields when the raid happened. I had no idea there was even a problem until I smelled the burning. At first I thought the villagers were having a barbecue. But the smell of smoke grew deeper. It wasn't the typical light and pleasant smell. The smoke was thick and dark and filled the sky."

"Did you know where your parents were during all of this? Did you find them?" Isabelle asked.

"I don't know. They were at home I think. When I realized something was wrong, I rushed home. The village was burning all over. People were running and screaming, only to be chopped down by machetes and swords. I froze." She paused and everyone waited in silence for her to continue.

"I was scared. I didn't see my parents anywhere. The area my house was in was fully engulfed in flames and the smoke billowed into the sky. I just ran away and didn't look back. I didn't know what else I could do."

"There was a city we would regularly trade with nearby. I remembered going there with my father a couple times while growing up. I convinced myself I knew the way. Maybe it was to comfort myself, to assure myself running was the best option, that I would be okay if I fled.

"Long story short… I had no idea where the city was. I got terribly lost. I wandered alone for two weeks. Luckily it was the rainy season and I had water. I was hungry but managed to survive off the little plant life I was familiar with. Eventually a merchant found me."

"So a merchant found you and took you in then?" Isabelle asked. "Did you live with them since you were thirteen?"

"No, they didn't take me in. In fact, they treated me like a burden and simply dumped me off. I've been homeless since I was thirteen and for a while lived off the scraps from taverns just like this one. When I was sixteen, I managed to join Adventurer groups as hired help. I slowly built up a foundation of EXP and at eighteen was high enough level to join those groups as a member."

Her story sounded like something out of a movie, a dark movie. My negative feelings towards her from earlier slowly melted away. What I couldn't understand was her shy temperament. How could someone who had to fend for themselves since thirteen act in such a way? Shouldn't she be strong? Outgoing? Decisive?

While telling the story, her voice wasn't shaky at all. She came across like a different person while talking about it—completely normal.

"I spent two years climbing the ranks and saving Zeny. I was twenty when I managed to save enough to secure a spot on a zeppelin. That was several months ago."

"That... sounds horrible," Isabelle fumbled out. I was entranced by Kimmi's story, so much so that she had managed drown out the surrounding patrons completely.

"Are you four ready to order? Oh, you don't have menus yet. Sorry, we're pretty busy tonight as you can see. I'll be back in a few moments while you take a look." A waiter passed each of us a pamphlet.

I suddenly didn't feel that hungry after listening to Kimmi's story. Life on Yetera would take getting used to.

"What should we get?" Aaron asked. The names of the food on the menu were meals I'd never heard of before. The three of us were stumped through and through.

"The Roda legs are pretty good..." Kimmi said.

"Roda legs?" Isabelle asked.

"Oh, it's a frog... a big frog... kinda. It tastes sort of like chicken."

"Doesn't sound like much," I said.

"Their legs are bigger than chicken thighs." And that was enough to convince us. We ended up all ordering some Roda legs and fried potatoes for dinner.

Enjoying some decent food and the merry atmosphere, we stayed to talk a bit later than planned. Luckily Broken Sword was still mostly empty and reserving Steven's room went without a hitch.

He arrived several hours after us. "I got everything," he said. "Tomorrow we depart for Tanyros."

Chapter 3: Frog Legs

"Gah, why is it so hot out?" Steven complained. He constantly grabbed at the hem of his shirt and fanned himself. Beads of sweat dripped down his chin and neck. The temperature here was a far cry from that on the beautiful Eastrath continent.

"Does everyone have everything they need?" Aaron asked. We each had a nice camping bag and I checked my own pack. The food, water, and miscellaneous materials were distributed evenly between the five of us.

"Looks good boss." Steven responded.

"Then let's get moving." It was early morning and the sun was rising into the sky. It was only going to get hotter as the day dragged on. The sooner we could get into the nearby forest the faster we would have some shade above our head.

Steven led the front with Kimmi just behind him. Aaron, Isabelle and I fanned out in the back. If anything untoward happened we were already in position to react according to our class roles. I remembered the advice Lady Briele had given to me very clearly.

Traveling on Eastrath had been relatively peaceful. We might expect to encounter a monster here and there but the chance of an encounter was very low. On North Maledith, however, she had warned that peaceful travel was impossible. I took her words as being without exaggeration.

"What should we expect around here?" I asked Steven. He seemed to be the most knowledgeable out of all of us. It was possible Kimmi knew just as much or more, considering the time she had spent here already. She just didn't seem like the talkative type.

"Most monsters are low twenties. They shouldn't be a problem for us at all. Don't worry, nothing will get past me," he boasted. I thought his statement would be true if we put him in a doorway. Nothing would get past for sure then.

Lady Briele hadn't been joking. We hadn't even walked twenty minutes out from Cape Tou before we encountered our first monster. I cast *Inspect*.

GIANT COCONUT CRAB	**LEVEL: 21**	**BEAST**
	WATER	
HP: 4801		**MP: 10**
	STR: 30	
	AGI: 10	
	DEX: 12	
	VIT: 20	
	INT: 3	
ITS CLAWS MAKE UP MORE THAN HALF ITS BODY WEIGHT.		

I wasn't expecting a crustacean, but perhaps it wasn't that surprising considering we weren't far from the coast. Palm trees and coconut trees towered on both sides of our pathway.

The monster was freakishly large and that fact made it look almost alien. Its eyes were beady and dark black. It came all the way up to Steven's thigh in height. The claws were so massive I wouldn't have been surprised if they could chop Steven in half at the waist.

The information from *Inspect* was broadcast to everyone in the party. The crab's brute strength and durability were its strongest point, while it was severely lacking in AGI. Steven pulled out his shield in front of him while Kimmi rushed forward.

"Stay behind at all times. It shouldn't be able to turn very well," Steven said. Kimmi nodded in response and took a roundabout way to positioning herself behind it. "Hey fella, look at me," Steven yelled at it.

This was our first encounter on North Maledith and was also the perfect situation to do something I had been dreaming about. *Ball Lightning*—I wanted to use it so badly in actual combat.

The crab felt the pressure from Kimmi behind and Steven in front. It slashed a claw out towards Steven and pinched, hoping to grab him. There was a cracking like thunder as it met nothing but empty air. I start to cast *Ball Lightning*.

Steven moved forward after the monster's first strike and stabbed out with his sword. It struck the hard carapace and left nothing but a thin white gash. The weapon had not even cracked the shell. It was at that same moment that Kimmi came in from behind and forced both of her daggers into the crab's back.

I was pleased with her reaction. She could read the flow of combat. She struck when the crab had no way to retaliate. Unfortunately, her two daggers were not powerful enough to pierce its shell. An AGI class that focused on maneuverability and not strength would have a hard time damaging this walking tank.

This was my fight to shine in. I wanted to impress my two new teammates. I was a mage. My unspoken promise to them was that while they occupied the monster, while they risked their lives in melee range, I would deal damage.

The ball lightning in my hand was fully formed and electrical snakes arced across the surface. I didn't have the exact distance but

I judged it to the best of my ability. I positioned myself carefully and tossed out the energy of the spell.

Aaron had also nocked a Powershot and sent it flying towards the crab's eyes. The monster's AGI stat wasn't great but its reaction time was stellar. To me, the arrow was merely a flicker. Despite that, the crab's eyes rolled back and a thick film covered them. The Powershot only managed to crack that film but didn't do any real damage to the creature's sight. The beady little eyes rolled forward again.

The crab let out a wet hiss and little bubbles foamed at its mouth. I thought it was maybe using poison but soon realized that wasn't the case. Aaron had just pissed it off.

My ball lightning reached the end of its travel phase and was now in that sweet four-to-ten meter range.

The first arc of electricity shot out and zapped the front left claw of the mob. An area at least a foot wide was immediately scorched black. Its reaction was to back away, and yet Kimmi was directly behind it.

It could have run away, but it wasn't that intelligent. The concept that Steven and Kimmi couldn't really do much damage to it wasn't something its mind could fathom.

The second zap of electricity came out. It was even stronger than the first. The entire left claw was smoking from the two strikes. To my surprise, Kimmi rushed forward again and raised her daggers. I was expecting another failure on her part, but my expectations were wrong. Her two daggers suddenly lit up and then pierced the crab's back.

The crab no longer cared that Steven was in front and Kimmi was behind. It wanted to flee at all costs and started to turn its burly body. Regardless, Steven was faster and managed to position himself in front of its path every time.

By the time *Ball Lightning* had run its course, half of the monster's shell was scorched completely black. Even better was that those areas had been weakened considerably after being burnt. Aaron managed to shoot arrows directly through into the soft flesh beneath and Steven dug his sword deep within too. The crab fell shortly after.

We grouped around the corpse once it had died. Unfortunately, there was no loot.

"What was that skill you used?" I asked Kimmi. It was definitely a skill as her daggers had glowed just before she stabbed down.

"Penetrate," she responded. Well, it had certainly worked exactly as the name suggested it might. There hadn't seemed to be much resistance to her second attack.

This was our first fight as a group and the first bit of EXP I had gained in a long time. Unfortunately, the EXP gain wasn't an impressive number to say the least. It would take quite a while to level off these crabs. On the positive side, the encounter went smoothly. No one ended up hurt at all.

In fact, the ease with which we dispatched the crab had been so smooth that we hadn't learned much at all as a group. This was understandable though. A monster of this caliber was simply cannon fodder. It wasn't always guaranteed we would be fighting just one monster at a time either.

The multiple-mob scenario was something we encountered shortly after.

"Are these Roda?" I asked. There were innumerable chicken-sized frogs blocking our path. There must have been twenty or thirty of them.

They were blue or green with splotches of exotic colors all over. Their large eyes stared in our direction hungrily. I cast *Inspect*.

RODA	LEVEL: 9 BEAST EARTH
HP: 925	MP: 10
	STR: 8
	AGI: 15
	DEX: 5
	VIT: 5
	INT: 5
A CARNIVOROUS RELATIVE OF THE TREE FROG. THEY PREFER TO HUNT IN PACKS.	

Just from looking the stats of one of the Roda it was clear why they hunted in packs. Individually they were incredibly weak. Their strength was in their numbers and twenty or thirty of these frogs could be a terrifying prospect. We didn't have enough bodies fight them all.

"Steven! How do we deal with this?" Aaron called back. It seemed that it had already become a habit for us to consult Steven on first encounters.

"I don't know!" he yelled back. Not great news.

"Kite backwards and stay together!" Aaron made his decision. Kimmi and Steven both retreated as we formed into a tight circle. The Roda hopped in our direction in response. Their tongues occasionally came out of their mouth as if licking their lips.

The direct result of us backing away was that the Roda ended up grouping together somewhat. They were far less spread out than when we had spotted them.

"Protect me for a moment." Aaron said. Isabelle and I knew what was going to happen. Kimmi and Steven looked on expectantly.

Aaron cast *Rain of Arrows* and blotted out a portion of the sky before raining death on the mobs. That single spell had thinned the number of Roda by two-thirds. Only those on the outer flanks weren't riddled with arrow wounds.

I also noticed a peculiar phenomenon. Some of the bodies of the Roda started to sprout vines that entangled them in place. This benefit was pointless since those hit were already dead, but it was an interesting development.

Those Roda on the flanks lucky enough to survive *Rain of Arrows* ignored their dying comrades. It wasn't that these Roda were more intelligent or had any form of plan. They were just focused on attacking us.

This was also when Kimmi showed a completely different side of herself. She brandished both her daggers and rushed to the right to take out mobs from the edge of the pack. It was honestly slightly terrifying to see her impaling and gashing every Roda in her path.

Stunned by the rogue's effectiveness, I didn't even bother to cast. Blood sprayed through the air with each stab and slash of her daggers. Her hands and legs had blood splattered all over them. Even her face was covered in a light drizzle of red.

She fought like a crazed demon, or someone who was releasing incredible, suppressed depths of anger and hatred. If I had seen her lick the blood from her dagger afterwards, I wouldn't have been surprised. Once all our enemies were dispatched, she became that meek little girl again.

"We should save some of this," Kimmi said nonchalantly. It was a reference to the Roda legs. "They are quite good." Her daggers were the perfect weapon to do the butchering so she was tasked with the job.

By the time she had finished hacking away at Roda limbs, Kimmi looked like a beautiful demon. *Is this the same person I felt would flee from battle? It looked more like she would run headfirst into the most deadly battle imaginable instead.*

"You should clean up," I coughed.

"Oh! Right…" she looked down at herself. There was actually so much frog blood that it couldn't have been comfortable. She wet a rag and spent several minutes wiping the blood off her face. My fear that the rogue would abandon us in a tough spot disappeared. The initial mild dislike I had felt for her personality was dwindling as well.

We didn't have many more notable encounters for the rest of the day. It seemed the journey from Cape Tou to Tanyros was a popular one. Since we had departed behind several other Adventurer groups, they were effectively spearheading the journey for us.

We happened upon a well-used campsite just before nightfall. "Feel free to set up camp nearby! The more the merrier!" A man yelled from another party. From the looks of it there was 4 or 5 different groups setting up at the campsite.

He wasn't wrong. The more Adventurers here the safer everyone would be and feel. It was my first night in the wilderness on North Maledith. We found an empty spot just nearby before setting up a little camp of our own.

Steven managed to find the trunk of a fallen palm tree that was mostly dry and brittle. He dragged it towards our selected campfire spot. It worked well as a seat for us to sit on. We huddled around the fire together.

"Shall we have the Roda legs tonight?" Isabelle asked.

"They won't hold long without some salt or frost magic," Steven said. Unfortunately, the only frost magic I knew was *Glacial Spike*. That spell wasn't a reliable or safe way to freeze things. Best scenario: I would mangle the legs with a jutting spike and ruin them.

Kimmi licked her lips, "Let's eat them tonight…" There was a hunger in her voice.

Something, something the blood of your enemies… I shivered just thinking about it. That couldn't be her intention…right? I pushed the grim thought to the back of my mind.

Steven started to take out a supply of seasoning and cooking utensils from his pack. They were utensils that neither Aaron, Isabelle, or I would have bothered to bring. I was grateful that he had done so, though.

Steven was an excellent cook and very soon the smell of our dinner (like roast chicken) wafted through the entire camp. I even managed to catch the glances of hungry eyes from the nearest group. We definitely weren't low on supply for the seasoning… and nor were we short of Roda legs.

"Should we share?" I asked. The hungry stares were becoming more evident. I didn't blame them though, it just smelled that damn good.

"We do have a lot and we won't be able to save them…" Aaron said.

I expected Steven to refuse outright, but instead he was expansive. "Bring them over. See if they have anything they can contribute and we can have a feast tonight!" His response was the exact opposite of my expectations.

The atmosphere instantly became lively. The camps that were originally spread apart and had an invisible barrier between them merged together. Burning logs and spare tinder were moved to the best of everyone's ability and Steven was the head chef.

Our tank sat over the fire sweating while working several pots and pans. It wasn't just Roda legs anymore though. There were hamburger patties being cooked, having been formed out of an unknown meat. Some sort of roast pork was generating delicious scents and there were even wild veggies and herbs. Steven had his hands completely full.

There were loud cheers as soon as the first Roda legs were passed out, "Long live Steven!" was the chant. The entire atmosphere went up another level once alcohol was brought out. There was something so amazing about it all.

The happy cheering and smiles made me feel alive. The positive attitude of the people all around made me feel so great that I couldn't contain my own laughter. Someone passed me a gourd which smelled like it contained a kind of beer.

"Heading to Tanyros as well?" he asked.

I took it but probably looked unsure of myself, "Yeah."

Why the hell not? I took a swig. That was definitely a mistake. The burn in my throat caused me to cough and nearly shoot the alcohol out of my nostrils. It was my first drink ever and it wasn't beer but something much more powerful.

"Haha, careful! It's pretty strong yeah?"

"Haha, yeah." I forced out through the coughing. This was something I would have normally been embarrassed about, but now didn't bother me at all. Instead, it made me laugh even harder. "We're gonna be heading to the mines." I said.

"Us too, maybe we'll run into each other." He held out his hand, "I'm Mark."

"Joseph." I reached back and shook his hand. Right after, I took another swig from the gourd before passing it back to him. Immediately after that, Isabelle brought over a pair of Roda legs and one of the burgers.

"Having fun?" she asked.

I looked at the people ranged around me. Everyone was chatting and laughing happily. The mood was great and the smell of cooked food elevated it even higher. Steven was still hard at work in the center, cooking as if his life depended on it.

One hand held a spatula while the other held a gourd of alcohol. He occasionally dumped the alcohol into the pan and then took a deep swig. Aaron was moving around introducing himself to each group and clearly enjoying himself too.

Aaron was normally so serious. Seeing him crack a smile and break into full laughter was refreshing. There was no doubt in my mind he was still doing his best to gather information during all of this. Even Kimmi had livened up a bit.

I took the two meals from Isabelle before finding a seat off to the side. I patted the spot next to me while beckoning Isabelle over. We sat down off to the side where there was a bit less noise. I grabbed my first Roda leg and bit in.

I had to admit it was even better than when we'd eaten Roda in the Tavern. Steven definitely had a gift for cooking good food, definitely for enjoying it too. "Things are gonna be okay," I said. This was the first time I truly felt that.

Optimism was a façade I presented to everyone. Deep down though, I never could shake a feeling of being in over my head. The sense I was an imposter was always looming and waiting to poke its nasty head up and scowl at me. In this moment, however, I felt so much better.

"Yeah," Isabelle said. I could tell her voice was a little shaky. It was a bit hard to see in the darkness if she was crying or not. I did though see her arm raise and wipe one of her eyes.

Perhaps it was the alcohol or my general feeling of hope, but I did something I'd never had the courage to do before. I put my arm around her shoulder and pulled her in close. This action wasn't made in a romantic way at all. Isabelle was beautiful, no doubt. She was more like a sister to me, though.

Given the circumstances, I had never thought about romance. There simply wasn't time. And this wasn't my intention at all. A part of me expected to be slapped or pushed away in rejection. Instead, our healer leaned in and let her head rest on my shoulder, her chestnut hair covering her face.

"I don't know when, but, one day… We'll figure out what happened." I paused. "I promise." That was my goal now. Why were we thrown into this world? Were my parents still alive? Was my brother still alive? There were so many questions to answer.

Isabelle sniffled and I felt her nod her head slightly. I didn't open my mouth to inquire what the specific problem was. There were just too many to cover. We had been suddenly thrown into a life-or-death situation and forced to survive. On top of that we were facing into a new world. There were enough problems we could go over them with a psychiatrist for ten years.

We sat in silence for several minutes before she stopped sniffling and seemed to have come to grips with whatever was bothering her.

"I'll keep you to that promise," she said.

"Count on it," I replied. "Let's get back to it." The party was still in full swing and people were getting even more rowdy. I went to Steven's side to see if I could give him a bit of relief from the cooking.

Instead of the heartfelt gratitude I was expecting, Steven simply shooed me away. It seemed he considered cooking sacred and wouldn't allow anyone to interfere. I could see a passion in his eyes as he marinated and seasoned every piece of meat.

As I moved around the camp and found myself being passed more and more of the alcoholic drink, the night slowly became a blur. At some point, having lost track of time, I fell asleep.

Chapter 4: Forest Troll

Aaron woke me the next morning. Those who hadn't drunk so much were waking their comrades from a stupor and taking down the camps. I had passed out on the ground and my head had been resting against a log.

I felt something warm and squishy under my arm and turned to see Steven cuddling up against me. I did my best to pull my arm from under his body. The bottom of my tunic sleeve was caked with dirt and the top was thick with sweat.

I gagged ever so slightly before turning to Aaron. He had a shit-eating grin on his face and was barely able to contain his laughter. I gave him a look that said 'I will hurt you.' It only made him laugh even harder.

We spent fifteen minutes cleaning up and packing everything away. A large portion of the night was a blur to me. There was no doubt I had a great time though. How else would I have ended up sleeping on the floor cuddling Steven if not?

"Any news?" I asked Aaron. Last night had been a party but I knew him well by now and that he had been using the event to gather information.

"Just the obvious, everyone here is heading to Tanyros. Good portion of them heading to the mines."

"Any of them taking a detour?"

"Nope, all of them are heading through the Elysian Fields," he said.

"Are we making a mistake then?" I asked.

"Let's talk about it as we travel."

Each group left in intervals so as to not crowd the group in front of them. There was plenty of room to fight. There was an upside and downside to this though.

The upside was the lack of monster encounters and the downside was the lack of monster encounters. We wouldn't be getting much EXP today. We might not be getting much EXP at all for the remainder of the trip.

This was a thought that normally would have bothered me a lot. I didn't feel that troubled by it now though. I always felt time was racing for me, that I needed to do everything quickly or I would miss my chance.

A part of me had realized last night that I had my entire life ahead of me. Yetera was only the next chapter. I'd take every day as it came. That didn't mean I didn't care about leveling or EXP though. On the contrary, I craved them both greatly. I'd learned a bit of restraint was all.

We didn't start the Elysian Field discussion for about an hour into our trek. The reason being was that Steven was like a walking zombie. I wasn't sure how much he had drunk the previous night, but it must have been a large amount.

"The four groups ahead of us are all going through the Elysian Fields," Aaron said. "With that in mind, should we reconsider it as well? It saves us an entire day of travel."

"I've always been for it," Steven managed a mumble.

I never had an opinion on this in the first place. Originally, Kimmi and Isabelle had been the most against taking any risk. Isabelle was definitely the most vocal one, though. It seemed Kimmi had warmed up to the idea since getting to know the other groups.

It was therefore just Isabelle still against taking the shorter route. Despite it being four-to-one, neither Aaron or I would pull the trigger and go against her wishes. That was always an option, but this issue wasn't so serious that we needed to do so.

If a situation was life threatening then a majority vote would be necessary to come to a decision: I would insist on that in a heartbeat. Here, though, Aaron tried to get a consensus by making a few points in favor of the shorter way.

"I don't know," she said.

"Just think about it for now," I said, "there are still two days till we reach the point where the routes diverge." Maybe she would come around on her own time. She nodded her head at least.

The four groups in front of us took all the available action. Monsters in the area that had any design on attacking us simply faded away into the surroundings. The consequence was safe yet boring travel.

The day dragged on endlessly. The weather on North Maledith was nowhere near as pleasant as Eastrath. The humidity was sky high. I found myself constantly peeling clothing off my skin. It seemed everyone else was doing the same. I looked forward to nightfall.

"Should we stay in Tanyros for a few days or head to the mines immediately?" I asked.

"We stay at most one day to restock anything needed and then leave," Aaron answered.

"I agree, there are a lot of people heading to the mines. We don't want to be left behind." Steven said.

"Will we be able to find a map of the mines?"

"There should be maps of the discovered shafts available for purchase. They're constantly being updated and the mine is constantly being excavated. It shouldn't be a problem."

"How many helpers should we hire?" Isabelle asked.

"If we want to make any reasonable progress and money, we should plan to stay down for a week. I think we should aim for two helpers minimum," Steven said. We were slowly ironing out any kinks in our plan during the downtime.

The sun sank gradually in the sky and darkness started to envelope our path. The groups in front came to a stop and formed together. We arrived after the camp was already setup, it was encouraging to see a spot had been left vacant for us.

Even the fire in the center was prepared and lit. Steven's cooking station was already being prepared for him. I was about to say something about not having any more food to cook when I saw the others hauling it out.

It seemed the groups in front had taken care to acquire dinner on the way. "It looks like it's gonna be another long night," I said.

The chants started before we even finished setting up our own camp, "Steven… Steven… Steven!"

I felt dismayed for him, being put under pressure to cook for everyone, but I laughed it off after seeing his cheerful reaction. He clearly liked the attention and loved to cook.

It didn't take long before a pleasant smell wafted over the entire camp. The temperature dropped to a comfortable level and the four moons high in the sky provided a beautiful backdrop. Again, the night began to blur as I ate and drank.

At some point, I found myself locking arms with Steven and dancing around the campfire. And later, I was chasing Aaron with a fireball after he told several people, including those I didn't know,

41

about the previous night's cuddling with Steven. That and my bold declaration of intending to become a renowned guild leader.

My head ached when I woke the next morning. Somehow Steven was cuddled into my arm again. I felt a bit of déjà vu. I didn't bother to drag my arm from beneath and instead rolled him like a marshmallow. He snorted, before farting in my direction. There was a moment I thought the loud volume of his own fart would wake him.

It seemed I had woken up a bit earlier than normal, as no one was moving around the camp. I stretched before moving into the wilderness to relieve myself. As I neared the camp on my return, I heard a branch crack behind me.

I whipped around, startled only to find Isabelle there.

"Sorry, I didn't mean to startle you," she said.

"Ah, no problem." I walked out from the shrubs "What's up?"

"Not much. I didn't sleep very well and everyone else is still passed out. It just felt a bit too quiet. It's dawn but there is no birdsong."

The grey sky was still very dim and there was a thin layer of fog hovering above the ground. Aaron hadn't even woken yet and he was usually one of the earliest to rise.

"Have you put any thought into the route change?" I asked.

"A little bit."

"We won't force you to, you know that. If you still don't feel comfortable by day's end then we'll take the detour."

"Okay…"

"But there's still something I should tell you. It was something Aaron said to me last night." I could barely remember the conversation to be honest. "The later we arrive the harder it will be for us to find good helpers, especially behinds several groups like this. I know that puts more pressure on you but you deserve to know. We'll all be putting in Zeny to afford the assistance."

"Did he go into specifics?"

"Well, there are a lot of factors. If we come in behind a lot of other groups, helpers will cost more, be lower level, and typically just lower quality. All the good helpers will be snatched up before we arrive. We might get lucky but it's more likely we'll receive the short end of the stick."

"It's that bad?"

"I don't know how bad it will be. Worst case scenario we delay our trip to the mines for a bit until more helpers become available."

"Sorry… I'm causing a lot of trouble."

"If we were back on Earth I'd be a bit more rushed over it. Time was of the essence there and monsters were growing stronger every day. That doesn't seem to be the case here. We aren't as rushed. Don't forget we're all in this together." Her mood seemed to cheer up a bit with my final remarks.

Regardless, she would need to make her decision soon. We would reach the break off point by mid-day. Once we passed that fork in the road there was no turning back. Either we took a left towards the Elysian Fields or we continued straight on past the shortcut.

The camp started to liven up some thirty minutes later. Heads started to poke from tents and people rolled along the ground. I had started packing earlier, before Steven or Kimmi even woke from their slumber.

Steven snored like an angry bear each time I nudged him to wake him. It was even harder to get him up than it was to wake up Richard in the past. Eventually both Aaron and I took turns rolling him back and forth. Only when it was impossible to comfortably return to sleep did he get up.

By then, two groups had already departed and we were fully packed to go. Steven rushed off into the forest for several minutes before returning.

It didn't look like we would be getting any action today either. We were once again the last group to leave. Steven remained a zombie at the front and I spoke with Aaron in more detail about the helper business for the mines.

According to the people he had spoken with, helpers constantly came and went. There were usually plenty waiting for a job. It wasn't often that several groups would come to Tanyros in a convoy like this. Most likely the first few groups would get the best pick.

You didn't necessarily want the highest level assistant or the person offering to work for the cheapest price. STR based classes were best as they mined the most efficiently. They could also carry a lot more weight. A few of them were good cooks too. That wasn't something we needed to worry about with Steven around though.

We had been walking for about three hours and the sun was high in the sky. We came to an abrupt stop as the group in front of us had stopped. The group in front of them had also stopped and there was some commotion ahead.

"Was that a yell?" It sounded as if someone was screaming ahead. It was too far in the distance to make out what was causing the ruckus. The road wasn't just a straight path either.

We were taking twists and turns through a dense forest-like maze. The only way to avoid getting lost was to follow the dirt and gravel road. It was unknown just how long ago this path had been crafted.

The commotion became even more prominent and it seemed the group in front was growing more curious, as were we. We decided to close the distance to them, "Any idea what's going on up there?" Aaron asked as we caught up.

"No clue. We stopped because the group ahead stopped," a woman said. We were on a bend in the road and couldn't see past the next group in front. We would have to walk up a decent ways to see what was stopping them.

I was inclined to do so, expecting a downed tree or an extended battle of some kind. But I hadn't even opened my mouth to say this, before a blood-curdling scream echoed from in front of us. The first yell could have been attributed to many things, this scream, however, was nothing like the first. I could hear the pure fear contained within. The scream continued and rattled through the dense trees before reaching us. Whoever made it was running in our direction. It suddenly came to an abrupt stop.

There was nothing but silence. It was obvious by now something wasn't right. The group further down the path were backing up slowly, coming closer to us. They were looking at something in utter fear.

"We should back up too." I suggested. It was impossible to know what it was around that corner that was causing the screams and the anxiety in the far group. The trees were dense and filled with shrubbery. We couldn't see directly through and beyond to the other side.

No one spoke in disagreement and we started to move back, step by step. Our eyes remained glued to the third group in line. By now they were turning in our direction and starting to run. It took a few moments before we could see what was causing the ruckus.

A giant turned the bend in the road. Its body was enormous and blocked the entire path from its left foot to right foot. The source of the earlier screaming was evident in its hand. Half a body was mangled in between the fingers of its clenched fist.

Blood covered the giant's lower jaw and beard. It dragged a club as thick as a tree trunk along the gravel. "What the hell is that…?" Isabelle asked. Neither Aaron or I had any idea either.

"That's…that's—" a man nearby couldn't even get the name out through his stammering.

"FOREST TROLL! RUNNN!" A member of the third group yelled while running in our direction. His shout seemed to stir a reaction in the Forest Troll. It took the mangled body in its hand and tossed it into the forest like a piece of meat.

The ruined body flew through the air before smacking hard into a tree trunk. The impact caused the tree to crackle like thunder. Whatever was left of the body turned to a paste on impact. The monster picked up its club and started to sprint in our direction.

The ground beneath my feet started to rock and tremble with each of its steps. Contrary to my expectations, the giant wasn't slow by any means. It picked up speed in a matter of seconds and was rocketing towards us.

"We have to go!" Steven yelled at us. The lethargy from his hangover was gone immediately. He rushed right through the middle of the group and started sprinting back down the pathway.

"We won't outrun it like this!" Isabelle yelled. The monster was gaining speed on us incredibly fast. It was possible that if the three groups turned and fought together we could kill it, but at what cost? Moreover, we just wouldn't get organized on this short notice.

If one group decided to bail and leave the other two as bait, matters would reach an unsalvageable level. The look on the faces around me made it obvious it was every group for themselves.

"Into the forest!" Aaron yelled.

It was clear we couldn't lose the giant on open ground. The forest would provide a bit of obstacle for its enormous body. We rushed right off the path and in among the trees, directly towards a deeper portion of the Elysian Fields.

There was no time for discussion at all. It was clear our decision was the right one. The Forest Troll scooped up a runner and squeezed him in its hand. "Ahh! Hel—HELP ME!" he yelled. There was a crunch as blood exploded out from within the Forest Troll's closed fingers.

It tossed the corpse like a ragdoll at another group. Two or three people were hit like bowling pins before toppling over. "Don't look back! Just run!" Aaron yelled at me. We couldn't waste any more time.

It was clear this violence wasn't about hunger. The monster enjoyed killing. The grin that covered its disgusting face proved that point. Hunting us was like a game. My lungs and thighs were burning.

The blood curdling screams behind us slowly faded away and I lost track of how far we had run

"Wait… stop, please." Steven was panting harder than anyone I'd ever seen. He keeled over and vomited. His face was entirely red.

"Thirty seconds, everyone catch their breath." Aaron said. We couldn't know if the Forest Troll would chase after us, what with other toys available to play with. Judging by the lack of commotion from the beginning of the encounter, the first two groups hadn't lasted very long.

"What in the hell was that?" Isabelle muttered quietly. I was wondering the same thing. The name Forest Troll only gave a label to that nightmare.

"Why was this not mentioned before we left?" I was also a bit angry.

"Wait… wait. I'll explain." Steven was still doing his best to catch his breath.

"Talk while moving," Aaron said. We didn't hear any movement behind us and started to continue walking at a steady pace.

"I didn't say anything about it because sightings are so incredibly rare." He looked at Kimmi who was a bit shaken, "You knew about it also, didn't you?"

"I did," she said. It seemed like both Steven and Kimmi were familiar with this monster.

"So why didn't you say anything? Shouldn't we be on the same page?" I asked.

"Can you blame us? There isn't even one reported Forest Troll attack per year. That's just how rare they are! Hundreds upon hundreds of groups use this route to Tanyros yearly." Steven was defensive.

"Could we have fought it?" Aaron asked.

"Absolutely not! Forest Trolls don't follow the same rules as everything else around here. They're an anomaly. So long as they are in the forest, they come and go as they please. That troll could have easily been twice our level. Even if we had put together all five groups we might have all been wiped out."

From the fact I couldn't hear anyone else in the forest, I felt that most of the members from the other five groups had been killed.

Ours had been the first to head off the path and we'd been lucky that the giant had chosen to take out the easier targets.

"How long till we can go back?" Isabelle asked. It seemed she was worried about the Elysian Fields still.

Steven shook his head. "We can't go back. It might not be chasing us but it will be in the area. Once it finds some prey to play with it will hang around. High level Adventurers are going to have to come wipe it out."

"So we just keep moving?"

"The Elysian Fields are this way. Even if it gets bored and decides to come after us, it won't follow us there. It won't leave the Forest, hence the name," Steven said.

"Will there be a problem entering the Elysian Fields here?" Aaron asked.

"I… don't exactly know. Most groups don't stay long and try to move through in a single day. We're still many hours back from the scheduled route. We can enter through here but we'll be much farther from Tanyros than normal."

"What are the chances the Forest Troll will come for us?" I asked.

"I'd say… very high. Once it hunts down the others, it will at least make an effort to find us. We didn't run very far. At best we'll be on even ground in the forest. We won't be able to shake it off us until we get clear of the trees."

It was looking more and more likely that we should head into the Elysian Fields as soon as possible. I was going to suggest a vote when we heard a crackling like thunder. In the distance, trees were collapsing and my heart beat fast as I could see the giant again through the tree trunks.

Its burly body pushed through the underbrush and weathered trees. It was stirring up a small storm as it moved in our direction. I grabbed Isabelle's hand and squeezed it, "It's gonna be okay. We have to go though!" There was no time for discussion.

We ran as fast as we could, hoping it was possible to keep the giant off us. There was no way we could contend with it as a group of five. The strength and speed it displayed was frightening. It clearly had a high level of intelligence as well.

Aaron pulled out the map as we ran and did his best to estimate how far off we were from the edge of the forest, "We should see the tree line in less than twenty minutes. Keep it up till then and we should be able to exit."

Steven was having the hardest time out of all of us. Not only was his equipment heavy he was terribly out of shape. "Can anyone carry anything else?" Aaron asked. We pulled bags off Steven to lighten his load.

Perhaps it was tiring, because the Forest Troll wasn't pelting along as fast as before, but it was breathing down our necks the entire time. Despite not gaining any ground on us, it showed no signs of giving up. In fact, I felt that it was secretly happy. It was like a cat playing with a mouse. We were entertainment.

Steven was on his last legs when we finally saw the sun shining horizontally through the trees. It was the tree line we were running towards. Just on the other side was the Elysian Fields.

Aaron and I both grabbed an arm and did our best to help support Steven over this last hundred feet or so. My throat, lungs, and legs were all burning like never before.

I could tell Steven had it even worse. His breathing sounded so hoarse I wondered if he was dying right then and there. His throat must have been dryer than a desert. We finally broke through the tree line.

My foot stepped onto lush green grass as the sun blinded my eyes. I didn't even have the time to take in the scenery. We shuffled a hundred feet or so out before Steven couldn't keep standing.

He collapsed into a heap and nearly dragged Aaron and I down with him. We turned back with trepidation. It took around thirty seconds before the Forest Troll poked out his ugly head. It looked at us menacingly but whatever magic ruled its existence meant it didn't dare step out from among the trees. It eventually turned back and disappeared into the forest once again.

Chapter 5: The Elysian Fields

"My God," I panted before falling flat onto my back. Everyone simply collapsed to the ground. Steven continued to heave as he breathed. He fumbled for his water gourd before pouring it into his mouth. The water caused him to cough even more as his big belly rose up and down.

"That was too close," he gasped at last.

"Way too close." I pulled out my water gourd and refreshed my dry throat. Only now the threat was gone could I take a better look around me. I was stunned into silence.

The Elysian Fields were… gorgeous. The sky was blue for as far as I could see. The grass in every direction was perfectly green and level: as if a gigantic hand sculpted had it with care. The only marks on the page of grass were tidy-looking bushes and the ruins of beautiful buildings that seemed to be strewn about randomly.

Despite them being in the middle of a vast open field, not a single stone looked out of place. The buildings were dilapidated and falling apart and yet looked incredibly clean. The old-style pillars and buildings reminded me of ancient Greek architecture.

Even in their destruction, the pillars looked as white as snow. There was a strong gust of wind that felt incredibly good on my skin. The wind created a perfect wave over the grassland before disappearing into the distance.

"This… is the Elysian Fields?" I asked. The way it had been described to me had made me think of it as a graveyard. A dark and daunting area with horror lurking in every direction.

"More beautiful than you expected, right?" Steven asked. He had finally managed to catch his breath enough to speak normally. Even Isabelle looked a little better as we realized where we were. The only word I could describe such a view with was 'heavenly'. The entire area felt holy.

"So what now?" Aaron asked. "Will we encounter monsters here?" Steven had mentioned ghosts before.

"It depends on our luck. Some groups pass through without a single encounter. If that happens then we can treat this as a holiday and enjoy the journey. If we aren't lucky then this place can be the scariest of hells."

It was hard to ever imagine this place being described in such a way. "Where are we on the map? Can we tell?" I moved to Aaron and everyone grouped around him as he unfolded the map.

"Those buildings sort of match up around here on the map, yeah?" Kimmi pointed.

"It looks like it," I agreed.

Steven didn't sound happy. "Damn, we're farther away than I thought."

"Is there a reason why most groups prefer to travel it in a day?" asked Aaron.

"I don't know the specifics, but I've heard you don't want to spend the night here." Steven said.

"Was there any reason why?" Isabelle expressed a concern we probably all had.

"Nope, most people follow the advice of those that came before them. It's how you survive out here."

"Well, with the distance we have to travel there's almost no chance we're making it to Tanyros in a day. We're going to be camping out tonight." Aaron said.

There was nothing but beautiful scenery in front of us. I turned towards Tanyros and saw only fields. All we could do was walk forward one step at a time.

Aaron folded away the map. "Are we good to start moving? Has everyone caught their breath?"

"Take your stuff back Steven." We gave back the bags he was responsible for. He accepted them reluctantly and took his position in the front of the group. We finally started to move.

One of the buildings was close by, "Can we take a look?" I was incredibly interested. It wasn't even out of the way. The closest was less than five minutes away from us. We only needed to walk straight towards our destination and take a short thirty second detour.

"I don't see why not," said Aaron, looking at the stone construction with curiosity. "We aren't in a rush anymore anyway." There was no chance we would be leaving the Elysian Fields until tomorrow. We would be here for one night regardless of our pace today.

We approached the building with caution despite seeing nothing out of the ordinary. It was never a bad idea to be more safe than sorry. Weather and time hadn't diminished the magnificent architecture in the slightest.

Untouched by the usual signs of wind and rain, the stonework was sculpted flawlessly. Every line was perfectly spaced and each groove was just the right depth. The archway had half an angel sculpted into it, the remainder had fallen off.

Despite it being in ruins, there was no debris anywhere. Not even the slightest bit of dust. The building itself was also flawlessly white. It wasn't grey and diminished at all.

"Does anyone come out here to maintain these?" I asked. It was surreal. It looked like the entire building received daily maintenance.

"Never heard of anyone coming out here to do anything," said Steven and Kimmi agreed.

"What's the problem?" Aaron asked.

"Doesn't this look a bit too clean to you guys?" I got a bad feeling. It felt like I was trespassing on sacred ground for some reason. "I've changed my mind about searching here, let's just keep moving." There was something prickling the back of my neck.

The last time I had this feeling was at the start of everything. It was my first quest and not respecting that feeling was part of the reason Veronica wasn't here today. I had learned to trust this uneasy feeling. "Let's camp far away from any buildings tonight." I said.

"What for?" Isabelle asked. "Did you find something?" She sounded stressed, and I was sorry I was making her fearful.

"Just a hunch," I said. It really was only a hunch. That, plus the fact it was incredibly weird seeing the spotlessly clean stonework given the current tumbled-down state of the buildings. That alone suggested something odd was going on.

Maybe the buildings themselves had been frozen in such a state for hundreds of years? There was no guarantee anything was maintaining them at all. The rules of this new world were still quite foreign to me.

It became clear just how far we had to travel through the Elysian Fields. The pace we were making on this flat and spotless grassland was remarkable, and yet there was never anything but more open field in front of us.

The view ahead went on and on forever like a mirage. No amount of walking seemed to bring the horizon any closer at all. The only way we could tell progress was being made was due to the buildings we approached and eventually left far behind.

There were two or three hours of sunlight remaining and I was thinking about the risk of being caught in the dark of night in these fields. Other Adventurers took care to enter the Elysian Fields at a point where they could reach Tanyros during daylight. Why did they always do that? Why did no one camp overnight here? The simple fact there was no reason to do so bothered me. As far as Steven or Kimmi knew, it was simply an unspoken rule. You didn't spend the night in the Elysian Fields. They didn't know why that was the case, just that it was.

Pioneers learned from those who came before them. Adventurers were similar in a way. Someone in the past had made a discovery. Word of their discovery spread enough to become a rule.

That rule was passed down without question until no one knew why it was a rule in the first place. If you asked someone: 'why don't you spend the night in the Elysian Fields?' you didn't get a straight answer. 'You just don't.' That's the best you would get.

That reason was good enough for most people. Was there any reason to inquire what was the danger from an empty field such as this? Many Adventurers had come through here and even visited these ancient buildings.

There was no value to be had here. No hidden treasure. The simplest reason was often the right reason. Staying the night in the Elysian Fields was not safe. That was all I could deduce.

The problem for us now was the lack of a safe option. We had been forced into the Elysian Fields far too early and now we had no choice.

"We take turns sleeping tonight." Aaron said, as though aware of my thoughts. It was a sound suggestion that no one disagreed with.

"I'll take first watch," I offered. That bad feeling was prickling the back of my neck. I wouldn't feel comfortable falling asleep before confirming the night was safe.

"Can you do it alone?" Aaron asked.

"Shouldn't be a problem." There was at least an hour of sunlight left. "Let's get camp started now then if we're not tight on travel time." It was a good time to stop. We were far enough from any of the buildings that I felt a bit more comfortable. "I want everyone to stay close tonight."

I couldn't shake that bad feeling at all. I didn't want a single person out of my sight.

"Kimmi and I will grab some firewood from the bushes while you set up camp," Aaron said. Steven got right to it and was already pulling pots and pans from his pack.

We had gorged ourselves the last two nights but still had enough food for another dinner and for lunch tomorrow. I setup all the sleeping bags directly next to each other, almost touching. Steven finished preparing his cooking setup when Aaron and Kimmi returned with enough firewood for the night.

"Stop dilly dallying and light the fire." Steven barked at me. He was aching to start cooking. I lit a fireball and got it going for him before giving him a bit of space to work.

Isabelle approached me looking anxious, "You'd tell me if something was up, right?"

"Yeah, I would."

"So what's going on? I can tell when you're paying extra attention to things. You've had that calculating look on your face for several hours now. Spit it out."

Up to now, I hadn't felt that my vague intuition of danger warranted a comment. No one else seemed to have noticed anything untoward. "I just have a bad feeling. Something isn't right."

"Like what?"

"I don't know. A prickling on the back of my neck. Like something is watching and waiting."

"Like a ghost?"

"Come on, I didn't say that. Now you're just being paranoid. It could be nothing, that's why I didn't say anything." Just as I spoke, I noticed something peculiar now that the sun was mostly behind the horizon. The entire grassland was coated with a low orange hue. "Where are the moons?" I asked.

"Huh? You're right." There wasn't a single moon in the sky despite there being absolutely nothing blocking our view. There wasn't even a star in the sky. Even in the forest we could see the stars and the moon between the branches of the trees.

The orange hue slowly receded along the ground until the sun fully vanished behind the horizon. The consequences of not having any moons or a single star in the sky became immediately apparent.

It was pitch black; just as dark as when we were maneuvering in the sewers under Egester. The light from the campfire only traveled a few feet, just enough for us five to see each other as we sat around it. The shadows from our bodies flickered and weaved. They eventually tapered off and disappeared into the darkness.

That bad feeling I had intensified several times over. I picked out several pieces of wood from the pile Aaron and Kimmi had brought and stabbed them into the ground before lighting them up like improvised torches.

The amount of light on the camp increased several-fold. We could finally see the heads of our shadows again and my anxiety abated just a little bit. With the exception of Isabelle, it didn't seem that the others were too concerned.

Steven was fully engrossed in cooking and Aaron and Kimmi were simply relaxing near the campfire. There suddenly a strong gust of wind that caused the campfire to flicker.

The gust of wind was stronger than anything we had experienced during the day. Several of the outer torches went out immediately. Even the central campfire was threatened by its strength. I lit a fireball and made sure to keep it burning. I then went and relit the outer torches.

The entire situation was alarming and yet no one seemed alarmed. I had never seen such total darkness before. Without our campfire you wouldn't have been able to see a foot in front of your face.

"Don't you guys think it's too dark?" I asked. Steven ignored me and continued to cook like a madman.

"It's a bit dark, yeah. What of it?" Aaron asked. He didn't seem like his usual self. Kimmi simply shrugged her shoulders as if everything was normal. Isabelle had already crept a bit closer to the campfire to get further away from that darkness.

"Shouldn't you summon your little helper?" I looked to Isabelle.

"Oh… right." Even she seemed a bit out of it. What was going on? She cupped her hands and then pushed forth before the little glowing fairy flew into the air. It hovered above us and gave a bit more light for a few brief moments. There was suddenly a strong gust of wind and the helper simply fluttered and disappeared.

Somehow Isabelle didn't seem concerned with that. In fact, no one was acting normally and yet what could I do but keep an eye on them?

"I'll keep watch with you," Isabelle said. "I can't sleep anyway." I was grateful. It seemed watching alone might end up being too much for me.

Steven whipped up a meal in record time before serving everyone. The more I watched Steven, Kimmi and Aaron the more I felt it odd, like they were locked in a stupor. My only solace was that the strong wind had died down.

Chapter 6: Escape from the Ghosts

The night was calm once again and all that could be heard was the crackling of the fire. I put a few more broken branches into the pit and got comfortable. Steven was the first one to enter his sleeping bag and doze off.

I didn't think too much of this. The running earlier today had taken the most out of him. Kimmi was the next to slip away, then Aaron. Eventually it was only me and Isabelle sitting on opposite sides of the fire.

I started to notice more and more about the world around me. It wasn't just the complete darkness; it was just too quiet in general. You couldn't hear the chirping of crickets or the hooting of owls. There was dead silence in every direction.

Isabelle ended up wrapping her arms around her shoulders in an attempt to keep herself warm. I wasn't quite at that point yet, but the fire definitely wasn't giving off that much heat. I put a few more branches in to keep it burning.

Gusts of wind came intermittently and the more I listened the more my hairs stood up on my body. The wind had a particular sound as it raced by us. I felt more and more like I was hearing hushed whispers each time it passed.

The feeling that something was watching me from the darkness grew so strong it was all I could think about. Yet it was impossible to see outside this ring of light from the campfire. The darkness was so strong it was closing in on us.

I lost my sense of time sitting in this dark and silent world. I couldn't be sure if hours or minutes passed. I started to hear things all around us. It wasn't just me; Isabelle heard them too. She jerked her head around in panic.

Footsteps: the sound of bare feet running across the grass, human footsteps. Someone was racing around us in a circle. At first it was only one, but then it was multiple, until dozens of figures were rushing around us in the darkness.

"You hear this? Right?" I asked. I did my best to seem calm but I was utterly terrified inside. Goosebumps ran up my entire back and tickled the nape of my neck. It seemed to me that the burning campfire was the only thing protecting us from an abyss waiting to swallow us up.

Isabelle nodded her head frantically and then scooted even closer to the fire. She was instinctually moving further away from the darkness behind her. The unknown was often the most terrifying prospect.

"Wake the others," I gave Steven a kick.

The footsteps racing around us came to a stop and silence reigned again. That didn't abate my anxiety though, in fact, it became even worse. My brain was screaming at me that something was wrong.

I felt an electrifying shock on my back. Something brushed against my shirt that was now thick with sweat. I saw Isabelle's face morph from something of fear and panic to utter horror.

"J… J… Joseph, behind you…" she stuttered and stammered. I felt it too. Something was directly behind me, breathing down my neck. I was petrified as alarms rang in my head endlessly. I also felt that if I turned around to look I'd be done for.

The figure just stood behind me. I could feel its presence inching even closer. Time seemed to stop for dozens of seconds before I felt its touch against my bicep. A cold and dead hand was creeping up my arm.

I couldn't move. My body was screaming. Eventually that hand climbed up the entire back of my arm and rested on my shoulder. Only after I could see that decrepit hand in my peripheral vision did my body finally react.

I jolted forward and closer to the fire. There was no part of me touching the darkness any longer. I looked back to see a hand floating in space and a fading pair of eyes. They eventually both disappeared into the darkness.

Isabelle put her hand over her mouth to stop herself from screaming. My attempt at calm was completely gone. I was spooked through and through. The area of my shoulder on which that hand had rested still felt cold to the touch, even sitting next to the fire.

I desperately fed more wood into the campfire and then forcefully burned it with a fireball. It became immediately obvious there was many more than just a few of these monsters. As the light from the fire flared outwards, more and more eyes became visible in the darkness.

Nor was it just dozens, there were hundreds upon hundreds of them. The eyes stared at us hungrily before backing away back into the darkness. My heart was beating out of my chest. I felt Isabelle dig her hand into my arms in fright.

Having proven hard to wake, Steven, Aaron, and Kimmi started to mumble in their sleep. Their faces contorted into frowns and scowls. It seemed as if they were all having nightmares.

"Mom…no, I'm sorry! I'm sorry! Please…" Aaron mumbled. He started to fidget and fumble even harder in his sleeping bag. I felt that if he hadn't been secured inside he would have rolled away into the darkness.

Kimmi started to hyperventilate and her face contorted to one of fear, before she screamed bloody murder. Whatever she was seeing in her sleep was terrifying her completely. Steven groaned in discomfort and twisted and twirled inside his sleeping bag.

"We need to find a way to wake them up," I said. This wasn't normal in the slightest, and I wasn't kind about it. I didn't hesitate to pour water on their faces before giving them a slap. Despite that, it wasn't easy to wake them at all.

Aaron jolted up at last, "What was that for?" He didn't seem pleased. His face was wet and his cheek was red. I had even pinched his nose a bit to stifle his breathing. It wasn't nice but it did the trick.

"Help us wake them! NOW," I said. He saw the fear on Isabelle's face and the seriousness in mine. We immediately worked to wake Kimmi and Steven.

Steven rubbed his eyes as we all huddled around the campfire, "What's the big deal?" He yawned.

"I think I found the reason why no one spends the night in the Elysian Fields." My voice was shaky and uncertain. The three of them looked at me expectantly. I lit a fireball in my hand and held it up. "Take a look." I tossed it out.

The fireball rocketed from our safe enclosure of light and into the darkness. It managed to light up a circle several feet around its landing point. Everyone's eyes widened in shock, no doubt mine as well. What we could now see was outside my expectations completely.

For the entire distance that the fireball had traveled there were human figures. They were lined up one after the other in the darkness as if in queue. They simply waited outside the light while staring in our direction.

My fireball caused a slight disorder in their ranks as they moved out of its path to avoid being in the light. There was no doubt in my mind they reformed and took their original position after it went out.

"WHAT THE HELL ARE THOSE?" Steven said. He didn't seem tired anymore.

"I don't know, but I think they are afraid of the light." A sudden gust of wind shook the campfire.

"Block the wind!" Aaron said. We would be swallowed up if the fire went out. We did our best to huddle around the campfire placing our bodies between it and the wind, keeping it alight. The issue was that sitting this close also hindered the distance the light from the flames traveled. The darkness was slowly closing in.

"What do we do?" Steven asked.

"How much wood do we have left?" Aaron asked.

"Not much." I had been adding it steadily to keep the fire lit. My sense of time was completely off and I didn't know whether the sun was due to rise soon or if the night had just began... "How long did you three sleep for? Do you have any idea?"

"No idea... I was having a nightmare," Aaron said.

"Me as well."

All three of them had suffered nightmares and as a result weren't sure of the duration of their sleep. The fire was working overtime to keep us out of the darkness. It wouldn't be long before we didn't have a source of light.

"I don't think we can stay here," I said. "We need to leave soon."

"How can we leave? They're everywhere." Isabelle said. It was the first time she had said anything since warning me of that figure behind me.

"We'll have to make torches and walk our way out," I said. "Aaron, pair up with Kimmi and start cutting up our sleeping bags for strips of cloth. There's enough wood here to make some torches." I turned to Steven, "Do we have any fat left from cooking dinner?"

"Ah, yeah." He shuffled through his pack before pulling out a glass jar with solidified cooking fat inside. Kimmi passed a dagger to Aaron and the two tore into the sleeping bags and revealed the cotton-like fibers inside.

They continued to cut the material into strips and began wrapping them around the tops of the broken branches. Steven smeared a bit of cooking fat to help get them started when ready. The intensity of the fire flickered and lowered during the entire preparation.

"Where are we heading for?" Steven asked.

"I'm not happy about the buildings, but I don't see any other options," I said. "There's something wrong about them but they might block the wind and we can try to get more wood as we travel too."

I wasn't sure we could go very far with our new torches but sitting here was certain death. I would rather take that gamble then wait for the fire to be extinguished and for us to be swallowed up by the slow advanced of these monsters.

"Kimmi and Aaron you two hold hands, Steven you're with Isabelle. Stick close and don't let go no matter what," I ordered. My fireball was a torch on its own and I didn't need to rely on anyone else for a light source.

"Which direction?" I wondered aloud; it was impossible to see our surroundings beyond a few feet.

"I think there was one that way?" Kimmi pointed. It didn't seem like anyone knew exactly which direction we were facing. It was entirely possible we would walk deeper into the Elysian Fields and miss a ruin, even while walking close by.

"I'll lead the path in front. You four stay as close behind me as possible." They each picked up their torch and then lit it in the fire. I used fireball and held it out in front of my face. I could see the eyes and bodies of the monsters slowly back away into the darkness as the reach of my magical light extended.

"Don't forget what I said. Stay close and don't let go." I started to walk forward. With every step I moved the numerous bodies in front of me receded. I was making a hallway through them, as the eyes in front of me shifted to my side and gave way.

Occasionally a decrepit hand would reach out in an attempt to touch me. When that happened I forced the fireball to burn even more brightly. The hand would instantly retract and the bodies I repulsed in that way fell quickly back into the darkness.

Almost immediately after I cleared the path, the bodies started moving closer and closer around me. I looked back to see Aaron, Kimmi, Isabelle, and Steven basically huddled together shoulder to shoulder. Their hands held the torches as far away from their bodies as possible.

We walked and walked but the scenery never changed. The moons never returned and neither did the stars. Pitch blackness lay in every direction. I started to doubt my plan. I couldn't even be sure I was walking in a straight line.

The torches were beginning to fade. I had no choice but to slow my speed and slip in between my friends. I burned my fireball as bright as possible to keep the darkness out. Our pace slowed to a crawl. I felt like we had been walking for an eternity.

All I could hear around me was the sound of our breathing. The entire world was muffled in silence. I felt like time was running out. This feeling was enough to drive me insane.

There was suddenly a new noise. It wasn't footsteps, or breathing, or hushed whispers. It sounded like sweeping, a rough broom brushing against hard concrete. It rhythmically scratched back and forth.

"Do you guys hear that?" I asked. It was like music to my ears: hope.

"Hear what?"

"I don't hear anything?"

It was unanimous. I was the only one who could hear the sound. As we had no other option, I changed direction and started to move towards the sound.

The scratching grew louder and louder in my ears and I picked up the pace. "What are you doing?" Isabelle asked. I was no longer going straight but had turned into the crowd around us.

"There's something this way. Trust me." I looked at the others. They were basically clinging to my clothing as their torches were barely enough to keep the sides of their bodies illuminated. Hands constantly reached from the darkness and brushed past them.

I didn't see it until we were just two or three feet away from its base. It was one of the decaying buildings. Our lights shined off its pearl-like appearance. The sweeping sound was coming from within.

"Why are we here?" asked Aaron.

"I don't know, something is inside," I said. There were a few stone steps emerging from the darkness. I took them and everyone followed me. The creatures that were waiting in the darkness didn't follow me: did they dare? This was the first bit of good news to have come our way since the night began.

The sweeping continued unperturbed. It was neither fast nor slow and each brush of the broom sounded exactly the same. I ascended the broken steps up to the interior of the ruin, aware of how heavy my own footsteps sounded and unsure of what would be waiting for us inside.

There was a garbed figure in the middle of a half-destroyed hall. Its entire body glowed in this pitch darkness. The glow caused a halo effect in the air just outside of its body. "Excuse me…" I called out quietly.

"What are you doing?" Steven shook me. He couldn't see the figure that I was seeing.

"Excuse me…" I was a bit louder this time. "Can you hear me?" The brushing suddenly came to a stop and the figure looked at me curiously for a moment. We locked eyes for at least fifteen seconds.

It was an old woman hunched over. Her attire was that of a maid, only colorful and bright and adorned with all sorts of instruments. "You can see me?" she asked.

"Yes!"

"Hmmm, it's been a long time since I've had visitors. Come in." Her voice was ethereal and faint. Yet I could hear it very clearly as if she had spoken directly into my ear. I took a step into the hall and the others followed me.

"Are you pulling a prank? This isn't the time." Steven was reprimanding me. In his eyes it was probably a completely silent hall and I was talking to myself.

"Shh, there's someone here," I said. "Don't be rude." I forced everyone inside.

"Have a seat." The figure leaned the broom against the wall and then sat down on the hard floor. I didn't hesitate and dragged everyone down with me.

"What are you doing?" asked Aaron. None of my actions were making any sense to them at all.

"They think I'm crazy. Is it possible you can show yourself or something?" I asked.

"I can't show myself but I can make my presence known," the figure said. She raised her hand and extended her finger and started to write something in the air. Glowing letters formed as she moved her hand. It was a language I didn't understand.

"You weren't kidding? Who's there?" I ignored Steven's surprised and even frantic reaction.

"Can you tell me why I can see you but they can't?"

"Hmm, that is a good question. All I can say is that the Elysian Field wears away at your senses slowly. The fact that you can see me and they can't means your senses are that much better than theirs."

"Might they eventually be able to see you?"

"Maybe…I'm leaning towards 'no' though. The fact that you can see me even after being worn away for so long is a testament to just how strong your sense is."

I asked the question that was bothering me the most, "Are we safe in here?"

"Those wandering spirits outside won't dare step foot in here. My master may not be alive anymore but he's not so weak to let those vagabonds taint his resting place."

Relief washed over me. "Do you mind if we spend the night?" I asked.

"You can spend the night but you need to pay your respects." She stood and then walked over to the end of the hall. There was an urn there resting on a mantle. The floor below was the only discolored part I could see.

I walked over and realized what the discoloration was. It was knee marks from someone kneeling there and praying. I got on my knees and leaned over before pressing my head on the floor below.

I felt strongly that someone was looking at me: judging me. I had an impulse to look up and at the urn but forced myself not to do so. It felt disrespectful, like I would be defiling something sacred.

I stood and insisted the others paid their respects as well.

"We'll be safe here for the night?" Steven asked hopefully.

"That's what she said." As far as I could tell she wasn't lying. There wasn't really a reason for her to deceive us in such a way anyway. I had a strong feeling that it wouldn't require much of her power to send us out into the dark night. "Don't worry about it and get some sleep."

The sleeping bags had all been destroyed so the others huddled into a corner and did their best to sleep. I took a seat in front of the urn and stared off into space. "What is this place?" I mumbled.

"Ah, how many years has it been now?" the maid asked herself. "I can't recall anymore." She bumped me with the base of the broom, "stand up."

I shuffled to my feet and stood in front of her. She was up to something but I couldn't tell what it was. Her hand held out the broom as if beckoning for me to take it.

"You want me to…?"

"If you're curious then start sweeping."

71

I took the broom and started to brush it along the floor back and forth. There was something very relaxing about the task. The surroundings started to fade as all I could focus on was sweeping the floor.

I didn't know how long that feeling lasted as I was lost in a daze. Suddenly, I was awoken from my stupor. A young boy wearing a robe and sandals bumped into me before toppling to the floor.

"Marcus! I told you to stop running and watch where you're going!" This was a female voice. I looked up utterly confused to see my surroundings had changed. The hall around me was no longer dilapidated but fully furnished and alive.

A woman came rushing down from a beautiful seat and scooped up the boy. She gave me a kind glance before turning back to the boy. "Marcus, what do you say?"

The boy twiddled his thumbs and looked at his hands before focusing his attention towards me, "Sorry Joseph. I didn't mean to run into you." His voice was low and discouraged.

"Oh, it's no problem. I should have been paying attention as well," I answered.

The woman gave Marcus a kiss on the forehead before putting him down, "run along." She turned back to me, "You're too kind to him sometimes. Don't be afraid to reprimand the young master."

Was this an illusion? I wasn't sure what was going on. I realized that I was now a maid-servant. "You're right ma'am. I'm terribly sorry." The words flowed smoothly as if I had practiced the phrase a thousand times.

"No need to apologize, you've always done well. Get me some wine and then call it a night."

I cupped my hands on my hips before doing a half-bow. I rushed out of the hall and towards the dining area.

The area of my vision wasn't limited to just this one building. There were numerous structures all around me. I was standing somewhere on the outskirts of a bustling city. There were servants and workers roaming frantically about. Even at this late time of night.

I shouldn't have known where the dining hall was at all, but my feet glided there without hesitation. *Am I in control or is this just a vision that maid wants me to see?* I couldn't be sure at all. The actions felt like mine, but my body moved on information I didn't have.

In the dining hall was the cabinet the wine was located in, the wine the mistress liked. These were matters that had never crossed my mind and yet my hands moved flawlessly. I rushed back with a tray containing a decanter and glass and passed it to the mistress. "When will the master return?" I asked.

"Seven days," she responded.

"A week? That's longer than expected." I responded without even knowing why I had any expectation at all.

"He's run into a bit of trouble. I'll need you to pay more attention to Marcus. You know how he gets when his father isn't around."

"Understood. I'll do my best." I clasped my hands and bowed before leaving the hall. Returning to my room, I was surprised to find it fully furnished with well-made items. It seemed that the old maid's status was quite high.

Before I knew it, the days started to pass like a blur. I was watching someone live their life from the inside. It was an absolutely astonishing phenomenon. It didn't come without problems, though.

I felt like I was losing myself. The only reminder of who I was came in the form of my name. 'Joseph' was the thought keeping me attached to my own consciousness. Otherwise, days went by with me identifying as the head maid of a rich and powerful family.

Scenes started to blur before my eyes like a slide show.

I was pouring wine for the master and mistress and listening to the master speak, "The king is becoming more erratic by the day, I fear for our family. The other families have already taken precautions to protect themselves."

"The king wouldn't harm us, would he? You two are like brothers," the mistress said.

"He hasn't been himself lately and I dare not say I can predict his actions. A king must be ruthless, you know this."

The scene before my eyes rapidly shifted. I was suddenly folding clothes in a beautiful courtyard. Marcus was playing in the grass while the master and mistress talked in hushed whispers, "The Calliope family has sent word. The king has made his move."

"What did it say?"

"The message is encoded so we won't know the entire story till tomorrow, but it is not good news." He paused. "The only word I could decipher immediately was at the bottom—irreconcilable."

"Do you have a plan?" she asked.

Time started to blur again and Marcus was no longer a young boy, but instead a young man. Seasons were coming and going and scenes continued to play out in front of me. "Of the ten great families only three remain." The mistress spoke with evident worry.

"I don't know what he's planning anymore. He keeps a distance even from me these days. It's out of my hands."

"We have never plotted behind his back! That must count for something!" She looked at the back of Marcus who was leaving the hall. "Please, for our child. Beg him if you must!"

"I have tried everything. He no longer sees me as the brother he once did. The only reason we remain today is the little bit of good-will he still has remaining."

"Should we flee?" the mistress asked.

"You can't! The palace guards are watching our every move. If you try and flee then our manor will be burnt to the ground before the sun rises. Promise me." He grabbed her and looked at her with the most serious of eyes.

She started to cry, "I promise."

The scene changed yet again and several years seemed to have passed. Marcus was no longer the stubble-less young man from before. The mistress had aged and even the master had grey streaks in his hair and beard.

"It's clear the lingering attachment he once had is gone. I know he will make his move soon." He sighed. "I can only apologize to the man I once was. I'm sorry that I kept it from you. I have been busy these last two years."

"What are you saying? What have you been planning?"

"I have gathered the remaining members of the fallen nine families. They have agreed to fight alongside us. In exchange, I will reinstate their names in victory."

"Thank God…" The mistress started to cry. "All these years I was so worried you had given up on our future… our son's future." Tears rained down her cheeks and dripped to the floor below.

For the first time, I started to feel emotions in this body I was occupying. I was originally just a viewer. My hands clenched hard and a feeling of foreboding welled up inside of me. There was another change of scenery.

The hall was crumbling and fire raged over the entire manor. I rushed outside only to see smoke billowing into the sky. Warriors in full gear ran to and fro hacking and slashing. It was an absolute blood bath.

"Joseph! Joseph! Help me!" It was the mistress. She was hobbling towards the hall with the master supported on her shoulder. His face was pale white and blood was gushing from his silver armor.

"What happened?" I asked frantically.

"He was stabbed, I don't know how badly. Hurry, help me get his armor off." We rushed him into the hall and unclipped his armor. The inside of his clothing was drenched with blood. The wound was much worse than what it looked like from outside.

There was no chance for us to save him. Blood was constantly coming out from his wound at the slightest touch. Messing with it would only kill him faster. He looked at me, "Joseph, please. I beg you take my wife and Marcus and flee." He was barely able to speak the words.

"What are you saying?" His wife was almost shaking him while crying. He didn't even look at her and continued to stare at me with those piercing eyes.

I did something unthinkable and grabbed the mistresses' wrist, "We have to go now. We can't stay."

"What do you think you're doing?" she yelled.

"Please punish me later! However, if we don't go now there won't be a later. We have to go." She resisted for a moment to stare at her husband. There was a moment when their eyes met and I could feel his life fade away.

Those dead eyes continued to stare through her and into the distance. It was only then that she managed to move her feet. "Where is Marcus?" I asked.

"He refused to stay put so we locked him away. He's on the first floor of the jail."

We rushed there without delay. I didn't have any fighting experience and avoided all the ongoing struggles as best as I could.

"Where is father?" asked Marcus when we appeared.

"There's no time for questions, we have to go!" I yelled. I had never raised my voice at Marcus before. I had always treated him favorably, despite the mistress's constant scolding that I should be harder on him.

He didn't retort in anger. My reaction showed him how awful the situation must truly be. We raced out of the jail and towards the surface. There was a hidden passage outside of the hall that led under the manor wall and into the forest.

The scene flashed again and we were rushing through the forest. Marcus was leading the way down the path while I was doing my best to support the mistress. "Hurry, they're just behind us! We can't stop now!" Marcus yelled back.

Guards were hot on our trail and chasing us through the forest. A sickening feeling was building in my gut that made me want to vomit. An arrow whizzed by my head and lodged itself into a nearby tree. Suddenly the scene changed again.

I was bound like a slave and standing off to the side of a giant spectacle. There was a large wooden platform with two gallows erected on top. Marcus and the mistress were tied and bound. Their heads placed through the slots as a guillotine blade rested high above.

My heart ached looking on. I wanted to be there with them on that platform, but I was not important enough to be executed publicly. The ropes were pulled and the blades dropped. The sound of two heads thumping followed by cheering filled my ears. I closed my eyes in disbelief.

The scene changed again. I was being shoved into that nearly destroyed hall. There were still remnants of blood and destroyed stone along the floors. A cold tea set and unfolded clothes rested in a corner of the room.

My hands and feet were tied. There was a silver urn resting on the mantle place right above where those two seats used to be. I stared in a daze until there was a sudden spike of pain on my aged back. A metal greave kicked me to the floor and I struggled to turn over.

The guard stood over me with his sword raised high. There was a menacing smirk across his scarred face. "Serve them well in the afterlife." He dropped the sword into my gut. The pain wasn't nearly as bad as the emotional turmoil this body was feeling.

I stared at the half-destroyed ceiling as my eyes glazed over. The view in front of my face slowly lost focus until I realized I was staring at the floor. A broom was still in my hand as I swept back and forth rhythmically.

Two wet tears splattered on the floor. I touched my face, "I'm crying…?" I asked. "What was that? What did you do to me?"

"I just allowed you to see some of my memories," the maid said. "Maybe you understand more now?"

Despite the visions having come in bits and pieces, I had slowly melded with that reality. That was an entirely different life from this one. There was once a civilization here, completely different to the one that existed today.

I turned and looked at the urn with longing. "Master…" I mumbled out. I found myself shocked that I was feeling this way.

"Don't worry. It will fade shortly. You're not quite back to reality yet and are still experiencing some of my emotions."

"That's all? That's good." I breathed a sigh of relief. I didn't want to feel like someone else. "How long was I gone for?"

"You were gone for a single sweep of the broom," she said. "What you saw was fifteen years of my life. You did better than I expected."

"Better than expected?"

"Well, I half anticipated that you would lose your sanity and forever be lost in the delusion that you are me," she confessed. "Yet my intuition was that this wouldn't happen, though."

I was angry but scared to lose my temper in front of her. Her power was on a level I couldn't fathom. "How long ago were those memories?"

"I don't remember anymore to be honest. Five hundred years? A thousand years? A thousand five hundred years? Master would remember better than I." She looked at the urn resting on the mantle. It was in the exact place I had seen in those visions. Not one inch to the left or right.

"Why? What was the point of showing me that?"

"The opportunity to share my feelings doesn't come often. A fleeting wish at the end of my life, perhaps?" She pondered. "My actions haven't been tied to reason for a very long time."

"Who—"

"No more questions. You should sleep if you want to get back to normal. Your brain is extremely overtaxed right now. If you aren't careful you could fuse parts of your memory with mine. That's the first step towards insanity."

How could I sleep like this though? I passed her the broom and walked to the wall before slouching over. Despite feeling torn, I fell asleep at once.

Chapter 7: Memory

"Joseph! Wake up or you'll be late!" A warm hand pushed against my shoulder and shook me awake.

My eyes opened gently and my mother's face appeared in view. There was a brief moment of confusion. "Where am I?"

"What are you saying where are you? You're about to be late is where you are, now get up!" she scolded. "You have work in an hour and your father is already there!"

I leaned up and rubbed my eyes. My thinking was foggy and I felt extremely confused. I was forgetting something important but couldn't put my finger on it. I rolled out of bed against my own wishes and put on my work attire.

I was a waiter at my parent's restaurant on my days off from school. Despite being the family business, I wasn't given any preferential treatment, "Hey dad."

"Didn't I tell you not to call me dad at work? I'm your boss."

"Sorry boss." I mumbled. This wasn't out of the ordinary. A lot of people referred to this as tough love. I didn't feel great about it.

"Get the team together and meet in my office. It's going to be a busy night tonight. No mistakes, understand?"

I nodded before gathering everyone up. The specials on dinners, alcohol, soups: we got the entire run down.

My feet were killing me by the time my shift ended. I slept like a rock that night and woke early for school the following day. I was unusually grumpy and agitated. Emotions that didn't make any sense welled up inside of me.

There was a chubby looking goof in one of my classes. The moment I saw him I felt elated. That elation slowly turned into annoyance and finally anger. I was on a roller coaster of emotions just seeing someone I'd never met.

That feeling of forgetting something was bothering me tremendously as well. I couldn't put my finger on it no matter what. I felt like that the entire week. Was I going insane?

I found out the chubby goof was named Jonathan. I also found more and more reasons to be annoyed. We were in a classroom of only twenty-four students and yet he constantly pulled snacks from his bag.

Chips, gummies, candy bars, you name it. He ate openly and loudly in class. Not only that, but he was also a complete slob about it. His lips smacked and bits of food debris went everywhere. He stuck his gum under the desk. He was an unhygienic freak.

That feeling that I was forgetting something important slowly started to fade away. I was becoming content with my life as it was. My anxiety and agitation were declining every day as I grew accustomed to my new school.

That was until one day I was walking down the breezeway towards my next class. There was a young man walking opposite me. He had a head full of red hair. It was short and reminded me of Velcro.

The man wore a basketball jersey with the number twenty-three. It wasn't only that, he towered over those around him. He was so damn tall that I couldn't help but look. He felt so familiar, like I knew him well.

Was it the feeling of meeting a long-lost friend? Was that what I was feeling? I suddenly felt like something was actively trying to bury that emotion away. It wasn't that I was being forgetful… something was trying to make me forget.

When I got home, I fought against this feeling and made the effort to look up the names of the members on our school basketball team. I found his picture there, and his name: Aaron. It was like a bomb went off in my head. I knew that was his name before I even read it under his picture. How did that knowledge come to me?

I reminded myself of this question before I went to sleep and took another glance at Aaron's picture before bed. I found myself having déjà vu often. Like these moments in my life had happened before. It was a daily occurrence.

That feeling started to come even more often. Until one day, all my memories were shattered. I was taking a table's order from a noisy group of college girls. The restaurant was near closing and mostly empty. Their chatter didn't bother me.

I took their order and started to walk away when I caught a piece of their conversation, "Why couldn't Veronica make it? What did she say?"

I felt a flood of emotions at the name Veronica. My head started to hurt as images of things that hadn't happened yet raced through my mind.

I stood frozen for several minutes before a realization struck me. *This is a dream… I'm dreaming. None of this is real…* Everything I was seeing had already happened. I had gone to sleep in that dilapidated building and had yet to wake up.

I started to hear my name being called. "Joseph!" It was faint and far away. "Joseph!" It came again a little louder. My name repeatedly echoed through the air and yet none of the ladies at the table could hear it. Even my father continued emptying the register without much of a care.

There was a sound like thunder and my name being called one final time, "JOSEPH!" I opened my eyes. My cheek was burning red. I raised my hand to feel the pulsing heat.

"Sorry… I might have slapped you a bit hard." Isabelle said. I looked around the brightly lit room. The sun was shining high above.

"Is she gone?" I asked.

"Is who gone?" Isabelle asked.

"Are you alright? Did you hit your head?" asked Aaron.

"You guys don't remember the ghosts and the danger we were in?" I sat up.

"We came here last night to sleep," said Isabelle. "And that's all. Are you sure you're okay?"

They didn't remember anything? The bodies? The maid?

I thought about that weird dream and wondered if it was a side effect of sharing memories. The dream was fading quickly and the feelings I'd experienced were no longer as intense. Aaron grasped my hand and pulled me to my feet.

"Do you know what happened to the sleeping bags?" he wondered.

I contemplated trying to explain and decided against it, "No idea."

"We should be in Tanyros by mid-day so it shouldn't matter that much. We'll need to get more supplies when we arrive though."

I glanced around the room and spotted the knee imprints just beneath the mantle. The silver urn was nowhere to be found anymore. Neither was the maid. I wondered if she was here watching me.

"Let's not waste time and get going." We departed the ruined home and stepped back onto the grassland. I didn't find the area beautiful anymore, not after last night.

"Where are we going?" I suddenly heard a voice I didn't recognize.

"Who said that?" I asked.

"Who said what?"

Isabella looked at me curiously, "No one said anything. Maybe you need to get looked at when we arrive."

"I said it." My heart stopped. I had a feeling that was similar to when lady Briele used telepathy. There was no one around us for as far as the eye could see. "Don't be alarmed."

I nearly stopped dead in my tracks. There was something inside of me… living… inside of me. *WHAT THE FUCK?* My brain started to scream gibberish.

"Calm down, calm down. You're right though, I am inside of you."

Who are you? I questioned. Whoever or whatever it was could read my inner thoughts. I suddenly felt the voice was familiar. The memories I received from that maid weren't completely gone from my head. *You're…*

"Right, I'm Marcus Chronis… but you know me only as Master. Arlene wasn't kidding. You're quite quick witted. I should have heeded her warning."

Warning?

"She told me I shouldn't rush to try and take control of your body." He sighed. "I should have listened."

So the reason I was forgetting the present and was reliving my past in my dream…?

"Right, that was me."

How could I raise my guard against an enemy inside of me? What could I even do to stop it? My hands were clammy and I started to feel dizzy. *Why would you tell me that?*

"Well, if it makes you feel better, I already failed." He coughed. "If I didn't fail… well I'd be you and you'd be… a dream, or something like that."

Did the fact this thing, Marcus, openly admitted its hostility show confidence or stupidity? What was I supposed to do in this situation?

"Relax, relax. I told you because I only had one shot at it. I failed. That's all there is to it." It spoke as if it didn't matter.

Like I can trust what you say.

"True, you can't trust me. So, I'll explain it to the best of my ability." He paused. "Last night when you went to sleep, I entered your body and tried to take control of your memories. If I succeeded I could put your consciousness in an endless loop. I would then use your current memories and live out your life.

"Unfortunately, I didn't listen to Arlene's warning. She said I should wait for an injury before attempting my strike. That was the plan… but when I got into your body…, I got so excited. I couldn't help myself and jumped right in." He sounded giddy.

"Anyway, it took a lot of my power to make an attempt. I failed at my strongest so how could I try again and succeed? I've been gathering that power for hundreds of years already.

"Arlene even forcefully injected some of her memories into you. She tried her best for my sake to weaken you. Alas, it wasn't enough." He spoke with regret. "Anyway, you're probably wondering why I can't try again."

Go on...

"I'm just a spirit residing inside of you. It's not possible for me to grow at a rate faster than you. You'll always be one step ahead of me. That's why it was my only chance."

What's the point of telling me this? It was like a criminal admitting to an attempted murder.

"Well, I'm hoping for the second-best thing. Mutual co-existence."

You want to live inside of me? FAT CHANCE. I'm gonna kick your ass out as soon as I find a way.

"Hey, just because I suggested that doesn't mean I'm all out of options. There's also the second option too."

Second option?

"Mutual Destruction. If you want to go down that route then I can definitely sacrifice the remaining power I have left to turn you into a retard. Shall we try it?" From having a joking tone, he suddenly became menacing. I didn't dare to call his bluff.

So what do you want?

"After seeing your memories I'm quite curious. Where are you from? That place wasn't Yetera. You're not from this planet, are you?" It was a shot right to the heart. I didn't know how to respond. "Well, I'll take your lack of an answer as my answer. For now, I'm just curious what the world is like now."

How long have you been dead?

"Hmm, around a thousand years? I haven't been awake that long though. It was around six hundred years ago when my consciousness suddenly awoke. Arlene's woke a few centuries after mine."

Then how could you know a thousand years have passed?

"Do you think you're the first Adventurer to visit my resting place? Of course not, there were even a few up-to-no-good that dug through my belongings. You can be sure I read their memories and turned them to retards." His tone was boastful.

There was something I wanted to ask Arlene but didn't get the chance. I never saw the use of a spell in her memories. No mention of levels, or monsters, or anything of the sort.

"Ah, right. I attribute those things as being the reason why I awoke as a spirit. You're right though, a thousand years ago when I was alive there was nothing like this. I don't know when it originated or how, but it couldn't have been too long after my death.

"The first time I read a person's memories took place a short century after I woke. Magical powers and the like were simply fledgling existences. It was a fresh and new concept that the residents of Yetera were slowly discovering. I can't imagine coming to life for any other reason."

So, something must have happened. Something on the planet changed.

"Right. It's anybody's guess as to what though. Even during my time there were crazy alchemists studying all forms of magic and sorcery. It never amounted to much though."

So just to get everything out—you're a thousand-year-old spirit that wants to reside in my body? After you tried to essentially erase my existence?

"It's not a bad deal, right?"

What about that isn't a bad deal?

"You won't even know I'm here. I can be quiet and you can pretend I don't even exist."

Sure, let's try that. Stop talking.

There was no response at all and I wondered if he would stay true to his word. I had been walking in a daze and wasn't sure how much time had passed. It was weird having a conversation in your own mind with someone else.

Not even five minutes passed before I heard his voice again, "Uhm… you never told me where we're going." He sounded embarrassed.

Didn't you say you would stop talking? That I could pretend you didn't exist? That I wouldn't even know you were there?

"You don't know how hard it is being cooped up in an urn for six hundred years okay? Tell me where we're going and I'll be quiet."

Tanyros.

The silence was short, "Never heard of it. Tell me what it's like." No matter how many times I acquiesced to his demands he didn't shut up. His silences only ever lasted a few minutes.

Eventually, we arrived at a towering and marvelous city with beautiful castle tops and I had found myself reprimanding him the entire trip.

"This is what you call Tanyros?" he asked.

I think so…

"This is the king's manor," Marcus said.

You're sure?

"Definitely; it's bringing back a lot of old memories. I wouldn't mistake it at all. Look right over there. That's his old castle." My gaze turned to a towering castle that pierced towards the sky. It was by far the tallest building, neatly buried away in a back section of the city.

"We're on the home stretch," Aaron said. "It shouldn't be more than an hour now."

"Isn't this a bit much?" Isabelle asked. She was right, it looked like several Disney Worlds side by side. The main castle was even more stunning and magnificent, especially as my expectations were low after staying in Cape Tou.

"Alright, our first priority is to find a map of the Tanyros mines and then recruit some helpers. It shouldn't be difficult to find some good recruits." Steven spoke the unfortunate truth. The Forest Troll had helped us out in that regard.

"This place looks exactly the same as I remember," Marcus said. "I feel like I'm thirty again." There was longing in his voice.

It was impossible to get his mumbling to stop. No matter what I said, or what I agreed to, he continued to ramble on incessantly. He was driving me to the brink of insanity. I found out that just ignoring him was the best method.

I chose to not respond to any of his questions and very soon he stopped talking. It seemed he was content with just watching through my eyes for now. I breathed a sigh of relief.

"There are so many people…" He gave one last thought.

The cobblestone streets were filled from one side to the other with people. Horses dragged carts here and there. Their trotting echoed through the crowds as the wooden carts rattled.

Numerous Adventurers lined the street side and hawked their wares. The patrolling guards seemed to ignore their presence unless they were blocking a storefront. There was too much to take in all at once.

Seeing the guards gave me a thought and I stopped two of them to report the Forest Troll; although they were skeptical at first, when the rest of the group joined in they were convinced and went hurrying away towards the castle.

"Where should we head for first?" Aaron asked. "We need mining equipment, camping equipment, food and then a few helpers."

There was a board in front of us at a fork in the road. A few people bunched around it curiously.

It was a basic map of Tanyros, one that was publicly available. Our group of five approached and took a look.

"We'll probably need to visit the mining district if we want equipment," said Steven.

"It looks like we'll be able to find the basic goods on King's Row. We can always ask where the best helpers hang out when we reach the mining district." Aaron had picked up the essentials from the map right away.

I backed him. "Let's get going then."

We started to meander through the crowds, doing our best to not get run over by the two-horse wagons. We quickly learned life in Tanyros wasn't slow. This was like the bustling life of a major city: get moving or get run over.

We followed the street markers until we turned down a dirty, cobblestone road. In front of us was a region that was in stark contrast to the beautiful scenery we just passed. The buildings were smaller and covered in thick soot.

The entire area looked more like a giant smithy than a city. Black smoke billowed out from buildings scattered in the distance. The air was thick with the smell of metal and burning charcoal.

Men and women covered in ash and soot worked just outside many buildings. They hammered molten metal before quenching it in thick buckets of black liquid. There were racks of their wares positioned nearby for any prospective customer.

We stayed close together and moved slowly, taking in every inch of our surrounding. Even when we stopped to take a look at a particular craftsman, they kept working unperturbed. It seemed they were used to these kinds of stares.

"How do we even choose?" I asked. There must have been dozens or even hundreds of blacksmiths here, forging equipment of all kinds. There were even tracks and mining carts being assembled at some smithies.

It was called the mining district but there was definitely more than just mining equipment being made. Almost every smithy we passed displayed swords and spears, even some lower-tier armors.

We kept walking around, no doubt with curious eyes.

"You all lost?" A voice called out, "Second time I've seen you come through here empty handed." It was a bald and burly man covered in a layer of black powder.

"Actually, we're looking to get some equipment," I said.

"Mining? Come over here and take a look." He beckoned. We walked over as a group. "What're ya'll looking for?"

"Everything… basically."

"Ah, new to the mines eh? We get new ones like you every few days." He brought us inside his small shop. It was much cleaner than I was expecting. It seemed he did most of the dirty work just outside.

"What do we need?" asked Aaron.

"Well for starters you're gonna want some pickaxes, that's the bare minimum." The shop owner took us to a wall that had a dozen or so pickaxes of varying sizes hanging on the wall. "If you wanna get more fancy then you're gonna want some mining rods and a sledgehammer. I have those over there."

Aaron nodded. "Anything else?"

"You should bring at least one good hand shovel. I also have some mining hats as well." He showed us a metal cap with a bright glowing gemstone inside of it.

"What's this?" Isabelle asked. She was referring to the glowing stone embedded into the metal.

"That's anlite ore, convenient isn't it? It's common as hell but the fact it glows makes it valuable still." The gem looked like it would serve well to illuminate a few feet in front of us in the dark mines.

"How much is it per cap?" Aaron asked.

The shop owner held up two fingers. "Two thousand Zeny per cap."

"How much total if we each got a cap, pick, hand shovel and then two mining rods and two sledgehammers?" asked Aaron.

The man paused for a few minutes and did some mental math. "I can sell the lot to you for twenty thousand. You pick the stuff you want right off the walls, too. Shouldn't be any issue finding one for the each of you."

Aaron looked back at us, "What do you all think?" I had no idea what it would cost us elsewhere. The man didn't seem to be taking advantage of us, but I couldn't be sure and no one else in the group seemed to be decisive either. 20,000 Zeny split between 5 of us was only 4,000 each. It was a small price to pay.

"The sooner we get a deal done, the better," I said. It seemed everyone agreed. Running around this district, fishing for the best deals did not seem all that smart, even if it eventually saved a few thousand Zeny. The faster we made it to the mines the faster we would start making some Zeny.

Aaron passed the man the twenty-thousand Zeny.

"Alright, feel free to grab the equipment you want."

"Any chance you know where we can find good helpers? We're also looking for a detailed map, too." I thought it worth a try asking this guy.

"The best helpers? The place you're looking for is the Golden Tap, a bar on King's Row. Anyone serious about mining hangs out around there. Most decent helpers carry a map with them as well. They don't depend on their handlers to do so. Can't put your life in someone else's hands, ya know?"

"Perfect, thanks." I turned to go.

"Name's Eric, come back if you need repairs! I do those as well."

We shuffled out the smithy and back onto the dirty cobblestone.

"That went better than expected," said Aaron, and he was right, we had managed to pick up all the mining equipment in one stop.

"King's Row, next stop?" asked Isabella.

"To the Golden Tap!" Steven said. I suspected his enthusiasm was in part because we were heading to a bar. We took to the streets and marched towards King's Row.

The sun was still high in the sky and the street we were looking for was far from bustling. Despite that, there were still plenty of customers mucking about. The hardwood creaked as we stepped in the front entrance. The smell of alcohol assaulted our faces.

There were groups spread around the bar randomly. I could see the packs of equipment hanging over their backs. Many had placed their gear directly on the table. Most of them, if not all, were miners.

We sat in silence for several minutes and yet no one came to take our order. The only thing letting me know we weren't completely invisible were the groups around us: their members occasionally took glances in our direction.

"Looks like we got ourselves a group of noobies here." A man called out before standing up from his table. The tone of his voice wasn't friendly at all, instead it was demeaning. He was looking down on us.

None of us spoke up to retort and instead I watched him. He started to walk in our direction, "The Golden Tap isn't a place for a bunch of beginners like you all. You should run along elsewhere." He slapped his hand down on our table.

I couldn't understand why he was being so hostile towards us. What was his reasoning for even suspecting we were beginners? Perhaps he was a veteran miner who frequented the Golden Tap?

"What's the problem? Are you the owner of this bar?" Aaron asked. His tone was neutral and non-antagonistic.

"The problem is you freshies think you can all just migrate to Tanyros and start mining." Little bits of spittle were flying out of the man's mouth. It appeared he was slightly intoxicated.

"Is there some reason we can't? I never heard of anything saying otherwise," Steven spoke up, again without a confrontational tone.

"You can't because I said you can't, chubby." The tall man put his finger right in Steven's face. His attitude was so disrespectful and demeaning I felt myself getting fired up. And I was not the only one: Steven's face was already turning red with anger.

A few of the patrons were looking at us with smiles while others seemed completely uncomfortable. This must have been a regular show. If he was trying to provoke us, he was doing a great job.

It looked like Steven was about to throw the first punch. I was preparing to use Glacial Spike when Marcus's voice stopped me. "Don't be rash." He said. "He's trying to provoke you."

I know that. What does it matter?

"He's out of your league. You see those three guys in the corner?" I turned my attention to a few snickering men with their bags resting on the table. "Soon as you all make a move they're going to jump in. Go ahead and keep summoning if you want your ass kicked."

This warning from Marcus was enough for me to stop and think logically. If our troublemaker was trying to provoke us then he didn't plan on throwing the first punch. Guards patrolled every street. Not only would we get our ass kicked, we might get in legal trouble.

I buried my anger and then reached out to Steven. I grabbed his shoulder and squeezed hard, "It isn't worth it," I said. Our tank's face grimaced as he buried the anger down and I felt his muscles relax. "Let's go," I added.

The man seemed disappointed at our reaction. Marcus was right. He was planning to give us an ass kicking. We had been pretty close to taking the bait. I stood and the others copied me. Then I squeezed my way around him before making my way back outside.

"What now?" asked Isabella. "That seemed like the best lead to getting some decent helpers."

"No problem, we'll be able to find some." Aaron was confident.

"Why did you stop me?" Steven asked.

"That guy looked drunk but he was looking to start a fight, and not because he wanted his ass kicked," I answered.

"Those guys in the corners were hiding weapons under their mining bags." Aaron backed me up. He was quite astute and had picked up on the danger too. He had never lost his composure from the get go.

We were about to walk off when a voice called out to us, "Hey! Wait up!" It was a man with a mining sack over his shoulder. His hair was long and dirty. The clothes he wore were mangled and torn all over.

"You guys looking for helpers?" he asked.

"How can you tell?" I asked.

"Well, most people coming to the Golden Tap when it's closed aren't looking to drink."

So that's what it was. There was no waiter because the bar wasn't open yet.

Isabella smiled at the guy. "Yeah, we're in need of a helper or two."

"Great! I'm interested and I know another miner who wouldn't mind joining an expedition too."

I remembered this man as one of the patrons from inside who had seemed uncomfortable during the entire encounter.

"We can talk about it, but first I have a question," I said. "What was that about in there? We definitely didn't do anything to provoke such a response."

"Yeah… that's becoming a bit more common lately. The man's name is Harvey and he's the leader of a mining organization that's been growing in size." The scruffy man gave a wry shrug. "Lately he's been trying to expand his influence by recruiting 'teams'."

"Recruiting them for what?"

"Well, that's what he claims he's doing on the surface. The reality is he's trying to monopolize as much of the mines as possible. He tries to intimidate and extort new teams like yours. He's been trying to get the royal family to sign off on mining permits. He says a lot of flowery words—"

"But in the end he just wants to be in control, right?" Aaron interrupted.

"Yep, he wants to extort the newer miners by forcing them to pay a premium to mine. A lot of the veteran miners feel threatened by the fresh blood and have joined up. Harvey's got considerable influence so the Golden Tap owner doesn't chase him out. In fact, he brings in a lot of business."

It was starting to make sense. "So why would you want to help us instead of one of Harvey's teams?" I asked.

"Well, the little bit of power their grouping has given them has turned them into some mean sonova bitches. They treat their helpers like dirt and offer the worst splits."

"First off, what's your name?" Aaron asked.

"George."

"And what's your cost?"

George seemed to think hard for a moment, "Fifteen percent! That's for me and my buddy."

It didn't seem like a bad offer. That left 85% of the split for us. Each of us would receive more of a split than theirs combined. Aaron remained silent while thinking.

George seemed to get a bit anxious, "Trust me, we're good workers. We've been running these mines for fifteen years. We know the ins and outs, even a few special spots."

"And what do you expect from us?" Aaron asked. I welcomed his question. It was best to lay everything out so no one was left disappointed later.

"First and foremost, we need protection, that's a given. You provide food and protection, and the trip is minimum one week."

"You don't need any equipment?"

"We have our own picks and mining hats. If you want to provide anything extra that's a bonus."

"What about these?" Aaron displayed two sledge hammers and mining rods.

"This is good stuff," George said. "Should help getting into those hard-to-reach places."

As he handled a rod and passed it back to Aaron, I noticed Harvey and his group of friends walk out of the Golden Tap.

"Hey George! Buddy!" Harvey called out. George jerked in fright, his entire body tensed up. "What are you doing over there with the noobs?"

"Hey boss…" George mumbled. "These guys were asking me about helpers."

"Ah, that's right. Didn't I say I had a group for you and your friend? Come over here and join us."

"Ah, boss, sorry. Already got plans." George said shakily.

"You have plans? What do you mean you have plans? We talked about this. Cancel your plans." Harvey wasn't cheery and friendly anymore.

"No can do. Contract is already signed."

"You signed? With these brats?" He asked. "Shouldn't be a problem then." Harvey turned towards us. "It seems there's been a misunderstanding with my friend George here. I'm just gonna need you to hand over his contract."

The pieces were coming together quickly. George somehow managed to shift the burden of responsibility onto us and removed it from himself via the idea of a contract. Obviously, contracts were a serious business.

"Sorry, no can do. George has already signed with us and we have no intention of releasing him from it." Aaron, as ever, was smart and improvised brilliantly.

Harvey's mood dropped several levels immediately. He seemed to be stuck between a rock and a hard place. We were in an open and busy street with guards patrolling on both sides. Not only did it seem that he couldn't ignore the existence of contract, but he also couldn't force us to hand it over either.

There was only so much big threatening words could do. The uncaring and calm demeanor Aaron presented made it clear that we weren't going to back down to Harvey's threats. Harvey cut his losses and saved some face, "Forget it. Let's go." He addressed his three men. They shoved through us and disappeared down the street.

George wiped the sweat from his brow and started to apologize immediately, "I'm sorry. I put that all on you but I didn't know what else I could do. If I didn't say we had signed a contract he would have hauled me away right then and there."

"Is it a labor contract?" asked Aaron.

"Right, it's an agreement of labor. The royal family distributes contracts with their seal and we just gotta fill em in. Not even Harvey dares to try and nullify one. He's wild but not so out of control he'll bite the hand that feeds him. The royal family could evict him in a day if they really wanted."

Aaron nodded. "So fifteen percent for you and your friend, food and protection?"

"And one week minimum of mining time." George added.

"Alright, where can we meet your friend and get these contracts signed?"

"He should be around in a while." George paused. "How are you so calm right now? Harvey might not act on you in the light, but in the darkness… he holds grudges."

I answered, "He was giving us a rough time when we had done nothing wrong. It was a damned if we do, damned if we don't kind of situation. If we were going to face the consequences regardless, we might as well have pissed him off somehow."

We left the conversation at that and went shopping to fill the time till George's friend showed up. We managed to secure new equipment and a surplus of food. George knew where all the shops were and his familiarity with Tanyros helped a ton.

Nearing sunset, we returned to the Golden Tap. While the hub-bub on the streets had died down, the Golden Tap was busier than ever. "Ah, there he is." George pointed. "Ryan! Over here." He yelled.

We all turned our head to see someone just as scraggly and worn down as George. The biggest difference was their age gap. Ryan was definitely not as old, and probably not as experienced. "Give me a few minutes to talk with him." George said. He pulled Ryan to the side and filled him in.

Once George confirmed Ryan was all in the two both signed contracts. Getting everything we needed to accomplish had taken a bit longer than expected and it was clear we needed to spend the night in Tanyros. George recommended a nearby inn and then headed into the Golden Tap with Ryan for drinks, agreeing to meet us in the morning.

Chapter 8: Into the Mountain

Our morning started bright and early. We met George and Ryan on the south exit of Tanyros as planned. They were packed and waiting for us to arrive. The guards didn't give us any trouble when leaving. The fact each of us carried a pack with mining equipment made it clear what our destination was.

George and Ryan were hired as helpers but were also doubling as our guides. They knew the lay of the land and the fastest route to the Tanyros mines. "It's a two hour walk west." George pointed at a towering mountain in the distance.

The path was so heavily frequented by humans that no monsters dared trespass anymore. The entire area including the regions outside of the mountain was rife with traveling miners. Despite that, it didn't seem like this amount of people could make even a small dent in the vastness of the mountain.

George showed us a map of the mines and it blew me away. The opening started midway up the side of Tanyros and then ventured an unknown distance underground. Even after many years of digging and excavating, the bottom had yet to be discovered.

The biggest issue was the growing strength of monsters the deeper you went down. The tight and winding paths slowly opened to humungous cavities with drops as deep as a hundred feet.

The thought of plunging one-hundred feet into the darkness caused me to shiver. Regardless, I was excited. We were going to be entering our first dungeon and potentially making great Zeny. For the last day Marcus had kept quiet and that helped lift my enthusiasm for the adventure.

The weather was beautiful and the two-hour trek flew by. As we approached the entrance of the mines, the ground beneath our feet started to shake and quake intermittently. A large crowd had formed outside the dark tunnel.

George walked forward, "What's going on?"

"Hey George. One of the veteran teams in the A shaft caused a collapse. They're doing their best to dig them out right now," a dust-covered miner responded.

"Are we shut out then?"

"No, just the A shaft for now." The miner looked at Ryan and our party. "If you're trying to get in then you'll have to take another route, though."

George nodded and headed back to us. "We'll have to take a small detour. It shouldn't be longer than thirty minutes."

"What happened exactly?" Steven wondered.

"The veteran teams are authorized to use dynamite. Seems like they made a mistake and ended up blowing a shaft and trapping themselves inside. It's an unusual event but it does happen."

"Is that gonna be a problem for us?" asked Isabella.

"Besides this little detour not at all. We weren't planning to use the A shaft anyway. We're heading down the E shaft. Just gotta make our way up the mountain a bit more and enter over there is all." George pointed upwards.

Isabella nodded in understanding and we all followed our guide up the side of the mountain. There was a thin and shaky route along the side that wrapped and winded around the cliff face. It was just barely wide enough for two people to pass side by side.

His estimate was spot on and about thirty minutes later we approached an open cave. There were several forking paths leading down into the darkness in front of us. Wooden plaques had been put up above each path.

They read A, B, C, D, and E. According to George we would be taking the E shaft. He pulled his map and showed us the spiderweb-like tunnels leading downward. It seemed every possible route was marked with one of these plaques.

The map was also marked with the letter E at this junction, I felt reassured that miners had developed this labelling system, it would be easy to get lost otherwise.

There was no point trying to mine at this well-travelled spot though.

George pointed to a small branch off the main tunnel. "We'll head down to E5 and start mining there. The area opens up a bit and we'll be around other teams. It should be relatively safe to start with."

We put on our mining caps and followed him down the dark and dreary tunnel. The walls around us didn't continue as rock, as I had expected, but instead turned into something crystalline. I couldn't help but run my hand along it as we moved downward.

"We call it crystal rock." George said, looking back at me. "No one has found a use for it; it's just a pain in the ass to mine through."

We descended for around an hour before coming to our destination. A wooden plaque was fastened above a tunnel that marked E5.

We entered inside and my claustrophobic feeling slowly dissipated. The tunnel grew wider and wider until we walked into an open shaft. Surprisingly, the walls here were not crystal rock. It looked like actual stone.

The ceiling was filled with stalactites that steadily dripped water. The air smelled slightly damp and moldy. The metallic sounds of picks smacking into dirt and rock echoed throughout the entire shaft.

George turned back to look at us, "Which one of you is the mage?"

"That's me," I answered.

"If you have any freezing magic I suggest you use it if we have to fight. The majority of monsters down here are hard as the crystal rock. The cold makes them brittle," he said. I took his advice to heart. I would be using Glacial Spike then.

George walked us along the shaft past other groups of Adventurers and miners and found an empty spot. "This is what we're looking for." He pointed at the wall, "crystal rock doesn't have minerals inside. We need to mine through rock or dig through dirt." The area in front of him was just a muddy, rocky spot. There was a stalagmite sticking out of the floor just next to it. Having struck at the ground with his pick George suddenly backed away, "Get ready!" He looked at me.

The only person not confused by his action was Ryan. I couldn't tell what was happening until the soil where he had started to mine began to pulse and tremble. A man-sized golem suddenly bust from beneath the soil and took a swing at us.

With impressive reaction time, Steven managed to block the strike with his shield. The noise of the blow sounded like a sledgehammer coming down on a sheet of metal. His shield rattled and his legs bent slightly. I cast *Inspect* immediately.

```
┌─────────────────────────────────────────────────────────┐
│  GRANITE GOLEM    LEVEL: 22        NEUTRAL              │
│                    EARTH                                │
│    HP: 6504              MP: 10                         │
│                  STR: 30                                │
│                  AGI: 5                                 │
│                  DEX: 5                                 │
│                  VIT: 20                                │
│                  INT: 5                                 │
│  A GOLEM MADE OUT OF THE FINEST GRANITE. WHO KNOWS     │
│    WHERE IT COULD POSSIBLY HAVE COME FROM?             │
└─────────────────────────────────────────────────────────┘
```

Following George's advice, I immediately followed up with Glacial Spike. The spike jutted from below and collided with one of the golem's legs. It didn't penetrate at all. The magical point actually broke off immediately.

The freezing ice, however, created a layer of frost on the golem's leg. That frosty layer slowly climbed up and towards its torso. Something I wasn't expecting happened immediately after. George used one of the sledgehammers from his gear and swung out from behind into the golem's leg.

His casual sledgehammer swing didn't meet with any resistance. Instead, the granite leg shattered into a million pieces before the golem toppled to the floor. I cast another Glacial Spike that connected with its chest and head.

George swung the sledgehammer down onto the monster's head which also shattered. A small gemstone came from within the head of the granite golem that George picked up before flicking to me.

I grasped it in my hand. It was an item. **Granite Control Switch.** I read the description.

The control source of a granite golem.

I couldn't help but marvel at how easily George had dispatched the golem. It was us who were supposed to be providing his protection. "You're thinking he's got hidden class abilities?" Marcus suddenly said. It was what I was thinking. "I can tell you that he does not." Marcus seemed to have insights into the world that were not available to me. "Even I don't know how he discovered its presence, though. Your guide backed away well before the golem came through the ground."

The battle had shown me how important local knowledge was. Without George's advice I would have foolishly been throwing fireballs at the golem. Steven and Aaron would have been tickling it with sword strikes and arrows. Maybe Kimmi could have done reasonable damage with Penetrate.

The fight could easily have been many times harder. George had made it look so simple that I felt utterly inadequate.

"It's fortunate you know a good ice ability. It gets a lot harder when they don't," our guide said.

"What's this switch?" I asked.

"No one knows, but it hints at something, doesn't it?"

It did. Something was controlling the golem. I suddenly felt a lot more excited about the item. Wouldn't it fantastic to have a granite golem under my control?

George and Ryan started to tag team the area the golem appeared from. Whenever they came across crystal rock they would grab the mining rods and sledgehammers. They would make a small groove with a pick and then place the mining rod inside.

One of them would hold it while the other smacked down on it repeatedly. Eventually the crystal rock would give and split right in half. They could then move it out of the way and continue digging deeper.

Sometimes, George would suddenly back away the narrow tunnel they were making and Ryan would follow. We learned quickly what that meant: a golem was coming through the bedrock. Ever since George's demonstration on the first golem, he just stood by and didn't intervene at all.

Knowing how to deal with the golems meant we made quick work of them. They varied in size but all had the same fatal weakness: bringing their granite body to extreme cold temperatures made them shatter like glass. Steven's strength was then sufficient to break their legs with a swing of his sword.

The first golem gave very little EXP, since George had done the majority of damage. The subsequent kills, however, all gave 500-600 EXP. Not bad at all for such an easy encounter. The only issue was they didn't show up very often.

Our two miners spent around thirty minutes on this one spot before backing away. I expected a golem but instead it was them throwing in the towel, George shook his head. "This spot's a bust, nothing here at all." We hadn't even found a cosmetic gemstone, let alone a valuable enchanting stone.

That was what the typical gems were called: cosmetic gemstones. They were used as the main focal point in jewelry. The royal family absolutely adored them and so did those passing through Tanyros.

These mines were an enormous source of wealth for the kingdom of Tanyros. It was unlikely the royal family would ever require permits from those wanting to mine here. The majority of wealth made from the mines ended up back in the city's economy anyway. Restricting access would have been like stabbing themselves in the foot.

George pulled the map from his bag and spread it wide. We watched his finger trace the path until eventually stopping on E5. I was surprised to find we were still so near the entrance. We hadn't even traveled halfway down the E shaft yet.

"Most of these areas have already been mined clean. I figured it would be a good idea for you all to get some experience first-hand before going deeper," our guide said. "It only gets harder as we go down, but I think you guys can handle it."

We were here for profits. A little bit of risk and danger was needed if we wanted to line our pockets. The granite golems we had encountered so far were nothing short of cannon fodder. It wouldn't be boasting to say we could deal with 4 or 5 of them at a time if need be.

"What do you suggest?" asked Isabella.

"Let's head down to E8 and try our luck there."

I could see enough of the map to tell at E8 was about halfway along the E shaft. The furthest marker I saw was E17. We were quite a ways from the deepest anyone had excavated.

Kimmi must have been wondering the same as me, "Are there people down in E Seventeen?"

"Probably, mostly veteran mining teams though, the guys that have been hanging around these mines for a dozen years." George paused. "I know I'm hired help but I won't be going down there unless you guys show some serious promise." It seemed the little bit of combat potential we had shown wasn't good enough to warrant mining that deep. I wasn't offended by his honesty.

In fact, I appreciated his straightforward attitude. George told us how it was and didn't beat around the bush. It seemed he had no time for dilly dallying in his old age. We packed away the few mining instruments we had removed and started to venture deeper along tunnel E.

The pathways tightened and widened as we ventured down. On our way down to E8 we passed several groups mining in the wider areas. Several times, George showed more of his expertise while we descended by stopping and raising his arm to halt us. Without fail a golem would morph out of the wall and block our path. Despite careful scrutiny of the environment, I still didn't understand how he was able to spot incoming enemies in the darkness and difficulties of the tunnel. Was it possible he had developed a detection skill over the many years of mining? It seemed like the best and only explanation.

George wasn't oblivious to my curiosity. "It's a skill." He said in answer to a question from Aaron. "There's a good few veteran miners who were once Adventurers like you all."

"Why'd you stop?" asked Isabella.

"Personally, I found I wasn't cut out for it. But a good chunk of us don't have a choice."

She frowned, "Like how?"

"You all seem new; so you just don't get it yet, but being an Adventurer costs money. You probably think you're going to be rolling in Zeny without a care in the world." He smiled. "Equipment cost money. Potions cost money, traveling costs money. The fees are endless. All of that money costs you time."

His first statement wasn't wrong. I did feel like things were looking up, that we would steadily grow our Zeny and it would be smooth sailing to Arturii. I continued listening. This was an older man's wisdom.

"There's a lot of reasons why people stop. Some get hurt and can't continue anymore. Maybe one day you want to start a family and raise a kid. It could be as simple as someone in a high place having it in for you."

"Regardless, you'll slowly learn that being an Adventurer costs a lot. And it's not just Zeny that you pay with. You have to give up your time, your health. You don't give up your time, your gear suffers, and your levelling suffers. You find yourself falling behind and being forgotten."

I never thought about it that way. Would a day come when my teammates were leaving me behind? Would I get hurt and have to stop only to find they weren't there waiting for me? I thought back to Richard. I had wanted him to come with us badly but realized eventually that time waited for no one. I wasn't an exception.

"Here we are, be a bit more prepared as we'll be encountering golems a lot more."

This turned out not to be the slightest exaggeration. It seemed the deeper you were the more intense the encounters became. Golems would pop up every couple of minutes and halt the mining progress of George and Ryan.

The flow of monsters and EXP was starting to become steady and hoping it was pushing my progress along, I checked my stats.

```
CURRENT EXP: 10045/49000     LEVEL: 20
           MAGE          FORMIDABLE
      HP: 1312/1312    MP: 344/498
              STR: 11
              AGI: 11
              DEX: 20
              VIT: 15 +2
              INT: 30 +14
           AVAILABLE: 0
```

111

The golems were giving around 500 EXP per kill and we had dispatched around twenty since entering. The overall gain felt like a drop in the bucket of EXP needed towards my next level. I wanted to venture deeper down. Looking at how bored Aaron seemed, I wasn't the only one who felt that way.

Probably, we were all chomping at the bit to get some more action. George, however, kept us from biting off more than we could chew. We moved down gradually, and George and Ryan made sure we were strong enough to protect them while they worked.

Only after demonstrating that a particular floor was something we could manage would they suggest we go deeper. It was honest progression and we followed his advice willingly. We would be down here for a week or more. There was little point in rushing on our first day.

We were on floor E9 and it was just past the mid-day mark when George yelled, "Got something over here!"

"Pass a shovel," Ryan said. We all grouped around the two miners, staring at the now mangled and destroyed rock. They had pounded it with their pickaxes and then beat on it with sledgehammers.

George took the shovel and began scooping and scraping away at the dirt. The stone below slowly came into view. It was smaller than a golf ball with green and blue hues covering the surface. Our helmet lights were reflected in the gem and made it shine.

"What is it?"

"It's an opal, purely cosmetic." George pulled it between his fingers and inspected it slowly, "This one's probably worth around two thousand Zeny. Not terrible."

"How can you tell?"

"Look at the stone closely. You see how it's kind of foggy and blurry inside?" He held it out for all of us to take a look, "people like 'em clear and almost see-through. The less foggy the better." He wasn't wrong. There was a grayish puff of smoke filling the inside of the stone. It didn't look clean at all.

The opal was our first discovery in several hours of effort. So far, the indications were that we were taking this mining business too lightly. There was a chance we would come out with empty pockets after a week.

"Do you think there's more in the area?" asked Aaron.

"Can't be sure. It's a good sign we have found it, though, because this means no one else has mined this spot. Let's focus our attention here for a while," George suggested. "Do any of you want to learn the ropes of mining?"

I was surprised to see Kimmi volunteer herself. She wielded her pick and stood beside George as he pointed here and there. He constantly gave her instructions and advice. The pick was nearly half the size of Kimmi and yet she wielded it effortlessly.

Her high STR stat was proving to be an absolute marvel. There was more power in her delicate frame than either George or Ryan could muster. She started to swing the pick down repeatedly. Soon a series of clangs rang out around us as it collided with crystal rock.

"Alright, when you reach a tough bed of crystal rock like this, you got two options," George said. "You either go around it, which is sometimes hard to do cause it can be real big, or you get out your mining rod and sledgehammer." He beckoned Ryan over who was carrying a sledgehammer and mining rod.

"You wanna make a nice indent in the crystal rock, the deeper the better. Then you set in your mining rod, if it isn't deep enough to hold on its own then get someone to hold it for you. Once it's in, you beat on it till it gives. Simple as that."

George held the mining rod in place for Kimmi while she started to hammer it in. She started off slow at first out of fear of missing. She would shatter his arm and hand without the slightest effort if she missed.

Eventually she started to pound on the top of the rod like a seasoned miner. There was a loud crack that echoed through the chamber, like the sound of a glacier breaking off and falling into the ocean. The mining rod had sunk several inches down. A clear indication the crystal rock had given way.

George looked pleased. "Take a look at what you found." There was something below the crystal rock.

"What is it?" I asked excitedly as George reached down for a gem.

"Looks like Peridot, a pretty good one." He twirled it in his fingers, "One of the better-looking ones I've seen recently. Once it's cleaned up should go for quite a bit." He passed the Peridot to Kimmi who was incredibly excited.

"If we go any deeper we'll start to see other monsters besides Granite Golems. We can go deeper tomorrow but for now let's keep focusing our luck here," George said. I was starting to grow bored with fighting just these Granite Golems but the two gems were evidence that settling in here could pay off for us.

The atmosphere became quite relaxed and we took turns trying our hand at mining. I was incredibly grateful that we had hired helpers. Kimmi, Aaron and Steven made mining look like cake, no doubt a consequence of their constant pumping of STR.

Isabella and I struggled to raise the pickaxe over and over. It was backbreaking work through and through. Although we had no indication that night was closing in on the world outside, my growing lethargy suggested it was late.

"How do we sleep?" I asked.

It would be a silly question if asked anywhere else, but here, a constant flow of golems came out of the ceiling and walls. When would there be any time to get a wink of sleep?

"We'll head back up to E Four," answered George, "there's a chamber up there for sleepers. Golems don't show up above E Five so it's safe. There are also helpers hired by the royal family that keep watch."

Deciding we were done for the day, we left our mining spot and made our way up to the less narrow shafts above, eventually finding tunnels with camps of Adventurers. Stepping carefully over body-filled sleeping bags and found an open area of our own to setup camp. I was hesitant to light a small campfire. George assured me it was okay. We were close enough to the cave entrance that smoke would drift up and out.

Dinner was a small stew, hearty and rich, enough to warm the body and soul. George and Ryan fell asleep in minutes. I found myself looking up at the hovering stalactites. There was a constant pitter of water hitting the cave floor.

I guessed that if you spent enough time down here it would all become white noise. The clanging of picks, the vibrations from the explosions, the constant droning of water, all amplified and echoed through every chamber.

I didn't know when I fell asleep.

Chapter 9: Into the Depths

George shook each of us awake. It was impossible to get used to, the same darkness we went to sleep in waited for us. It would be incredibly easy to lose track of time here.

"Once we pass E-ten there will be more than just golems. The wildlife that has been living in these caves for hundreds of years has slowly been driven downward from the surface. They are rare but present."

As if to illustrate George's warning, we soon found ourselves battling new creatures.

CAVE SALAMANDER LEVEL: 26	BEAST EARTH
HP: 7652	MP: 75
STR: 20	
AGI: 20	
DEX: 10	
VIT: 30	
INT: 3	
A GIANT SALAMANDER. IT LOVES MOIST PLACES.	

```
POISONOUS CENTIPEDE        LEVEL: 10        INSECT
                         POISON
    HP: 1825                    MP: 10
                         STR: 5
                         AGI: 15
                         DEX: 15
                         VIT: 5
                         INT: 2
   A POISONOUS CENTIPEDE. ITS BITE WILL MELT HUMAN FLESH.
```

The latter creature was a centipede that was entirely white and could be found crawling along the stalagmites. We almost didn't notice it as we passed by. Luckily, George was paying careful attention. It wasn't a serious danger by any means, but its strength lay in stealth, and its vicious poison which could have been a problem had it caught us by surprise.

```
ROCK SNAKE        LEVEL: 24        BEAST   NEUTRAL
    HP: 5193                    MP: 15
                         STR: 15
                         AGI: 20
                         DEX: 15
                         VIT: 15
                         INT: 5
   A SNAKE THAT BLENDS PERFECTLY WITH THE SURROUNDING
                         ROCKS.
```

There were also an endless number of vampire bats that screeched overhead. Even the golems coming through the walls and floors became more frequent. It was a full-time job to protect George and Ryan while they mined.

Despite how frantic and rushed the situation felt for us, George and Ryan looked quite relaxed. I only hoped their attitude would slowly rub off on to us. We were too new to this underground world.

Our group turned out to be more adaptable than I thought. We learned to go with the flow and take the rush as it came. We quickly learned the weaknesses of every creature in this cave and divided our responsibilities accordingly. Besides Glacial Spiking the Golems, I didn't have another significant role and steadily played my part as we ground away.

CONGRATULATIONS! YOU HAVE REACHED LEVEL 21. AS A REWARD FOR LEVELING UP, YOU HAVE BEEN GRANTED THREE STAT POINTS!

I had been dying to see these words for what felt like ever. The constant source of monsters to dispatch was heavenly. I didn't ever want to leave, and suspected I wasn't the only one feeling that way. We had even received a new skill book for Aaron.

BOOK OF ENSNARING ARROW LV. 1
CAST TIME: 2 SECONDS
MP COST: 8
DISTANCE: -
DURATION: 10 SECONDS
COVERS AN ENEMY IN VINES THAT RESTRICT ITS MOVEMENT.

The word 'ensnaring' sparked a memory from an earlier encounter. It was while fighting that horde of Roda. Some of the corpses had vines growing out of them, similar to how I imagined this skill would work.

"Don't you have a skill like this already?" Kimmi asked Aaron.

118

She had taken the words from my mouth. Out of all of us she had encountered the vines the most. She had been like a blood-thirsty demon as she hacked and slashed every Roda to pieces, plus she had seen them up close on looting them afterwards.

Aaron held out his quiver, the one which had dropped off the Ancient One back on Earth. "It's this thing: as far as I can tell it imbues my arrows with special properties. One of them seems to give the arrow a bit of life. The vines growing out is a side effect."

If the two effects could stack that would provide quite a bit of crowd control. A duration of ten seconds wasn't as long lasting as Shackle but it didn't seem there was any damage threshold. We hadn't run into any enemy we needed to CC thus far but I was interested to see how this would work.

CURRENT EXP: 55/51000	LEVEL: 21
MAGE	FORMIDABLE
HP: 1342/1342	MP: 344/506
STR: 11	
AGI: 11	
DEX: 20	
VIT: 15 +2	
INT: 30 +14	
AVAILABLE: 3	

I opened my stats with more hesitation than ever before. The levels weren't coming quickly anymore. These three points were worth their weight in gold. In the end I decided holding onto them was currently the best option.

The days passed quickly with the constant stream of monsters to kill. Unfortunately, our luck wasn't that good. Over the course of six days, we found several more cosmetic gemstones, but no enchanting stones at all. Even George seemed upset at this terrible rate of return.

The rate at which we were finding material was pitiful. If it kept up, at the end of one week none of us would be happy with the haul.

So we started to travel deeper still and soon found ourselves on floor E15. I couldn't tell if George genuinely believed in our ability to go deeper, or if he wanted more Zeny. The miners down here were all veterans. None of the helpers were hired, either. They were all part of one team, Adventurers and helpers. They routinely came down together.

I noticed more and more of the stares we received from other miners were unwelcoming. I received many unfriendly gazes that made it clear that we were looked down upon. I had a bad feeling about the hostility of those around us.

This must be why Harvey was so successful in recruiting. All of these veteran miners disliked the fresh blood. There wasn't an ounce of comradeship in their eyes and it seemed to me that if it wasn't for the presence of George they even might try to get rid of us.

I didn't doubt at all they'd give him a hard time after our contract was up. I could imagine the conversations: "us veterans gotta' stick together." They'd pat him on the back over some drinks. Meanwhile Harvey would sit in the back like a snake, laughing as he gained another pawn to his cause.

I shook off that thought and focused back on the task at hand. I needed to be quick with my reaction on Glacial Spike. I wasn't even needed for the non-golem monsters. Whenever a golem came up, George, Ryan and I would take care of it together.

The close presence of so many other experienced groups dealing with the spawns definitely hurt our EXP gain compared to operating in a tunnel by ourselves, but it was the only way to keep things under control. The other groups all around us were doing the same things as us. They were even merrily chatting and laughing as they took on the occasional mob.

Another day passed just like that, and we finally had a bit of luck. We managed to find one enchanting stone, a piece of Phlogopite. This was a solid 20,000 Zeny gain: enough to pay for the materials we had bought before leaving. Not that anyone wanted to leave. None of us were fully satisfied and wouldn't be until we were well ahead.

We eventually found our way down to E17. It was a large open cavern filled with a dozen teams. There was enough space for dozens more. Wildlife crawled through the darkness and maneuvered through the many twists and turns.

The cavern tapered off at the lowest point to a single hole. This appeared to be the frontier, the furthest point anyone had managed to reach in their excavations. Careful not to go too close to the edge, I looked into the pitch darkness below. It was a hole of unknown depth and I felt like I was looking straight into the abyss.

We picked an empty spot and started to excavate. George and Ryan were careful with their strikes. Fortunately, the floor below us was still at least several feet thick. We weren't at risk of collapsing our floor.

I noticed the groups around us slowly exit E17. They didn't leave all at once so nothing seemed amiss at first. The teams mining beside us gradually dwindled until there was only a few left. I wasn't the only one who noticed, "Hey Lucas, what's up? Where's everyone heading?" George called out.

"Ah, George, can't speak for the others but we're gonna head back for some lunch and probably pick another shaft." The miner's voice was a bit shaky, maybe tinged with a bit of guilt. By now I understood something was wrong.

"Should we head out as well?" George asked us. It seemed the situation wasn't comfortable for him either. Being the last team in cavern did not feel right. Not only that, the pressure on us from spawns was rising.

"Right after this Crystal Rock," Ryan had placed a mining rod in the ground and was preparing to slam down his sledgehammer, "I see something below." This was an exciting prospect and all of us, myself included, were blinded by greed.

Unfortunately, before we got to find out what was under that Crystal Rock, I heard the sound of a wick burning. It was the miner, Lucas, whom George had spoken to. He was at the entrance to the cavern where a stick of explosive had been shoved into a groove in the narrow pathway.

His intention was obvious, to trap us in this cavity, this tomb. "Sorry George." He yelled. He really was. I could hear the remorse in his voice. Did that matter though? Not really. His apology didn't stop him from throwing even more explosives directly into the cavern and towards us.

No one said a word. It was obvious what we needed to do. We had to get away, and yet there wasn't anywhere for us to go. "Run! Now!" I cried. Steven bashed his shield into the Poison Centipede we were fighting and sent it hurdling away from us. His action managed to buy us some time and we immediately ran towards the far end of the cavern. The only cover that might provide us with protection from an explosion was that of the many stalagmites poking from the floor.

My heart was beating out of my chest as I crouched beside one of the large mineral rocks. It felt like an eternity before that first explosion went off and in the meantime the centipede was attacking Steven, making it hard for him to stay in cover. Then, like crackling thunder, the rocky entrance collapsed. It didn't take much brain power to realize we were now trapped. I braced myself for the next explosion.

Time seemed to crawl and the only sound I could hear was my own beating heart and the sound of that burning wick. The explosion came and I felt the heat and debris blow by my face. Even the stalagmite wasn't enough to keep me protected.

My ears started to ring and it was all I could hear. I could still feel the quaking of the wall, the growing cracks. The room was falling apart.

It was no surprise, the explosion creating so much extra pressure with nowhere to go. Well, there was somewhere to go—the empty cavity below us. I imagined what the sound would be like, a gigantic room sheering off from inside the mountain. I couldn't hear it, but I could feel it.

Suddenly my body felt weightless. I was in free fall, nothing around me but darkness. I didn't know how long I fell, but the eventual splatter didn't come. I landed on something hard, my ribs hurt from the impact.

Water surrounded me on all sides, I was stunned. It was pitch dark again, a truly perfect darkness. My sinking body was the only indication to which way was up or down. My ringing ears suddenly popped.

The breath caught in my throat was torturous. I shrugged off the shock and swam towards the surface and breathed in deeper than I ever had. My gasp echoed inside the entire chamber. I couldn't even fathom just how big it was.

My mind raced as I looked around me, listened for any movement. I lit a fireball in my wet hand and held it up. I would be the light in this dark tunnel. The sounds of people surfacing rang out around me. They took huge gaping breaths before swimming towards the light.

"Joseph!" Their voices called out one at a time until they swam to my side. I felt incredibly fortunate, and as a group, we were. Even Ryan managed to come back up and swim to our side. George, however, never resurfaced.

Only after that initial adrenaline had worn off did I realize just how cold the water was. We couldn't stay here very long or we would freeze. Ryan was definitely struggling already.

"Swim till we find a shore," said Aaron. "Go in different directions." It was our only option.

I was a torch in this dark chamber, and as long as I had the ability to cast fireball, we wouldn't lose each other. We started to swim in opposite directions, eventually Isabelle's voice rang out, "Over here! There's solid ground." I turned and started to swim in the direction of her voice.

Our clothes, our gear, even our food was fully soaked through. Some of it could be salvaged, but the bread and dried cheeses were completely ruined. We tossed them into the dark abyss. Starting a fire was the highest priority: otherwise we would freeze.

I managed to light a campfire and we huddled around it. We removed our outer clothing and set them aside to dry. Our words echoed endlessly beyond and up. I wasn't sure just how far down we had fallen, or how big the cavern was.

Isabelle summoned Heirophant's Helper so that we would see a little more of our situation. It definitely helped illuminate the area around us, but it couldn't travel far enough away from Isabelle to reach the ceiling or even one of the cave walls.

There was only one way to find out the size of the cave, and so I enlisted Aaron. He nocked an arrow and placed a tip wrapped in a rag into the fire. It started to burn brightly and he aimed directly up and fired. It soared and soared before eventually colliding with the ceiling.

Some vampire bats were startled. They shrieked and then flew through the air. The displaced wind from their flapping wings created a sound as loud as a blowing wind. We weren't alone down here. George had warned us clearly; the wildlife grew bolder the deeper we went.

It was hard to gauge the distance in this darkness, but we must have fallen over two-hundred feet. It felt like a miracle that most of us had survived the fall, or possibly our survival was a testament to our increased physique.

George was not so lucky. I mourned for him. The miner had taken us on against the pressure of his peers. And he'd been murdered for it. George had been the most experienced of the two miners and had been very patient with us. Maybe even, had begun to like us, as we figured out how best to fight the mobs here. Now he was gone and I would never relent against those to blame.

Ryan was clearly hurting, but took George's passing better than I expected. Was it unusual to lose someone down here? I couldn't be sure. He was keeping himself composed and trying not to show his grief. All the same, I noticed him wipe a tear away.

I started to feel guilty. If George had never gotten involved with us, then this wouldn't have happened. He was a good guy as far as I could tell. Were there loved ones to miss him? He had never mentioned a family even once; I realized how little I knew about him.

The loss of bread and cheese hurt, but we could ration ourselves and stretch what we had that a bit further. This was only our third day in the mines, and we had brought enough food to last a week.

The more pressing issue was the mobs in the cave. It was alive with movement. There were sounds around us that weren't made by the vampire bats, or water droplets, or even the still falling debris. The walls crawled, slithered, and hissed. With such a mountain to climb, I was hard pressed to see how we could get out of here.

"If we are careful, we have enough food and water to last a week," Aaron said. "Surely someone will find us by then?"

"No one will come looking," Ryan looked up. "It's nothing out of the ordinary; a tunnel has collapsed. Those veteran miners never saw us. There's no reason too, either. Judging by the drop off, the work on the E tunnel will stop here. A new shaft will be dug at a different angle."

"The more pressing issue is the monsters around us." I couldn't see them but I could feel their stares of hunger. It was nonsensical that we hadn't been swarmed yet, there must be a reason, and so we looked.

The answer came quickly. We weren't on solid ground at all, but just an island in a large lake of water. We had yet to find the true cave floor. I pointed this out.

"I guess that explains why nothing is coming after us," somehow Kimmi managed to sound enthusiastic.

We needed to go, but we couldn't leave. Our only protection was also a cage that trapped us. We were currently drying our clothes but would need to go for a swim again soon. Were we even ready to contend with the monsters waiting in the dark?

"If no one is coming to find us then we need to find a way out. What we need most is ideas," observed Aaron.

Ryan pulled the now soggy map from his bag and spread it on the dark ground. I held my fireball above it to provide more light. "I can't say for sure how far we've fallen, but the closest shaft at this depth is shaft C."

"So, you suggest we try and connect with another shaft to ascend?"

"I don't see any other way. There's no way we can climb up from here." The distance from shaft E to shaft C didn't look all that far, but we had to be sure that there was solid rock between us and our goal, a place we could rest. The water was so cold, even a strong swimmer wouldn't last too long in it.

"How sure are you they connect?" Isabella wondered and Ryan shook his head.

"Not sure at all. It would be great if we find a pathway and don't have to dig that hard, if we're unlucky we hit a solid wall. If that happens, we might be better off digging up into D shaft."

My sense of direction was already off. We needed to get our bearings first. We couldn't just dig out of the side of the mountain if we went the wrong way. By now we were deep underground.

"Can you try and get an arrow up top again? I need to see where the blown opening is," Ryan asked.

Aaron nodded his head and continuously nocked arrows, lighting them in my flame and sending them arcing upwards until we had a decent idea of the structure above us. "Shaft C should be that way then." Ryan pointed.

If we were lucky there would be solid ground nearby and a pathway to walk on. We hoped and prayed while Aaron lit his arrow and shot it into the darkness in the direction Ryan wanted us to go. What we saw was less than ideal. There was no solid ground for as far as the arrow went. Only more water.

The good news was we didn't see a dead end. We would, however, still need to swim through the murky abyss. Hitting a dead end after swimming was my big fear though. The water was cold and quickly sapped your strength. What if I didn't have the energy to come back?

We would need to swim purely with our legs as well. If we wanted to keep our now dry clothes from getting soaked once again the packs would have to remain in our arms above our head. It wasn't going to be easy.

"I'll lead the front with a fireball. Isabelle you keep Heirophant's Helper around everyone else," I suggested.

Holding my pack and a fireball would be near impossible. I opted to lead the front and swim with my pack on. I would just dry them again. Fireball would help me dry my clothes quickly. It wasn't a problem if I was the only one who got them wet.

Steven looked hesitant. "When should we go?"

The day was still relatively early, not that the light reached down here. I could just tell by the fact that I was still full of energy.

"As soon as possible." Time was of the essence. We needed to get a foothold if we wanted to make it out alive.

I stuffed my clothes back into my pack and strapped it around my back. "Follow behind me; close." I looked back at their nodding heads and fear filled faces.

Chapter 10: Further Depths

I took the leap of faith and plunged into the water in front of me. My head was only underwater for a moment before I resurfaced, finding that I was able to reach the ground with my feet. I lit a fireball with one hand and wiped my face with the other. It was chilly as hell.

On seeing me able to stand, the others didn't risk diving in like I had. They each sat on the little island's edge and dangled their feet in the water before gently wading away, arms up high. This way they could keep the packs above their head and safely dry.

I turned away and saw that in the direction we needed to go the ceiling dipped dangerously low. After a hundred meters or so, it was just a few feet above my head. There was a thought droning through my mind no matter how much I pushed it to the side. Something I dare not bring up: what if there was something in the water with us?

We had managed to get out of the water safely the first time, surely there was nothing to fear? I couldn't help but look down at the pitch-dark water. I couldn't even see my torso just several inches under.

I was experiencing a kind of fear that could drive you insane. Was I swimming here waiting to be pulled under? To feel a tug on my leg and then be dragged below the surface, unable to regain it, until I took my final water-filled breath?

I shook off the horror and slowly waded further on. There was no noise but the sound of our bodies swishing through the water and chilled breathing, that and the occasional drip. We were moving at a snail's pace, and rightfully so. Staying above water carrying a pack of supplies on your head was not easy.

"There's a construction ahead," Marcus spoke up for the first time in days. I didn't see or feel anything, but I had learned his senses were extremely keen. If he said there was something, there was something. I didn't even need to ask before his answer came, "I don't know what it is either."

Regardless, it made me hopeful. My biggest fear was swimming into a dead end only to return empty handed, chilled to the bone, and lower on energy than we started, without an ounce of progress.

I suddenly saw something in the distance. It looked like a wall, but there was a bit of illumination coming from the water below it, though I was so low in the water I couldn't get the angle to see what it was. Nor could the others behind me have even seen the faint light, my fireball blocking their vision completely.

My swimming suddenly felt a bit easier. I didn't need to exert much strength to move forward.

"There's something up ahead." I was sure now; the wall in front was lit up quite clearly by whatever was the light source. The wall, however, seemed to be a dead end: it looked like we would need to turn around. I grew quite disappointed.

I found myself drifting forward as if part of a current: something was wrong now. This body of water seemed stagnant but it was flowing, and the pace was picking up. I was moving against my will towards that glowing wall.

I wasn't the only one to notice either. Steven called out, "this isn't such hard going."

131

"Do you hear that?" I was suddenly anxious. There was a distant sound of rumbling waves, water crashing into something over and over. It was weak at first but steadily grew in intensity.

The wall was coming closer and my line of sight improved: the water wasn't touching that distant wall. The wall rested just a few feet away and the water dropped off.

The pieces came together; it was a waterfall. We were drifting towards a waterfall that dropped even deeper down. "Turn back! It's a waterfall, we have to turn back!" I yelled at them. We had gotten too close; it was too late.

I was only a few meters from the edge and couldn't fight the quickening current. A quick glance showed me that all of us were being funneled from this huge shaft into this little drop off a dozen feet wide. The strength of its pull was not something we could contend with, even with both arms and legs.

My mind drew a blank. There was no way out of this situation and I found myself sinking below the surface, sucked by an irresistible current and freefalling.

Thankfully, I didn't fall for long. I wasn't shocked or stunned and had the presence of mind to move out of the way, lest someone land on top of me. I was amazed, my eyes could see under the water. Not due to some change of my own, but from the room we had entered.

It was another large cavity, but instead of the darkness we'd experienced above, it was brightly lit. A rainbow of colors was visible in every direction I looked. I was confused for only a moment before I thought back to that little smithy and Eric. This was all anlite ore. The entire chamber was coated with it, and lit the whole area as bright as day.

I swam to the shore and watched as my teammates plummeted off the waterfall and into the spring below. *Spring, huh?* It was the same water as above, and yet I referred to it so differently. The contrast between light and dark made the water seem a lot less dangerous.

This waterfall was nowhere near as high a drop as our first. Everyone landed with a splash below and safely swam to shore. Their attempts at keeping their packs dry had failed miserably, and yet their expressions showed their mood was looking up.

All around us were bright beautiful colors. Green algae and plant life covered the stalactites and stalagmites, making them feel like tall trees. Gemstones of every shape and color plastered the walls and floors. We were in an underground jungle.

Ryan looked around with eyes wide as saucers, his mouth could barely form the words, "Those…those are rubies, and those are diamonds and amethysts…" his mouth mumbled through the names of dozens and dozens of gemstones before coming to a stop. He was basically shaking in excitement.

It wouldn't be fitting to call the cavern an underground jungle without there being monsters. I could see they were present as well, except they seemed content with their positions. There were different creatures huddled around clumps of gemstones; they eyed us with hostility but made no move to attack.

"This… is a treasure trove." Ryan was twirling, water flying off his clothes as he took the sight in. "We're rich…"

"It looks like we'll have to fight for it," I said. "It doesn't seem like they want to give up their wealth."

"I didn't know monsters could be seduced by pretty gems," said Kimmi.

133

There was a strange power in some of these gems. The creatures in this cave were probably gaining some benefit from them. Else they wouldn't guard them like this.

Marcus suddenly rained on my parade, "This isn't what I'm feeling. There's something else here."

I don't feel anything though, and Arlene praised my senses.

"I'm a spirit. You can't compare yourself to me."

I started to look around the chamber but couldn't find anything out of the ordinary.

"Let's come back to reality for a moment." Aaron said. "All we've gained is a bit of light and some potential wealth. We still have to get out of here... and as far as I'm concerned, we've made negative progress."

He wasn't wrong. We were now deeper underground than before.

Aaron continued, "Let's get another fire going, dry out our clothes and take a look around in the meantime."

The sudden excitement from having moved from darkness to this bright light had temporarily drowned out the chill in my bones. It was returning now and a fire was a good idea.

We setup a little camp and then started to move around the chamber. Agreeing not to take any gems, we didn't want to reveal our hidden designs on the monsters' piles of wealth and instead took care to avoid provoking them.

There were salamanders and snakes wrapped around clusters of gems as if they were the warmest sunstones to bask on, while the centipedes weaved in and out of the lush green plant life. Only now, with such abundant light, could their appearances be easily seen.

The cave's salamanders were bright red and as big as a komodo dragon. They weren't dry like a lizard but were slimy instead. There was a sheen to their gooey-looking skin. Their entire bodies pulsed and bulged as if breathing through every pore on their bodies.

The rock snakes were no longer a shade of black but instead a mix of colors: brown, red, grey, and their skin also changed colors according to that of the stones. If they weren't wrapped tightly around such bright gems they would be hard to make out on the cave floor.

The centipedes were just a brighter shade of white. Their bodies were almost translucent in this brightness and looking at them made my skin crawl. It was possible to see their organs beneath their bleached carapace.

Steven called us all over to a dip in the chamber. The only way out was down a slope to where an entire new area opened up to us. It wasn't a drop but more of a gradual decline, similar in descent to a staircase. Something we could easily walk up and down without much trouble.

My attention was immediately focused on what rested inside the chamber. The cavity was also filled with gemstones, but in the center was a chair. Not a chair of gemstones or rock, but a chair made from the body of two Granite Golems.

They had morphed and formed in such a way to create the base, and the support, and even the two arm rests of a chair. There was a man sitting atop it, or maybe it wasn't a man. It was a human-like figure who calmly rested there.

Its arm was formed into a hook that held up its chin. Its legs were crossed as it leaned back, seemingly bored. There was no skull above its head, so it wasn't a boss. But it was definitely out of the ordinary.

"This is what I sensed," Marcus said.

The Granite Golem chair proved one thing. This thing in front of us either controlled the golems, or had connections with whatever did. Moreover, we couldn't continue progressing towards shaft C without getting past it.

We were stuck between a rock and a hard place. There was no going back up as we couldn't ascend the waterfall. There was only this unknown foe in front of us.

What do you think? How strong does he look? I sent my thought to Marcus.

"This is definitely what I was feeling before and he is out of your league." This wasn't the great news I was hoping to hear. "The gap isn't that wide, but it may not only be him. I may have been quiet but I wasn't sleeping, y'know? You still have those cores right?"

I did, nearly a hundred of them, in fact. Marcus was spelling it out for me and I wasn't so dumb as to not understand. This thing wasn't that strong on its own… but it was potentially the summoner of the Granite Golems.

If I understood Marcus correctly, the majority of its strength would be in the minions it could control. Up until now we had only encountered Granite Golems, but how many might come at a time? And were there other types of golem? If he was already out of our league on his own, what of him plus the golems he summoned working together?

This was just speculation on my part. Plan for the worst, hope for the best.

"Is there a way back? Can we go around him?" Steven asked the obvious questions.

"We walked the entire chamber and this is the only path out; there's enough room to go around him but look at his eyes. He's watching us and I'm worried he'll attack," Aaron replied.

Kimmi had a bloodthirsty look in her eyes. "Can't we just kill him? He's not even wielding a weapon."

"I wish it was that simple," I said, "it's possible he's the one spawning those Granite Golems. If that's the case, we'll have more to deal with than just him."

Steven wanted to go around, Kimmi wanted to go in daggers out, and overall, we had no plan.

"Is there any way we can find some sort of weakness? Maybe develop a plan to engage him?" asked Isabella.

"I don't think so. The golems can go through walls. If that's the case, terrain really doesn't matter much. It's possible we get one attempt only." The alternative to failing that attempt weighed on my mind heavily. I didn't say the words, but I didn't need to. If we weren't strong enough to take him down, we'd all die here.

"He's quite far away. Maybe he won't come up the slope after us? Doesn't that area around his chair look sort of like an arena?" Ryan had been quiet during our discussion but offered perspective on something no one else had commented on.

The man's chair rested dead center of the lower level. He was sitting on an elevated platform about ten meters across. The entire area did look like an arena designed for battle. It was only a guess, but it was the best lead we had.

That small observation gave me hope. Maybe we could retreat from this room in the face of defeat. That defeat wouldn't mean death, and we could try again. The level of the area and the fact he wasn't a boss should mean he wasn't unbeatable.

We were a five-person group, just slightly lower level than the monsters in this area, we also had Ryan. Surely, we had a chance? At least I hoped so.

"How long can we wait? Realistically?" asked Steven.

"With the food we brought... we have about a week before running out if we're responsible." Aaron looked at the salamanders and snakes and centipedes strewn about, "if we get creative... a lot longer. There's also a water source right there."

If absolutely necessary, we could survive down here for a while. That was assuming these monsters were edible and that the water was drinkable. All of this hinged on the idea we would have more than one shot at the figure in the chair.

"Will anything change if we try to get past him today or tomorrow?" asked Kimmi.

"Not really," I responded; it would just be a whole lot of sitting around.

"Then let's get to it after our clothes dry." Kimmi was itching for a fight. I started to wonder where that shy and reserved attitude had disappeared to. When it came to battle, she seemed like an entirely different person: angry and bloodthirsty.

It took an hour huddled around the fire to dry our clothes and the moment of truth was quickly approaching. "Should we send Steven in alone?" This was something I saw Lady Briele and Bryan do. "You can get an idea if we can go around. Or if he attacks, of that guy's skills while we keep a distance. We'll be in range to help if needed."

Steven seemed uneasy at the suggestion, but Isabelle reminded him she would still be able to heal him. We just wouldn't be focusing our firepower and would instead wait before coming in. "Fine, I'll do my best."

"We can use that time to find any weaknesses or patterns," said Aaron.

"Is there anything I should do?" Ryan asked.

"You can be a neutral pair of eyes. Keep an eye on any changes outside the arena." Our focus would be tunneled. Any changes to the environment, arena or room might go unnoticed.

"Let's go then." Steven stood up first.

We approached the slope and then started sliding down carefully. The floor wasn't inclined too much, but it was covered in moist algae and smooth cave floor. The traction was non-existent. It was more difficult to descend than I'd imagined.

The human-like figure was waiting for us when we steadied our feet. In response to our approach, he had risen from his golem chair and was standing posed as if in expectation of battle. Despite that, he didn't make any effort to run towards us and was waiting for our move.

We started to spread out as we moved in his direction. We ended up in a half circle by the time Steven reached the 'arena'. It wasn't exactly an arena but a gradual rise in the floor. It was a large platform with the throne at the center.

As Steven began his attempt to skirt around to the side, his step was unsteady, his sword and shield in hand. The figure in the center suddenly smiled and a voice came from his throat. It was a language I'd never heard before. There wasn't any malice in his voice, it was whimsical and curious.

I felt Marcus stir with excitement. It was something I hadn't felt before, "Are you here to free me?" Marcus said. I was confused for a moment and then realized… he was translating. Marcus could understand the man's words.

How could I explain this to my companions? Was there any reasonable way to tell them I knew what he said? Did it matter? I buried the distraction to the back of my mind and watched Steven reach the critical half-way point. My breath was caught in my lungs.

Chapter 11: An Impossible Battle

Watching our tank navigate the short, one-hundred feet distance seemed like an eternity. Steven didn't rush and the creature didn't step away from his chair. He stood there like an uninvolved spectator and watched as Steven tried to get past him while always interposing his shield.

Eventually the pressure was too much, and Steven couldn't walk calmly anymore. He started to run to the far side and a yell escaped his throat. Immediately, the man on the platform rushed to intercept him and Steven braced himself. The closer the two figures got to each other, the more the differences between them became apparent. The enemy figure was human-like, but his proportions were a huge contrast to Steven.

He was nearly half-a-body taller, somewhere around nine feet tall. The muscles of his forearm and legs were as thick as Steven's torso: an absolute freak of nature.

You would think with such a burly body it would be hard for an attacker to miss him, but he had no problem evading Steven's first strike. He even managed to retaliate flawlessly. His sledgehammer like fist pummeled into Steven's shield.

With a sound akin to a car crash, Steven went tumbling like a ragdoll and rolled around ten feet away. Steven was a big guy, moving with incredible inertia. To somehow stop his rush, and then instead send him ten feet back… It was a frightening showcase of strength.

"Not yet!" Aaron yelled. I was aching to jump in. Kimmi had bloodlust in her eyes as well. We couldn't though. We had learned nothing and Steven was still fine as well. He crawled back to his feet and wiped some of the mud and plant life off his body before going forward again.

This is what Einstein called insanity: doing the same thing again and expecting a different result. But what could Steven do? He needed to draw out some weakness, some flaw, something that gave us any semblance of hope.

Our fighter was outclassed completely and instead was used as a boxing bag. His shield started to whine with every punch and the scrapes and bruises on his arms and legs started to drip with blood. Isabelle had already healed him several times.

"Waiting isn't going to change anything!" I yelled, and it was the truth. We needed to force a reaction. The fight had started and while I could be a bit more cautious, I still needed to act.

"Fine, go!" Aaron yelled.

My first goal was to get in range and cast *Inspect*.

Skill has failed. Insufficient level.

He wasn't a boss, which meant he was at least a three-star unique, or super unique. The depth of his abilities were still unknown.

Aaron nocked an Ensnaring arrow and shot it, while Kimmi rushed like a phantom to the far side of the unique opponent. Aaron had always impressed, so I was hopeful for his shot. I suddenly felt like we were children trying to beat an adult.

The figure caught the Ensnaring arrow with his bare hands. I witnessed the vines start to sprout beneath his clenched fist. They attempted to climb up his arm when his hand clenched tighter. The arrow snapped and green goop escaped from within. He had squeezed the life out of the vine.

I started to cast Glacial Spike with the hope of hindering the man's movement. Steven was already approaching from the front and Kimmi was midair behind his back. Her daggers started to glow and I thought we would finally deal some damage.

The daggers were coming down when a Granite Golem came from the floor below and bore the brunt of the dagger strikes. A fist as big as Kimmi's torso came hurtling back like a hammer. She did her best to cross her arms in front of her chest. The strike still sent her flying like a cannon ball.

She tumbled across the floor a dozen times and showed no signs of movement. It was then that my Glacial Spike came from the floor below and stabbed into the figure's leg. There was no big re-action, and it wasn't a victory for us. Kimmi was in an unknown condition twenty or thirty feet back.

Aaron didn't need to be told at all. He strapped his bow behind his back and rushed to Kimmi. Isabelle was already making her way around as well.

Steven stopped rushing forward and instead held his ground while they worked to recover Kimmi. The unique mob turned his attention towards me and then revealed his first ability. Granite Golems started to sprout from the floor all over the platform.

There wasn't just one on each of us, or each, there must have been thirty or forty of them. The situation had turned from bad to worse. There was no way to fight in this situation at all.

Aaron was already carrying Kimmi on his shoulder while run-ning back with Isabelle. I rushed towards Steven and did my best to dodge the sledgehammer-like hands raining down from all directions. The Granite Golems were not agile by any means, there were just so many of them.

The attacks from the golems were like an unceasing wave moving in our direction. There was no need to call for a retreat, we were already rushing off the platform and towards that slippery slope we had descended. I looked back at the unique to see that he hadn't moved.

The frost from Glacial Spike was still on its leg. It could have shattered it with a simple movement but didn't. Maybe it couldn't? I had to turn my attention to escaping the golems. The slope in front of us was daunting.

"Hold her!" Aaron passed Kimmi to Steven and nocked an arrow. He shot it with incredible force into the slippery cliff wall. Vines started to sprout and climb across. Ensnaring arrow was acting like a ladder for us to climb up. That was Aaron at his best: quick thinking in a crisis.

We grabbed the vines and dug our heels in while we climbed back up. The Granite Golems were just twenty or thirty feet behind us. It was a struggle with Kimmi being unconscious, but luckily Ryan was waiting for us at the top.

He reached down and helped to pull us up. The Granite Golems behind didn't continue to chase us and then retreated to the platform where they morphed back into the floor. The unique sat back down in his chair and resumed a pose at rest that looked extremely bored.

"How is she?" I asked.

Isabelle shook her head. "I don't know, lay her down!"

We carefully removed the daggers clenched between our companion's fingers and laid her flat on her back. There were deep dark bruises on her forearms where she had blocked the blow.

Isabelle casted multiple heals and the discoloration faded somewhat. Eventually, Kimmi squinted before opening her eyes wide. The majority of damage was on her arms and luckily, they weren't completely broken.

Her reaction time was good, "I managed to kick off the Granite Golem just as his strike hit me, else I think my hands would have snapped in half." Her arms were still shaking. Once we knew she was okay we retreated farther away from the opening.

"Did we discover anything?" asked Steven.

"After I did a bit of damage to him he summoned the Granite Golems," I said.

"He didn't move off the platform the entire encounter. And his feet seemed to glide along it; he didn't raise them once," Ryan's information was arguably the most important.

Aaron double checked, "Not once?"

"He didn't so much as lift a foot during the melee. He only twisted his upper body to face Kimmi and used his arms." This was important information, but created more questions than answers.

"So, either he can't raise his feet, or he chose not to," mused Aaron aloud.

Kimmi, coming back to her usual self, joined in, "And what would be the reasons he wouldn't separate his feet from the floor?"

"Well... is it some sort of challenge to him?" I offered. It wouldn't be wrong to feel like we were being played with.

"Or there's something special about the platform that's granting him power," said Aaron.

That was also a possibility. Similar to how these monsters around us hugged their mounds of gems. Surely there was benefit to be had from a connection with a power source?

Checking again, I couldn't see anything unnatural about the platform. It just looked like a raised part of the cave floor, thick with dirt and plant-life.

I said, "If he can't move off it, then he doesn't need to be tanked. We can safely take him down with ranged attacks."

"There's still the issue with all of the Granite Golems. They're incredibly tough without your Glacial Spike assisting."

"It doesn't seem like he holds my archery in high regard either," muttered Aaron.

"And if he can leave the platform, but chose not to? What about that scenario?" Kimmi looked as disconsolate as we probably all felt.

"He might get weaker if we force him to move," I suggested encouragingly. I really needed to tell the others about the man's desire to be free. First, I had questions for Marcus.

"Maybe that granite throne grants him control of the Granite Golems?" asked Isabelle.

Aaron nodded. "That's an interesting possibility. If we could remove him then we wouldn't need to deal with the golems."

"He wasn't weak by any means; I was getting my ass kicked." Steven was rubbing his now battered shield. Regardless, a scenario without dozens of golems assaulting us was obviously the better one.

"Realistically, what's the best-case scenario for us?" asked Aaron.

After a pause, Isabelle answered, "I think the best case scenario is that he can move. And hopefully moving either limits his control of the granite golems or removes that ability completely."

"Agreed," I said.

I turned my attention inward to Marcus. *How can you understand what he said?*

"He was speaking my native tongue."

And you're sure he said, 'Have you come to free me?'

"Absolutely sure."

I racked my brain. This lent credibility to the suspicion the figure couldn't move off the platform. But maybe it meant he just couldn't leave the cave. If he was trapped here, then what trapped him? There were too many questions and no answers. Once more I considered telling the group. It didn't feel right holding back information that could be crucial, especially not from Aaron, my longest companion and best friend in this world.

"Knowing he can speak a tongue that's nearly a thousand years old doesn't help anyone," Marcus barked. "I can say for sure no creature like him existed like that back then, not nine feet tall." Marcus could feel my irritation, "I want to know just as bad as you do!" he finished.

Exposing Marcus and explaining the situation might not push us any further in our knowledge of the encounter. The questions would be endless, and I couldn't be sure how they would react to having a spirit residing inside of me, let alone taking me hostage.

Is it possible for you to speak through me? If it wanted to be free, maybe there was the possibility of striking a deal?

"It might be possible, but how would you explain that?" That was the crux of the problem. I didn't even need to say it for Marcus to understand: if exposing him was our only option, that was what I would do.

"How outclassed did you feel Steven?" Aaron asked.

"It didn't feel good, but it wasn't something a few levels of STR couldn't fix."

The most obvious solution to this problem was to increase our power. Heads turned as we looked at the many creatures littered around the cavern.

The Centipedes were worth almost no EXP, but the Rock Snakes and Cave Salamanders gave a decent amount. Not that any of them could compare to the Granite Golems we'd been able to grind. None, however, had come through the walls or floor to strike us. Gaining our next levels would be a long slog against these mobs.

"It wouldn't hurt to try my hand at cooking up some snake and lizard," offered Steven. He was right. If we were going to be down here for a while, we needed a new source of food. I had to admit they didn't look very appetizing.

"We should be able to deal with them without Kimmi, too," said Isabelle, "she's going to need at least another day before her arms are in any fighting shape."

Ryan looked greedily at the gemstones embedded into the cave floor and walls, "We can start mining too."

"I'm not sure we should yet," I said.

"Why not?"

"It looks like the only thing keeping those beasts from devouring us is their mounds of stones. The only reason they refuse to move is they're afraid they'll lose their spot."

"We'll find an opportunity to take what we can later," said Aaron.

I assumed all of us were interested in the gemstones. We just needed to be as smart as possible about the situation. There was no escaping this cavern just yet.

We approached a Cave Salamander huddled between a stalagmite and the cave wall. His belly rested atop of a colorful mound of anlite ore. He hissed as we approached and showed his teeth.

The reptile was extremely hostile as we approached. Like a mother protecting a nest of eggs. It didn't want us coming anywhere near its little treasure trove. Its mouth remained wide open as saliva dripped from its maw. We drew cautiously closer.

I wasn't afraid of this single Cave Salamander, that wasn't my fear at all. My biggest fear was that the surrounding Salamanders would assist once we engaged this one. With an anxious look on his face, Aaron nocked an arrow and after looking from one person to the next, focused and shot directly into the salamander's side.

The monster rushed out from behind the stalagmite and directly towards us. Steven halted its approach with a body check from behind his shield, while I cast a fireball. It was instantly obvious that fire was the bane of this creature. Its entire body was slippery with a coat of moist goopy slime that now burned with a blue flame.

"Don't use your ensnaring arrow or whatever," Steven said. "I don't want it to ruin the meat." We had backed up a decent distance away from the cave wall and yet none of the other monsters showed any indication of assisting.

They couldn't fathom that they were on the list. They looked on as if to say *better him than me*. I don't know why but I suddenly caught myself chuckling. Wasn't this the perfect example of human nature?

They came first for the Cave Salamanders, and I didn't do anything, because I wasn't a Cave Salamander. Then they came for the Centipedes, and I didn't do anything, because I wasn't a Centipede. Then they came for me, and there was no one left to do anything.

This was their destiny, and yet they didn't know it. Steven and I ended up dispatching the Cave Salamander as a duo. We managed to leave its body intact.

"Shit, it's so slimy!" Steven complained. He picked it up before carrying it back to the spring.

Once there, he tossed it into the water and then started to furiously rub the goop out.

"Guh, did you really need to do that? We're gonna have to drink that," Isabelle gagged.

"What do you want me to do, huh? You wanna come over here and rub this shit off?" He acted up, to indicate how disgusting he felt the job was. I could only laugh at his exaggerated expression of distaste.

The goop slowly fell off the leather-like skin and swirled away into the spring. It didn't take long before I couldn't even tell the goop was ever there. The thought of drinking that water, however, still made my stomach churn.

When Steven was done he pulled the Cave Salamander from the water and plopped it on the floor. The skin beneath that slimy goop was leathery and rough and filled with pores. He got to work with a knife.

Watching him butcher the reptile was far from pleasant, but there wasn't much by way of alternatives. His work was impressive and eventually he returned to the spring to wash the remaining blood from the carcass.

The meat itself looked lean, and more white than pink. It was a color I'd never seen before, and yet it didn't smell bad at all. Steven was like a mad scientist as he prepared several different ways to cook the meat.

He hung some over a rack to dry for jerky; fried a bit in a pan with some fat; and charred a piece directly over the campfire. I had to admit, the smell was pleasant.

"Alright," he said at last, "everyone have a taste and tell me what you think."

I was the type of person who would try anything once and had no qualms about it. I picked up a skewer and bit into the charred meat. I was disappointed. Not that it tasted bad, but that it tasted like… very little. It was flavorless.

I took a piece fried in fat and found it much more enjoyable, "This is my pick," I said. It seemed like that became the consensus as everyone worked up the courage to eat the lizard. It being tasteless was actually not bad news.

It was much better than it being disgusting. We could add flavor, but not take it away. "Shall we try snake next?" Steven was sharpening his knife while eyeing the closest Rock Snake. We quickly got back to work.

Chapter 12: Round Two

The remainder of the day passed by quickly and it turned out the Rock Snake tasted much better than the Cave Salamander. It was less of a pain in the ass to clean as well. The only downside were the numerous bones you needed to pick from its meat.

That in itself provided some form of enjoyment, like cracking crab claws for that little bit of meat. You needed to work for your meal, and that made it taste just a bit better. At least that's how it was explained to me by Steven. I didn't see the appeal.

The best news was that nothing actively assaulted us. If we picked a target and killed it, a new creature would take its place. Nothing came at us unless we took a gem. We tested our theory and dragged a gemstone away only to find this did trigger the approach of monsters from the walls.

As long as we left their precious gems alone, they didn't seek us out for any trouble. They also didn't mind when we killed their buddies. It seemed they actually preferred it. There were more creatures than there were materials. In a way, we were helping them: at least that's what I told myself.

I felt myself getting tired and realized it wasn't easy to fall asleep in such an environment. The lighting never changed, and it wasn't exactly dim. In fact, it was bright as hell, twenty-four seven. We elected to have someone keep watch while the rest of us took turns trying to sleep, and that job turned out to be mind-numbingly boring.

There was no room for imagination. Everything around you was exactly as you saw it. The night was long and when not on duty, I only managed to fall asleep when my eyes could no longer stay open.

Waking up to the sound of a waterfall was a new experience, and I learned to enjoy the vigorous noise it provided. It was always there, never stopping. I wondered where the excess water was going.

Not that this question mattered, as I had no intention of holding my breath and swimming through underwater tunnels. I would rather be eaten alive by Cave Salamanders then ever risk that terrifying prospect.

The hours turned into days, which passed extremely slowly, and the EXP came even more slowly. It seemed like this speed of leveling was my new reality. Only on the third day of being stuck in this cavern did I level. And then we were already starting to exhaust the wildlife around us.

> **CONGRATULATIONS! YOU HAVE REACHED LEVEL 22. AS A REWARD FOR LEVELING UP, YOU HAVE BEEN GRANTED THREE STAT POINTS!**

There were a few new discoveries to be happy about as well. Kimmi had received a new dagger.

> **SNAKE'S FANG: ENCHANTED WITH DEADLY VENOM. THE FANG OF A VERY POISONOUS SNAKE. ONE DROP OF VENOM WILL KILL YOU.**

She wasn't allowed to use the new weapon on the Rock Snakes though. We had deemed them our main source of food, and we couldn't have her spoiling the meat with her poison.

The biggest haul from the days of grinding were actually several skill books, all of them very promising.

> **BOOK OF CHARGE LV. 1**
> **CAST TIME: 0 SECONDS**
> **MP COST: 6**
> **DISTANCE: 12 METERS**
> **CHARGE AT YOUR ENEMY WITH IMPRESSIVE MOMENTUM.**
> **GENERATES A CONSIDERABLE AMOUNT OF THREAT.**

This went right to Steven with no questions asked. He would never have to yell while pitifully rushing a monster again.

> **BOOK OF BLEND LV. 1**
> **CAST TIME: 1 SECOND**
> **MP COST: 10**
> **DURATION: 5 SECONDS.**
> **COOLDOWN: 60 SECONDS.**
> **BLEND IN WITH YOUR SURROUNDINGS, FADE TO NOTHING.**

This was arguably the most mind-boggling and interesting skill we found. It went to Kimmi of course and we all eagerly wanted to see it in action. Once used, her body slowly faded until completely invisible. Only after I felt a tap on my shoulder several seconds later did I understand she had moved behind me.

It was a perfect skill for an assassin. I wasn't sure how much use we could get out of it right now. But it was a great ability none the less.

```
BOOK OF ICE NOVA LV. 1
CAST TIME: 2 SECONDS
MP COST: 45
DISTANCE: 2 METERS
SUMMON A NOVA OF ICE WITH THE CASTER DEAD CENTER.
FREEZES NEARBY ENEMIES.
```

This was the most useful ability of the four we found. Not because it was my ability and I was biased or anything.

```
BOOK OF MENDING LV. 1
CAST TIME: 2 SECONDS
MP COST: 10
DISTANCE: 5 METERS
SLOWLY HEALS WOUNDS OVER A SHORT PERIOD OF TIME.
```

This was a HoT, or Heal over Time spell. Before gaining the book, Isabelle only had one healing ability. At all times, she needed to carefully consider who was the priority for her healing. The new skill would allow her a bit more flexibility. It would have been perfect in our battle with the mysterious figure, when she could have thrown it on Steven while she rushed to rescue Kimmi with Aaron.

I had two level's worth of stat increases still sitting waiting for me to allocate them. I still wasn't sure what attribute I wanted to increase.

I decided to continue holding my stat points. Glacial Spike had also reached level three as a result of constant usage.

The cast time had increased by a full one second and the MP cost had nearly doubled. The distance went up quite a bit as well. There was no doubt the power also changed. I was also incredibly interested in Ice Nova.

Moving away from the rest of the group, I decided to cast the new spell. Suddenly, a wave of ice pulsed outward with me at the center. The air grew chilly and the ground beneath my feet froze to a solid ice. Everything within a short two-meter distance was frozen solid.

I was hyped until I realized just how short range the freezing area was. I was basically required to be in melee range. I guessed that made sense though. It was the only way to add any sort of balance to the area-of-effect ability.

155

Although it had been slow going, I felt content with a level every three days, especially given the skill drops, but Aaron had watched my experiment with Ice Nova and was immediately on his feet.

"This solves a big problem for us: the Granite Golems," he said.

Up until now, I had needed to Glacial Spike to target the Granite Golems one at a time before we could easily dispatch them. I now had an AOE ability that could accomplish the same weakening effect as Glacial Spike but on several golems at once. There also happened to be an abundance of Granite Golems.

"The boss doesn't move off the platform… so why don't we try to gather up the golems and AOE them down?" Aaron suggested. "Here's how we'll do it…" He explained the plan in detail. As was often the way, I felt confident after listening to him. It definitely seemed feasible. If it worked we could increase our leveling speed significantly.

And leveling up enough might prove to be the way to defeat the unique figure blocking our path. The combination of a lot of spawns who were vulnerable to cold with my new AE was a rare opportunity if things worked out the way we hoped they would.

While we descended that slippery slope once again, Ryan remained up top looking anxious. We spread out as we approached the mysterious man, but only the bare minimum to avoid anything untoward happening. The unique stood to greet us; as if scripted the same words as last time came from its mouth.

Our feet touched that raised platform, our arena of battle and then Steven cast Charge. He arched his body and pointed his sword tip forward. The previous scene did not repeat itself. His speed and momentum were a level higher than previously.

Even the unique, with his impressive strength, couldn't send Steven flying out, although he did stop our tank's charge.

Meanwhile, Kimmi had rushed forward alongside Steven and then used Blend. She disappeared into the surroundings as if never existing in the first place.

By the time she reappeared, her daggers were already piercing his back. There was no hesitation as she kicked off and skillfully evaded that fist flying back. As expected, the Granite Golems were summoned and began to appear all over the arena.

This was the most crucial part, and the most dangerous. Everyone rushed together and gathered between the arena and the slope back to safety. Granite Golems came from close and far to swarm us.

Steven did his best to keep the closest golems off us, "Now!" he yelled.

I cast an Ice Nova and the surrounding golems froze in place. The ice climbed up their rocky bodies and froze them solid.

They shattered like champagne glasses from every dagger, sword, and arrow. The ten golems around us exploded into dust. There were still thirty or so remaining moving towards us, slowly.

I felt hesitant about standing still for so long. Being on the move seemed like the safest play, and yet we needed to keep our distance from the figure. This area was the closest position to our escape route.

We allowed golems to gather around us and repeated the process three more times at the cost of nearly 200 of my MP. It was worth it: the amount of EXP we received was mind boggling. The question now was would he summon another batch of golems?

The answer was no, and my anxiety about remaining in one spot for so long was building. He suddenly raised his hand and pointed towards us, I moved without thinking. It was a good thing too that I did.

A stalagmite as thick as my body pierced directly through the rock and almost six feet into the air. Getting impaled like that was instant death, and just the very sight of it was grim to think about.

"Retreat!" Another stalagmite had burst through the floor where Steven had been standing a moment earlier. The attacks were constantly rumbling from below and bursting through the ground towards the ceiling. We didn't look back before rushing to the cliffside. Aaron fired another arrow to create hand and foot holds and we ascended safely.

I felt such an incredible rush, in just five minutes of combat I had received 40% of my level. The gain didn't come without its risks though, as those stalagmites demonstrated clearly. If I had moved any slower that 40% EXP would have cost my life.

Knowing the danger didn't make me feel any less excited. In fact, I was so hyped I wanted to go again immediately. I had enough MP to do that whole spawn of golems one more time.

"That was twenty-thousand EXP!" Steven was panting.

"Will he summon them again?" wondered Isabelle.

The only way to find out was to go again, and so we did. We repeated the encounter just as before. Time seemed to slow immediately after Kimmi struck her daggers down.

Our opponent raised his hand and out came those Granite Golems. Those beautiful EXP-filled rocks. If this was a game we would be banned for exploit abuse, and luckily it wasn't. The encounter went cleanly as before and we retreated back up top.

My MP was almost thoroughly exhausted, but my EXP bar was nearly full.

```
CURRENT EXP: 44075/53000                    LEVEL: 22
              MAGE              FORMIDABLE
        HP: 1372/1372      MP: 14/514
                   STR: 11
                   AGI: 11
                   DEX: 20
                   VIT: 15 +2
                   INT: 30 +14
                 AVAILABLE: 6
```

The decision of where those 6 stat points should go suddenly became a lot easier. I put them into INT, bringing it to 36+14 and my MP to 50 from 550.

"Can we go again?" Kimmi asked, looking at me.

"I can only cast Ice Nova one more time." I pleaded. "It's forty-five MP per cast and I just have fifty, what do you expect from me?" I was aware that I had become the bottle neck preventing my group from getting free levels. They decided to let me rest while they ground out the necessary EXP for me to level again from the surrounding monsters.

```
      CONGRATULATIONS! YOU HAVE REACHED LEVEL 23. AS A
    REWARD FOR LEVELING UP, YOU HAVE BEEN GRANTED THREE
                      STAT POINTS!
```

```
CURRENT EXP: 11275/55000        LEVEL: 23
            MAGE        FORMIDABLE
        HP: 1402/1402   MP: 61/558
                STR: 11
                AGI: 11
                DEX: 20
                VIT: 15 +2
                INT: 36 +14
             AVAILABLE: 3
```

Even with that extra level, I was thoroughly spent. It would be several hours before I regenerated enough mana to go for another run. Regardless, the EXP per hour was mind boggling.

I suddenly didn't feel trapped in this cavern, and in fact I felt that we were lucky to be here and that I didn't want to leave. At least not until we'd made the most of the opportunity. We headed back to our little fire, which I noticed was growing worryingly low. We didn't need it for light, but the bit of warmth it provided was pleasant.

There wasn't anything we could burn down here. The wood we brought was only for cooking, and yet we had been burning through it at a steady rate. We were left with no choice to put out the fire to save it for food and deal with the chilly cave air.

The biggest downside to our new strategy was that the Granite Golems did not ever seem to drop items or skill books. No one complained even a bit about that though.

For some time there had been radio silence from Marcus. I had a strong feeling he was keeping me in the dark about something, that he understood something more about the unique located in the room below. But his silence was welcome.

The problem we had of dispatching the unique vanished as well. Our intention wasn't to defeat him anymore, but to farm his summoned golems for as much EXP as possible. My MP stat was the only limit to rapid progress, and that caused the others to get incredibly creative.

"There must be a more efficient way," mused Aaron. There probably was, and every Ice Nova saved was another cast. We were using four casts per cycle, totaling 180 MP. That 180 MP was worth around 20,000 EXP.

It would be tough to find a single person who would complain when presented those numbers, but they were currently obtainable for us. It was human nature to want more than what you had, and so they pushed even harder.

I decided to lean back and close my eyes as resting granted me an MP regeneration boost. It was also something they suggested readily. I wasn't allowed to use any other spells. They didn't even want me to move around.

Aaron strongly believed that if we could somehow mob the entire forty golems together, we could dispatch them easily with one Ice Nova and his Rain of Arrows skill. That was probably true on paper, and dispatching frozen Granite Golems wasn't ever the problem.

The issue was how to easily group them. They weren't fast by any means, but they were bulky. My Ice Nova cast range was merely two meters, and I didn't feel comfortable if something went wrong. Forty golems would be smashing granite fists onto my head.

It increased the risk to a tremendous amount. None of us would survive being mobbed by so many golems, and yet that was required to make Aaron's plan work.

"Instead of one pull why don't we do it on two? That should be easier since they spawn at every corner. Bottom first, and then top." This was my counter-suggestion and it still made me uncomfortable. Because one group or two, I would be in the center of this mess of golems.

"We can try it tomorrow." I suggested. It would take at least that long for my MP to fill; we wouldn't be wasting any time. Everyone agreed and our next encounter was the following morning.

Chapter 13: Andino

"Same plan as before, we change positions after though." Aaron walked to the bottom middle of the platform, instead of the bottom right. "Instead of a golem group spawning on us, we'll be in between two spawns. Realistically, the two groups should meet at the same time with us in the middle."

The pattern of the fight went exactly as he planned. The golems met perfectly with us in the middle and I cast Ice Nova. Aaron followed that up with Rain of Arrows and cleanly dispatched all the golems on one side while Kimmi and Steven took care of the other.

The remaining two packs were moving incredibly slowly and I felt hesitant again about standing still. I had a fear of things stabbing me from below. Sezhul was my first bad experience and now this situation was making me relive it. Despite my worries about being struck by a magically appearing stalagmite, it didn't seem like the mysterious figure used his casting ability until all the Granite Golems were dead. We still hadn't managed to make him move out of our way but that didn't seem like a priority anymore. We were all content with farming the event for EXP.

Despite our incredible leveling speed, the days passed slowly. Mostly because we could only level for a short period of time before I ran out of MP. All the same, the levels started to pour in and my dissatisfaction with being trapped underground disappeared almost completely.

CONGRATULATIONS! YOU HAVE REACHED LEVEL 24. AS A
REWARD FOR LEVELING UP, YOU HAVE BEEN GRANTED THREE
STAT POINTS!

CONGRATULATIONS! YOU HAVE REACHED LEVEL 25. AS A
REWARD FOR LEVELING UP, YOU HAVE BEEN GRANTED THREE
STAT POINTS!

CONGRATULATIONS! YOU HAVE REACHED LEVEL 26. AS A
REWARD FOR LEVELING UP, YOU HAVE BEEN GRANTED THREE
STAT POINTS!

CONGRATULATIONS! YOU HAVE REACHED LEVEL 27. AS A
REWARD FOR LEVELING UP, YOU HAVE BEEN GRANTED THREE
STAT POINTS!

CURRENT EXP: 13050/65000   LEVEL: 27
MAGE   FORMIDABLE
HP: 1672/1672   MP: 111/626
STR: 11
AGI: 11
DEX: 25
VIT: 20 +2
INT: 41 +14
AVAILABLE: 0

It was hard to complain with this sort of progress. At least, until
it stopped being so impressive. We were at least 5 levels above the
Granite Golems, and that seemed to be the tipping point for an
EXP penalty. Even with my entire MP pool we weren't guaranteed
a level per cycle anymore.

The added fact that the golems dropped no items started to become an issue too. Equipment was a large part of our power. It was time to move on, and that meant defeating the unique figure. After a discussion indicated we were all thinking the same, we agreed to wait for me to recover my MP and then we would make our attempt at getting out of here.

I was proud of us as a party. We had found ourselves in a terrible situation and managed to overcome it. To not only survive, but to go on and take advantage of such a poor situation: it spoke wonders to our potential. I slept like a rock that night.

"Is everyone feeling confident?" Aaron asked in the morning. We were much stronger than our first attempt. At that time, we had to flee almost immediately after the granite golems spawned. Now we farmed them while casually chatting. It was time to move on and escape this cave.

"My MP is full," I said.

"Mine as well," said Isabelle.

Aaron strung his bow. "Same strategy as before. Once we down the golems and he starts casting stalagmites, keep moving. We don't know what his abilities will be after that. Survive above damage."

Everyone nodded in understanding and then we all descended towards the arena.

The start of the fight went flawlessly, as we were so familiar with it by now. And it was such a contrast with our first attempt. Steven charged without fear and went blow for blow with the figure, without being shoved back.

Steven's shield still buckled and whined, but his legs held fast. Aaron, Isabelle and I moved into position directly in the bottom middle of the arena while Kimmi used Blend. She vanished before inflicting the opening damage and triggering the Granite Golem spawn.

We all quickly regrouped and moved as one unit to dispatch the 40 golems. Two Ice Novas, two Rain of Arrows and the hacking and stabbing of Steven and Kimmi accomplished this easily.

Stalagmites were imminent.

"Spread out and keep moving!" Aaron reminded us. We were venturing into the unknown. I had leveled considerably, and it was time to try again. I cast *Inspect*!

```
SPECTERANDINO*** LEVEL: 32       HUMANOID
                      NEUTRAL
     HP: 95825                MP: 155
                  STR: 50
                  AGI: 15
                  DEX: 25
                  VIT: 65
                  INT: 15
 THE SPECTER OF ANDINO, AN ANCIENT FIGURE. HOW LONG HAS
             HE BEEN TRAPPED DOWN HERE?
```

I could Inspect him now, which taught me that the level range requirement for the spell was either 5 or 10. I had been 11 levels below the figure on my first attempt.

Specter Andino pointed at each of us, seemingly at random. Stalagmites the size of our bodies rumbled from below and burst through the floor. We were expecting these attacks and were already prepared. Steven even managed to charge back in range and tank.

This revealed that as long as someone was in melee range, the specter didn't seem to be willing or able to cast the stalagmite spell. I was finally able to safely cast without worrying about being pierced from below. Both Aaron and I began bombarding the figure with spells and abilities.

Steven held his ground as boulder-like punches slammed down onto his shield. He blocked every strike but was still taking hundreds of hit points of damage just from the shock of the blows. Even so, the HoT from Mending was enough to heal the damage.

Andino was simply exchanging blows with Steven while we obliterated the unique mob from range. Even Kimmi was sneaking in attacks here and there, while avoiding any counter-attacks. The fight was going smoothly.

Was this just a gear and level check? As long as you could tank the damage and sustain MP for healing abilities you could defeat him?

No matter how favorable the situation seemed, I had no intention of letting my guard down. Despite the figure not casting stalagmites again after Steven held his aggro, I didn't stay in one place for longer than a single cast.

My decision was the correct one, but it didn't matter. Andino suddenly raised both of his hands and rock hands reached from beneath the floor. The hands grasped every portion of the arena and locked each of us in place.

I had been expecting some sort of stalagmite follow up. I kept my eyes glued to Andino who was in the center. Suddenly, he vanished.

Fast! Without the slightest warning Andino appeared beside me. He loaded a full punch and all I could do was turn my body and brace my arms with my staff. The punch came like a ton of bricks.

My energy shield caved and cracked immediately before his hand crashed into my staff and eventually my two arms. The force was so incredibly strong the stone hands grasping my ankles shattered and I flew like a bullet across the arena and into the cave wall.

My vision was swimming as I peeled myself off the wall and collapsed to the ground below. I coughed several times, the deepest causing blood to speckle from my throat and onto my hand. I felt like I could barely breathe.

I looked down at the indent running across both of my arms: proof of just how hard the staff had dug into my skin on impact. I wasn't sure if either of them were broken. There was a strong tingling itchiness racing through both of them, as if I had been electrocuted.

CURRENT EXP: 13050/65000	**LEVEL: 27**
MAGE	**FORMIDABLE**
HP: 372/1672	**MP: 276/626**

STR: 11
AGI: 11
DEX: 25
VIT: 20 +2
INT: 41 +14
AVAILABLE: 0

It had been a 1,250 DMG attack. 1000 of it was taken directly to my HP pool and 250 was absorbed by my energy shield. Slamming into the cave wall with such speed had done another 300. I was in bad shape.

Isabelle was still trapped and couldn't race to heal me. "Hold on!" I heard her yell. I fumbled for a white potion before downing it and added a bit of buffer to my health. If Andino teleported to me again and struck me it wouldn't be enough.

Aaron took a big risk and nocked arrows, accurately shooting the braces trapping Isabelle's feet. She rushed to me once free and he did the same for everyone else, eventually freeing himself last.

I felt that warm sensation that comes from receiving a heal and an even warmer touch. Isabelle helped pull me up from the cave floor. Little bits of rocky debris were still stuck in my back, some of them deep enough to draw blood.

I had never felt so bad before. My entire body was aching from the pain. *Had I hit my head?* I really couldn't be sure, but Isabelle had managed to heal me back to full HP. I hadn't died and now was no longer in danger of dying. I struggled to my feet and stepped back onto the arena.

Steven cast Charge once more and immediately closed the distance with Andino and the fight resumed again. The strike that had nearly killed me terrified me completely.

We had finally made Andino move his feet, as he began battling in earnest. His kicks caused the entire chamber to quake and Steven was getting pushed back. Mending was no longer enough to keep him topped up and Isabelle had to cast direct heals.

Andino was attacking ferociously as we continued to bombard him. I realized now that bosses weren't the only fearful monster. Three-star uniques were terrifying as well. We were definitely at the limit of what a party of 5 could face on their own. Past this you would need to form a raid.

Miraculously, despite the storm of attacks, Steven was holding on. His shield was in tatters and we would no doubt need to replace it once returning to Tanyros. One way or another, the fight was coming to a close soon.

Vines started to climb up Andino's legs as Aaron had successfully landed an Ensnaring arrow. The intensity of the specter's attacks slowed as the vines tightened and clenched around his legs, then up his body.

Andino suddenly stopped his assault and raised his hands again. The stone hands were coming and I knew it. I started to cast Glacial Spike in a 50/50 gamble. Less than a second later I felt my ankles being gripped and I cast the spell into the ground at my side.

My gamble paid off as Andino appeared beside me. Glacial Spike jutted in between us just before he could strike. His fist pounded into the icy barrier between us and shattered it into a million pieces. Energy shield flickered repeatedly as bits of icy shards bombarded me.

I had cuts on my face, arms, neck and legs, but this was still better than taking a full blow from his fist. Within a second of that I was free. Aaron had already started nocking arrows to destroy the stone braces holding me in place.

Steven intercepted Andino with charge and the fight came to a close just like that. Even though Steven's shield was mostly destroyed, Andino's abilities seemed spent. Eventually, he let out a sigh that sounded like relief, before falling to one knee.

The specter's appearance slowly morphed until the nine-foot body was no longer present. A ghostly man instead took his place: a fine-haired gentleman with luxurious clothing and a coronet atop his head.

My heart dropped as I thought we would have to continue our fight. Marcus suddenly spoke up with urgency, "Quick! Go to him!" I felt that Marcus was hiding something from me but I did as he asked, intending to get the full explanation after.

Chapter 14: Andino's Story

I rushed over to Andino due to the pleading of Marcus and against my better judgment. Naturally, the others were concerned, "Careful!" cried Isabelle. I came to a stand in front of that ghostly figure. Foreign words escaped his mouth.

I couldn't understand, but he was telling a story. It wasn't a story for me, but instead for Marcus who was inside of me. Could he sense Marcus? I didn't know if the fact I was getting a speech was a response to my simply being there or some deeper issue to do with Marcus.

I 'listened' for what felt five minutes before the figure ceased speaking. I felt conflicted. There was a storm of emotions raging inside of me. Marcus was in turmoil and his mental state was affecting mine.

The ghost slowly walked away. It turned to look back one more time before fully vanishing into the cave wall and disappearing. Loot then spawned where the nine-foot giant had been. The fight was definitely over.

As soon as the ghost walked away, the others started to rush to my side. Everyone was excited to distribute the loot, so speaking to Marcus would have to come after. Four items floated in place waiting to be claimed.

> ### Ethereal Cloak*: AGI +5
> A THIN ALMOST TRANSPARENT CLOAK, IT IS INCREDIBLY DURABLE AND LIGHTWEIGHT.

"Perfect for Kimmi?" suggested Steven. There wasn't a need for any discussion, and she accepted it excitedly.

> ### Frenzy Blade*: STR +4 VIT +4
> HOLDING THIS WEAPON PUSHES YOU CLOSER TO THE EDGE. YOU FEEL YOURSELF GOING BERSERK.

The sword was a great new weapon for Steven. His shield was nearly destroyed in the battle with Andino but he still looked very happy to be ahead overall.

> ### Holy Chapeau**: INT +5 VIT +3 Healing Effects +5%
> THE FRONT IS ADORNED WITH A BEAUTIFUL CROSS. YOU FEEL CLOSER TO THE GODS WEARING IT.

This was one of the best items I'd ever seen drop and would definitely push Isabelle's heals to another level. The INT and VIT were incredibly tempting for me, but my gear was still quite good and the healing bonus would be wasted. I had no issue with her taking it.

The final item was a skill book.

> ### Book of Summon Granite Golem
> ### Cast time: 2 Seconds
> ### MP Cost: 75
> ### Duration: 60:00
> ### Cost: Granite Switch

This would bring us a Granite Golem as a temporary ally at the cost of one Granite Switch. None of the golems from the Andino encounter had dropped any Granite Switches, but we had at least 60 from our grinding before that. The MP cost was huge, but that wasn't a problem to me at all as I felt the benefits, especially in certain situations, would definitely prove worthwhile.

A quick look around the others showed they all expected me to take the book, so I did.

In great spirits now, we discussed the fight that had just happened, praising Steven's bravery, but I was glad too that Isabelle called me quick-witted for my interposing a Glacial Spike when needed. All throughout the chat, I felt a little distant from my friends due to the turmoil that Marcus was creating in my thoughts.

I would let Marcus calm down before questioning him. He was still agitated, and I could feel it. There was also the pressing issue of getting out of this cave. With Andino gone the chamber was now ours to explore.

"C shaft would be this way." Ryan pointed while leading us to the distant wall. It was lush with algae and plant-life. There wasn't a single opening to be found. In fact, the entire chamber was sealed tightly shut.

"What now?"

"We can try to make our own path." Ryan suggested. While it would be slow, we still had a stable water and food supply. There was no risk to our well-being, just an immensely time-consuming task ahead of us.

"Why don't you summon your golem?" suggested Aaron.

Kimmi looked up at me. "Yeah, can't it travel through walls?"

That was an interesting idea. My mind had been so focused on the 1-hour duration and limited uses I would have with it that I had assumed the summoning would only be for battles.

"I'll have a go." I tried to cast Summon Granite Golem.

I racked my brain for what had gone wrong and then realized it might be that having a Granite Switch in my inventory wasn't sufficient. I pulled one out and held it in my hand before casting again.

My suspicion was correct. A golem appeared from the floor. The switch in my hand, as if possessed, moved on its own before burying itself in what would be the golem's head. Eventually it stood before me.

I found myself disappointed. I had been expecting a burly and magnificent Granite Golem but instead received... this. It was smaller in every way than the mobs we had been fighting, a miniature version. The significance of the reduced size of golem was very clear: it was weaker in every aspect in comparison with the dungeon bred ones.

I considered whether this might be a result of my having a beginner's skill, one that might rise and lead to my being able to summon more effective golems. I checked my mastery page and could see Summon Granite Golem was there, but there was no level at all next to its name. There wasn't even a progress bar. That was strange.

"Why's it so small?" Isabelle asked. My pride took another jab. I was already feeling insecure about my golem.

I coughed, "I don't know. It was born this way." There was something miraculous about it though. A feeling I couldn't quite explain. I could... inhabit it. It was as though I had its senses, the minimal ones a sentient piece of stone might have: all to do with vibration and touch, rather than sight.

"Let's try it out." My new-found ability to access the senses of the golem made me excited, I was optimistic. We hurried to the far wall towards C shaft and I willed the golem to enter the wall. It morphed directly into the stone and disappeared.

The feeling the golem was projecting to me was now a tightness, a restricted feeling. I learned quickly what that meant. It was surrounded fully by rock, there was no open cavity. I willed him to go on even further.

I could feel his location in the wall, his direction, his distance. I moved him forward slowly and then felt a liberating feeling. He had found an open pocket, it was possibly another cavern. "There's around five feet of solid rock in the way before there's a cavity."

I continued to walk my golem forward and he was still unrestricted. He was like a remote-control robot, except I was able to direct him with my mind. Eventually I couldn't move him forward anymore. Not because he hit another wall, but I'd reached the limit of my control. It seemed twenty feet was the farthest he could be away from me.

"How long would it take us to dig an opening wide enough to crawl through?" Aaron looked to Ryan. He was the resident expert and the only one who could know the answer.

"Five feet of solid rock will take us hours. Going sideways is a lot harder than going down. There is little assistance from gravity in swinging your pick sideways. It's all about your own strength."

As I continued to consider alternative solutions, I could see that everyone else was looking at Steven. I didn't want to be stuck here for weeks, trying to escape like a captured rat. Acknowledging the unspoken request, Steven picked up a pick and began hammering away at the wall. Ryan joined him.

The process was mind-numbingly slow. Little bits of the cave wall broke off here and there as they etched marks in the stone. It seemed to me that Ryan was maybe under-exaggerating the time required to break through: it could take days to get through this five-foot section.

Marcus had seemed to calm down by now and I focused my attention inward towards him. *What was that about earlier? What did he say? Did he realize you were inside of me?* The entire situation left me feeling confused. Marcus was keeping something important from me. I felt vulnerable because while I couldn't know what he was thinking, Marcus could read all of my thoughts. There was no hiding from him.

"Do not be anxious, Andino didn't realize I was inside of you. He just didn't fathom you couldn't understand his speech. I guess that's reasonable considering he's been trapped down here one thousand and twenty years."

That's not much longer than when you died...

"As young men we were inseparable, the best of friends. Over the course of a dozen years we became friends on the surface, and enemies in secret. I always wondered why he suddenly changed, became so cold."

He was... the king?

"Right, the king who was attempting to destroy the ten families and... eventually succeeded."

So what did he say? You still didn't explain.

"King Andino said that one day on a hunting expedition, they discovered this mine. They ventured inside with curiosity and came across a stone. It was beautiful and lustrous. He wanted badly to gift it to his wife. He kept the stone close to his heart, it was to be a surprise.

"They often returned to the mine over the course of several days. His nights became long and arduous, his sleep was rough. Nightmares haunted him and he was tired every day. The night before they planned to depart for home, he had the best sleep ever. His dream was everything he could have ever wanted.

"The dream showed him growing old with his wife and they had many sons and daughters. The kingdom was prosperous and without worry. The snakes in the capital weren't out for his head and no one was plotting. He didn't want to wake up, and so... he didn't.

"When he eventually did wake up, he was in this cavern, wasting away. His days were spent in boredom and turmoil. He had no sense of time and no way to escape. This platform was his prison and he couldn't leave.

"He realized he had a strange power, the ability to summon those golems: they didn't make him feel any less lonely. He made himself a throne and he sat at it while watching the years pass by."

"One day there was an explosion, it shook the entire cave and the reverberations could be felt even here. He wasn't scared, he was excited, but what could he do? He was stuck here and couldn't leave.

"So he looked to his golems, he wished they could be his hands, and he could send them out. To his surprise they could leave, they could travel through the cave walls and upward, but they could never reach the surface."

So that's why they can't go past E5... It was similar to my own twenty-foot restriction, although it seemed Andino's range of golem control was much further.

"He came to learn through his golems that the explosions were caused by humans. He saw a glimmer of hope tinged with darkness. He wanted to know so badly what happened to the outside world: what had happened to his wife, his children, his kingdom. And so he willed his golems forth. At first their goal was just to communicate with the humans, to beckon them deeper to meet him, he learned very quickly that was futile.

"The Adventurers wielded strange magic and had no intentions of coming along quietly. They killed his golems on sight and cared only for the beautiful stones. So he was no longer gentle and instead attacked with force.

"Those coming into the cave grew stronger and stronger and Andino's attempts to capture them grew harder, but at last his golems brought him someone from the outside world. The truths he learned from his prisoner did not put his heart at ease.

"His wife was dead; his kingdom destroyed; the families of his friends all ruined. Worst of all was the reason they always gave: 'It was the fault of the mad king Andino.' But how could that be? He knew he had been trapped here the whole time.

"Andino was furious, and in his rage killed the Adventurer who gave him that information. He strongly believed the story to be lies, and yet it was reinforced time and time again as future captives were brought before him. The mad king Andino was the cause.

"How could he not believe it? Was his proof of being trapped here not supernatural enough? The Andino the people loved and revered was here, stuck below this mountain. While the Andino people feared terrified his kingdom.

"Years continued to pass and those he dragged down had less and less information. Some had not heard even his name. 'Do you know the mad king Andino?' he would ask. 'I do not,' was always the response.

"This struck at his heart, for he knew that his kingdom was no more. And yet, it was oddly liberating. He did not want to be remembered, even though that man was not him, it was him. That liberation did nothing to free him from his current predicament.

"He was trapped here, with no end in sight. He continued to summon golems to pull humans below, he wanted to be found, to be freed. Yet, he could not let go. The thought of being known as the mad king Andino left his mouth sour, his heart dead.

"He spilled out the following words in defeat: 'That Andino is not me.' Those were his final words before walking away and disappearing.

My heart was heavy, a mixture of Marcus' effecting my emotions and the sadness of the story. I could not imagine being trapped for over a thousand years, let alone knowing someone had taken my place with ruinous consequences.

I hope you weren't planning the same when you tried to possess me…

"I just wanted freedom." And yet that didn't make me feel any better about the circumstance.

What happens if I die? It was a sudden thought that crossed my mind. *What happens to you?*

"I also will die." It felt like a wall was slowly coming down. Marcus had given useful advice many times since entering my body. Despite that, I couldn't trust him fully yet.

"I understand and will earn your trust."

The turmoil Marcus was feeling dissipated slowly and was eventually replaced by relief. In his view, his uprising against mad king Andino had been unconscionable. They were supposed to be brothers for life, through thick and thin. Now he appreciated that the man he betrayed was not Andino after all. It was a small victory that accounted for very little in the great sweep of time, and yet it made Marcus feel happy again.

Chapter 15: The Power of Ice

I brought my golem back through the wall in an attempt to speed things up. Maybe it was possible he could bring me through with him. This attempt proved to be a fruitless endeavor that left me dirty and wet.

My body wouldn't pass through regardless of how I willed it. It seemed that using the picks was the only option available to us. As I got used to the constant banging that became a white noise, my mind wandered.

I thought about life back on earth, school, pointless things that helped fight off the boredom. Eventually those thoughts were boring as well. There had to be a way through this cave that wouldn't require hundreds of hours of labor. I couldn't even be sure our picks would last that long.

Then, as I thought of the possibilities for each skill, and how could they get us through the wall, it struck me. The rocks were moist and filled with liquid. Every strike caused a splatter of dirt and moisture. There was a way and that was to take advantage of the fact these walls were filled with water. Water expands when frozen, and that process does more than just shatter rocks.

Water turning to ice expands so strongly that it can shatter metal pipes. "Hey, back away for a second." This was worth a shot. I aimed at the pitiful crevice they had excavated and cast Glacial Spike.

The others watched as an icy spike appeared in the gap and shattered as it impacted the rock.

"That didn't work," Isabelle complained. My goal wasn't to use brute force at all, and so I ignored her and allowed the ice to remain in the crack.

I cast another Glacial Spike, and then another. Finally, on the third cast I heard a noise. It was a cracking sound, deep in the rock. A hairline fracture traveled from the opening and up the wall, and then there was more cracking.

The water inside the stone was expanding with a force much stronger than our little picks could deliver. The cracking continued for dozens of minutes before coming to a stop. "Try again." I urged.

Everyone had heard the splintering sounds coming from inside the wall, and everyone could see that the stone was suffering splits. There was now an expectation we could do this. Steven and Ryan started to swing their picks hard again and pieces of wall came away much more easily. They eventually picked up sledge hammers and started smashing into the wall that way.

Chunks constantly fell off as the entire wall looked brittle. It had already cracked and separated inside and merely needed some nudging to dislodge. The progress in just those short few moments was more than the previous hour's worth of work.

I repeated the process again and eventually we were through that five-foot wall in a little under three hours. A far cry from Ryan's expectation. It was a hole we would need to crawl through, but no one would complain.

Isabelle sent Heirophant's Helper inside and Steven followed behind it. The space we'd made was tight fitting for him to get through and we needed to push him from behind. Eventually we were all inside the new cave.

The cavern beyond the wall was dark and claustrophobic without a monster in sight. The entire area looked like one big, sealed room. The ceiling was low and the cavity end was nowhere in sight. That was good news for us as it traveled in the direction of C shaft.

We reached the far wall and it was my turn again. I was forced to use another Granite Switch and summon my golem. I sent him into the wall ahead, and then above, and to either side. I was looking for any possible openings we could take advantage of. I eventually found one.

It was another opening but this time even smaller. It wasn't even large enough for the golem to be able to stand up straight in. That alone meant we would need to crawl through it on all fours. Turning around to stop wasn't an option though.

There was potential and that was enough. None of us expected to get out of here in a day. The mineral and gem filled cave still waited behind us. We just hadn't mined it yet in fear of the resulting attack. Only when we secured our exit would we do so.

We excavated for three days before hearing a familiar sound. In the distance was the clink of pick on stone. There were people close above us! The vibrations came through the wall and even – once we were quiet enough to hear it – a faint suggestion of conversation.

It was time to collect our spoils, and so we returned to our camp once again. By now we had increased the hole in the cave wall so Steven could get through comfortably, and he had become somewhat of a miner himself.

As they set about gathering the valuable stones under our protection, Steven and Ryan chatted happily while they dislodged every mineral and gem. Their reactions grew even more exaggerated.

"Oh my, check out this ruby, come Steven, come look!"

"My God, Ryan, it's beautiful, we're rich!"

"No wait, I've an even better emerald here!"

And they continued in this vein with ever-growing enthusiasm.

The monsters in the cave didn't like our plundering, but they had no choice. We settled any disputes quickly: a few arrows here, a few spells there.

At last, our bags were completely full to the brim with valuable gems. So full that Ryan couldn't even estimate the total wealth we had accumulated. Our one-week trip had turned into something like three weeks. The wealth we would be able to return with, well it might take a lifetime to accumulate, or a couple. I wasn't the only one filled with a sense of achievement. As we made our way out, I could see that everyone had smiles.

When we broke through the final, thin, wall and found ourselves in the C 22 shaft, we received wide-eyed stares from the people nearby. All the other teams stopped what they were doing to look at us: it wasn't every day that miners came up from below. The startled looks we received were entertaining. A few veteran miners came over and poked their heads into our hole and realized we had come from very far down.

There was nothing to say. I was exhausted, we all were, and only when freedom was so close did tiredness hit me like a ton of bricks. There was also the situation with Harvey to consider now we were back among those who had tried to kill us.

"He's done for." Ryan said. "Once we report our findings to the royal family, they'll send out their own workers to confirm."

"We don't have any proof though." I didn't think it would be so easy.

"Of course we do." Ryan jingled his backpack. "This is proof. They also can't use explosives willy nilly. Every explosion is recorded, no exception. We report Lucas and they confirm he used explosives in E-Seventeen on that day, it's over. He'll spill the beans in a heartbeat."

"Is it safe?" wondered Kimmi. "The royals won't take our gemstones?"

Ryan shook his head. "Going through them will cost us a bigger cut, but it's the safest method for exchange by far. This might be a life-time of wealth for a mining team, but not for the royal family. They have thousands of miners going through there every week. Taking our wealth wouldn't be worth blemishing their reputation over."

I was convinced. Who else besides the royal family could do a transaction of this size anyway? And anyone who could, besides them, most likely dealt in shady business. Although Steven and Isabelle had reservations and I could see Aaron thinking things over, Ryan assured us that the royals would treat us fairly.

The fresh air felt so foreign to me. I was used to the moist and cool cave air below. The smell was clean and refreshing. It made me realize I never wanted to step foot in another mine again.

It wasn't just the air either, just walking on solid ground was difficult. My body had grown accustomed to the constant bumps and contours of the caves, of the need to always watch my head. The trek back was a refreshing one where I felt myself grow back to my full height, unconstrained by fear of a knock.

We kept a low profile all the way to Tanyros. It was unlikely Harvey had any idea yet that we had returned, but news would spread about a mysterious six-person team emerging from below shaft C 22. Eventually the pieces would come together and people would come looking.

Unfortunately for those wanting us dead, we had a plan. Shops constructed and run by the royal family were all over Tanyros. They didn't give the best rates, but they had a reputation for being completely fair. New miners could visit them without the slightest clue as to what their harvest was worth. They wouldn't take advantage.

We found the nearest and approached the clerk at the counter.

"Exchanging gems ladies and gentlemen?" he asked with a smile.

Ryan responded by plopping his sack down onto the counter-top. There was a glass-like jingle as the contents shuffled within.

The man was astonished and an avaricious expression grew over his face as he spread the gems along a velvet cloth, "This is a good harvest! How long were you down?"

We continued to place our bags down on the counter-top one after the other. Eventually there were six bags crammed with gems on the counter-top. The clerk's face was now showing amazement and even panic. "Uhh, excuse me, I've never seen... I'll get my manager!" Clearly it wasn't normal for so many valuable gems to come in at one time. He returned a moment later, "He wants you to come to the back."

We followed the clerk around the counter and entered into a back office. It was a cozy little room the six of us had to squeeze into. A gentleman with long, black hair rested behind a desk. He was doing some paperwork, but his office job didn't quite suit him. His physique was rugged and muscular, almost like a fighter.

"My employee says you have a lot of gems for trade, let's see them." And so we did. We piled our bags upon his desk till he needed to stand to see us. "Uhh, we can't pay you for these, I'll get my manager!"

He started to scribble some notes and then whistled hard. A young man rushed into the room through a side door. "Go now,

185

be quick about it. If you waste any time I'll dock your pay!" The gentleman was all smiles and deference. "Sorry about that. I hope you don't mind waiting a few minutes." He wiped sweat from his brow.

There was something oddly pleasing about this. The way the clerk and manager acted as if they were on thin ice. Would the next person come and tell us the same thing before shuffling off? We didn't need to wait long.

The next man who arrived fit the part. He was scholarly and well dressed. The air about him was refined. "Leave us," he said to the manager. Just like that, he commandeered the office for his own use.

I didn't have positive feelings about the rich and powerful. They were snobby and stuck up, they treated others with contempt. He didn't have any of that, and it wasn't an act. I could see it in his eyes.

"Nice to meet you all, I'm Keith."

"Nice to meet you," said Aaron.

"First things first, and sorry if this comes off the wrong way, how did you obtain this? It's not common for a group to bring in such a haul, and for that reason I need to ask."

"Well…" We allowed Ryan to narrate the story. He was familiar with mining terms and his knowledge of who was there and at what time far surpassed ours. They could cross check his story and confirm it much more easily than if I had tried to explain it.

Where I did feel I could add something to Ryan's account was to describe the encounter with Specter Andino. I didn't reveal his true origins though, for now the existence of Marcus would remain my personal secret. It wasn't that I couldn't trust my teammates either.

There was nothing to be gained by telling them except endless torment and annoyance. I didn't want to experience the nonstop questions or even having to play telephone. There was no doubt in my mind once he was revealed he would take it upon himself to pester every single one of them and they would constantly want to check for his opinions.

And if I refused to pass on his thoughts to them in his stead, well I'd probably be the one pestered instead. I wanted to avoid that situation at all costs.

Keith was taking note of the entire story, no doubt jotting down the important names of each person mentioned as well as locations and descriptions. He only spoke when Ryan was completely finished.

"Alright, I will say for now that I don't deal with judgement and punishments. My job is to simply calculate the wealth of these gems. However, I have noted down what you have told me about the attempt to kill you and I assure you it will be sent to the right people."

"How long do you think it will take to see results?" asked Ryan.

"I shouldn't be saying this, but Harvey is already on thin ice. This isn't the first time we've received reports of misconduct. This, however, if verified, would be the worst I've heard so far. He doesn't hold the royal family in high regard at all." There was an audible disdain in Keith's voice.

"Anyway, let's get to the calculations. Judging from what you've brought it may take me a few hours. You're free to stay and watch or you can come back later. I assure you nothing will be missing and all will be accounted for. Here is the seal of the royal couple." He raised his hand, on which a large ring had complex design. Ryan leaned in close to study it and nodded.

"I have a request if you don't mind," I said.

"If it's something I can fulfill I'd be glad to."

"I want to know the last recorded price a piece of Orichalcum sold at."

"I don't know off hand but it shouldn't be hard to get. I'll have one of my men take care of it. We'll both know when you return."

"Thank you."

I turned to the others with my spirits high, "I kind of want to eat something other than snake or salamander."

Kimmi nodded. "Let's find a place then."

"Do you know somewhere good Ryan?"

"I do."

We took to the streets and eventually filled our bellies. I ended up ordering the juiciest, greasiest, hamburger possible. I didn't even know what creature the meat was from, and yet it was so delicious.

I ate until my stomach was bursting at the seams. I hit the meat-wall and surpassed it. My nose was runny and my body was sweating. After that phase came the extreme lethargy. They basically had to carry me back to that exchange shop.

We returned to find Keith had tallied everything nicely. The gems were all sorted into separate piles: emeralds, rubies, diamonds, peridots, pearls and so on. He passed us a slip of paper sealed with the royal family's emblem. He also signed his name below.

There was a number on it. The amount of money that the gem-stones we brought back were worth: 975,000 Zeny. I was blown away as was everyone else. "Take that to the royal bank on King's Row. You can exchange it there. Also, the last known Orichalcum sale was two weeks ago in Arturii. He looked at a slip and read the contents aloud. Sold for seven-hundred and fifty-thousand Zeny at auction."

That… was an astronomical number. I couldn't help but glance at my party members. I was confident Aaron and Isabelle would help me in purchasing one, but I couldn't be sure about Steven or Kimmi.

I couldn't deny we had grown closer as a team. When we had first met Steven, he was arrogant and boastful. Looking at him now it seemed he did that to protect himself. No doubt being rejected by team after team had taken a toll on him. He was just a goofy kid like us and he was a good tank, no question.

Kimmi had been shy and reserved, almost to an annoying degree. Now she talked happily and wasn't afraid to share her opinion. She also scared me quite a bit. It felt like her bloodlust in battle was growing with every fight.

I suddenly felt less lethargic. This was everything I wanted to have back on Earth. My feet were gliding as though full of energy as we went to the royal bank where we exchanged the slip with shaking hands. Ryan would receive 15% and each of us would receive 17%. I was suddenly 165,750 Zeny richer.

Ryan wanted to celebrate, and his enthusiasm spilled over to Steven. The two somehow managed to convince us to join them. Where better to celebrate than enemy territory?

The sun was just coming down and the Golden Tap was absolutely bustling. It was filled to the brim and we barely managed to squeeze inside. This time it was definitely open. The bar itself was packed along its entire length with people leaning over each other for drinks.

There wasn't even a place to sit and so we ended up huddled in a circle in the center of the room, looking quite out of place.

"Ryan! Where's George at? You're never in here without him." Someone called across the busy pub.

Ryan was at a loss for words. How could he respond in this situation? 'Harvey conspired to kill us and George died in the fallout.' Something like that?

An explanation wasn't needed because our presence was already recognized. Harvey was sitting in the corner and even Lucas was at his table. His little deed seemed to have gained him quite the promotion.

There was no smug look. No demeaning eyes that wanted to embarrass us. Lucas had a look of terror on his face. Harvey just seemed confused. He glanced at Lucas and then back at us several times. Was he wondering if we were ghosts?

The look of confusion on Harvey's face quickly devolved into one of anger. It wasn't directed at us, however, it was directed at Lucas. Harvey showed no sign of wanting to engage with us. I made eye-contact with him and gave him a smile: a smile empty of warmth.

Even while I was watching Harvey grip Lucas at the shoulder, multiple guards forced their way into the Golden Tap.

"Out of the way! MOVE! ANYONE BLOCKING OUR PATHS WILL BE DETAINED." They plowed through the half-drunk patrons with ease, despite the congestion.

Harvey's reputation had preceded him. The soldiers maneuvered through the Golden Tap and directly to his table. Lucas wasn't spared as the guards took the both of them in one quick swoop. Somehow, Harvey managed to put a look of being wronged on his face. I wanted to know what would happen to him, so I asked a soldier.

"Don't obstruct me in my duties, citizen."

"I'm glad to see you here. I was one of those he tried to kill. Do you know what will happen to him?"

"Jail. Jail for a very long time. He thought he was too important to be brought down. But the king and queen have had their eye on him for months. He'll be put away for a very long time and quickly be forgotten.

Our trip to Tanyros had been more profitable than any of us could have imagined. We were all level 27, Kimmi had even managed to hit level 28. The pockets holding our Zeny were fat and burning hot. It was truly time to move on. Our next destination: Arturii.

Chapter 16: The Marsh Ponds

The only downside to our having journeyed to Tanyros was its location. It was located in the opposite direction to Arturii and we would now need to travel that distance back.

"Should we hire a coach?" Steven asked.

"Too expensive, let's just walk," Isabelle said. "And a coach won't save us much time, only provide a bit of luxury."

I didn't have any opinion on this. Sleeping on a hard cave floor was still fresh on my mind. A sleeping bag in the grass was nothing in comparison.

"Should we stop by the Magma Caves or Marsh Pond on the way?" Aaron asked.

"Did you just say the forbidden word? THE FORBIDDEN WORD?" groaned Kimmi and I knew what she meant.

"I've seen enough caves for a lifetime, I'm good," I said.

Aaron laughed. "Alright, well what about the Marsh Pond then?"

"I'll think about it on the way… I'm a bit done with damp environments too." I was sort of a bit done with everything. So much stress and action had been packed into our Tanyros trip. I needed some time to absorb it all. Maybe I would feel differently when we got to Marsh Pond.

"Do you think the Forest Troll is taken care of yet?" wondered Steven.

"Who knows? Probably." Aaron was perhaps a little nonchalant, considering how dangerous that monster had been.

We retraced our steps through the Elysian Fields and as we did I felt a sense of nostalgia. It was weird though, being the only person who could remember what actually had happened that night.

I wasn't sure if they would believe me if I told them anyway. There was also Marcus. 'Hey you guys, so there's this thousand-year-old spirit living inside of me. Yeah, Marcus Chronis, one of the heads of the ten great families, I'm sure you've heard of him'. That conversation wouldn't go well.

This time we opted to take the proper path and passed through in a single day.

When we left the Elysian Fields and moved into the trees, it soon turned out the Forest Troll hadn't been taken care of yet. There was a sign along the main pathway into the forest: BEWARE: FOREST TROLL RECENTLY SIGHTED. That's all it said.

Would the troll still remember us after three weeks? Would it attack us regardless? There was also a part of me itching to give him a go. "Hey, will we fight if we see him?"

"Yes."

"No."

"No."

"No."

It wasn't a surprise to me that the only person who answered yes was Kimmi.

Fortunately, or unfortunately, we didn't encounter the troll on our way back. In fact, the trip was relatively uneventful.

The monsters we met on our travels had a keen eye for danger. They would burst from the dense foliage and give us a quick glance before darting off. It wasn't worth it for us to chase them either. None of them would have provided us with much EXP.

We reached Cape Tou before nightfall and ended up sleeping in warm beds. The stockade village was an intermediary halting place for a bit of supplies and more information. And what we learned from the other people there was that the problem of disappearances in Arturii hadn't gotten any better. In fact, the situation had only grown worse. People were now finding bodies of entire parties on occasion. All terribly mangled and ripped to shreds. A statement had finally been issued by the Adventurer's hall and we were told a summary of it: *We can't say for sure what the creature is, but it is an anomaly. It is much higher level than the areas it roams.*

The monster destroying Adventurers sounded like the Forest Troll only more terrifying.

We were also told about Adventurer killers: those looking to take advantage of the mayhem. Adventurer killing was heavily frowned upon, but a few groups took it upon themselves to murder and rob other Adventurer parties. How could they be caught with so many groups disappearing? It was easy to slip through the cracks. This was a tumultuous time for Arturii and North Maledith as a whole.

Somehow or another we all felt these problems too big for our small little party. We were unable to alter the blowing winds and rising tides. Our journey to Tanyros had been enough of a detour, and so we hardened our resolve, we were going to Arturii.

We did, however, decide to visit the Marsh Ponds for some EXP on the way. It just so happened to be around our level, and there were no reported incidents. While it was a three-day journey to the Marsh Ponds, they were more or less in the right direction:

going there wouldn't take more than half a day out of a direct route to Arturii.

"What kind of baddies are we gonna fight at the marsh ponds?" Kimmi was already chomping at the bit.

"Well… swampy ones, those and the poisonous insects," Steven said.

"Blegh. Why is everything poisonous and insectuous? Can't we just find some normal enemies to kill." Kimmi was sick of it, so was I to be fair.

"Is insectuous a word? I don't think that's a word," Aaron objected.

"If it isn't a word, it is now, courtesy of me."

"Insectuous, it has a nice ring to it." I confessed.

Kimmi grinned. "Right? I think so too. I'm quite proud of myself."

"Have you all thought about what you'll do when we reach Arturii?" Isabelle asked a question I was afraid to ask.

"I figure we'll find some missions and work our way up the ranks." So, Steven didn't have any intention of leaving us, that was great news.

"What about you Kimmi?"

"Kill monsters." She coughed, "ahem, with you guys of course."

I felt relieved at her answer, our party would remain intact.

"Maybe some of the swamp life will be tasty," she added with a wink.

"Please stop."

"What? Don't you think the Rock Snake was decent? I cooked it pretty well, right?" Steven looked at me as though aggrieved, but he was teasing me.

"I think I'm gonna' vomit." The entire three-day trip was merry just like this. The journey was quite destitute though. In our three days of travel, no one else was en route to Arturii. In reflecting on this, we realized the situation might be a bit worse than we thought.

The smell of the distant beach and ocean air faded, eventually replaced by something… else. It was a murky, dirty smell that penetrated my nostrils and came to rest at the back of my throat. The smell was foul, but in a unique kind of way.

The air was humid and mosquitoes pestered us constantly. That alone made it clear we were close to the Marsh Ponds. The distant trees slowly morphed into something else entirely. Thick algae coated the entire area in green.

The tree trunks developed ridges that were covered in a multitude of colors. It seemed the water level reached quite high up on occasion. Their roots were exposed and covered with debris scorched white by the beaming sun.

The canopy was incredibly mottled. Sunlight speckled across the forest floor, occasionally illuminating the murky marsh below. Eventually, our path ended and only a wooden dock awaited us. There was a single sided sign that read 'Marsh Pond' in dirty black letters.

Sloping down to the surface of the marsh, the decking became a path of weathered wood that creaked and groaned with every step. There weren't any railings at all. At most two people could walk side by side before risking falling in.

"This… doesn't seem very welcoming," said Steven. The rest of us held our judgment, but if there was any place worse than a damp cave… it could be this place. We walked with anxious steps on the faded planks.

The decking bent and buckled under our feet and I felt there was a real risk that any misstep would cause one of us to fall right in to the fetid water beneath. Our surroundings came alive as crickets chirped and frogs croaked. It was like an orchestra performance where every instrument played high notes of its own choosing. All of the noise was topped off by our constant slapping and cries of, "God damn mosquitoes are everywhere!"

There was something eerie, almost surreal about this all. If, somehow, I forgot this was Yetera, I might be able to convince myself I was just living in a swamp down south back on Earth. We walked for around thirty minutes before our scene finally changed.

The swamp remained the same, but the decking we walked upon eventually tapered off into a maze of shacks and wooden buildings. There was a city built just a few feet above this muddy water. It looked like an absolute ghost town.

There was one skinny man, however, standing at the end of the path who greeted us. "Ya'll come here to visit the Marsh Pond?"

"Aren't we here already?"

"Naw, this the outskirts. Ya'll still got a good couple hours in 'fore you make it there. I reckon it's quite late though, might be wise to call it a night. I got some rooms."

It was true that the occasional hoot of an owl had intermingled with the orchestra of insects and amphibians. The sun was already descending and there was maybe only one or two good hours left before the only thing in the sky would be four moons.

Aaron looked around the group then back to the man. "We're interested."

"Great," He started to shout out at the top of his lungs, "Babe! Babe!" and it wasn't long before a woman with an uncanny similarity to him appeared. "Babe, show these gentlefolks to they rooms. Also, if you guys want some supper we be cooking in this hall right here."

We were expecting a shack for each of us. That wasn't what we got though. The woman showed us to a place that was a large, almost summer-camp-like, building with bunk beds lining either side. This was our 'rooms'.

"Well, it's just for one night." Steven shrugged.

"I guess," I said. It was easier to go along with the offer than complaining, and so we did. "But if this is what they consider 'rooms', then what will 'supper' be?"

We ended up all heading over to the dining hall and were surprised to find no one else but us. We were the only group in this little section on the Marsh Pond outskirts. This wasn't what I was expecting. The impression I'd gotten was that plenty of other Adventurers around our level would have been here.

Supper turned out to be normal despite my guesses. There was a casserole and an assortment of wild veggies all grown on the marsh pond. Steven was quite interested in these and spent his time pestering the wife about ingredients and seasoning.

"Is there anything we should know about the ponds before we go in?" Aaron asked her.

"Well, first thing is I noticed you boys swatting at skeeters the whole time. I'm surprised you came here without any repellent. They'll drive you insane real quick. Also, you're gonna' want a good map, that's a given."

"Do you have one?"

"I don't sell no goods here unfortunately. There's a shop on the way you can get everything you need. Called Arnold's Alchemy 'n' Supplies, he'll have yer map and also the green herb."

"Green herb? What's it for?" asked Isabelle.

"You guys really coming here with no knowledge whatsoever? I don't know if yer confident or just stupid. You each needa' eat some green herb everyday just to ward off poison. It won't save ya if you really get bit bad but most of the insects that nick ya won't cause anything but some itchin'."

"Is this shop on the main path in?" Aaron was rubbing at one of his own itches.

"Yeah it is," she paused. "At first, I thought you was all some bold Adventurers come ta sort out our troubles, but it's clear you guys don't know nothing at all. I don't know all the details but something bad happened at the pond recently."

That was worrying news. We were under the impression the Marsh Pond had been unaffected by the changing tides: the player killers and the new monsters.

"Arnold knows all about it though I'm sure." She turned to her husband, "Hun, let's call it a night already, I'm tired. Excuse me, everyone." They left us in the hall to ourselves.

"Who was it that said the Marsh Pond was fine?" Isabelle had an evil glint in her eye.

"Uh, me…" It was Steven.

"How do you want to die? Slow and painful? How about painful and slow?"

"Let's relax," Aaron said. "We're still on the outskirts, we can still leave."

For once, I disagreed with Aaron. I felt we'd come this far, we may as well try to find out a bit more. "Why don't we listen to what this Arnold guy has to say first?"

Aaron nodded. "Anyone oppose?"

No one did, and just like that we were agreed to head off the next morning.

There wasn't a single moment during the night the crickets stopped, or the frogs stopped, or anything stopped. I don't remember when I fell asleep.

We formed up in a dense fog that covered the swamp and reached almost to the bottom of the decking. It was like we were walking on a bridge above clouds. The mosquitoes weren't nearly as active right now and our trip was a bit less annoying.

We walked for around ten minutes from platform to platform. All we found was just more and more lodging that seemed to be completely empty. There really wasn't anyone in the whole outskirts besides us and the residents who lived the land.

Eventually, the lodging was far behind us. There was an hour of travel with nothing but the single path in front of us and nature surrounding us. "Did we miss it?" I asked.

"He did say it was on the path inward, let's go a bit further." Aaron said. So we did, and he was right. There was a little offshoot from the wooden path that traveled thirty or forty feet out. A single building sat there.

It was as old and rickety as the rest. Moss and plant life covered every inch of the building, so much so that you might think it was part of the swamp itself. There was a sign board dangling out front on rusted chains. The image on the sign was a shoddily drawn alchemy bottle.

"This must be the place?" asked Kimmi.

"Should be," Steven was at point.

We walked up to the building and shuffled up the short steps to the front door. The boards creaked and groaned, even the door squealed as we opened it. Behind the counter was a decrepit old man with the wildest beard I've ever seen.

"Are you Arnold?" said Steven.

"Who's askin'?"

"Sorry, we're here to buy some goods and get some information."

"Then yeah, I'm Arnold." He suddenly leaned off his stool which was much higher than I had expected. He was so short he disappeared behind the counter. We waited a few moments before Arnold hobbled to the front and stood before us.

"Whatya need?"

Aaron spoke, "First, we want to know some information, it's about recent events at the Marsh Pond."

He looked at us with a curious gaze, "If the information bad you still gonna' buy some goods?"

"Uhh... probably not," Aaron confessed.

"Then ya gonna' have to pay for the information."

"Fair enough."

"If you decide ta stay after n you buy some goods I'll refund ya how 'bout that?"

"That works, how much?"

Arnold held up five fingers.

"Five hundred?" asked Aaron.

"Thou'"

That seemed like an astronomical amount for a bit of information. We didn't have any choice though.

Aaron reluctantly handed over the five thousand Zeny and Arnold ushered us over to a table in the front of his shop. "People have been fleeing the Marsh Ponds in droves for the past five days. They occasionally come through here and pass the information along. Is this all your first time in the swamp?"

"Yeah."

"Aight then. For the baseline: the deeper you go into the ponds, the stronger monsters get. Most of the time they don't venture out on their own and they mind their own business in their own territory." This was starting to sound oddly familiar.

"Basically, the monsters deep inside the swamp have been pushing out regularly, and way farther than normal."

"What kind of monsters? Higher level or what?"

"Uniques, super-uniques, parties been getting wiped out and the whole place is unstable. It hasn't reached this far yet but who knows." Arnold looked around at the shop he must have called his home for so many years, "I might even hafta run on outta here eventually."

"Can you tell me why people even come to the Marsh Pond?" I wondered aloud. It was hard to make a judgment on if the risk was worth the reward. The monsters here were our level. It could get dangerous fast.

"It's a good leveling spot and a great place for resources. You saw the shop sign didn't ya?"

"We did."

"That's my name, Arnold the Alchemist. The amount of herbs you can find in here for special potions and medicines is innumerable. It's a treasure trove." So there were Zeny to be made. I was immediately inclined to give it a shot. Not only was I itching to level, I really wanted to grind out the remaining Zeny needed for the Orichalcum.

"Where would you go, if you were us, and wanted to get those herbs?"

"There's a camp about two hours from here. It's where all the people currently venturing into the Marsh Ponds are residing. Sort of a last-ditch effort to keep the monsters from spilling out."

"Should we give it a shot?" asked Isabelle. It was the question on everyone's mind.

"Ya can always visit the encampment and retreat if ya aint cut out for it. Just don't go too deep," Arnold said. I wasn't sure if this was his honest opinion or if he just wanted to sell us more goods.

"I'm in," I said.

"As long as we can find something for these damn mosquitoes I'll give it a shot." Isabelle also weighed in to support the risky option.

"Will I get to kill stuff?" Kimmi asked, "if the answer is yes then I'm in."

From his nod, it was clear Aaron would go along with me and Isabelle. We were just waiting for Steven to decide.

"Do any of the swamp monsters taste good?" asked Steven.

"Woo boy, you ever try some fried Snailigator tail? Some of the best eating you'll ever have." And I could tell by the interest in his eyes that was enough for Steven. "Anyway, if ya'll are gonna' head in I got what you need."

"Well it seems we are," said Aaron. "We heard something about a green herb. We also need a detailed map, best you have."

"Green herbs yeah, you wanna' ingest 'em everyday durin' mornin'. Gives you a certain resistance to the toxic insects in the swamp. Now that's not to say you're immune. If you get a bad bite then you're in for some trouble and you'll need somethin' more powerful. As for the map, I got dozens. I also got that repellant this lady was talking about."

Arnold wasn't joking. He was a one stop shop and eventually we had enough supplies to last in the swamp for two-weeks. The price tag was a lot less than I was expecting, only 12,500 Zeny.

Business wasn't exactly booming for Arnold lately given the circumstances.

"What do we do with the green herb?" asked Isabelle.

"Ya' don't wanna swallow it. Just put it in your mouth and give it a chew. Suck on it for a while."

I tried some, which eventually ended up a little clump of tasteless mush between my gum and teeth. Regardless, I kept it there to ensure I got the most out of it.

We took off deeper into the marsh and headed for the encampment Arnold spoke about.

Chapter 17: The Marsh Camp

About halfway to the encampment we saw our first team and they were heading in the opposite direction to us. One of their members was being carried on a make-shift stretcher. His entire body was covered in sweat, as if experiencing a terrible fever.

Their expressions were downcast and none of them gave us so much as a hello or a welcoming glance. Based on this group, the situation faced by Adventurers was going to be even more difficult than we'd been led to believe. Somehow, that made me even more excited than before.

I wasn't sure what I was expecting to see when we reached the camp, but I was pleasantly surprised. It wasn't just built on top of wooden platforms but was actual solid ground. We went across to a short clearing of tall weeds beyond the end of the decking.

On the other side of the grass curtain were tents spread all over the dirty ground. Puddles of water filled the mud that people constantly walked through. The entire area was surrounded by wooden barricades that deterred monsters from venturing to attack.

Through an open gate I could see that beyond the encampment was more swamp but with solid ground too. A walkable path wound and twisted through the water, following the course of the higher ground. The end of the path was shrouded by the sheer amount of plant-life; it was impossible to see further than a couple hundred feet.

The mood in this camp was dreadful. Most people were crest-fallen and walked with their heads held low. Then too, I noticed that there was blood present on the barricade spikes.

Despite the problems, there were a good thirty or forty people moving about. A few of them were drinking from flagons around a campfire and seemed to be doing their best to stay merry. Others just rested in their tents.

"Newcomers?" A woman asked while walking into our path, but not in a way that was aggressive or confrontational. She held a clip-board with some paper. I couldn't see what was written on it.

"Yes." Aaron answered for us.

"Alright, come with me I'll show you where we have some camp space." It seemed she had some role to do with logistics, and so we followed behind her.

"The mood seems pretty bad…" I observed.

"Mood's always bad, even when it's peaceful, like now. I'll give you a warning though, and don't forget it, it ain't the days you need to worry about, it's the nights. Past three or four, we've been hard at it until dawn and nearly overwhelmed at that."

"Is that why everyone is in their tents?"

"Yep, most of 'em are sleeping right now. Few of 'em are trying to take the edge off before bed." She was referring to those drinking around the campfires.

We arrived at our little plot of land. It was less than ideal as the ground was completely uneven. Not only that, muddy water lay just outside where our tent opening would be. We were also dangerously close to the barricades.

"Can't we get… a safer location?" I wondered.

"Sorry, there's no space and to be honest, no location is really safe." She walked away and left it at that.

Isabelle shrugged. "Guess this is what we get."

There wasn't much we could do about it but suck it up or leave.

"We're already here… let's see how it goes," said Aaron.

And so we ended up erecting our tent and putting the things we didn't want to carry on our persons inside.

I was at a loss as to what to do. My instinct was to go into the Pond to grind EXP, and yet no one else was doing so. When I found her to ask why, the logistics officer gave a simple response, "You can venture into the Pond but I wouldn't recommend it. You won't be getting any sleep tonight, I promise. If you do decide to go, don't go too far."

It was still early in the day and I felt it shouldn't be a problem to at least take a look. We ended up exiting the camp and into the open swamp. This was a completely new experience for us. Forewarned, we made sure that every step was slow and measured.

There was a thriving ecosystem all around us. Yet, there was nothing to be found besides the insects and frogs. No monsters; nothing attacked us. We couldn't find anything of interest. We walked the outskirts for thirty minutes before walking back empty handed. Presumably, we would need to wait till night time to see the monsters.

We zipped up our tent and did our best to conserve energy. It seemed this would be another sleepless night. I found myself with absolutely nothing to do but lay there staring at the green tent top. It was also hot as hell.

"Do we really wanna do this?" I asked.

"I'm having second thoughts as well," said Steven. "This is kind of hell."

From beside me, Aaron said, "We should at least give it one night."

207

"Fine, one night."

The day was hot as hell, long as hell, and boring as hell. Only when the sun was beginning its descent did people start to come out from their tents. The entire camp suddenly came to life. I suddenly felt like it was the 1940s and I was going to war.

We were camped out behind enemy lines, waiting for a relentless night ambush. It was exciting in movies but definitely not exciting to live it out. Campfires were lit and food was cooked: it was the equivalent to breakfast time. *You don't eat now, you won't get to eat*, seemed to be the message. We joined in with the 'festivities' and ate our own dinner.

Eventually the logistics officer sought us out. "Alright, here's the deal. Your party will be responsible for this little section. Everyone staying at the encampment has to put in the work. If you run or leave, you ain't coming back."

We were required to hold a short, ten-foot section along the barricades. There was nothing special or particular about it, just another section of wall, the same as any other surrounding the encampment.

The crickets came alive and the owls started to hoot. This short moment of cheerfulness passed as everyone got up from their seats around the campfires. Weapons were drawn and all conversation stopped.

We waited in silence for dozens of minutes with nothing happening. "What are we doing?" I whispered.

"Dunno, copying everyone else?" offered Kimmi.

And we were. The regulars should know better than us, so, naturally, we prepared to follow their lead. It was nerve racking waiting in silence. Eventually there was a new noise mixed among those of the natural nightlife.

A sound of rustling bushes and weeds became audible in every direction. The water surrounding the camp started to resound with splashes. Creatures large and small were plunging in and out of the swamp water, creating the impression of a large number of rushing monsters.

It felt like there was an army just dozens of feet away from us among the bushes beyond the barricades we faced. The fact we couldn't see them made it even more tense.

Steven drew his sword, hefted his shield and positioned himself to our front. Isabelle summoned Heirophant's Helper and had it rest in the air just above Steven's head. A little of the night's darkness receded.

One of the larger creatures on other side of the stockade had finally reached the shoulder-height weeds in front of us. The fronds started to rattle and shake as if alive. Something burst through before colliding with the barricade.

The monster resembled nothing like I had ever seen before. I couldn't compare it to anything on Earth at all. It was just a large and goopy-looking… tree-swamp-monster thing. Its body was covered with algae and peat. *Inspect* told me it was a beast known as Swamp Growth.

```
SWAMP GROWTH    LEVEL: 29        BEAST   EARTH
        HP: 7812            MP: 70
              STR: 35
              AGI: 10
              DEX: 22
              VIT: 38
              INT: 5
A MIXTURE OF SWAMP AND NATURE THAT HAS COME ALIVE.
```

Despite having such a large body, it attacked in odd ways. It went to punch out at nothing but air and its hand extended before wrapping around Steven. His sword didn't strike out to retaliate against the body of the monster but cut away at the hand slowly swallowing him up.

Our tank's entire shield was completely covered and most of his left arm. Kimmi was already behind the Swamp Growth and stabbing down. Even with Penetrate her daggers simply entered inside the creature's body and didn't seem to do any meaningful damage.

I had learned to love Glacial Spike. Not so much for its damage, but for the incredible utility it provided. Jutting through from below the floor a spike of ice pierced directly through the monster's lower leg and into its chest.

The lower part of its body froze and then Aaron shattered it with an arrow. I thought that would be it. The body flopped to the floor; yet it didn't die. Instead, the body began to grow outwards again until it was good as new.

"We need to find its weak point!" Aaron yelled. I had seen this before in games, monsters that had immortal bodies and a core or central weakness. Without destroying or damaging that specific weakness you dealt no meaningful damage.

The vulnerable point of this monster, assuming there was one, was clearly not in the legs or lower body, which meant the upper chest or head were the most likely places. "Aim for the chest or head!" I called, even though I knew this was easier said than done. The upper body was wide and the size of the core was unknown.

Glacial Spike was incredibly useful, but not in this situation. It would never reach farther than the lower body. I instead switched to Fireball, which, I discovered also dealt only superficial damage that was quickly regenerated. I didn't have any ability that could dig through the outer layer of goop and find the core. I was completely nullified in this encounter.

Luckily, Aaron had just the right ability. He primed Power Shot and released an arrow to the dead center of the monster's chest. The entire middle section of the creature blew open and for a brief moment we could see something: a mess of roots the size of a human head just below the right shoulder.

The opening Aaron provided quickly closed up, but that was enough. We had found the core, and Kimmi didn't miss her opportunity. She used Penetrate and cut cleanly right through the shoulder and slashed the mess of roots to pieces.

The goopy muddy swamp monster collapsed before splattering to the ground like someone dumping out a bucket of mud and grass all over the floor. The dirt splattered and freckled all of us with dark blotches.

That was only the beginning of a long night. The distant sounds of monsters rushing the encampment continued. The other groups were fighting all around us. No one was giving any ground.

Monsters continued to force their way through and up against the barricade.

SNAILIGATOR	LEVEL: 27	BEAST WATER
	HP: 5565	MP: 10
	STR: 40	
	AGI: 15	
	DEX: 5	
	VIT: 25	
	INT: 5	

ITS MASSIVE JAW AND ARMORED BODY BOLSTER INCREDIBLE ATTACK AND DEFENSE.

I could actually compare this creature to something on earth. It crawled along the floor like an alligator. The difference was its massive head, which looked disproportionate to its body. There was also a shell-like armor going from its neck and over its back. This aspect of the creature reminded me more of a turtle than a snail.

Fortunately for us, the snailigator's defense didn't seem to work well against magic. It managed to chomp at Steven a few times before Ball Lightning did considerable damage. Its big head proved to be just for looks and the monster was thoroughly shocked into a stupor. Steven managed to stab directly through its skull and finish it off.

Coming through the undergrowth and over the stockade were not just these large and monstrous creatures. Even the more docile and normal wild-life was rushing the encampment. It was almost as if they were being controlled, or something deeper in the swamp had forced them out.

The fortunate news was the normal wild-life was easily dispatched. Aaron only needed to release an arrow to take them out. The rest of us continued to focus our attention on the more threatening enemies.

SWAMP WASP*	LEVEL: 30	INSECT EARTH
HP: 19373		MP: 45
	STR: 20	
	AGI: 40	
	DEX: 5	
	VIT: 40	
	INT: 5	

A GIGANTIC WASP RENOWNED FOR ITS INCREDIBLE SPEED.

To call the wasp gigantic was an understatement. An insect the size of your thumb on Earth here towered over Steven. Its flapping wings sounded like a mini plane propeller. The stinger coming from its abdomen pulsed as the tip poked in and out.

'Sting' didn't do justice to the type of attack of this insect, 'impale' was more appropriate considering the size of the wasp's stinger. There was also no doubt in my mind it was poisonous. Every God damn monster was poisonous here…

This was likely to be a costly battle, something we all desperately wanted to avoid. Panacea was expensive and Steven could very well end up using multiple doses if the fight dragged out. Still, I only needed him to hold out for a few seconds. I started to cast Meteor Storm.

It had been such a long time since I had last used the spell. A suitable situation had never presented itself, but now seemed to be the perfect time for the spell. There was this gigantic wasp as well as numerous less-threatening monsters rushing up and against the barricade.

The dark sky lit up as a burning ball of fire descended from above. The first meteor came down and hammered directly onto the wasp's head. The resulting impact was massive, and even startled those groups either side of us.

The meteor shattered only after dragging the wasp into the muddy ground. The impact of the spell didn't stop there as a second came crashing down. Nor was I the only one hurting the wasp. Aaron was nocking arrow after arrow and pelting the now cracking carapace with his missiles.

The second ball from the Meteor Swarm managed to push the giant insect a bit further into that muddy mess and only half of its body was still above ground. I constantly cast Fireballs and threw them out. By now, the wasp had zero mobility to even move or retaliate.

The wasp was dead by the third meteor strike, but there was no stopping the spell. It came down and struck the ground sending out a mess of debris. The weeds rattled as hundreds of tiny rocks jetted through the air.

The nearest monsters to the blast were riddled with holes. The barricades made dull thuds as debris slammed into them. Even a portion of the surrounding weeds fell over as the rocks sliced through them like a scythe.

The fourth bolt from the Meteor Swarm cleared the entire area ahead of the barricade of anything living. There was finally now a bit of breathing room to be had. For once there weren't any monsters trying to force a way over the barricade. The commotion had even attracted the attention of other groups of Adventurers and I saw many faces turned towards us.

That was a tall order to accomplish. They were constantly battling for their lives at every barricade opening; all their actions up to now had suggested they thought there was no time for distraction. To have them pay attention to what we were doing was quite an achievement.

We waited in silence for the impending wave to continue crashing into us. The moment of reprieve allowed Steven to wipe the dirty mud splattered across his face and arms off. I popped my water gourd and drank as quickly as I could, the others seeing this did the same.

It became clear that the lull was not normal.

"What's going on?" Several voices called out from the different groups. Not because there was too much action but because suddenly the siege had stopped. The rustling had ended, the sound of charging footsteps had ceased.

The impending tide receded into the swamp as if it had never been there. From the expressions of amazement and hope all around, this was a new development not seen before. For the past three or four days, we'd been told, every night had been a battle to the death till dawn.

I wasn't so naïve to think it was my Meteor Storm that had changed the pattern of events, something big was probably unfolding deep in the Marsh Pond. This abrupt reversal could have happened whether we were here or not. A new phase in whatever was evolving here.

The sudden change seemed to flip things on its head. What should everyone do with no monsters to fight?

Going out in the swap in pitch darkness was tantamount to suicide. With no one at your back, with no barricades to protect you, dying was the most likely result.

"Is it a trick? They're gonna come back once our guard is down." Someone in the group to our right shouted over.

"We can't relax, they'll be back soon." Again, a voice from another group. No one was willing to accept the latest change, and for good reason. Making a mistake at this junction would be the end. Outrunning these monsters built for the swamp was not possible.

Thirty minutes, and then an hour passed with no sign of a renewed attack. There was nothing but normal swamp sounds. It seemed the tide of monsters had truly retreated into the darkness. Only then did people group around campfires and sit down.

The chatter grew more lively, and the same question continued to pop op, "What do we do now?" The answer was staring us in the face, at least our group at least. We were tired as hell and ready for a night's sleep.

Aaron sought out the logistics officer and made a request, "We're going to try to get some sleep. If there's any change to the situation then wake us up." We weren't running or fleeing, and so she could only agree. I was exhausted and falling asleep came easy.

Chapter 18: The Scent of Danger

We woke later than normal the following morning. A thick layer of fog that reached to my knees hovered over the camp grounds. There were a few people still out and about, but most had gone to sleep at daybreak.

The situation change left everyone stumped and no one could say for sure if there would be another attack tonight. I felt that if the attack repeated itself in the same fashion as last night, there was no point in staying here. The EXP gain for the time we'd spent was miniscule. Not only that, the best way to get wealth here came not from killing monsters but from finding the rare resources located in the Marsh Pond. It was time to make a judgment call.

"I think we should vote to either leave the Marsh Pond completely... or venture into the Marsh Pond and abandon this encampment." I honestly didn't mind either choice but was going to vote to explore: the situation here was clearly changing, and that meant there was an opportunity.

"I... don't know," Steven shook his head.

"It's a big gamble." Aaron said.

"Right, and with great risk comes great reward," I said. "We would be the only group to make the move. So whatever is happening, if there's a payoff it would be ours for the taking."

Isabelle said, "I'm willing to trust your judgment, but I'm still undecided, so why don't we do it this way: we head in and if things don't favor us, we leave immediately."

I agreed. "I think that's fair. What does everyone else think?"

"If we're willing to retreat if things look bad, I'm for it," Steven said. Kimmi nodded and so it was decided. We started to pack our things and pick up our tent.

The logistics officer came over and confronted us, "Are you leaving? If you abandon the camp you won't be coming back."

I looked her in the eye. "We are leaving, but not the Marsh Ponds. We're going to be heading deeper in." Our decision startled her. This wasn't fleeing, and there was no way if we returned she could refuse us as deserters. We were more like valiant warriors charging headfirst into battle.

"If you want to get yourselves killed then I won't be the one to stop you. If you do come back, this will be your spot, so don't forget." It seemed we wouldn't lose our position. Not that we cared very much for it.

"Did everyone chew a green herb?" asked Aaron.

"Ah, I forgot, good catch," I replied.

Our packs were loaded, my mouth tasted like medicine, it was time to get moving. Those still awake watched us depart in confusion; they were probably wondering why we were rushing to our deaths.

I didn't feel that way though. At no point the previous night did I feel the situation was out of our control. We had dispatched every enemy that came quite easily. Now we had the additional help from the fact it was daytime.

Whatever the challenges ahead, I felt that we would handle them well and if we found ourselves out of our depth, would be able to extract ourselves. My trust in Steven had grown dozens of times since we had met him. There was a shadow of Bryan in him, a reliable tank. He wouldn't walk us into a situation that he felt we couldn't handle. Even when Steven didn't feel comfortable, he still stood up for the challenge.

Isabelle's heals were on another level and in all the grinding we'd done together, her awareness in battle had increased greatly.

Then there was Kimmi. I was wrong about her from the get-go. Kimmi did run in battle, but not away from it. She was the first to dive in headfirst. When she did, she left you with an impression of bloodshot eyes and red hair, and it was then I truly felt she was a battle demon.

Aaron was the pillar of our team. He was reserved and quiet, but only because he silently analyzed every aspect of a fight. He was always looking for that edge to give us any advantage possible.

Our feet touched the swampy ground below. The fog was so thick it was hard to see the ground beneath each step. There was no choice but to follow the thin and winding paths available to us, lest we wade through water.

The plant-life grew thicker and thicker as we trod deeper. Mosquitoes buzzed like flies all around us. Luckily the repellant did a fantastic job at keeping them off us. Otherwise, the clouds of insects looked dense enough that the mosquitoes would eat us alive.

As the fog cleared we started to notice monster tracks all over. They went both ways and were freshly embedded in the earth. The steps were everywhere, big and small. Some were larger than possible for any monster we had yet encountered.

The wildlife seemed non-existent, which was anything but ordinary. From what we'd been told about this region, even just thirty minutes into the swamp and we should have been presented with numerous encounters. And yet nothing happened, nothing at all.

It wasn't until we had walked for a solid hour that we encountered our first monster. It was another Snailigator resting in a low pond. The majority of its back was out of the water but its head wasn't visible.

Aaron nocked an arrow and shot cleanly into the swamp on a course to where its head would be. The monster raised its snout and rushed in our direction to where Steven stepped into its path and met it. Ball lightning seemed to be the right spell here. Every electrical shock sent it into a stupor that made dispatching it a piece of cake.

For some reason, the monsters had withdrawn deeply into the Marsh Pond. Instead of finding this area littered with low tier creatures to fight and gain EXP from it was mostly a barren wasteland and the Snailigator was our only encounter.

There was suddenly a smell in the air, strongly contrasting with the smell of filth and slow decay. It was sweet, almost delicious smelling. Like the finest candy you could buy. I found myself becoming intoxicated.

It took me a moment to realize that I was losing my sense of reason. This smell, whatever it was, had such a strong attraction, such a pull. "Does everyone smell that?"

"Smell what?" asked Steven. I was once again reminded of Arlene telling me my senses were a step above those of my friends. It was either that or I was crazy.

"You're not crazy." Marcus said. "It's not a delusion."

After so many days of silence, it was comforting to hear him give me assurance, but also troubling. The fact my senses were better meant the scent was having more of an effect on me. The feeling it gave me was a strong desire.

I instinctually wanted to travel in the direction it originated from. When I thought about animals being much keener to smell in general, things were starting to come together. The question was why?

"Nothing. I thought I smelled something sweet." And everyone accepted this, despite the entire area smelling like a mixture of trash and decay. There was no proof as of yet the mysterious scent would become a problem so I didn't bother going into detail about it.

We walked for another hour before Isabelle spoke up, "Something smells sweet."

"You smell it too?" By now, the smell was already getting to me. It was itching at the back of my neck. I felt like an addict and I was worried how it would be if we continued.

"I can help you suppress the effects of that scent," Marcus said. I knew he was telling the truth, but it was still scary to know he could have that kind of impact on my will. I could only agree to Marcus or explain to the others why we couldn't continue, and so I allowed him to interfere. In a way it was sort of like a test of trust.

"Let's see what it is." And so we started moving in that direction. It was no coincidence that scent continued to grow stronger and stronger the deeper we went in. Whatever the source was, it lay deep in the Marsh Ponds, maybe directly in the center.

Kimmi was the next to smell the scent, and then Aaron, lastly it was Steven. Isabelle was clearly growing agitated and impatient.

"Relax, you're not acting normal," I said. Only then did she realize it was exerting a controlling appeal.

"Is this why all the monsters are missing?"

"Probably." It was the only logical explanation. The reason for something pulling us so deep in still bothered me immensely. Even with Marcus's assistance the desire to hurry towards that sweetness grew intense and agitating. It was tempting me with every step.

It was around the point that I was thinking of calling a halt that we saw the first peculiar thing. Two monsters were facing off against each other. This wasn't a territorial dispute at all. There was so much free real-estate to occupy. It was a fight to the death for some reason I couldn't discern.

The two monsters mauled and brutally fought with their lives on the line. There was no survival instinct, no hesitation, no retreat after a display of prowess. They traded limbs like playing cards without a care of the damage, and eventually, there was a clear winner.

Unfortunately, that victor was so badly mangled and damaged that it succumbed to its injuries soon after. The scariest development of all was what happened after.

Both bodies remained ten or twelve feet apart, completely lifeless. Normally, they would remain there until scavengers came and picked them clean before time washed them away. That was my expectation, but the reality was quite different.

Finger-sized vines broke through the loose and muddy soil before plunging deep into the flesh of the fallen monsters. These vines attached little suckers all over the bodies and then began to pulse and throb as they sucked the corpses clean.

Just like that, two enormous bodies were turned to skin and bone. The innards had been liquefied and then swallowed up. The vines disappeared into the earth and then didn't resurface.

"What… in the hell was that?" I said aloud.

We were all too worried to move forward. It was impossible to know if these vines were part of a monster of the swamp or something related to that sweet smell.

We took a wide birth around the incident and found more incidents of monsters fighting each other, more battles. Every time the conflicts followed the same pattern; there was an obvious disconnect from reality. No monster showed a desire to live, only one to fight to the death. That was when my mind connected the dots.

This sweet smell, whatever it was, was bringing these monsters here. Why? To fight to the death, and once they did so, the creature responsible absorbed the corpses for nutrition. What was the end goal though? Was this just a boss?

Something we learned very quickly was the vines didn't bother to show themselves unless the monsters were dead. Was it possible that the plant responsible for these vines was actually weak?

It was also possible my estimations were incorrect. I didn't feel any desire for bloodlust, or a desire to fight, I only felt a desire to acquire that sweet smell. Was there a reason the monsters would fight to the death and we were left unaffected?

I spoke up. "I think they're fighting over whatever that sweet smell is."

"Me too. It's not that they are completely delusional or under the control of that smell. Whatever it is, they value it more importantly than their own life," Aaron observed. "And if whatever is producing that scent can appear so valuable to these monsters, then it clearly has a value for us too."

And so I came to understand there was indeed a treasure in the Marsh Pond: it was whatever was providing the source of that scent.

"So why now, for the creature or monster that's releasing the scent?" Steven was searching for answers.

"To grow," Aaron said. "Something has triggered a change in the swamp, right? Well, that change is the growth of a plant with the scent. It now wants flesh and it is using the scent to attract its food. The monsters under the influence understand there can only

223

be one victor, and so everything is an enemy. Every new encounter is a fight to the death. The loser is absorbed as nutrition."

"Are you suggesting there's a powerful hunting plant growing here?" I asked.

"I can't think of any other reason. The plant is attracting monsters here. They are fighting and then get absorbed. It clearly needs that absorption to grow. Something that the monsters will fight to the death for can't be ordinary."

"How much further can the source of the scent be?" The attraction was already so strong and we had only encountered a fraction of the monsters that should be in the Marsh Pond. To go any further in and expose ourselves to more influence from the scent and put ourselves in the path of monsters would risk an absolute blood bath. We might very well lose our ability to resist and find ourselves battling to the death for the scent just like the other creatures. We didn't even know what 'it' was for sure. How long did we even have to find the plant before it achieved whatever it was trying to do?

The fact that it was still absorbing nutrients and monsters were fighting with no clear core plant in sight suggested it wasn't ready. That might mean we had a certain amount of time to make our move.

Any encounter we had from here on out would only end in one way: destruction. There would be no pause and weighing of options, attack or not attack, it would be do or die. We needed to be fully prepared for every foe.

Despite our reservations, the idea of a 'miracle fruit' producing a magical scent was too tempting to pass up, and so we continued to move towards it. An increasing number of devoured monster corpses were a testament to just how brutal this effect had been. The skin and bones of mobs of all types were everywhere.

The good news was that nearly every living monster we encountered was either in battle or heavily wounded and recovering. Despite that, they showed no hesitation in trying to attack as they limped in our direction. The resulting fights were easily managed.

My desire to find the source of the scent continued to grow stronger. Was I succumbing to the effect? Or was it the prospect of gaining control of a very rare and powerful magic? Soon we encountered our first 'real' enemy. It was a Swamp Wasp, and it revealed something peculiar. Either some monsters were not affected to the same extent by the attraction of the scent, or stronger monsters resisted the effect more easily.

The reason for that thought was the presence of another monster nearby: a particularly large and unusually colored Snailigator. The Swamp Wasp and it seemed to coexist peacefully, and they weren't battling to the death. Did they have a level of intelligence that said fighting now was pointless? Were they waiting for some kind of endgame here?

Aaron proposed that we take on the wasp without using our most powerful spells as if we were approaching some kind of boss fight, we didn't want to attract unnecessary attention, and we didn't want to tip off our best strategies. The fight therefore really put Steven's tanking ability to the test. The wasp continuously zipped side to side, as fast as the blink of an eye. Steven had to do his best to keep it focused on him while Aaron fired arrows and Kimmi looked for the chance to launch a surprise attack.

The monster occasionally stuck out its abdomen and its stinger shot out like a piston. Otherwise, it leaned its mandibles forward in an attempt to grip Steven with them. They weren't the wasp's main weapon, but were so powerful that they could definitely snap off an arm.

It became obvious Steven coped better with strong monsters compared to fast ones. He was at a clear disadvantage, and without the use of taunt would have been unable to keep the aggro. He didn't seem able to retaliate in the slightest.

Perhaps because of his lack of experience with this type of situation, Steven's inability to hit the wasp led him to grow frustrated. The fact his enemy was easily evading all of his swipes and making successful attacks while Steven was unable to land a blow, caused his anger to boil over. All at once, he gave a roar of fury rushed forward haphazardly.

I knew at once this was a bad idea; the stinger was too fast. Patience was needed here. Before my warning had even been formulated, let alone shouted, the wasp had taken advantage of the way Steven had opened himself up and it stung the side of his chest. The stinger passed directly through the flesh in his underarm and out the other side before retracting back.

Death could be that quick and none of us hesitated at all to unleash our best spells. Stealth was no longer important here when Steven's life was in the balance. I cast Glacial Spike while Aaron shot out Ensnaring Arrow. Isabelle had already healed Steven, but that wouldn't remove the poison in his veins.

Our two-pronged attack provided a brief moment of reprieve as Kimmi did her best to drag Steven back. The wound was deathly close to his heart and the veins under his skin were already bulging and discolored. His eyes were bloodshot and blood started to drip out of his nose and mouth.

A Panacea was pulled and he used it immediately. His attack had been a costly mistake, and one that he maybe should have learned sooner. Steven was completely rattled at that moment. I knew that feeling. I had also been at death's door due to poison.

Seeing the blood in Steven's eyes enraged Kimmi even more. She suddenly blended into the surroundings before appearing behind the swamp wasp. It was still tied down by Glacial Spike and Ensnaring arrow.

Her daggers glowed bright before she slashed across its neck. There was just a moment of silence and peace before the head fell off and plopped to the floor along with the body. The wings and limbs continued to twitch and wiggle. These unpleasant movements continued for some time till it was fully dead.

"Are you okay?" Isabelle asked. I looked at Steven who was barely able to get up off the swamp ground. He was leaning on one side.

"…I think so. Shit, that was close. Sorry for scaring everyone."

"Lesson learned. Sometimes you'll encounter an enemy you can't hit, that's only normal. You can't excel at everything," said Aaron.

It was true. He could either be strong and tanky, fast and tanky, or strong and fast. He just didn't have enough stats to reach that trifecta yet.

None of us rebuked him for his mistake, and that was only natural. Steven was our teammate. I reached out my hand and helped scoop him off the ground. He slowly wiped the dirt off his body.

Chapter 19: The Source

Nearby was the large Snailigater: it was unusual in having iridescent purple lines in its skin. Nor did it attack us or show any signs of aggression and instead, after our battle with the wasp had ended, the monster started to walk away. This was an odd behavior compared to the other monsters, but it made sense from a survival point of view.

As with the other dead monsters, vines appeared from the swamp below and quickly latched onto the wasp's body. These sucked even more vigorously until almost nothing was left. It seemed stronger monsters provided even more benefit towards whatever was absorbing them.

As we moved on, I could hear the dying throes of many monsters in the distance. Every step closer to the scent caused our desire to grow and grow. I was starting to worry whether we would retain the judgment to turn around if we needed to.

It seemed elites of a certain level had the ability to resist the desire. By the way they watched what was happening to weaker monsters but did not get involved, they understood something strange was happening, and avoided battling to the death. Only the weaker cannon fodder continued to battle deep inside the Marsh Pond.

Eventually, we could see the source of commotion. It was a towering tree in the distance, so large that it blocked a portion of the sun. Despite being so many miles away we could still make out every branch and bend.

There was suddenly an electrifying shock that traveled through my body. My eyes focused on a particular branch of the tree. Something dangled there, something magnificent.

It was a kind of gem which was miniscule in comparison to the tree, but which made the tree even more marvelous. All the vines and their feeding energy were being funneled towards it. So much so that the gem glowed brightly. It was completely pink and sparkled like a ruby.

My mouth instinctually watered just looking at it. It was impossible to gauge its size from such a distance, but it had to be at least the size of a watermelon, maybe even bigger than that. "Do you see it?" I asked everyone.

Everyone was staring with expressions of awe and desire. It was beautiful, that's what my brain was telling me. I wanted it right then and there, and so I kept moving. The world around us was shrouded in haze.

My goal was singular as I moved forward: I had to obtain that miraculous fruit. The roars coming from deeper and closer to the tree, however, helped erase my stupor. My hair stood on end. I knew the creatures making that noise would smash me to a pulp in one hit.

Yet, my feet kept moving and we began fighting to force our way past the constantly arriving creatures. The monsters striking out at us were all small fry: Snailigators; Swamp Growths; Moss Ooze; and we also took on any wounded elite we could get our hands on.

Our journey eventually came to a stop as a mass of monsters appeared in front of us. There must have been hundreds sitting around, patiently waiting, each in a small patch of its own little territory.

They noticed our presence but didn't make a move. All of these creatures here had sufficient a level of intelligence to know that getting wounded now would hurt their chances of obtaining the fruit. They opted to wait patiently for whatever development was under way.

There were so many monsters here I didn't recognize. The ones resting closest to the tree seemed ultra-rare. A few gave me chills just glancing at their spikey backs and sharp talons.

"This… can we do this?" Steven asked. It was a good question, and it seemed he was the only one thinking with a clear head. His senses seemed to be the worst out of all of us, and perhaps he was getting the least impact of the temptation of the ruby-fruit.

"I don't know," I confessed. By now the desire I felt was burning. Marcus had woken up and was working hard to keep me from losing my cool and rushing blindly towards that towering tree.

"We have a chance… maybe," Aaron said. "It will be a blood bath. I can resist the scent at least to the extent of being able to be strategic about which monsters we take on." He looked at those daunting creatures deeper in. "If they can be drawn into fighting each other, maybe we can make a move then."

"Will we have our senses by then though?" I asked. It was apparent that distance wasn't the only thing affecting this attraction. My desire was growing stronger just sitting here and waiting.

"How long will we have to wait until something changes?" Isabelle licked her lips.

"I don't know." And yet there was nothing to do but wait. The situation around us felt so incredibly strange. There was no doubt we would be mauled and ripped to shreds in moments if every creature here were to attack.

It was also clear we weren't viewed as a serious threat. At most we got a passing glance from a monster, before it returned its attention to the gem-fruit that was slowly engorging and growing brighter.

Eventually the attraction from the gem-fruit would grow strong enough to where nothing would have the power to resist. That was the feeling I had, and yet this was good news. No matter how good my sense of smell was, these beasts living in nature were going to be more affected than me. I would be the oriole behind the mantis.

We waited for what felt like eternity before there was a sudden change. That pink gem high in the tree suddenly pulsed. I felt a gripping at my heart as the desire it invoked in me spiked to an unbelievable level.

The monsters around us grew agitated as well. Their hair stood on end as growls and groans escaped their throats. There was a blood lust in their eyes and it seemed a crisis was near. We also jumped to our feet in preparation.

Our motion was a little spark that started the fire. Everything devolved into pure chaos as every monster turned to its neighbor and rushed at it. It was like two armies crashing full speed into each other.

We weren't exempt from the action at all. A towering and furry beast turned in our direction and attacked us. Good! I could tell from the eyes of my friends that they were also hungry for battle.

```
┌─────────────────────────────────────────────────────┐
│  SWAMP YETI*      LEVEL: 31          BEAST  EARTH     │
│            HP: 27310        MP: 10                    │
│                    STR: 50                            │
│                    AGI: 15                            │
│                    DEX: 10                            │
│                    VIT: 70                            │
│                    INT: 15                            │
│  A TOWERING BRUTE COVERED IN THICK ALGAE AND SWAMP   │
│                    SLIME.                             │
└─────────────────────────────────────────────────────┘
```

The palm of a hairy giant hand was as big as Steven's shield, still, he managed to brace his legs for impact. His heels dug in deep to the muddy ground and slid back a few inches when the swing of the Yeti landed. Despite its force, he had blocked the blow.

I wanted badly to cast Meteor Storm, it would be the perfect way to dispatch this Earth monster with one spell. Marcus's voice shook me awake, "Don't do it."

Why not?

"Don't look more threatening than you need to be. If you perform such a miracle then won't you be a major threat? Can you guarantee these monsters won't eliminate you as a group? The enemy of my enemy is my friend."

It was a troubling thought, and some of the monsters had shown at least a basic level of intelligence. I opted for a Fireball and started to chuck them out repeatedly. The yeti in front of us had a high HP pool and impressive defense.

Not only was the monster's body large and muscular, it was covered in thick fur that acted as a barrier between its skin and our attacks. Not to mention the layers of algae and dirt and moss that had accumulated over the years.

There was good news too, though. It didn't seem like it had any special abilities at all and simply brawled with Steven in close range. As long as he could hold his own, it was only a matter of time before we would dispatch the Yeti.

Isabelle was timing her heals perfectly and never let Steven's health dip below half. We were whittling away at this giant, one fireball, arrow, and Penetrate at a time. Eventually that burly body collapsed and those familiar vines sucked it up.

We had an incredible advantage in this wild scenario. As long as Isabelle had MP we entered every fight as good as new. The monsters around us didn't have that luxury. Most of them were already sporting new injuries.

The lure of the scent only grew stronger with each passing moment and each falling monster. The pink gem-fruit was calling to me now in frequent pulses and the desire to eliminate any foe that could potentially steal it away surged up in me.

Only the roars coming from the creatures closer to the tree trunk could shake my hazy mind. Those monsters were on another level. I don't know why we thought it was a good idea to continue, but we did.

It was probably an aspect of the gem-fruit's enchantment, but I just knew this was a once-in-a-lifetime opportunity. This situation was something that could change your fate, something that could change your entire direction in life.

The next elite to come at us was a spider.

```
┌─────────────────────────────────────────────────────────┐
│  POND SPIDER*      LEVEL: 32        INSECT  NEUTRAL      │
│              HP: 31272        MP: 10                      │
│                    STR: 35                                │
│                    AGI: 25                                │
│                    DEX: 45                                │
│                    VIT: 40                                │
│                    INT: 7                                 │
│  THE STRANGE PADS ON ITS FEET ALLOW IT TO WALK ON WATER. │
└─────────────────────────────────────────────────────────┘
```

This was the first time I had come across any monster with such high DEX. It was also the first time encountering one with eight legs. Fortunately for us, one of its front legs was already cracked and leaking bug juice.

Several of its eight eyes were damaged and or completely gouged out. It was in a sorry state from the get-go. Despite that, we couldn't afford to underestimate the spider at all. Insects tended to be poisonous, especially in the swamp.

The reason for its high DEX stat became immediately obvious. The four front legs were all considerable weapons that could be used more or less at the same time. Each struck out like lightning towards Steven.

Even the cracked and damaged one was a weapon, and arguably more dangerous. The gooey blood splashed onto Steven and caused his skin to sizzle. Isabelle quickly healed the damage while Mend assisted in keeping him topped off.

Insects like this—ones with hard exteriors and soft underbellies—were my most hated enemy, so I loved to kill them. Somehow, they were always poisonous and just a pain in the ass in general.

Steven hacked and slashed while doing his best to keep the splashes of blood away from his face. Aaron used Powershot and managed to take out another two eyeballs. By now, the spider's vision was almost completely blind on its right side.

That allowed Kimmi to make her move with ease. She blended into the surroundings before appearing just before the four right legs. Her daggers glowed and she sliced through the connecting tissue of each limb.

The spider screeched in agony as the limbs were sliced clean off. There was nothing left supporting it on one side, and it fell over with a smash. The remaining four legs shuffled frantically but could only manage to spin it along the ground.

The fight ended with a Glacial Spike right through the chest cavity of the monster. There was nothing to stop it, and the spider was now incredibly close to the ground. The shard of ice jutted straight through its body and out the back.

To my surprise, no vines came from the swamp to devour the corpses. It seemed even they knew how poisonous and corrosive its blood was. The body would sit here until something that could stomach it came by.

I wiped the sweat from my brows and wasn't the only one to breathe a sigh of relief. The fights were going smoothly. We were at a clear advantage, an advantage that was only growing.

The remaining monsters were covered in their own blood. Their limbs were broken or mangled, their eyes were gouged. Some even had traces of teeth marks where massive jaws had been locked onto their body.

"It's starting to look rough." Isabelle said. She pulled a blue potion from her inventory and then gulped it down. I wasn't quite at that point yet, my MP resting at around 70%. She was constantly healing Steven through every beating.

The area around us was beginning to thin as a few clear victors emerged from the hundreds. By now my desire was burning to an uncontrollable level. I could feel nothing but greed. Marcus was constantly assisting me to restrain that impulse.

We were so close. I wouldn't forgive myself for failing at this moment. *Don't let me lose control.* I pleaded with Marcus, but only for my own comfort. I could tell he was already using everything in his power to keep me from going over the edge.

The extraordinary fruit was growing plumper by the moment. The sweet smell was intoxicating to an unimaginable degree. In a dirty and disgusting marsh like this, the scent of the ruby-fruit was of heaven itself.

The added weight from its growth caused the thin branch the fruit was dangling from to bend and droop. It was like a heavenly hand slowly lowering it towards me for consumption. I understood now, once it drooped to the ground, it was ready for someone to pluck it and eat it.

The gem fruit was sinking lower and lower, and all the monsters around started to move even closer to it. We too pressed inward towards the trunk, towards the really goliath creatures of unknown level and strength. To them, we were like ants.

They didn't bother to look at us, or the other creatures. They focused on their opponents of equal strength. It was obvious they were sturdier than anything else in the swamp, and possibly didn't even belong here. Since the beginning battles, none of them had perished yet.

They were in rough shape, but so was everyone. Physically, we were okay, but mentally we weren't. I was feeling the pull of the gem-fruit the worst and even Isabelle was panting heavily. Her cheeks were red hot.

There was nothing more tempting than the miracle fruit to me at this moment. Even living paled in comparison. My thinking was absolutely wrong, and Marcus was constantly whispering in my ear.

"Calm down." He repeated it over and over. We'd miscalculated in coming this far. Marcus had underestimated the pull of the scent, and his own ability to help me.

I already knew it by now: I was lost. I had to have it. Regardless of anything, I would get it. My eyes were locked to that beautiful gemlike fruit sinking ever so close to the ground. Nothing could make me look away from it.

There was suddenly a mournful cry, full of regret and despair. It seemed Isabelle had momentarily escaped from her stupor, leading to a brief moment of realization, but not me. Nothing could shake me at the moment.

A goliath came crashing down so hard the earth shook. Dust and mud and debris flew through the air as if a building had collapsed. A plethora of vines slithered out of the ground before feasting upon his flesh.

The miracle fruit grew plump at an alarming rate: this was it. It was coming now, like a divine being. The victor of that fight, a T-Rex kind of beast standing near the trunk looked in our direction.

The triumphant goliath then turned in the direction of all the remaining beasts and let out an ear-shattering roar. I felt like my soul was being torn asunder. Just the sound from its cry had dealt damage to us and Isabelle showered us with heals to help us recover.

Several of the more injured monsters bled from their orifices before collapsing. The miracle fruit grew plumper in response. Others, somehow in command of their desire, realized this was not their trophy to claim and rushed off into the distance.

Steven, who was the most lucid of all of us, came to a sudden realization. "We can't do this, and I won't. That thing will kill us all…"

It seemed that roar had already shaken Aaron and Kimmi awake as well. I knew it was bad when Kimmi readily agreed, "We should retreat."

I couldn't look away though. It seemed Isabelle was struggling as well.

"Let's leave while we can," Aaron said. I ignored his words and started to run towards the fruit like a madman.

"What are you doing?" Marcus yelled, but I didn't care. This needed to happen, no matter what.

"JOSEPH!" Aaron yelled. It was already too late, I had long ago crossed the threshold of no return and chasing me would get them killed. Looking back, I could see Isabelle had a yearning expression before she suddenly lurched towards the fruit as well.

"Grab her!" Steven cried and together with Kimmi they managed to restrain her before pulling back.

Did I feel bad in that moment? That they didn't chase me? I couldn't be sure, but maybe. My mind wasn't working right, and that's what was so dangerous. I felt lucid, I felt completely justified in my actions.

I wasn't alone in my charge though, other creatures of the swamp rushed forward as well. We were rushing towards a grinder, and I wasn't the first to arrive. The beasts faster than me were like decoys.

They were scooped up in one hand by the goliath and ripped in half, or even tossed like a ball into others. Yet I wasn't looking to fight and win, I was looking to plunder the fruit. I was insignificant in this, a weak human.

I couldn't stand toe to toe against any of these monsters, and maybe that was why I could get so close. I ignored the burning in my legs, the burning in my lungs, my parched throat. None of it mattered.

The world around me didn't exist, only that beautiful fruit hanging there. I had long ago blocked out Marcus completely. Nothing he said was getting through to me at all. I ran with a singular goal in mind.

Time was passing so slowly, but suddenly I found I had reached my destination. I was under the miracle fruit and it was sinking right to my grasp. The size of the pink gem was more impressive than I had imagined it to be from afar.

It wasn't a fruit at all, but something else. The size was staggering, at least as big as my torso. It was almost perfectly see through with a pink hue to it, perfect in every way.

I lifted up my hands like a newborn begging for milk. This was the best moment in my life, I truly believed that. There was contact and I felt an electrifying shock through my entire body. Several lifetimes of enjoyment couldn't compare to this feeling.

The texture of the heavenly substance was completely different to that of my expectations, and defied common sense. It was soft and jiggly like Jello, yet maintained a perfect shape. I couldn't hold back and dug my hand into the interior. It disappeared with no resistance.

The pink and gelatinous substance wiggled in my hand as I forced some of it into my mouth. Its taste… there was nothing to describe it. It didn't have a taste, it had colors, so vivid and beautiful. A moment of relief washed over me.

I realized there was nothing left around me. Nothing but that goliath of a monster we had no chance against. Its claw was already halfway towards me. This was a moment to regret, and yet I didn't.

My mind was still so fucked up I only felt happiness, and peace. Even as that giant claw smashed into my body, as my bones broke, as the world spun around me, I felt grateful. I felt elated, I felt satisfaction. My world turned black.

Chapter 20: Rebirth

"Is he alive?" this was a voice I wasn't familiar with. My eyes slowly opened to see a group standing in front of me. It was a party, but not my own. I turned my head to look around and could find no one but these strangers. I was still in the Marsh Ponds, but the monsters and the gem fruit were gone.

They were a party of four: three men and one woman. I tried to make out their classes by their dress and equipment and could clearly pick out those of the three males. They were a tank (with a massive shield), an archer, and a healer. The female, however, was hard to read: she was a caster of some kind, but her clothing looked peculiar.

"Hey, are you okay?" she asked.

"Move away from him…" the tank warned.

I didn't know what I was expecting. Not Aaron and Steven and Kimmi and Isabelle; wherever I was, I knew they wouldn't be here. It was no fault of theirs: my decision to try and run past the goliath had been completely suicidal. Of course they weren't here.

Despite to everything that had happened, my body felt great. It felt light and easy to move, even my robe felt more comfortable than usual. I looked at my hand and realized it was clean; my skin was fairer than it used to be, more muscular even. This wasn't making sense.

The group was watching me as if I was a wild animal, "Sorry, who are you?" I asked. I sat up a little and they all took a few steps back. "Something happened here and I got lost." I made up a lie.

"Right, there was some commotion here that's why we rushed out here. Can you remember anything?" the tank said.

"It's all a blur. Ah, did you see another party?"

"We saw another party on the way out, yeah."

"Red head? Fat tank?"

"Yes, that was them."

"Did they say anything?"

"Nope, we tried to ask them what happened and they didn't even acknowledge us. Seemed the mood wasn't too good."

"Was that your party?" asked the girl. I nodded my head in response. "Must be why they were so upset; probably thought you had died." That really was likely. I realized the party window was gone, I could no longer see their names and if they could no longer see mine, it was the obvious conclusion.

I was originally the leader of our group, so perhaps the disappearance of it was a range issue. Hopefully, I could catch up with them, although my feeling was that at best they would be at the encampment. "How long ago did you see them?"

"We passed by them three days ago, on the way into the Marsh Pond," the tank answered.

My heart sank. Three days? I was out for three full days? Things weren't adding up.

There was no doubt in my mind I should be dead right now. That palm that hit me was big enough to squeeze me to a pulp. At the very least, every bone in my body should be broken.

I started to inspect my body and realized there wasn't a scratch on me. Not even the smallest of discomfort anywhere. In fact, I felt better than ever before. I felt brand new. Naturally, I checked my character sheet.

```
CURRENT EXP: 56740/65000      LEVEL: 27
            MAGE        FORMIDABLE
        HP: 1972/1972   MP: 686/686
                STR: 21
                AGI: 21
                DEX: 35
               VIT: 30 +2
               INT: 51 +14
              AVAILABLE: 0
```

My mind drew a blank. My stats… they were so high. Every single stat was 10 higher than before. That was more than 15 levels worth of stats… and all I did was eat a handful of that miracle fruit? How was I even alive?

"Actually, you did die. We both did." Marcus spoke for the first time since I had woken up.

What are you talking about?

"I'm telling you after you blacked out… I felt us die." And yet here we were. The miracle fruit was… more insane than I could have imagined. Did that mean I was literally reborn? A phoenix among men?

"I don't know about that, but the magic in that fruit definitely saved us both," Marcus affirmed.

I stood up and started to wipe the dirt from my clothing. The desire to chase after my party subsided slightly after I realized they were three days ahead already. Since I knew their destination, I didn't panic. I felt there was a good chance I'd be able to find them in Arturii.

The most pressing issue was that of getting out of this swamp. My new stats made me feel superhuman, but that wasn't enough to get out of this swamp alone. I scanned the party in front of me carefully.

They were only four, so there was an open spot for me. At least it was possible to get their assistance, if they were willing to help me. "Are you leaving the Marsh Pond anytime soon?" I asked.

"Actually, we only just arrived and aren't planning on leaving for a while," said the tank.

It wasn't the news I wanted to hear, but there was nothing to it.

I thought again about the difficulty of getting out of the swamp on my own. It definitely wasn't a smart idea to attempt it. Would leaving now or a few days later change that much?

"Why don't you join us? It isn't safe for you out here alone," said the girl.

"Claire…" the tank had a tone of voice that said he felt it was inappropriate for her to make that decision on her own. "Sorry, we need to talk about this in private." He looked to me.

"No problem." I could understand it. He was the thoughtful type, like Aaron, someone who weighed each option carefully. There was no guarantee I wasn't dangerous. I watched them walk several feet away, before they huddled together and began a low-voiced conversation.

Despite their efforts to be quiet, I could make out bits and pieces of their conversation:

"He'll die if we leave him out here alone."

"We don't know him."

"Let's give him a chance, its four versus one anyway." It seemed a few were hesitant and rightfully so. Yet they decided to give me a chance.

I accepted and the party window became available to me. The four of them were each level thirty, their classes available for me to read. The female, whom I knew as Claire now, was an enchanter.

I remembered having heard about this class, but she was the first person I saw to have it. The other three classes were as I had guessed.

"What's your name?" asked the tank.

"Joseph."

"Nice to meet you, this is Lucas, this is Donald, I'm Mitch and that's Claire." He gestured as he spoke. Lucas was the healer, Donald was the archer, and Mitch was the tank.

"Nice to meet you all." I gave them a heartfelt and appreciative smile. "How long will you be staying out here before returning?" I asked. Joining with them already seemed like it was the right choice.

Mitch seemed to be the decision maker of the group, "We're gonna stay for three to five days depending on what we can find. The area is a bit irregular at the moment."

"Have you been here before?" I asked.

"This is our second trip to the Marsh Ponds so we know a little bit."

"It'll be fine, stick with us we'll take good care of you." Lucas said. At least they seemed like good people. The healer's words put my mind at ease.

Once I was fully recovered, it seemed incredible to me that gigantic tree was nowhere to be seen. All remnants of the mythical tree and the miracle fruit were completely gone. The area had been torn apart in a massive level of destruction, yet the evidence to indicate that a battle had ever taken place here was nowhere to be seen. The hollow carcasses were all gone; all except that of the Pond Spider.

It seemed the traffic in this area wasn't too high. That thought was supported by the fact I hadn't been eaten while sleeping. Assuming my body been here the whole time. "Where are you heading now?" I asked.

"We're going to head towards the tar pits." I was familiar with the name, as I had seen it on the map before. They were north and a bit east of the center of the marsh. We weren't that far from them.

"When we came through we didn't run into many monsters," I said.

Mitch nodded, "Right, we haven't seen much either. Everything we did run into was an elite or unique though. Seems only the strong monsters survived whatever that recent event was."

We started to walk towards the tar pits. I kept to the back, so as to avoid getting in their way. It became immediately apparent they were much more knowledgeable than our group had been.

"Isn't that more Silver Moss?" Lucas asked.

"It is!"

As far as I was concerned the plant they were talking about just looked like dried out moss that had been in the sun too long. I couldn't really tell the difference between the moss they were excited about and any other.

"There's Gator Leaf right there too!"

They were moving from place to place collecting all sorts of strange plants and moss. I just looked on curiously, unable to offer assistance.

After watching for a while, I could sort of understand that there was a slight sheen to Silver Moss, but not why the green stems they pulled out were called Gator Leaf. "Why is it called Gator Leaf?" I asked aloud.

Claire brought an example back to me. "Do you see the shape? It's kind of jagged around the edges like some teeth, but not only that. For some reason it's only found in Snailigator ponds. The Snailigator wasn't there though."

This made sense and we had run into a Snailigator in a foot-high pond like this one as well. We just didn't know what we were looking for at the time. There was probably some Gator Leaf in there as well.

"What's it for?"

"Gator Leaf is one of the ingredients in Strength potions." There was a lot I didn't know still and perhaps she was thinking the same, because she asked: "Where are you from?"

"Ah, a little town called Elesham on Eastrath."

"Hmm, never heard of it."

"Me neither." Lucas was close enough to be listening in.

"Yeah, it's very small and out of the way. I wouldn't expect you to."

I let the conversation drop there, mainly because my thoughts kept wandering back to my new stats. I was only level 27 but had as many stat points as someone who was level 45.

My fingers were itching for some action. I wanted to fight, and my next level wasn't far off either. Two elites would be enough.

I didn't need to wait very long.

We came across a Pond Spider that was in fighting condition. Either it had remarkable recovery abilities, or it had avoided being caught up in that massacre of three days ago. I cast *Inspect*.

POND SPIDER*	LEVEL: 33	INSECT NEUTRAL
HP: 35272		MP: 10

STR: 35

AGI: 25

DEX: 45

VIT: 40

INT: 7

THE STRANGE PADS ON ITS FEET ALLOW IT TO WALK ON WATER.

"Woah." It seemed Mitch had never seen *Inspect* before. He was obviously surprised at the new flood of information presented to him. For me the interest was that this Pond Spider was a level higher than the one I had encountered previously.

Should I assist them or just watch and wait for them to tell me it was fine to help? They had invited me to party. I felt I should at least pull my own weight.

Mitch went forward to meet the Pond Spider and I immediately noticed a difference between him and Steven. Mitch focused on using his shield much more than Steven.

He almost never stabbed out with his sword and instead chose to bash into the spider. Not only that, the shield was absolutely huge. It could double as a door. The benefit of that became immediately obvious.

There wasn't much of Mitch's body exposed and even though the spider's legs struck like lightning, they couldn't land on him a single time. Instead they drummed against the shield and scrabbled around its edges.

Claire was the player I was most interested in. She was an enchanter and I'd never seen one in action. Her hands started to glow and her clothing fluttered. Some ancient words came from her mouth that I couldn't even pronounce if I tried to copy them exactly. Several treants grew out of the ground and then rushed at the spider.

Their hands morphed into wooden spears that stabbed and prodded. That wasn't the only attack from the spell though: vines came from the floor and wrapped around the spiders legs and immobilized it in place.

Donald hadn't used a skill yet, and only after the spider was trapped in place did he lean back and nock his bow. As the archer pulled back the string, the bow gave a sound like I'd never heard before, a rising, high-pitched whine as though it were an aircraft accelerating for takeoff. The entire bow glowed with flame before he released an inferno directly at the Pond Spider.

The fiery missile caused a massive explosion directly in the monster's face and scorched every eyeball to nothing. Their teamwork and skill usage was impressive to say the least. In a matter of moments, the spider had been blinded and also couldn't move.

I started to cast Glacial Spike and realized that my hands were moving fluently, my thoughts flowed flawlessly. It took a single second before that icy glacier jutted up from below and embedded directly into the spider's underside.

Mitch remained in front and had bashed the spider's skull silly. That door-like shield was a hammer that constantly smacked into that skull till it went mushy. The spider collapsed to the floor and didn't move again.

It wasn't that the spider didn't have any abilities, it was just that this group never gave it the chance to use a single one. There was a giant door in its face until its limbs no longer worked, and then it was fully blinded.

This was what you called synergy. Their skills all worked together and formed a singular goal. That goal came even before defeating the spider: first to disable, then to kill.

"That skill you used, it's pretty useful!" Mitch said.

"Ah, yeah, Glacial Spike, it's good." I really wasn't used to getting compliments and didn't elaborate. "Your style of fighting, what would you call that?"

"Hmm, I don't really have a name for it. I sort of understood long ago I wouldn't be really dealing damage. I started using my sword less and less. It just sort of worked out. I don't have as many openings anymore but I usually bring the mobs to a stop."

It also seemed that enchanters really did control nature to a certain degree. It would be rude of me to ask if that was the extent of her abilities. Still, it was impressive none the less. She could deal damage, tank with her treants, and also had decent CC: a jack of all trades.

"I wasn't sure if you'd want me to join in," I said.

"Feel free to cast what you like. I don't think you'll take the aggro off me." Mitch gave me the go ahead, and that made me feel a bit better. It was weird to have felt so untroubled by a battle. I always felt incredibly worried for Steven watching him tank.

It wasn't just that Mitch looked safe behind his mighty shield, there was also a disconnect between me and the group. I didn't know Mitch well and the thought of him getting hurt didn't put me quite on edge in the same way. Somehow it felt like a business agreement we were in. Perhaps over the course of a few days that feeling would change.

"How different is the marsh compared to the last time you came?" I asked.

"Night and day… Last time we didn't even make it this far in. There were just too many encounters."

I'd seen for myself that the miracle fruit had reaped an incredible amount of monster lives. Perhaps not restoring any of them. In my eyes the gem-fruit had been something heavenly, but maybe it was more like a devil fruit to monsters.

We were walking along peacefully when I noticed something in my peripheral vision. It was a small dot growing in size rapidly and I felt my world slowing down. Claire was walking by my side and if I dodged the incoming object it would surely hit her.

There was no time to say anything at all, I grabbed her with both arms and pulled her back. She let out a squeal in fright and everyone turned back to me in confusion. Donald looked angry: he was the one questioning my motives earlier.

He was about to speak when the object that we barely dodged smashed into a tree trunk in its path. There was the sound of impact and then cracking. The tree collapsed with a thud. No one could even ask what was going on before the foe appeared.

It looked like a Swamp Wasp, but there were glaring differences. First was the size. It was bigger in every area possible. Second was the color. It had odd stripes running all over its body. A new stinger suddenly emerged from its abdomen.

It was clear now what the missile was: the wasp shot a stinger from its abdomen like a bullet. I didn't think I'd have been able to react in time if my AGI wasn't currently 21. I cast Inspect.

```
┌─────────────────────────────────────────────────┐
│  FEMALE SWAMP WASP**      LEVEL: 34      INSECT   │
│                    EARTH                          │
│       HP: 79373          MP: 115                  │
│                  STR: 36                          │
│                  AGI: 52                          │
│                  DEX: 5                           │
│                  VIT: 43                          │
│                  INT: 5                           │
│  A MORE DANGEROUS AND CAPABLE SWAMP WASP, HER     │
│  INCREASED SIZE ALLOWS HER TO CARRY AND PROTECT HER│
│                   EGGS.                           │
└─────────────────────────────────────────────────┘
```

This was going to be the real test. I was anxious about how they would deal with this monster. Locking down slower monsters was much easier than dealing with something as agile as this. This wasn't going to be easy.

I could see the confusion and hostility clear at once from their faces to be replaced by urgency as they immediately all moved into position. Mitch was quite quick and managed to move in between us despite being the farthest away. He didn't hesitate to cast *Taunt* and pull the initial aggro.

Donald, Lucas, and Claire spread out from his position as though by instinct. It looked purposeless but they were far enough apart to avoid any unnecessary enemy AoE abilities but still assist each other quickly.

The high AGI stat of the wasp was nothing to scoff at. Her abdomen stabbed out over and over, attempting to skewer Mitch. It pulsed disgustingly as the stinger inside pumped in and out like a piston. Sparks flew off Mitch's shield as he stepped back one foot at a time.

Claire started the fight by spawning her treants as usual. She also summoned a strange man-sized plant. It grew from the ground and had a vicious looking mouth filled with layers of sharp teeth.

The plant swayed hypnotically while also taking gaping bites towards the wasp. The wasp simply fluttered to one side or the other in response. Its movements so quick there was only a green blur back and forth.

There was no way I could accurately hit it by targeting with a spell, so I chose to cast Arcane Missiles instead. It was something I'd not used in a long time, but one of the benefits of the skill was its ability to lock on to an opponent.

The missiles were bolts from the void and tracked the target. One after another they formed in the air and rushed in the wasp's direction before smashing into it.

Claire seemed to be going all out as another two treants grew out of the ground. There was now Mitch, four treants and a single man-eating plant surrounding the wasp. The area available for its maneuvers was growing tight.

The vines Claire had used on the spider wouldn't be effective here as the wasp hovered above the ground at chest height. There was zero chance they would be able to latch on and grasp it.

I wasn't sure what Donald had been doing, his bow was pulled taut but he didn't release the arrow at all. There was no indication he was even using a skill, not that I could tell at least.

One of the treants moved in and stabbed out with a spear-like hand. The wasp dodged as normal before teleporting right next to its head and pumping its stinger a dozen times throughout its body.

The entire head and chest of the treant had been shredded to pieces and it collapsed on the ground before despawning. The plant tried to retaliate in that moment and bit nothing but air.

Fortunately, Mitch wasn't just messing around and was ready for the wasp's return. He managed to slam that metal door into it.

That blow sent the wasp off balance slightly and Donald suddenly released his arrow. It seemed that he had been waiting for this moment so as to guarantee a hit. I watched the arrow fly through one of the wasp's wings, very close to where it attached.

It was a hit, but it was also a miss. I realized now that Donald was attempting to take out one of its wings. Without its mobility this wasp would be nothing to worry about at all. Yet he had missed the one chance Mitch provided and the wasp might not present another.

So far, we had managed to confine the Swamp Wasp to within an area about ten feed wide. Despite that being fairly tight, the wasp was the queen of that little area and was in complete control. We were fighting at its pace.

Nor did it seem that Arcane Missiles was that much of a bother to it. Its body didn't even react to the bolts hitting it. I couldn't tell if the carapace was too thick or the skill too weak. Luckily, I had a good ability for small enclosed areas.

I started to cast Meteor Storm. This was the perfect opportunity and the spell had never let me down. The circle glowed around me bright red and that fiery meteor spawned in the sky above. My DEX was only ten points higher, but my cast felt so smooth.

The first of the bolts came crashing down unexpectedly and even startled Mitch. Fortunately, the wasp didn't have eyes on the top of its head and that fiery ball of rock connected cleanly with its head. I watched in slow motion as the rock started to crumble and shatter while the wasp was pushed closer to the ground.

There was a moment of struggle and I really thought we would put it on the ground, I was wrong. The wasp fluttered its wings even harder and zipped backwards and out of the enclosure. The three remaining meteors hit nothing but air and ground.

The swampy ground had little bits of fire burning on it and now there was considerable distance between the wasp and us. There was a short moment when I thought the wasp would simply flutter away and cut its losses.

That wasn't what happened. The abdomen started to pulse and throb harder than before and a stinger extended a worrying distance out. Suddenly, the stinger exploded out like a bullet directly towards Claire's plant.

It was a pinpoint shot that severed the stem and caused it to flop over and turn dead brown. The man-eating plant was gone just like that. That wasn't the end either. It shot out two more stingers and accurately dispatched two treants. There was only a single treant remaining.

Mitch started to move in its direction just before the last stinger was shot. It became clear if you didn't tank it in close range it would continue to pelt you with these bullets. Unfortunately, he didn't arrive quickly enough.

The last stinger shot directly towards Claire and I thought that would be it for her. "Barrier!" Lucas yelled. Immediately after, a glowing shield formed in the air and the stinger crashed directly into it.

The barrier managed to stop the stinger halfway through as cracks spread out from the impact. The missile fell to the floor and embedded a ways into the muddy ground. Nothing about it looked like a stinger. It looked more like a straightened elephant tusk.

Mitch arrived immediately after and re-engaged the fight. Our attempts up to now hadn't been for nothing. It seemed shooting the stingers required considerable energy. There was also a piece of wing missing and burn marks across the top of its head.

Donald had been charging up another shot and let it fly immediately after. It was another good hit and although not a critical one, he managed to cut off another chunk of the damaged wing.

The wasp's flying was unstable now, and moving to one side was considerably slower than the other. We had hindered its incredible speed enough for me to feel confident to begin throwing out fireballs.

Donald stopped channeling whatever skill he was using before and began nocking arrow after arrow. Each one connected and embedded a bit into the monster's carapace and abdomen. The damage was building quickly.

I started to cast Glacial Spike and the jutting ice came from below and scraped past the side of its abdomen. A bit of chill traveled up its body and restricted its movements even further. We were nearing the end.

Mitch was relentless with his shield and continuously bashed out and threw it off balance. There was an air of panic in the wasp's movements as it realized it had bitten off more than it could chew. The remaining treant managed to stab out its hand spear and penetrate directly into the side of the wasp's chest.

The wasp jerked away and bug juice shot out from the wound. There was a horrible noise coming from its mouth that made me wince. I thought it was going to shoot out poison but instead entered what seemed to be its dying throes.

The wasp used the last of its power to retreat back away from Mitch. There was more pulsing in its abdomen and I realized it was going to shoot out one more stinger, one more dying shot: it had opted for mutual destruction.

I could see the panic in Mitch's face as he rushed as fast as he could to intercept the incoming attack. The stinger was like a soccer ball and he was the goalie. Unfortunately, he was too slow. Who was it going to be? Who would it target?

My hair rose and a chill ran up my back. It was targeting me, I was sure of it. The bloodlust it was emitting was tangible enough for me to feel. Was this more of my new senses coming into play? I contemplated summoning a Glacial Spike to block the way and decided against it.

The stinger on the ground nearby showed the missile would tear through Glacial Spike like a hot knife through butter. It would only block my vision and slow my reaction time. The abdomen pulsed one final time before that stinger launched in my direction.

Time seemed to slow as I saw that white tusk-like bullet hurtling in my direction. Everyone seemed slow, the panic still clear as day on Mitch's face. This feeling was so surreal, like I was slowing time myself.

I knew I wasn't, but the effect was nearly the same. My mind was moving at a million miles per hour and I knew exactly where that stinger was going. I tilted my left shoulder back and turned my head as it flew past.

The speed and force of the stinger was such that I could feel the breeze across my face. I had managed to stare death in the face and live to see another day. The stinger tore through the shrubs behind me before embedding itself into a tree.

Mitch reached the wasp almost immediately after and finally used his sword to stab out. It entered mid-way through the abdomen and he ripped it straight down spilling the contents.

Donald also shot his final arrow directly into the head of the wasp. It struggled to stay afloat before falling to the ground. Its

257

wings and twitching limbs only stopped a few moments later. The fight was finally over and I let out a sigh of relief.

> **CONGRATULATIONS! YOU HAVE REACHED LEVEL 28. AS A REWARD FOR LEVELING UP, YOU HAVE BEEN GRANTED THREE STAT POINTS!**

I could immediately see a few items hovering there. The normal excitement with drops wasn't there for me at all this time. This wasn't my party and I wasn't expecting to receive any items. At least I had managed to get my level.

> **CURRENT EXP: 2560/67000   LEVEL: 28**
> **MAGE   FORMIDABLE**
> **HP: 2002/2002 MP: 469/694**
> **STR: 21**
> **AGI: 21**
> **DEX: 35**
> **VIT: 30 +2**
> **INT: 51 +14**
> **AVAILABLE: 3**

I wasn't even sure what to do with these three points. What was I even lacking at the moment? The extra 10 VIT and 10 DEX really put me ahead of where I needed to be for my level. I decided to put them into INT, bringing that stat up to 54+14.

I walked over to where they were sorting the loot. There was only one skill book remaining when I arrived.

"Aren't you curious what dropped?" Claire asked. She was holding a skill book and I figured it was an enchanter spell.

"No, it's okay."

"Well… that's a shame, this was for you."

"Well, that changes everything, let me see it." I was a simple man, what could I say? She passed me the skill book and I started to read it.

BOOK OF CREMATION LV. 1**
CAST TIME: 3 SECONDS
MP COST: 35
DISTANCE: 7 METERS
SUMMONS A PILLAR OF HELLFIRE TO INCINERATE YOUR ENEMIES UNTIL NOTHING REMAINS.

The Cremation spell definitely sounded cool as shit. I learned it immediately and actually felt incredibly grateful they would consider me worth a share of the loot. I had helped them defeat the wasp, definitely, but I was confident they would have done so without me as well. The book was definitely worth a considerable amount.

"Thank you, everyone," I said. The sense of enmity from before seemed to have disappeared from their minds and they were all smiles now. Only Claire looked troubled. She knew just how fast that stinger had been going. It had bolted right before her eyes after all.

"Are you really only level twenty-seven… no twenty-eight?" She asked with some suspicion.

How could I even answer that question… it was right there in the party window. "What do you mean?"

"Well, how should I put it…" She moved a bit closer to me and started to squeeze my arm. I felt like she was inspecting a specimen and I had to admit my body wasn't the same it had been before my encounter with the gem-fruit. My arms were no longer flabby and thin. "You don't seem like a mage."

There was real substance there, I was lean and muscular, no doubt a result of having 21 STR and AGI. There was a power buried in my small frame, explosive power even. My reaction time was not something a mage would normally be capable of.

Claire was right. I figured that not offering an explanation would be the best option. There was nothing I could say that would reduce her suspicion of me. Not that she was hostile, her manner was only curious.

We took off and headed for the tar pits once again. There was another lull while we travelled, during which I grew incredibly bored. Donald, Mitch and Lucas were ahead, always conversing quietly with each other. Occasionally, however, one of them stole a glance at me.

I suddenly felt there was something they weren't telling me. They constantly scanned the map in their hands as if looking for something very specific. The tar pits were absolutely huge and that region wouldn't be hard to find.

There shouldn't have been any reason for the careful attention to our exact position. They suddenly came to a stop up ahead.

"What's up?" I asked.

Donald swallowed heavily. "Ah, we're just trying to get our footing."

Yet it didn't seem like they had come to the tar pits to gather random herbs.

"He's gonna find out soon anyway, just tell him." Mitch suddenly smacked Donald in the arm.

"What?" Donald protested.

"What's he talking about?" I looked at Claire.

Donald shrugged. "To be honest… we weren't just coming to the tar pits without reason. I'm sure you met Arnold before."

"Yeah."

"He made a request of us; he wants us to recover a rare type of grass—Star Grass."

"So, what of it?" I didn't know anything about Star Grass or Arnold's quest.

"There are reports of an above-ground cave somewhere near the tar pits that has Star Grass inside."

She... she said the word I didn't want to hear, "A cave? So, we just find it and get the grass and then we can get out of here?" It seemed this journey wouldn't be three to five days if that was the case.

Claire answered, "That's the idea, the problem is we can't just go in and take it. His source claimed there's a Lunar Ape guarding the entrance of the cave. It desperately needs Star Grass for its growth and definitely won't give it up peacefully."

Mitch suddenly interjected, "The Lunar Ape is a super-unique monster, the closest thing to a boss encounter. Normally we wouldn't bother trying with our small party, but... there are rumors it was injured recently and is still recovering."

It seemed their good will from before was in preparation for this. "What's the Star Grass for?"

"It's a rare ingredient for a special potion that increases your EXP gain for a certain time." This was an effect I'd never heard about before. Being able to level faster sounded like a luxury for the rich: the potion must be expensive and so must the ingredients.

"You're planning to sell it to Arnold?"

"Right..."

I didn't know these people well enough and I also didn't know the value of Star Grass. Demanding a solid cut in the profit perhaps would be fair, but this was their mission and they might resent me trying to elbow in at a late stage. And they did me a favor not leaving me on my own. "How about this, I'll help and ask for no cut in the Star Grass. In exchange, I get first pick at one item off the Lunar Ape."

That should be a reasonable request. One item out of the many that would drop wasn't pushing my luck. If they couldn't agree to that then I'd simply take my chance on getting back solo.

Donald was about to speak when Mitch stopped him, "That's fair, as everyone will be risking their life for this. First pick is yours; you have my word."

Can you feel anything? I asked Marcus.

"It doesn't seem like he's lying." That was enough for me to go forward with the plan. Worst case I could leave and try my luck in the wilderness alone. I wasn't completely defenseless. There was still an inventory of potions at my disposal.

"How far are we from the cave?" I asked.

"According to the information, we're looking for an above ground cave past the northeast corner of the tar pits. No more than two minutes past."

"We're still quite a ways out then." We still hadn't reached the tar pits yet, although we weren't far off. It would be another hour on foot at the very least, depending on any encounters.

Chapter 21: Lunar Ape

As we got closer to our goal, a thick layer of fog covered the land. It was so incredibly dense it was like we were walking on clouds. We could hardly even tell the tar pit was there when we arrived. Apart from an occasional glimpse, the thick black goop was completely obscured from view.

The smell of sulfur assaulted our nostrils. That was the main indication that we had arrived. Visibility was awful and our speed of travel slowed to a crawl.

Pungent odors assaulted us and the temperature climbed as we grew closer to the pits. I could hear the constant popping up of bubbles as the tar boiled and brewed. The entire area was unpleasant to be in. Hot, sticky, and stinky.

We took a moment to find our bearings, a task which was definitely harder than normal. Based on the shoreline and surrounding area, we were on the west side of the pit. Following the shore north and then east was our best bet, and so we did.

Claire turned out to be extra useful in this situation. On Earth, such tar pits would be uninhabitable, but on Yetera monsters lurked within the region. By casting her vines along the shoreline, she covered us from incoming attacks. If any monster tried to sneak out and snatch one of us, she immediately knew. Even better, the vines restricted the attacker and allowed us to easily defeat it. The vines were the hook and we were the bait.

We hadn't walked beside the pits for even five minutes before we got our first bite. It was a dog-sized, hairless creature. Black toxic goo covered every inch of its body; only its eyes were uncovered for us to see.

Claire's vines constricted the monster completely, and regardless of how it struggled it couldn't break free.

"May I?" I asked. The monster was a small fry, nothing we needed to be worried about.

"After you," Claire answered. And so I started to cast Cremation. My high DEX reduced the cast time from 3 seconds down to 2 seconds. A pillar of fire came from the ground and completely engulfed the creature, which began to squeal and squirm its way out of the flames.

I did wonder about Claire's vines and whether I might damage them too, requiring her to recast more often, but my fear was unfounded. They simply disappeared into the dirt and avoided the fire completely.

The creature only managed to move halfway out before the remaining half of its body disintegrated and eventually crumbled to ash in the flames. Its head and shoulder regions were still covered in burning tar. The remains smoldered there and left a bad taste in my mouth.

The power of Cremation had proven better than I expected, particularly the height of the flames. Even monsters that could fly would have trouble avoiding the pillar, as it rose over ten feet in the air. I couldn't really ask for much more than that.

Our surroundings slowly changed their nature. The plant life was just a thin layer over the exposed earth and some of the bushes and grasses were just lifeless husks. It seemed the thick smell of smoke and sulfur had polluted the banks of the pits.

I started to notice carcasses of all sizes as we reached the top of the tar pits. There were bones big and small, some bigger than anything I'd seen before. A few were even fresh kills as the attached rotten flesh demonstrated.

"This should be the spot." Mitch announced. We couldn't have been far off. The source claimed the cave was just two minutes past the north east corner of the tar pits. Well, that's where we were. Trying not to breathe the noxious air too deeply, I scanned the surrounding area.

The fog wasn't helping at all. It morphed and swirled into the little bit of remaining plant-life and hindered our vision completely. We were walking towards the Lunar Ape cave completely blind.

Mitch looked back at me and the others, then signaled with his hand. It was time to get in position and prepare for battle: whether we fought the ape right here or encountered it in the cave, we would be prepared.

There was a nervous tension filling me up. My adrenaline was starting to pump and I loved this feeling. It was growing rarer by the day. I was slowly becoming desensitized to monster encounters.

We stayed in our current formation and entered the tree line. Mitch was careful with every step and constantly checked on our positions. Less than thirty seconds later I saw what we were looking for.

The stone in front of us was like a miniature mountain than a cave. It was like a giant's mouth waiting to swallow us up. Nothing but darkness could be seen while looking in. Even the fog swirled and disappeared into the abyss.

"Should we try to pull the ape to here?" asked Claire.

"It may not come out if it's injured... we'll have to go to it," Mitch replied.

"What if it isn't injured?" I wondered.

"Then we run."

I had never seen a super unique before. I could only take their word for it when they said it was the closest thing to a boss encounter possible. I anticipated that even Specter Andino would pale in comparison to this fight.

Their whole plan depended on how injured the Lunar Ape was and I tip-toed forward wondering if their intel was reliable or if I was just moments away from death. Eventually, the cave opening was directly in front of us. I could only see a few meters in, before the darkness swallowed everything up.

The opening had to be over thirty or forty feet wide. The incline was shallow, so we wouldn't be traveling deep underground, just a meter or two below ground level. Despite that, the temperature was distinctly colder as we crossed the threshold.

Claire summoned a fairy similar to Isabelle's Hierophant's Helper and sent it out and deeper into the cave. A green hue coated the walls and floor. I scanned every nook and cranny for a foe.

The bats inside shrieked before dropping from the ceiling and flying out of the cave. Their screeching could be heard repeatedly as they darted in the distance. Only after they were some distance away could we hear anything else.

What we heard then was a loud breathing, the kind of troubled breathing from someone short on breath: hoarse and rough. It was the Lunar Ape no doubt, but I couldn't see it. At least it did sound injured.

If it had heard us, it had no intention of moving out of its resting place. Was it listening and waiting for our arrival? We walked deeper and deeper.

It seemed to me our plan of running if the ape was too strong wasn't going to work. The cave floor was uneven and rocky. Added to this difficult terrain was a slickness created by a thick layer of algae. I could tell already that the floor was going to be hard to maneuver upon at speed.

We turned a bend in the cave and finally I saw the Lunar Ape. It was a building-sized primate with white fur. The entire creature somehow shined like the moon. It was illuminating the darkness.

The monster showed its fangs and let out a growl that made my heart tighten. This was one of the beasts from closer to the tree that had lost its fight and had eventually fled. There was no doubt that it was out of our league.

Fortunately, the information that the ape was injured wasn't wrong. Parts of its white fur were covered in dark, red blood that faded into the darkness. One of its arms was possibly broken as well. It dangled at an odd angle from its shoulder.

Mitch measured his steps and presented himself with open arms to the Lunar Ape. Donald pulled his bow back and started to launch arrows right away. The ape simply stared at us, as if we were merely pests. The look of disdain in its eyes was evident.

Despite that, Donald continued to shoot arrow after arrow, I even started to chuck out fireballs. The Lunar Ape started to grow more restless and was reaching its breaking point, with an expression that said: when had such insignificant little shits disrespected it so much?

This was his lair, his sanctuary. I felt that in his eyes we were no stronger than flies, striking haphazardly at him, and at a time when he was injured. He suddenly beat his chest with the only usable hand remaining and screamed.

I felt my ear drums pop and even a bit of liquid seemed to come from within to leak onto my lobes. It was a shout that shook the soul and made every inch of my skin tingle. This was serious shit; Mitch wasn't kidding when he said our lives were at risk.

Even so, I had become addicted to the adrenaline high. My hands were shaking, not with fear but excitement. This was what it felt like to be alive. Something I craved so badly back on Earth. It was right here in front of me.

The Lunar Ape finally tired of our ineffective assault and rushed forward on both feet. It looked odd watching him waddle towards us like a duck. The broken arm meant it couldn't easily travel on all floors.

The other arm came swinging out like a baseball bat and hit directly into Mitch's shield. I could hear the impact; I could even feel it as the air brushed past me and stirred this stagnant cave. The armor on the tank's boots gave off sparks as he slid back, scratching across the cave floor.

Mitch had resisted the attack with his own strength, but that wasn't enough. The terrain wasn't on his side at all. His metal boots slid even further till there was no traction keeping him on the ground. He flew into the side of the cave like a rocket.

He coughed up a mouth full of blood before falling to the ground and kneeling. His breath was heavy and he was panting hard. The hit was nothing to despise. I took the brief opportunity to cast *Inspect*.

LUNAR APE***	LEVEL: 36	BEAST	NEUTRAL

HP: 215457   **MP: 10**

STR: 69

AGI: 25

DEX: 30

VIT: 82

INT: 22

A LUNAR APE, A UNIQUE BEAST ABLE TO HARNESS THE POWER OF THE MOON.

Those stats were out of this world. I'd never seen an HP number that high before. And the sort of STR score that meant it would be as easy for the ape to squeeze the life out of a person as it would be for me to squeeze a lemon.

The Lunar Ape was thoroughly enraged right now and was taking all that fury out on Mitch. Our tank had been barely able to get to his feet when the Lunar Ape reached him. We needed to retreat right now; we couldn't fight it in this cave.

The ape's fist was swung and I was expecting Mitch to splatter on the wall. Lucas, however, was already prepared, "Barrier!" he yelled. That thin sheet formed in the air directly in front of the ape's fist. There was a moment of pause before it shattered like glass.

Despite that, the resistance the magical barrier provided allowed Mitch to raise his shield. The next strike didn't send him flying into another wall but pushed him back a dozen feet. Donald was prepared and together with Lucas, grabbed Mitch before rushing for the cave entrance. "Retreat!" He yelled.

Our probing had been a complete failure. This Lunar Ape didn't fuck around. Despite its injuries, the monster had the strength to back up its anger. There was no chance we could fight it in here.

Despite feeling my feet nearly go out from under of me a few times, we sprinted outside the cave and eventually lay Mitch down on the thin swap grass.

"How is he?" Claire asked.

"He's okay, he just needs a little bit to recover from the shock. I've already healed him to full."

Mitch only opened his eyes twenty minutes later. He didn't jerk up in surprise but instead laid there as if contemplating everything that happened. "We miscalculated," he said. "We need to drag him out."

I was convinced that we couldn't defeat the mob. Period. But I didn't know the hidden cards they held. I kept my mouth shut and allowed him to speak.

"Let's smoke him out," Mitch suggested. "He can't stay in there for very long if we light the whole place up."

This was a good idea and there was plenty of fuel in the vicinity as well. Dozens of half-dead trees surrounded us. Then there was an entire pit of black sticky tar that burned beautifully.

"And after that?" I asked.

"I think I can take his strikes on solid ground. There's no footing in there, I can't even see my steps."

"Will smoke affect the Star Grass?" I asked.

"A little smoke shouldn't be a problem."

Well, it wasn't my problem anyway. I wouldn't be getting any split of the Star Grass.

We started to prune the nearby trees and then dip them in the tar pits. Just pulling them back out was a difficult challenge. The tar was sticky, like gum in hair. It took a solid hour before we acquired enough material to properly smoke him out.

The Lunar Ape was still in his little cavity when we returned. As long as we didn't provoke him, he seemed unwilling to rouse himself. Instead, he sat back there and stared at us menacingly. We started to toss the tar covered branches deeper in.

Eventually there was a nice pile of goopy branches just two-dozen feet in front of the Lunar Ape. Even without the fire it produced a pungent odor that made my nose wrinkle. This was our only option to get him out.

"Is everyone ready?" I asked. It was my task to set it ablaze and there was already a fireball burning in my hand.

"Do it." Mitch said. And so I tossed out the spell. There was a miniature explosion from the debris. The fire danced excitedly for a few moments before mellowing out. Thick smoke disappeared towards the dark cave roof.

The Lunar Ape let out a vicious growl. It sounded absolutely pissed but didn't move forward to attack us. All we could do was wait, and so we headed back to the entrance.

"Do we have a backup plan if this doesn't work?" I asked.

Mitch shook his head. "Nope, it's just this. We don't have anything that could lure it out." A dozen minutes passed before a pitch-black smoke started to whirl over the cave lip and into the sky above. It was absolutely toxic smelling, worse even than the background stench of sulfur.

Still, there was no commotion from the cave and we grew worried our plan had failed. More and more thick smoke continued to pour out until there was a steady stream of it. Suddenly, there was a commotion.

There was an annoyed growl from the cave and the sound of hurried footsteps. The Lunar Ape rushed from the darkness and I

271

couldn't help but chuckle slightly. Its entire coat was covered in a layer of soot.

None of the previous majesty was there. It didn't glow softly in the dim light but instead looked like it had spent a week in the coal mines. The ape beat on its chest and puffs of black soot exploded into the air.

"Get ready!" Mitch yelled. He was already rushing in the direction of the ape and the fight was going to begin. His plan to use smoke had paid off and we now had it above the surface and on solid ground. Could Mitch really contend in strength? I was about to find out.

Our tank put both hands behind his shield and leaned forward in his charge. It took his entire body weight and the forward momentum to stop a single-handed slap. Regardless, Mitch still lost ground. His boots dug into the muddy soil and left a large indentation.

Four treants rushed forward and vines came from below to grasp the Lunar Ape. Claire had also summoned something new: a large tree golem with gigantic tusks. It had a few similarities to the Swamp Tree.

The Lunar Ape didn't panic in the face of us ants in front of it. Its leg muscles bulged and literally snapped the vines trying to restrict it. His only working hand swung out like a blade and smacked all four treants away a dozen feet.

A pillar of hellfire burst from the ground below its feet and began working on one of its legs. The fire left the monster startled but its body was much sturdier than I expected. The white fur didn't even discolor or burn as it hopped out of the flames.

There was a bit of smoke from the heat, but no noticeable damage. Mitch rushed forward again and slammed his shield into the ape. This time, the large fist didn't swat but instead grabbed the entire door before lifting Mitch off the ground.

There was no doubt if the other arm hadn't been broken the monster would had been able to flatten Mitch into meat paste. Fortunately for us, the Lunar Ape opted to try to slam him into the ground one-handed. Mitch was raised a decent height into the air when Donald made his move.

An arrow that created a sonic boom in the air and visibly deformed the space around it shot directly into the arm raising Mitch. The shot was like a jolt of electricity that caused the Lunar Ape to drop Mitch.

That wasn't enough to get our tank out safely though. He fell to the floor on his ass and managed to raise his shield just before the lunar ape kicked him like a soccer ball. There was a dong sound as foot and shield connected and Mitch went rolling away.

The treants had made their way back now and were suicide gripping the Lunar Apes legs. The tree golem was two-thirds the monster's size and punched repeatedly into the ape's lower chest, sinking a wooden fist in deep. Yet the damage I was hoping to see didn't come.

Instead, there was a smile on the Lunar Ape's face. It flexed the muscles of its chest and pushed the tree golem's fist out of its flesh. The tree golem was grasped by its wooden arm and then launched like dead wood into a nearby tree.

The Lunar Ape turned its hatred towards Donald and started to rush in his direction. It seemed Mitch didn't have any aggro control. To my surprise, Donald didn't seem startled at all and instead started to fade into the surroundings before disappearing entirely.

This was a skill eerily similar to Kimmi's Blend. The problem was, I reckoned I would be next on the list. The ape could be on me in a moment. I pulled a Granite control switch from my inventory and held it in my hand.

As I feared, the Lunar Ape jumped right in front of me and as it thumped to the ground, I cast Summon Granite Golem. The ape's hand formed into a fist and collided with the Granite Golem just as my conjuration came from the floor. The granite golem simply exploded on impact. It was only good for giving me a second of breathing room. I turned and rushed away.

The ape wasn't done with me just yet. Donald had yet to reappear from his ability and Lucas still had a cool down on his Barrier. I was running for my life. There was no way I could outrun the monster, even with its injuries, so I swerved to come past Mitch in the hope that when he got in range he could taunt the ape back onto him.

So far Mitch had been nothing but a punching bag, but I couldn't see any discouragement on his face. This fight seemed par for the course as far as he was concerned. He was built to take damage and nothing else and this gave me hope.

Mitch suddenly let out an ear-piercing shout from his throat. It was no doubt a special skill and the Lunar Ape didn't like it at all. The Lunar Ape focused its sole attention on Mitch without a care for the rest of us. Whatever the skill was, it generated a lot of threat.

Donald suddenly reappeared and I also now had some breathing room. I started to chain cast Glacial Spike as fast as I could. Ice constantly jutted from the floor below in an attempt to penetrate that thick and sturdy hide.

There was now a bit of blood coming from one of the legs and a thin layer of frost ran up its coat. Mitch was still holding his own despite the Lunar Ape attacking in frenzy. Donald had spent that time repositioning himself.

He was now on the opposite side and directly behind the Lunar Ape. He loosed an arrow that glowed a special color. It burrowed into the Lunar Ape's neck. The Lunar Ape suddenly grew sluggish and its eyes hazed slightly.

That arrow looked to have carried some sort of tranquilizing shot, and the monster's attacks slowed considerably. I switched from casting Glacial Spike and instead cast another Cremation. That flame of fire rushed from hell and started to scorch the ape from underneath.

The Lunar Ape was still sluggish but the sudden heat and pain shocked it awake. It tried to rush out of the pillar of flame when Claire's tree golem grasped it around the waist and held it in the fire. A wail of despair and fury escaped its mouth.

Its left leg's fur was completely scorched off and the skin beneath was boiling red. Cremation went through its full duration and I was about to cast another when the ape managed to break free. It was thoroughly pissed now.

The Lunar Ape grabbed the tree golem and didn't toss it but instead bit into the golem's shoulder before ripping it in half with its injured hand. That was the end of Claire's summoned support. The fury in the monster's eyes expression turned into something tangible.

As the ape's eyes turned a dull and cloudy white, an odd feeling washed over me.

YOU ARE AFFECTED BY LUNAR RESTRICTION.

This was a status effect I'd never heard of before. I checked my stats and confirmed they were at the levels they should be. The debuff had a different effect then. I quickly learned what it was.

275

My body felt heavy and lethargic. Gravity didn't feel the same to me at all. And the others seemed similarly affected, Mitch was having it the roughest with his heavy equipment. He could barely move from the position he was in.

I was sure that if my STR and AGI hadn't been double what they were before my death and rebirth, I'd barely be able to lift the staff in my hand. Fortunately, I could still move if needed. Donald was also having a relatively easy time. Claire and Lucas weren't so lucky.

The treants were out for the count now. They weren't destroyed, but they just didn't have the power in them to contend with such intense gravity. It was impossible for them to even support their own weight and they collapsed to the ground.

The Lunar Ape remained in front of Mitch and kicked and slapped furiously. There was a single benefit to this increased gravity: Mitch was sturdy like a rock. It was even harder to push him back but was obvious that it was all he could do keep the door-sized shield raised.

Lucas was showering him with heals constantly. This wasn't the worst-case scenario at all, and I finally felt this was a winnable encounter. One of the monster's leg was covered in boils and blistered, while blood dripped from random places all over its body.

The Lunar Ape quickly grew tired of attacking Mitch. It demonstrated its impressive strength by lifting him up despite the increased gravity affecting him. It then hurled our tank like a ball into a nearby tree.

Mitch hit the tree and caused it to shatter into pieces. Blood exploded from his mouth and he fell feebly to the ground. I could see the struggle it took for him to just raise his arms and head. Lucas continued to pour heals into him.

I was half expecting the Lunar Ape to charge wildly but instead it did something else. It grabbed one of Claire's treants and then looked directly at Lucas. I suddenly had a bad feeling and started moving in his direction.

The treant was thrown like a fastball directly towards him. "Barrier!" The cool down must have just come up and the treant smacked into the barrier before crashing to the ground. The Lunar Ape didn't stop there and scooped up another.

He was eyeing Lucas again and I knew what had to be done... I didn't want to though. *Fuck, this is gonna hurt.* I managed to arrive just in time to grab Lucas. The treant smacked directly into my back and sent us both tumbling away.

My back felt broken and I couldn't even move. Lucas managed to crawl from below me and heal me several times.

ENERGY COAT HAS REACHED LEVEL 2.

There was an unexpected benefit in my sacrifice.

My sacrifice had been the only option in the situation. Without Lucas this fight couldn't have continued, plus I could be healed. I had been fairly confident that with my stats the blow wouldn't kill me. The bones of my back cracked a few times as I stood up again despite the discomfort. The extra gravity definitely wasn't helping.

Donald managed to shoot another tranquilizing arrow into the Lunar Ape.

YOU ARE NO LONGER AFFECTED BY LUNAR RESTRICTION.

The pain in my body faded slightly as the stress on my battered frame abated.

I managed to stagger a bit closer to the fight. Mitch was already back at the ape's feet and trading blows. The two remaining treants

277

rushed on in, while Claire focused her attention on the scorched leg of the beast. The vines that originally were stretched and snapped by its muscles came into existence again and focused all their attention on its damaged leg. Their squeezing caused a white liquid as well as blood to squirt from its limb.

It was obvious what needed to be done: focus all of our firepower on that one leg, and so we did. Donald used that first skill I had witnessed and sent an inferno at the leg. It didn't burn as intensely as my Cremation but still did considerable damage.

The two remaining treants did their best to chain him down. Their arms grasped the healthy leg and forced the Lunar Ape to use its bad leg to move. Blood constantly dripped and ran from beneath the scorched skin.

Mitch also chose this time to use a previously hidden skill. A faint red light covered his body and he grew in size. He must have gained two feet of height immediately, his muscles started bulging. He now came up to the ape's lower abdomen.

The force of his shield blows grew considerably, and even the Lunar Ape couldn't push him a foot back in retaliation. We were making considerable progress and the Lunar Ape was now on the back foot.

My mana was running low after taking the treant hit for Lucas. I chugged a mana potion and held nothing back. This was our opportunity: do or die. I cast another Cremation immediately underneath the Lunar Ape's groin. The fire came from below and a scream I'd never before heard escaped its throat.

The treants locking its legs in place caused it to tumble as it struggled away from the fire and the Lunar Ape actually fell on its back. The two treants immediately despawned as Claire focused all her attention on summoning more vines.

They slithered from the muddy ground and started to tightly wrap the Lunar Ape's arms and legs. It was now lying flat waiting to be sacrificed. I cast another Cremation directly under its back.

The hellfire was no doubt burning right up against its skin. The ape struggled crazily on the ground but couldn't free itself from the restraints. Mournful wails escaped its throat. I couldn't even imagine the amount of pain it was experiencing. Donald made sure to tranquilize it again and weakened it even further.

Suddenly, the air seemed to thicken and the entire area became stagnant. Mitch grasped his sword with both hands and then kneeled onto the floor before stabbing his blade into the earth. I was utterly confused.

A sword of immeasurable size appeared just above the Lunar Ape, as if coming from another dimension. It came down with a blinding light and pierced directly into the chest of the Lunar Ape.

The sword dug in with no resistance and cleanly executed the monster. The Lunar Ape lay there motionless, not even a bit of life remained. It was finally over.

"Thanks for that save," immediately Lucas rushed over to my side.

"No problem, can't finish the fight without a healer."

"Still." He scratched his head, embarrassment covered his face.

"Is everyone okay?" Mitch was the worst off. It seemed like he could barely keep standing once the skill he been depending on had worn off. Apparently, there were after-effects to that skill which drastically weakened you. The increased size and power wasn't for nothing then.

"What was that arrow you were shooting?" I looked to Donald.

"Drunken Arrow."

"Is Mitch gonna be okay?"

"Yeah, he just needs a few hours to recover. Berserk takes a pretty heavy toll on your body when you use it."

Everyone was grouped around the Lunar Ape's corpse and I started to inspect the loot.

NATURE'S PEACE**: STR +4, VIT +7, DEX +1
A BEAUTIFUL RING FULLY FORMED IN NATURE. IT IS TOPPED WITH A BLOOMING ROSE.

LUNAR BROACH***: INT +1, GRANTS LUNAR BLESSING LV. 1
A BEAUTIFUL BROACH SHAPED LIKE A HALF-MOON. IT GLOWS WITH A WONDERFUL POWER.

TYRANT'S BREASTPLATE*: STR +10, VIT -2
THE BREASTPLATE OF A MAN WHOSE ONLY GOAL WAS TO HOLD ANOTHER MAN DOWN.

MOONLIT STAFF**: INT +7, DEX +5, MP REGENERATION +3 PER 15 MINUTES.
A STAFF WITH A CRESCENT MOON ATOP IT.

I looked at all four items and was torn between just two of them: the moonlit staff and the lunar broach were the only two items I could make use of. I'd never seen or heard of an item like the broach that granted a skill.

I noticed that almost everyone was eyeing the broach greedily, and they knew more than I did. If the broach ended up being not great, I could sell it at Arturii and work towards the Orichalchum.

"I'll take the Lunar Brooch," I said. There was some disappointment in their faces.

"Take it, we had an agreement," Mitch said. I scooped it up and held it firmly in my palm. It felt magnificent in my hand, slightly warm to the touch.

Claire took the Moonlit Staff and Mitch ended up taking the Tyrant's Breastplate and Nature's Peace. It was a huge upgrade for him and his ability to tank. The mood of disappointment quickly passed and Mitch at least looked jubilant.

"Let's head in and find the Star Grass," he said. That was all that was left for this endeavor. I followed behind them and focused my attention on the lunar broach. It said it granted a skill called Lunar Blessing.

I checked my skill sheet and found it there.

> LUNAR BLESSING LV. 1 (FROM ITEM)

The skill didn't have any EXP bar or anything, so the max level was 1. I read the description.

> LUNAR BLESSING (PASSIVE): 5% OF DAMAGE TAKEN IS GAINED AS MP WHEN HIT.

This seemed kind of flat on its own, but I saw at once that it had incredible synergy with Energy Coat, which coincidentally had hit level two in this fight. I checked Energy Coat as well.

> ENERGY COAT LV. 2 SUMMON A COAT OF ENERGY TO SURROUND YOU. WHILE ACTIVE, 35% OF DAMAGE TAKEN IS TAKEN FROM MP BEFORE HP. EXCHANGE IS 0.8 MP: 1 HP.

I'd gained 5% more damage absorption and 0.8 MP per absorb. That was a considerable increase in ability. The downside to leveling it was quite intense though, actual pain. Leveling didn't seem to be the result of simply being attacked either. The harder the hit the more level it gained.

ENERGY COAT LV. 2 0/2000

During that fight, Energy Coat had gone from /300 to /2000 which meant I wouldn't be getting level three anytime soon. I couldn't complain with such a great ability anyway. My focus shifted back to the present. We were under the hood of the cave.

There was thick black soot along the cave floor that coated the green algae. The earthy moldy smell was replaced by the smell of burning. There was nothing else to describe it. We started to walk inside.

All the other information around this quest had proven right, so optimism was high among the others, even though no one had spied any Star Grass. We couldn't check before as the Lunar Ape was very protective of its little area.

Defeating him then searching the area had been the only option available to us. The spoils were good regardless, and no one had ended up seriously injured. In my eyes this was a successful mission, even if Arnold never received the Star Grass.

We turned the bend in the cave and could see the low burning debris on the cave floor. It was just embers now; the resting place of the Lunar Ape was a dozen feet behind it.

Mitch wiped the sweat from his brow, one arm was still resting over Donald's shoulder for support, "Let's go." He swallowed heavily. From his tone, this was evidently a huge moment for them. I realized now the Star Grass was more valuable than I had appreciated.

We walked with anxious steps around the burnt pile of timbers-fcfaz and tar and descended deeper into the cave. It was difficult to not slip and we eventually made our way to the far wall. There were random items and souvenirs here kept by the Lunar Ape.

The treasure was mostly destroyed armor and weapons, nothing of value but some of the items still looked nice. There were even a few cosmetic gemstones. We started to dig through every nook and cranny but couldn't find any Star Grass.

"What's this?" I asked. I burned a fireball brightly in my hand. In front of me there was normal boulder but I could see it was blocking an opening of some sort. "If the Star Grass was that important to the ape then it should be in here, no?"

The others rushed over and took a look. This seemed a likely spot for where he kept his most valuable treasures. The boulder was his safe, protecting the cavity behind it.

"Let's move it," said Mitch. And so we all grouped on the right side and started to shove.

This was a boulder the Lunar Ape would need considerable effort to move, let alone us. We struggled hard but still couldn't move it. We were stuck and couldn't budge it an inch. "What do we do?" Claire asked.

"There must be a way. Let's think about it for a few minutes." I had already considered Glacial Spike and decided it against it. There was no guarantee any Star Grass in the vicinity would survive such cold temperatures. I also didn't have any equipment to smash the boulder.

"I can summon my golem again in twenty minutes," Claire said.

"Let's wait for it." Mitch agreed.

"So what did Lunar Blessing do?" Lucas asked me.

"I gain a small amount of MP when I take damage," I answered.

"Ah, okay." This seemed to dampen his enthusiasm immediately. Non-tanks weren't enthusiastic on the idea of taking damage.

Neither was I to be fair, but together with Energy Shield it would help minimize some of my MP loss.

I caught myself looking at Claire's moonlit staff. The staff would have been the more immediately effective upgrade for me. Still, as Energy Shield leveled higher the broach would become more useful. It was such a unique effect I doubt I'd find anything similar for a long time.

When the twenty minutes were up, Claire summoned her Tree Golem and it walked up to the plate. It bear-hugged the rock and then pushed with all of its weight and strength. There was a scraping sound as the rock rubbed into the cave floor.

The golem didn't seem like it was having an easy time and eventually gave up moving it completely. Fortunately, the boulder had moved enough for a small person to squeeze inside. We all looked at Claire.

She was a trooper, and didn't complain at all while she struggled and wiggled to get through the gap. "It's in here!" she yelled.

"Bring it out!" called Mitch.

After another struggle to get out, she emerged with dirt all over her hands and clothing. One of her hands was holding a patch of grass. It wasn't just any grass though and that was obvious from its appearance alone.

The grass in her hand sparkled. There was an odd hue of glittering light as if stars were raining down on it. The name 'Star Grass' was well earned. Claire handed it to Mitch who immediately stored it away carefully in a box.

Lucas asked, "Was there anything else inside?"

"Nope, it was just the Star Grass."

This went to show just how highly the Lunar Ape valued Star Grass: to move this huge boulder back and forth and only store the Star Grass inside.

There was nothing left for us here, and I was super ready to get out of this cave.

The mission had gone better than anyone expected. They had allocated 3-5 days for this mission and yet we managed to get it done before sundown. There was around 1-2 hours before nightfall. We would be spending a single night out here at the very least.

Our trek back was slow as Mitch was still recovering. Donald had to support him the entire time. Normally they wouldn't even risk moving like this, but the Marsh Pond was in such a peculiar state.

One good night of rest and Mitch would be good as new anyway. It was crazy to think so little time had passed since that first night at the encampment. Well, in terms of my own perspective. The three days I was unconscious didn't count as far as I was concerned.

We ended up camping directly under the four moons and starry sky. Unfortunately for me I didn't have my pack or anything. I settled for sleeping on the ground. It wasn't a great night.

Mitch was in top condition the following morning. Sadly, it didn't even matter as our entire trip back remained uneventful. People started to pour into the Marsh Ponds in droves. The lack of monsters really aided in their ability to find valuable herbs.

That contributed to our encounter-less journey back. Every monster nearby was claimed by new Adventurer groups trying their hand. Even the encampment was lively and packed to the brim. The demoralized mood of days ago had completely disappeared.

Arnold's alchemy shop was bustling when we arrived. He had to put up a CLOSED sign and pull us to the back. "Was my information good enough?" he asked.

"Yes, we managed to get the grass."

"Ten percent off as agreed then; hand it over."

Mitch removed the Star Grass from its box and passed it to him carefully. Arnold examined it carefully for a dozen breaths. "It looks in fine condition." He passed Mitch a hefty sack of Zeny, and then another. My eyes would have popped out of my head if there had been a third. "Good doing business with you, now skidaddle. I got customers." He sounded just like a grumpy old man.

When we left, Claire asked me, "Where are you headed next, Joseph?"

"I have to head to Arturii. That's where my party will be."

"Right, I hear it hasn't been peaceful lately. You should hurry as fast as you can."

"Are you all not going to Arturii?" I asked.

"Unfortunately no, we have business elsewhere," Mitch said. "Feel free to stop by the Disciples headquarters. We're a new guild but they should be able to provide some help if you give my name."

"I didn't know you were guilded," I confessed.

"Right, things haven't been the most stable lately. We chose to keep it a secret until things blow over. No reason to bring any trouble to ourselves."

This made sense. Humans were fickle creatures that fought over benefits of all kinds.

"I should be fine on my own, let's part ways here." I started to shake everyone's hands. "I appreciate your help and kindness."

"Ditto."

"Travel safe!" It seemed I would be on my own for the three-day journey to Arturii. I wasn't sure if I should be worried or excited.

Retracing my steps from the Marsh Ponds filled me with nostalgia and longing. One week had passed since our departure from Cape Tou, to me it only felt like four days though. I couldn't help but wonder how they were doing. *Did you all make it safely to Arturii?*

A part of me was also incredibly afraid. What if they had made it to Arturii and replaced me already? What if no one was waiting for me? George's speech during the Tanyros mines expedition continuously repeated in my thoughts.

Chapter 22: Metropolis

On my first day of travel towards Arturii, I found myself walking in an anxious stupor. By all accounts I had died. There was no doubt everyone had saw seen me get hit by that beast. Marcus too confirmed that we had died. How long did my friends have to wait before my name disappeared from the party window?

What would I do if I couldn't find them when I arrived at Arturii? There were so many scenarios plaguing me. All I could do was put one foot in front of the other, one step at a time towards the new region.

The stares I received along the way were anything but pleasant. It was awkward feeling that I was standing out and drawing attention. Everyone else traveled in full parties and I could see from their glances and expressions that the people I met were wondering why I was alone: was I a high-level Adventurer or just a lost stray?

There were a few parties that were considerate enough to greet me and express concern. Unfortunately, they were all going in the opposite direction: having left Arturii and making their way towards Cape Tou. From the anxiety and disbelief I encountered, I started to doubt if I could make it on my own. There must be good reason why it was so unusual for individuals to make this journey.

On the second day I figured out why no one traveled alone. A group of three Adventurers ambushed me on the road, "Hey, traveling to Arturii? Where's your party?" A fighter in plate-mail probed.

I was of the mind to ignore them completely, but they blocked my pathway and wouldn't let me pass. "Careful." Marcus said. "They're up to no good." And yet it was three on one.

"Do you have friends coming through here?" said their cleric.

"They're a few minutes behind me," I lied. I hoped that would be enough to deter these people from harming me.

It wasn't. "Well it's good we'll only be a minute," said their third party member, a rogue-type.

They rushed me from three directions and I hadn't a chance. Soon, I was pinned to the ground. The rogue held a blade against my neck. "Hand over your Zeny or we'll slice your throat."

A part of me was tempted to disobey, "Listen to him." Marcus said. "He means it." And the stories of people taking advantage of the chaos resurfaced. I would surely become another statistic for the 'monster' roaming about. They would never face justice. Should I die in vain?

And so, I gave away all my savings. I felt it wouldn't stop there either. They were going to strip me clean of everything, all my magic items.

Hey! What are you doing?" Another group of Adventurers appeared behind me and shouted at them.

"Shit!"

"Let's go." And they took off into the surrounding trees. Not before every bit of Zeny I owned was gone. The Orichalcum felt farther away than ever. It was disheartening to see that the people of Yetera were filled with snakes and weasels, just like Earth.

"Are you okay?" asked a female ranger.

"Yeah…" I mumbled. Losing the Zeny hurt more than a stab wound would have. It was everything I worked for since beginning this entire adventure. I had been frugal too.

"Where's your party?"

"I don't have one."

"Walk with us then, Arturii is only a night off."

Of course I was willing to join them but wasn't in the mood for talking and although I really should have made more of an effort to express my gratitude, I was just in too dark a humor: hundreds of thousand Zeny, painfully acquired with weeks of grinding, questing and sacrifice, all gone.

The sight of Arturii in the distance managed to lighten my mood considerably. It was a magnificent city, more impressive than I could have imagined. I knew it was big just from the map, but this beyond my expectations.

As far as I could see, the city was like a fortress. There was no doubt a dozen or more towns the size of Tanyros could fit inside its walls. I felt that my entire time in Yetera until now had only been a journey to this starting point. Arturii was it: the metropolis that all serious Adventurers arrived at to begin their journey in earnest.

The scale of the city only continued to grow bigger and bigger as I got closer. I couldn't even think of a fictional city that was as vast as Arturii; I'd never pictured anything like this place in my imagination, that's how grand it was.

Every fifty feet the walls were topped with a guard post. Heavily armored guards stood side-by-side on every section of the wall, overlooking the wilderness surrounding the city. Nothing could escape their eyes and everyone who wanted to enter had no choice but to funnel into a check point at the enormous gates.

"Entrance is a thousand Zeny!" a woman in a uniform demanded from a booth beside a raised barrier.

I was in trouble. "I was robbed… I don't have any Zeny at all."

"Get out of the line!"

"Is there no other way to come in?" I asked.

"Wait till we aren't busy!"

And so I did. Having said goodbye to the party who had escorted me, I stood next to the wall for a good thirty minutes as people went in and out like ants. Eventually, there was a lull in the action and I rushed over.

"Is now a good time?" I asked the woman as politely as possible.

"Fill in your details." She handed me a sheet of paper similar to the one we filled out in Cape Tou. I accepted it happily before jotting down all my information and handing it back to her. "The fee will be deducted from your next mission. Try to not get robbed again!" She finally allowed me entrance.

"Thank you, really thank you." How pathetic would it be if I got stuck just outside of Arturii after overcoming all the challenges up to now? Over a measly thousand Zeny. I passed by the booth and under the wall before stepping out on the other side.

Arturii was a fantastic looking city with amazing architecture. The buildings were clean and functional. They weren't fancy but seemed instead to be designed for efficiency and height. They towered into the sky in every direction.

I looked around me and realized I had no idea where I was. There were innumerable buildings, many of which had no markings. The small shops would provide me no help. Unless you were buying something, the patrons ignored you completely. There was no free lunch in Yetera.

I could walk for hours and get nowhere, that's just how big the city was. "Excuse me!" I stopped a well-dressed man who was heading to the exit booth. "Can you tell me where I can find a public map?" I needed something similar to the signage board in Tanyros.

"One block over." He pointed with his finger and then continued on his way. I didn't even have time to say 'thank you' before he was out of sight. I rushed one block over and spotted a mess of people.

I had to force myself through several parties before being able to see the board properly. The map was huge and covered a frame that was many times larger than that of Tanyros. I scanned and scanned until finding the 'you are here' dot.

I was at the easternmost entrance, the far right on the Arturii map. The buildings around me were all marked. There was no space, however, for details so they were simply indicated as 'inn' or 'shop' or 'potions' or 'blacksmith'.

The more I looked at the map the more I realized just how many inns there were. I could spend a week checking every single one: finding Aaron and the others was going to be much more difficult than I expected.

I noticed buildings tagged 'guild' and many of them also had another name beside the tag. These were often listed beside an incredibly large building, no doubt indicating really powerful guilds: Tyrant, Power, Valkyrie, Abyss, the list of names went on and on.

Those that were simply marked 'guild' seemed to be new buildings or recently acquired buildings that hadn't been updated yet. My only lead here was that Mitch and Claire had mentioned that they were members of the Disciples guild and that I could look them up when I got to Arturii. I scanned and scanned until I found a small, inconspicuous building with Disciples guild tag on it.

My best option seemed to be to go there and ask for assistance. There was very little I could do with no Zeny and no information. If I didn't act at once, I'd be sleeping in the streets. I wasn't sure if that was even allowed in Arturii in the first place.

I couldn't help but scan all the buildings and people around me. Arturii was like one giant festival. People were everywhere, on every street. It was loud and colorful no matter where I walked.

My only option was to go with the flow of the people around me, else I'd find myself pushed over. It took a while to navigate the currents of the streets but eventually I made it to the Disciples building.

"Hi there." I said to the woman behind a counter: she was in her thirties, had short dark hair, in the practical cut of an Adventurer and held a pen in slender but strong-looking fingers.

"Fill out the form if you're looking to join." The woman didn't even bother to look up at me.

"I'm sorry, I'm not interested in joining."

"Then what are you here for?"

"Mitch said to come here if I needed some help."

"Mitch again?" she mumbled under her breath. "I'm busy, so spit it out. How can we help?" She was obviously reluctant but at least I had her attention.

"I need to find my party; they should have arrived in Arturii three or four days before me."

"Are they members of the Disciples?'

'No. They aren't in a guild.'

And you didn't set a rendezvous point?"

"No…"

"Alright, well, there are places for people to reconnect who have lost each other. Also spells. I need names; classes; levels; descriptions, detailed descriptions. Don't leave anything out if you want to see any results." She passed a blank sheet of paper over the counter. I took it and began providing descriptions for each of the members of my old party.

"If our senior members can't find 'em with this… then you'll be on your own. So add in everything that makes them unique."

"I understand."

After I'd spent what felt to be an hour, making sure to mention all the armor and items my friends had owned when I last saw them, she took the paper and continued to mumble under her breath, "…I'm gonna chew you out when you get back…" When I didn't leave she looked up again at me curiously, "Is there something else?"

"Ah… I was robbed on the way here and don't have any Zeny for a room."

She looked at me with eyes of disbelief, as if someone could actually be this hopeless, "Fine, fine. I can put you up for the night."

"Thank you!"

"One night!" She made clear. I nodded my head excitedly. As long as I could reunite with my party then everything would work out, they had plenty of Zeny and would support me. She looked down at the paper. "Where is your own name and information?"

"Oh? I didn't know you needed it."

"If we find your party, then how can we contact you?"

"I'm Joseph."

"Alright Joseph, I'm Susan." For the first time I noticed smile lines around her thin mouth and grey eyes. She wasn't naturally this severe. "Don't think you can take advantage of our guild 'cause of Mitch. He's just a little squirt around here." Susan disappeared into a back room with the paper and eventually returned with a key in her hand. "Here's the key to room two-o-five. If you lose this, consider it forfeit."

I held onto the key like it was more precious than my own life. It was a place of refuge in this bewildering city and a guarantee of safety during the night. For now though, the day was still young and I wanted to explore and learn more about this massive metropolis.

I was about to leave the front entrance when Susan called to me, "Want some orientation out there? I'll be off in five minutes if you want to wait for me." I was thoroughly confused. This sounded like a kind gesture, one that was quite different from the attitude she had displayed up to now.

Naturally, it would be a great advantage to have someone who knew the city show me around, so I waited. She took a bit longer than five minutes but that was fine. It hadn't yet reached midday.

"Sorry, replacement was a bit late," Susan said with a smile.

"No problem. Where do you want to go?"

"Hungry? Let's get some lunch." I didn't bother saying I had no Zeny, she was clear on that already. The only food I'd eaten since leaving the marsh pond was the result of stranger's kindness. I was famished.

"Thank you. Lead the way." And so we walked out onto the bustling streets. There was a huge difference between walking blindly and walking with confidence. Susan maneuvered the crowds like a proper resident and in five minutes had traveled the same distance that had earlier taken me twenty.

"This is my favorite restaurant," she said. It was a modest establishment, similar to what I'd consider a Ma and Pa shop. The traffic was fleeting and the building itself seemed more old-school than was typical for the city.

I followed her inside and we took our seats off in the corner. There were silverware and menus placed on the table, it was oddly similar to something I would see back on Earth. I picked up the menu and started to browse through.

"What's wrong?" Marcus suddenly woke up and asked, "It feels like you just saw the most unbelievable thing in the world." He wasn't wrong. I felt shocked. The names of meals on the menu… they were all familiar from my hometown back on Earth. Pork chops; spaghetti and meatballs; meatloaf; it continued on and on.

This was too impossible to be a coincidence, "What will you order?" I asked.

Susan smiled. "The pork chops are my favorite." I wanted to see the food to believe it, so despite her recommendation, chose something different.

"Uhm, the spaghetti and meatballs." And so she ordered for both of us. My heart was in my throat as I waited. What did this mean?

"Tell me about Mitch and how you met," asked Susan.

I was happy to still my wild thoughts by telling her of my own encounter in the Marsh Pond, my 'getting lost' from my party, and eventually my being found by Mitch and Claire and the others. I went into great detail about our journey to the tar pits, our subsequent battle with the Lunar Ape, and finally the recovery of the Star Grass.

"Star Grass eh? Seems he's doing quite good for himself." I had felt that this was her interest from the get-go, to find out whether Mitch had returned with Star Grass, but I could also find out some information from her as well and talking about the ape had reminded me of a question I had.

"Can I ask you something?"

"Sure."

"What's the difference between an elite and a unique mob? Or even a super unique." This was an issue that had never made completely clear to me.

Susan laughed. "Of all the questions you might have asked me, I didn't expect that one. Well… I'll put it in Marsh Pond terms so you can understand better. The Swamp Wasp for example, a one-star elite, is known as an elite not a unique because there are many of them scattered around the Marsh Ponds.

"However, the Female Swamp Wasp, *is* a unique monster. That's because throughout the whole Marsh Ponds, there is only ever one spawned at a time, just her. The Lunar Ape is the same way, there is only one Lunar Ape. He was a super-unique though, and that was because of his star rating.

"Three-star is the highest level of difficulty on unique and elites. Uniques with the three-star rating are known as super uniques. It's important to understand that unique are also elites, but elites are not always unique. Does that make sense?"

Her explanation laid it out quite well. "Yeah." Uniques were essentially one of a kind. "And above that is a boss?"

"Right. Super unique are the highest tier of monster below a boss monster."

"Are there tiers of bosses?"

"If there is, no one has ever seen it before." Our food was coming out on plates just as she finished explaining. Her pork chops rested in front of her and the semblance was impossibly similar to the food of my town. They were breaded and sizzling, even the smell was identical.

My spaghetti and meatballs were spot on. I wasn't sure if the meat was the same, but the presentation was identical. This was more than just naming a meal with no understanding. This was cooked by someone who had experienced these things before.

"Do you know the shop owner?"

"Not well, he's a bit reclusive. His cooking is good right?"

297

The taste of my meal was exactly right too. I would be hard pressed to tell the difference between authentic Earth food and this, "Yeah." There was information here waiting to be uncovered. "Has the shop been here long?"

Susan had a mouthful of her own meal. "Mmmyeah, long as I can remember."

"Is it possible I can meet the chef and give him or her my regards?"

"You'd think so, right? Strange thing is, one time I asked to meet him, I wanted some recipes, this one most of all. But the staff wouldn't even ask for me. Seems he doesn't meet anyone."

I looked at the door to the kitchens. Perhaps if I could leave some cryptic message or indication I knew about where he was from, then he would meet me. I flagged the idea for my 'to do' list but felt was probably better to hold off for now and concentrate on finding Aaron and Isabelle and the others.

I finished my meal and waited for Susan, feeling some trepidation when the bill came out. She wasn't setting me up was she? Definitely not, "Are you worried I'm gonna make you pay?" It seemed my worries were on my face. "You told me a good story, that's enough." I nodded my head in relief.

"Anyway, thanks for the good time. I like people who enjoy their food as much as you obviously did. And your account of that battle with the ape was something else. So Mitch is off the hook. I'm not gonna' scold him for bringing yet another stray to the guild. I have things to do now, you know your way back to the guild for later?"

"Uh, yes. Thanks for the meal." And just like that we went our separate ways. I was once again alone in Arturii without a purpose or direction. It was an oddly liberating feeling, as if time had stopped and nothing I did this day would matter at all.

Chapter 23: The Lonely Swordsman

I decided to just walk towards the nearest large buildings, most of which were guild halls. A good many of them were marked on the public map from earlier but seeing them in person allowed me to appreciate their magnificence. These were the leaders of Arturii and the North Maledith continent.

Eventually I came upon the Adventurers' Hall: one of the biggest buildings of them all. My feet felt locked in place for a long time as I watched people swarming in and out. It was intimidating. Tomorrow I would return, hopefully with news of my party. I turned around and headed back to the Disciples guild and called it a night.

There was nothing like sleeping on a proper bed. I'd never really become used to the cold and dirty cave floors, or the damp ground of the swamp. I had to think back to just before leaving Tanyros to recall the last time I had slept on a bed.

I slept like a rock that night.

I woke the following morning to a knock on the door. My eyes were still crusty as I rolled out of bed. My feet were unsteady as I opened the door, "Hello?" I asked.

It was Susan, she held a slip of paper in her hand. "This is the information we found. Hopefully, it's enough."

I opened it with shaky hands and started to read the contents. There was a group matching the description. They checked into an inn four days ago, three blocks out from the Adventurers' Hall.

"Do you know where this inn is?" I asked.

"What's the name?"

"*The Lonely Swordsman.*"

"Ah, I've heard of it. I can show you." She pulled a map from her inventory and then spread it onto my bed. "Right here."

I scanned the location a dozen times over, memorizing exactly where it was. The city center was fresh in my mind and I could visualize in my head what street and block to turn on. I felt very confident I could find it.

All the stress and discouragement of these past few days vanished. The only thought on my mind was reuniting with my friends, my party. "Thank you, thank you so much." I grasped Susan's hands and nearly shook her arms off. It was time to go.

"Hey, Joseph." She caught me in the barrier between my room and the hall.

"Yeah?"

"Good luck." She smiled.

I rushed off like a bat out of hell.

I was deathly nervous as I approached *The Lonely Swordsman*. Just because my friends had gotten a room here didn't mean they were still here. They were always quick to move and there was a chance I had already missed them.

The door opened as, despite the early hour, a half-drunk patron stumbled out. I slipped by him and inside the dining area. I could hear that my voice sounded fraught with nervousness as I started a conversation with the innkeeper. "Ex-excuse me."

301

"What'll it be?"

"Actually… I'm looking for my party. Have you seen a tall red-headed man? Hair kinda looks like velcro."

"Velcro? Don't know anything about this Velcro you speak of but I know who you're talking about. He was a nice guy. The whole group of 'em went upstairs around thirty minutes ago?"

"Really?"

"Yeah. Don't let me find out that you're lying and playing games."

"Absolutely not. They are my party."

"Second floor, room twenty-four."

"Thank you."

Holy shit! I had found them, they were here. I raced up the staircase and exited on the second floor. The wooden floorboards creaked as I rushed towards room 24. My stomach tightened: I could suddenly hear their voices on the other side of the door.

I knocked and held my breath.

"Someone at the door." I heard Steven say. There was some shuffling before it opened. It was Aaron. Beyond him was Kimmi, Steven and Isabelle.

My heart was stuck in my throat and I didn't have any words. I couldn't imagine how they were all feeling. They had seen me die; they knew I was dead. The surprise for them must be much greater than the emotions I was feeling.

Aaron stared at me with the widest eyes I'd ever seen.

"Who is it?" Isabelle asked. Aaron was blocking the doorway and no one but him could see me properly.

"I'm… back." I managed to mumble out. I heard Isabelle fumble off the floor and rush to the door. She must have recognized my voice. Isabelle grabbed Aaron by the arm and shoved him out of the way.

"Sorry everyone…" There were tears in my eyes. I was ashamed in my actions, that I had put everyone in this position. It was all coming to the surface now.

"You IDIOT!" Isabelle started to tear up and she punched me hard in the chest. "We thought… we thought you died! How could you do this to us?"

There were no words I could say to respond her. My actions had been selfish. In my defense though, I wasn't in my right mind at all. "I'm here now." It was all I could say. Both Aaron and Isabelle pulled me into the room and sat me down.

"What happened?" Aaron asked.

It was time to tell the story again, but this time I didn't need to lie at all. I told them about the fruit, about the stat increase, about meeting Mitch. There was nothing I left out. There were highs and lows throughout.

Steven was dismayed as I got to the end. "You got robbed?"

"Yeah…"

"Well,' Aaron looked around, 'I'm sure we can each pitch in a couple thousand Zeny so you can at least pay off your debt and rent a room." They each gave me 3k Zeny and I felt grateful. I was not longer destitute.

"What did I miss while I was gone?"

"Honestly… not much. We were conflicted on finding a new party member these past few days. Besides taking a look around we didn't get anything accomplished."

Isabelle was keen. "Now that you're back we should probably look into accepting some missions."

"Why wait? Let's do it now," said Kimmi. And so we headed downstairs. I stopped at the counter to get a room and then exited the inn. The four of them were waiting outside for me. Just looking at them again was like a dream.

We weren't far off from the Adventurers' Hall and got our place in line. The hall reminded me of Egestor but on a much larger scale. The building had rows and rows of lines with clerks behind every counter. People lined up in expectation of getting their turn at accepting a mission.

"Names, classes, levels," the clerk behind the counter asked. We updated him on our details and he found our records. "Seems you guys have been busy: nearly seven levels in a month? That's pretty good."

I nodded in response but said nothing. Most of that gain could be chalked up to our exploit at the Tanyros mines.

"Unfortunately, you guys are currently the lowest rank in the city. You'll have to work your way up the missions slowly."

I suddenly had a feeling of déjà vu.

"Can we see the list?" asked Aaron. "I hope it's not just delivering supplies around town."

Kimm's excited look had already turned to one of despair. Like me, she interpreted his words to mean menial tasks and plenty of non-combat shenanigans for us to choose from.

"Now, now, don't be so quick to judge. Anyone who can make it to Arturii has some ability. Even the lowest ranks will have missions suited for your level. Both combat and non-combat."

"Can we borrow this for a while?"

"Sure, you can have a seat over there."

And so we began flipping through the rank F missions looking for something that piqued our interest.

Steven tapped the sheet. "This one here is an escort mission, twenty-five-k Zeny for five days of work: Arturii to Cape Tou."

"Pass." I had seen enough of that scenery. It was also only 1k Zeny per person per day, nothing impressive to say the least.

"What about this one?" said Isabelle. "Recover lava rocks from Magma Caves."

More caves, everything was a cave. We ended up passing on that as well.

"Let's try to do one in a territory we haven't explored yet," I suggested. We flipped dozens of pages before coming across one that seemed passable.

Aaron put his finger by a short entry. "This one looks good."

It was a protection mission. There was farmland located north east of Arturii that helped supply some of the food the city required. Lately there had been increased attacks on the farmers from predators.

Multiple groups of Adventurers were required to work around the clock to ensure a good harvest. The beneficiary was the Arturii City Council itself; there was no doubt we would be paid.

"How about it?" he lifted his red head out of the way and we all looked at the mission again.

"What does it say about the living situation? Will we be fed?"

I felt affectionate towards Steven on hearing this question. It was so characteristic of him.

Aaron read aloud, "Food and lodging will be provided. Minimum of one week's service. Payment delivered upon successful completion."

The whole mission was 75k Zeny, which was not bad for a single week of work. Food and lodging provided, open farmland. This could be like a mini vacation for us.

"Let's accept it," I said, to nods from Isabelle and Kimmi. And so we went back to the clerk and signed up for the mission.

"Alright, take this slip to the northern guard's station. They'll arrange a wagon for your transport."

"Should we leave immediately?" Kimmi wondered.

"Then what did I rent a room for…?" Welp, it seemed like a little of my Zeny was going to be wasted. I probably wouldn't have been troubled by it, except for having come to appreciate the importance of even small amounts from the time I'd had none.

We made our way to the northern gate and then consulted the guards running the booth, "We have a mission." We passed them the slip.

"Alright," one of them came around to the front. "I'll get everything in order. Feel free to wait over there."

The bench he gestured to was outside the city walls. And so we took a seat in part way to the wilderness. It was intriguing watching all the different Adventurers arriving and departing from Arturii.

Around thirty minutes later the guard called us over, "Your ride is here."

Along with the others, I climbed aboard a two-horse wagon. The driver wore shoddy clothes and looked like a farmer. "You the new batch?" He spoke as if we were goods being transported.

"Yes," Steven answered for us.

"Alright, hop in the back and get comfortable. It's about an hour trip." An hour? Honestly, that wasn't a distance we would have had any problem traversing ourselves. The road was bumpy and I felt myself being tossed around the back constantly.

My footing felt completely off after arriving. I had become accustomed to the constant rocking and rattling and nearly fell over when stepping down.

"Here we are," the farmer said. "You'll be starting immediately." He pointed at a far-off building at a corner of the farmland we had come to. "That will be your home for the next week, the section of farm there is also your responsibility."

"What should we look out for?" asked Aaron.

"Anything that tries to come through that fence. Most of the time the attacks happen at night, so you might want to fix your schedule: any animal deaths on your watch come out your pay."

Now that information hadn't been in the specs and wasn't good news at all.

'That section' of the farmland turned out to be a huge area marked out with white fencing. It was definitely not a zone we could easily watch on our own, especially at night. It seemed our work was cut out for us.

The farmer left us to ourselves and we ended up walking to the far corner of the region we were responsible for unattended. The building assigned to us was a farmhouse. It wasn't anything special but definitely had a homey feeling to it.

The entire outside of the house was whitewashed. There were two wooden steps leading up to the porch and above all of that was an overhang to provide shade from the sun. Lanterns dotted the corners to provide that extra bit of light at night time. To top it all off there was a rocking chair on the porch. I could imagine a farmer sitting here smoking a cigar and looking over his crops.

There was no lock at all on the front door and so we made ourselves at home. It was two stories but just had two upstairs rooms, each with two beds. One of us was getting the short end of the stick and would have to sleep on the couch downstairs.

"Let's rotate someone out each night, that's only fair," proposed Isabelle, "starting with Joseph, since he gave us such a shock." And so that was the suggestion we went with. Whether we slept this night or during the day tomorrow, I'd be in the living room on the couch.

We dropped our packs and walked around the wooden fence that marked our zone. It was important to inspect every little bit of it. If there was a weak spot, or even a gap in the fence, we needed to know about it. The animals depended on us, and we depended on them for our Zeny.

It was only now that I took a good look at what they were. I honestly couldn't recognize them at all. They looked like cows but were covered in a thick fur, which made it seem like they'd been crossed with sheep. The animals huddled around the pasture in groups and kept to themselves. It was surprisingly quiet and they paid little interest in us.

"We should really request more supplies, especially lanterns," observed Steven.

He was right. It was going to be too dark to see much of our area once the sun disappeared behind the horizon.

"I'll go ask if he has lanterns, some rope and maybe some bells," I volunteered. Not only did we need to light up the fence, we would want to install our own security system. Luckily for us, the farmer did have a few cowbells and plenty of lanterns.

We went around as a group attached lanterns at fixed intervals along the fence. At the end of the process I felt we should be able to see anything trying to sneak in and act accordingly. I had also tied the bells to the rope and strung it up along the top bar of the fence. Anything that bumped into the fence would cause a jingle.

"How should we take positions?" asked Kimmi. Staying to-gether would leave too much ground uncovered. It didn't help that the farmer gave us no real indication to how bad it got at night. We ended up splitting into three uneven teams.

Aaron and I took one section, Steven and Isabelle another. Kimmi suggested she defend a spot on her own and the thought clearly made her excited. She was the least likely of us to take damage and no one complained.

Back at the farm, the dinner we were brought was actually great, until I was told exactly what it was. They had fed us the remains of cattle that had died the previous night. Whatever had been left on its corpse. The thought of the savaged animal gave me an unsettled feeling. It was definitely added incentive to do my best come nightfall.

The veil of night slowly came down on us. The warm spring day became a cold spring night and we all took our positions.

Aaron and I ended up in the pasture a-ways. We did our best to avoid any manure on the ground and found a decent spot on which to sit down and wait. My eyes trained on the white trim fence and the darkness just beyond. "It could be a long night," I said.

"A tired one, too." We hadn't slept during the day, so this first night would probably be the worst. If there was no action we would be sitting here in boredom a long time.

There was a jingle in front of us as something moved over the rope. We both stood in anticipation when a furry little head poked through the white trim fence. It was just an average-looking fox.

"You got it?" I asked. I felt a tinge of regret.

Aaron nodded his head and stood, before loosing an arrow. The fox let out a yelp and we heard the rope tingle again as it rushed off. "That was aimed in front of it; the fox will be fine." Seemed Aaron felt the same way as me.

The majority of the night was like this. Just a lot of non-threatening predators looking for a meal. Was there a reason they were being attracted to this farmland? There were more than you'd expect. I made a note to ask if it had always been the case that so many foxes, weasels and opossums had tried to cross the fence.

Still, 75k for such menial work still made sense. If it was expected to be dangerous then we should have got more. At least that's what I was telling myself. In a way, this could be like a vacation. I leaned back and stared at the starry sky.

Hey Marcus?

"What?"

What's your goal now? You found out what happened to your kingdom... and your family. What's next? Living in my body with no free will of his own couldn't be comfortable, although he never made any demands to me, besides being allowed to co-exist in peace.

"I want to know why. Why did it all happen?"

The source of magic?

"Right, something happened."

I was also curious. It was a thousand years ago that King Andino had been imprisoned. There must have been some form of magic at that time, just unknown to the people of Yetera.

The time frame didn't mash up with my own departure from Earth, but I refused to believe this system had no bearing on my own situation. That was my own goal. To find out why I was here. If our quests were related in any way, Marcus would find his answer as well.

"Oh, I forgot to mention something to you," I said to Aaron.

"Yeah?"

"I visited a small restaurant in Arturii and found something peculiar. All of the food they served were meals from Earth; meals too

310

particular to have been a coincidence. They even had the aesthetic and flavors right."

"Did you meet the owner?"

"No. And that's another thing; he doesn't allow visitors."

"We can get to him if we wanted to I bet. Let's get a footing in Arturii first though."

"Right." There was suddenly more jingling. Dozens of foxes poked their heads through the fence and seemed to want to make a jailbreak.

I suddenly felt a bit less guilty at the thought of dispatching them. This was going to be a pain in the ass.

Chapter 24: Night Battles

Three days passed quickly without any developments of interest. The only threat to the animals was that of local predators sneaking their way through the fence in an attempt to snatch cattle. I couldn't figure out why they weren't just hunting local wildlife.

It was only the third night that we started to see a change. We encountered our first real monster coming through the fence.

GHOST WOLF	LEVEL: 31	BEAST SHADOW
	HP: 6660	MP: 25
	STR: 33	
	AGI: 35	
	DEX: 10	
	VIT: 32	
	INT: 5	
AN ETHEREAL WOLF. THE MOONLIGHT SHINES THROUGH ITS TRANSLUCENT BODY.		

This was just a regular monster, albeit on the faster side than most. I managed to shackle it in place, which allowed Aaron to use Ensnaring Arrow. The wolf died in a single Cremation after that.

We were preparing to sit back down when the farmer hollered at us, "Get your party and head to the east gate. We got an emergency!"

"What about the cattle here?"

"Don't worry about it. I'll be bringing them south right now. Just get to the east gate."

We rushed to Isabelle and Steven.

"What are you two doing? Why aren't you at your post?" asked Isabelle.

"There's some kind of emergency, let's go. We're needed at the east gate. We'll get Kimmi on the way."

When we arrived at the east gate it was immediately apparent why we were needed. There were dozens upon dozens of shadowy-looking figures. They almost didn't appear to be real.

```
SUMMONED SHROUD WALKER  LEVEL: 30       SUMMON
                    NEUTRAL
        HP: 7311              MP: 0
                    STR: 30
                    AGI: 20
                    DEX: 5
                    VIT: 35
                    INT: 1
     A SUMMONING OF NAZTASHA THE SHADOW PROWLER.
```

"New guys! You take the north side!" Someone from one of the parties already here shouted at us. We turned our attention to the left and moved into position. There were Summoned Shroud Walkers coming over the fence all over.

These figures were so black they almost faded into darkness. There was just a thin shadow line behind them from the light provided by the four moons. Something else that was fascinating was each one looked different.

Their body shapes were varied completely. Some looked like bears, and wolves, and foxes. There were even some giant Roda— the giant frogs that had fed us for part of our journey—and other natural wildlife. They were strewn about in front of us all over.

313

Isabelle Summoned Hierophant's Helper and sent it out in front of us, abating some of the darkness. Steven positioned himself directly under the glow and we stared at the incoming shadows. They were all summons which only meant one thing: something or someone was in the darkness beyond this fence, bringing the monsters into existence.

Regardless, we could only deal with what was in front of us. No caster could summon forever. Eventually, the summoned creatures would be defeated and perhaps then the real foe would show itself; if it did not simply retreat.

Steven charged towards the nearest Shroud Walker and stabbed out. It had a bear-like figure and deep, penetrating red eyes. His sword went directly into its chest and something extraordinary happened. The chest separated and allowed his sword to pass directly through.

"They can morph their bodies?" Isabelle exclaimed. This was bad news for us.

Steven was constantly growing more accustomed to battle and didn't stop his attack there. He followed the stab up with a shield bash. Luckily, the mob's ability to rearrange its shape had limits. His bash connected cleanly and sent the Shadow tumbling back.

Kimmi appeared directly behind the Shadow and sliced horizontally from both sides. The Shadow made an attempt to evade but another limitation became clear. It wasn't possible for the Shadow to break apart entirely, it always needed to be connected at some point.

This was their weakness and fortunately Kimmi must have intuited this. Cutting the Shadow in half caused it to immediately disperse. The first Shadow died just like that.

Kimmi and Steven were the only two with sharp weapons that could slash in such a way. Aaron and I needed to be more creative. We worked together to dispatch the next Shadow.

The arrows Aaron loosed simply flew through the Shadows as they morphed their malleable bodies to avoid any impact. He modified his strategy and instead shot an Ensnaring arrow directly at the feet of a dark, giant fox.

The vines quickly climbed up its body from below and wrapped it tightly. As the Shadow attempted to morph and change its body to move through the vines I cast Cremation. That beautiful pillar of fire came from hell and incinerated it in place.

It was good news that magic worked against these summoned creatures and Aaron had found a way to be useful. We were all effective at killing the Shadows and we worked quickly to dispatch the foes in front of us. The problem was they kept coming.

More and more Shadows continued to come over the fence like one endless wave of darkness. It was a flow that didn't seem like it was going to let up anytime soon. I was starting to question the logic that an individual caster could only summon so many creatures before growing tired. *Naztasha the Shadow Prowler* was the source, according to my *Inspect*: but who was that?

We battled late into the night. My mind was already foggy from the lack of sleep. The Shadows were still coming over the fence. Suddenly, there was an ear-piercing howl that chilled me to my core.

I was expecting the worst but presented with the best. The Shroud Walkers in front of us slid backwards and withdrew into the darkness before retreating over the fence. It was finally over. However, the culprit behind the summoning remained out of sight.

We had been battling for several hours already. Everyone was thoroughly exhausted, no doubt including the groups holding the other sections of the east gate. We walked back over to the others.

"What was that?" asked Aaron.

A warrior answered. "Don't know. It's the first time seeing it. Even the farmer never heard about anything like it."

"So this isn't what we signed up to defend against?" I asked.

"Not specifically. There have just been a lot of intrusions and cattle being snatched during the night, nothing about summoned monsters."

Eventually the farmer responsible for this patch of land returned, "What happened? Did you defeat the evil killing my animals?"

"No," said the warrior, "whatever was behind that attack has fled."

"So you're saying it got away? What are we paying you for!" he yelled. It didn't seem that he understood the severity of the situation.

Aaron gestured to calm him. "We held off a big attack… sorry the opportunity didn't arise to find out who was behind it." I admired Aaron's approach. The farmer was essentially the employer and we couldn't respond to his attitude by being disrespectful and cutting ties with him if we wanted to be paid.

"Well, there's nothing can be done about it now. You all that came over to help get back to your areas. There's still a few hours before sunrise."

When we returned, the cattle in our area had not yet made it back. It seemed the farmer had packed them away for the remainder of the night. He wasn't taking any chances at all. "I'll have them back out tomorrow night. You guys should sleep now while you get the chance."

None of us had a single complaint about getting some sleep. We welcomed it openly and returned to our farmhouse. I took the couch as agreed and drifted into a stupor.

It was mid-afternoon when I woke. Aaron was already out and about moving around. "The farmer stopped by earlier with some news."

"Yeah?"

"He said be prepared for a repeat of last night. We're to be ready to go at a moment's notice." I guessed it would be silly to consider the attack of the previous night to be a one-off incident, especially with the summoner not defeated yet.

Naztasha the Shadow Prowler... This mob was likely to be a super-unique, with its ability to summon hordes of minions. The problem was... what if it was a boss? There were just two other parties here with us.

The Golden Thief Bug back in Egester would have been around level 35. For that battle, there had been fewer total useful people than three groups of five, but they had been considerably higher level than the boss. Well, at least on our front. We were all level 27 and 28 only.

The level gap was enormous, at least for our party. I couldn't be sure about the other two parties and what their level was. The mission was one of the lowest grade; it wouldn't make sense for the other parties to be vastly superior to our own.

"Did someone report last night's incident to Arturii?" I asked. It was important reinforcements were on the way. I wouldn't throw my life away for some cattle if it came down to it, even if retreat meant mission failure and the penalties that came with it.

317

"I asked. They passed along the information. The farmer doesn't know how Arturii will respond so we might be on our own another night."

I sighed while lying back down. Things were getting complicated.

We ended up in a meeting with the other two groups. As we were the last group to arrive, we allowed the others to take the lead.

"Aaron is it?" asked the warrior who we'd met last night.

"Yes."

"I'm Troy. Alright, in case of a repeat of last night your group will hold the same area as before. We don't know anything about Naztasha the Shadow Prowler but if it shows itself, we'll band together and fight it together." He looked around the room. "Who are the other tanks?"

Steven raised his hand. "Me. Steven."

There was one other, a woman, Magella.

"Alright, you two will be my backup if it comes to it. We'll take the encounter slow. Outside of its ability to summon we have no information about the summoner, it might be a raid encounter." He looked at everyone. "Regardless of where it appears, our formation won't change. Melee will only move on my call."

It seemed Troy was used to being in leadership positions like this and no one had any complaints with his approach. Our group was essentially follow up for his party, and that was fine.

We started to walk back and prepare for nightfall.

"Do you think it will come to that?" asked Steven.

"To what?"

"A boss encounter."

"Have either of you been in a raid before?" I looked at Kimmi and Steven. Aaron and Isabelle and I had all raided the Egester sewers.

"No..." they both said. Steven was obviously nervous. He'd never any been in a situation where he'd been back up tank for anyone. The pressure was definitely on him more than the rest of us.

"It'll be fine." Aaron patted his shoulder. "You just need to be there to pick up the aggro if something happens. Otherwise treat yourself as any other melee."

Night rolled around and we found ourselves sitting in our separate groups on the cold grass. The crickets were out in full force tonight. A cool breeze gave me the chills and I wished there was a fire burning in front of me.

The occasional fox and wolf would try their hand at sneaking through the fence but they always ended up failing. Aaron stopped showing mercy long ago, as regardless of how many we killed, more came. There was just no end to their intrusion.

The sun had been down for about two hours when we heard a commotion at the east gate. There was no need for the farmer to get us. The Shroud Walkers had returned in full force. We raced to our position and started battling.

There was no obvious difference between the night before and tonight. It was just a bit on the chilly side.

Defending against the summoned mobs was back-breaking work. The EXP wasn't half bad, but many of the Shroud Walkers flowed away when injured, which meant we didn't get all the kill EXP that we could have. There were so many, that we couldn't consider changing approach and counter-attacking. Instead, we remained on the defensive.

I didn't want to go anywhere near the fence, especially with something more menacing waiting beyond. To our right, however, the farthest group must have felt differently. Because they started to push their assault towards the fence. They were wiping out every Shroud Walker in their way. My occasional glance left me feeling impressed. They were stirring up a ruckus.

Steven started to feed off their enthusiasm. He was growing more aggressive as he too pushed towards the fence.

"Stay back," I said.

"Yeah, don't go near the fence," Aaron agreed.

Not even ten minutes passed before an ear-shattering scream assaulted us. My eyes darted to the side just in time to witness the result. Of the farthest group whom had pushed up the fence, four of them were retreating in a frenzy.

The problem was, they didn't have their tank, Magella, with them. There was a dark spear the size of a human with flickering black flames on it. Its entire shaft pierced directly through her chest and pinned her to the ground.

She wasn't struggling or resisting at all and looked lifeless. That wasn't all though. There was a moment of silence before a slim, pitch back hand came from the abyss and grabbed her. It was more like a paw than a hand, with long razor-sharp claws.

The lifeless body was scooped up and the dark spear faded away into nothingness. We heard a loud, bone-shattering crunch. My body felt frozen with fear, I was covered in goose bumps. There was a constant wet and mushy crunching noise.

I hadn't seen it all, but the basics were clear. She had gotten too close to the fence and that shadow spear had impaled her. Her death was quick... but being eaten didn't sit well with me.

Everyone stopped and started to move away from the fence. We had always known there was more of a threat than just these Shroud Walkers, but we hadn't given our opponent its due respect and somebody had just died for it.

The third group, the one led by Troy, backed away slowly from the direction of the chewing sounds. The noise stopped and suddenly another shadow spear materialized in the sky over there. It was thrown directly at Troy. To my surprise he managed to raise his shield and deflect the blow.

The grass nearly exploded from impact and that was everyone's queue to run. Whatever it was, we couldn't fight it in the pitch-black darkness. And it seemed that its first meal had not satiated its hunger.

More shadow spears started to be flung out randomly at Adventurers. It was time for a full retreat. This mission was not worth our lives at all. We backed away over fifty meters before the spears stopped flying at us. It seemed they could only reach so far.

The Shroud Walkers didn't care for us anymore and instead latched onto those cattle too stupid to have run off. They took five or six of them and pulled them towards the fence. Once there, spears repeatedly shot out and impaled each animal.

A single hand scooped them up and no doubt placed them directly into the mouth of the monster as the sounds of it chewing resumed. After the sixth cow was eaten, the Shroud Walkers dispersed and the night returned to normal.

"What are you all doing? You're getting paid to protect the cattle, not feed 'em to the monsters!" Rightfully, the farmer was pissed, but 75k Zeny was chump change for an encounter on this scale.

"Apologies," said Aaron, "but we didn't sign up for this. Whatever that thing is, we need more people." And that was the truth.

321

Not only could we not see our opponent, it could instantly kill us with a single attack. We still didn't know what we were fighting.

"This was issued as only an F-rank mission," said Troy.

"Tch, you're all I got," the farmer had a tone of complaint in his voice.

"Then I suggest you send a more detailed report." Troy started to walk with the farmer. "Do you have the details on everyone? Make sure to mention it killed a tank in one hit."

Tensions were high, naturally. The party who had lost their tank wanted nothing more to do with the mission and immediately accepted the penalty. They would have headed to Arturii that night if they weren't afraid of the beast lurking in the dark night.

Arturii would take at least another day to respond to the incident and so the farmer decided that packing away the cattle was the best course of action. That meant we would have no duty for the next two nights.

I ended up in a second-floor bedroom for the second night. Despite having the option of the night to sleep through, we kept our schedule flipped. If reinforcements came, we might be resuming night battles.

The window was open and allowed a cool breeze to blow through the room. I rested my head while keeping lookout from the window. The Shroud Walkers did return and we got ready to abandon our post. The cattle had already been removed from the area.

But the summoned mobs only walked a ways in and then meandered about mindlessly. Naztasha never set foot over the fence, if it even had a foot. It was a long and boring night. I didn't gain any information by watching from afar.

When I woke up mid-day there was still no news from Arturii. The cattle were allowed to graze during the day but shuffled away again for another long night. There were still only our two parties.

The day of departure was coming up quickly. I couldn't help but think it was an anticlimactic ending. Another uneventful night passed with the same ending. The Shroud Walkers could make it over the fence but Naztasha never showed.

Chapter 25: Naztasha the Shadow Prowler

The following day two new parties arrived and the farmer decided it was best we resume duties. They were briefed immediately on the situation and given a solid piece of advice: stay away from the fence.

None of the five of us were feeling comfortable. The shadow spear was on our minds. I feared for Aaron and Isabelle most. I was confident in dodging it myself, but was not sure if Isabelle could do the same.

If they were caught by surprise, Steven and Kimmi would also be susceptible. As long as they looked out for the spear attack, then Steven could perhaps block and Kimmi might be able to evade it.

"Stay near me," I told Isabelle and Aaron.

I didn't care if we had to be holding hands the entire night, I couldn't allow them more than five feet away. Isabelle didn't have any skill like Barrier. This situation made me realize that as a party we were severely lacking in defensive abilities.

The sun came down and we had an extra party on our right-hand side. We were stronger than on day one and that alone provided some relief. Crickets started to chirp and the four moons spread out across the sky.

Like clockwork, Naztasha arrived. Not that we could see the summoner, but the Shroud Walkers appeared. The way they moved was incredibly unique, as if sliding along the ground like a puddle. Their bodies morphed from the shadow and flowed towards us. No less or more than any night before. We were already prepared for battle.

I couldn't understand the point of this attack at all. Was this just for food? I refused to believe a mob of this strength and caliber couldn't hunt in the woods outside Arturii. If that was the case, what was its purpose attacking the farm?

An hour passed in what felt like minutes. No shadow spear was thrown and matters looked promising. Just one more night of this and it wouldn't be our problem anymore. Fighting an enemy with no face was unsettling.

There was suddenly a crack in the air. Like the sound of glass slowly shattering. It was coming from near the fence; a sound that was completely out of place.

"Look at the sky!" I yelled.

There was a thin line running through one of the moons. It wasn't that the moon itself was cracking, but there was a film, or some sort of barrier. Suddenly, everything made sense.

It wasn't that Naztasha refused to walk over the fence, or was even scared to do so. There was a barrier surrounding this fence. But then what did it mean when these Shadows passed though the barrier? When these lesser monsters were able to cross?

Was there a threshold? Monsters over a certain level or strength couldn't penetrate? Or of a certain density, which was why only very translucent creatures could slip in. That was the only thing I could imagine making sense. The sky directly in front of me was shattering after all. What else could it be but a massive barrier?

The cracking grew more intense. The moon in the sky had hair-line cracks running all over it, like a spider web. In fact, the entire sky was cracking above our heads. A dark hand reached up and blotted out one of the moons before digging into the barrier.

The hand grasped a chipped portion and pulled back. There was now a man-sized hole floating there. A second dark hand reached into the other side and then pulled it apart. There was an explosion of glass and refracting light as the barrier crumbled.

My desire to see what Naztasha looked like crumbled almost immediately. The reality was I didn't like what I saw at all. One 'hand' stepped over the fence and then another. The entire figure was dark as night with burning red eyes.

The face of our enemy was pointed, with a snout and piercing white teeth. These stood out vividly against the black backdrop. It was a gigantic-looking fox and had three tails. Naztasha was as big as a farmhouse and oddly nimble-looking.

Worst of all was the sign above its head. There was a red skull floating there which symbolized one thing: it was a boss, and that was bad news for us.

There were a few moments to make a decision.

"Do we run?" Steven asked.

"Can we run?" I asked. Would we even be able to get away? The situation was elevated to a serious level. Would we be punished for fleeing? Arturii depended on the livestock behind us, that much was certain.

Troy suddenly slapped several times on his shield, "Get in formation." He yelled. His party was standing firm behind him. His display of courage seemed to rally the others and we rushed to the call.

"Aaron, Isabelle, stay near me." It was highly risky to take on this boss, but at the same time it did seem like the best option. I would, however, never forgive myself if either of my friends were impaled by a shadow spear. Especially knowing I could have prevented it by being near them.

They didn't show any hesitation and stayed by my side.

Troy moved in to engage, "Deal with the Shroud Walkers!" he yelled. His plan seemed to be to allow him to feel out Naztasha and see if there was anything we could discover, while we held back the Shadows.

We were aggressive in our attacks and dispatched the Shroud Walkers quickly. That was when we finally saw where they came from. Naztasha leaned low as if to pounce and opened her mouth.

Naztasha exhaled and the Shadows seemed to come from within her. It was a breathing summons. They flooded the field immediately and were all dangerously close to Troy. This wasn't an ideal setup in the slightest.

Troy started to back away in response and realized he couldn't do so. The moment he removed himself from Naztasha's melee range, one of its three tails curved up like that of a scorpion. It then aimed directly at a random person and shot out a shadow spear.

Luckily, everyone around was solely focusing on absorbing information. As soon as the tail started to move irregularly and that shadow spear formed, people were ready to dodge. "I need back up tanks!" Troy yelled.

I felt scared for Steven, but he needed to make a move. The Shroud Walkers were closing in on Troy and he still needed to contend with Naztasha. The constant swiping and biting meant he had no time to deal with anything else.

If the off tanks couldn't alleviate that pressure, he would be swallowed up figuratively and literally. Isabelle had already moved to one side of me and was casting heals on Troy. I didn't know how much damage he was taking, but it had to be considerable.

I wouldn't let Steven hear me say it, but Troy was definitely a better tank. His movements and reaction time were crisp and clean.

He never took a direct hit and the alteration between attacking and defending was well-timed.

The biggest question was if these Shroud Walker summons would ever stop? If we could somehow just have Naztasha to deal with, the fight might be possible. We only had four healers here for four tanks.

"Range go ahead! Melee stay out!" Troy yelled. That was my and Aaron's cue. I moved in range and started off by casting *Inspect*.

| SKILL HAS FAILED. INSUFFICIENT LEVEL. |

The message was anything but assuring.

This was a boss whose level was greater than 38. We were vastly under-leveled for this encounter, but we were too far committed now. Leaving at this point would doom a large portion of these parties to death. Was I a monster for thinking it was still the best option?

I cared about my party, my friends more than anyone else. Despite that, I resolved to give the battle my best shot before it came to giving up. And as well, I didn't want to be known as a coward or deserter.

My first spell to test the mob's response was Cremation. When the spell landed, I managed to catch a glimpse of its flames below Naztasha's belly. I knew just how fiercely the fire burned and how devastating the damage could be.

Despite that, Naztasha didn't show any interest in stepping out from the spell effect. Either the damage was too low or the boss's resistance too high. I focused my attention towards the right front paw instead. It was constantly swinging out at Troy.

I chain cast Glacial Spike on the front right paw. Ice constantly jutted out and burrowed between the fingers. Only after the fourth cast did I see the slightest signs of blood and a small amount of frost on Naztasha's pitch black fur.

A bit of blood was akin to a scratch for these monsters. There was no doubt in my mind we were in for a lot of trouble. It wasn't just me casting either.

The casters in every party were throwing everything they could muster. It was a complete and utter shit show and yet Naztasha showed no signs of slowing her attacks. We were steadily losing ground.

Troy was doing his best to remain stationary, but every swipe dug his heels a bit deeper and pushed him a bit further back. In just a couple minutes of this, his back would be up against one of the farmhouses.

"Melee in!" he yelled. There was a risk involved in calling them now, but the timer was finite. The healers only had so much MP before they ran out. I could see the calm composure on Troy's face had faded somewhat. The damage he was taking must be immense.

It was then that I realized I had to try to turn this around in increments. Defeating the monster was the end goal, but you could win small victories multiple times before then. I could try to take out its vision, its mobility, or its attack power. Any one of those things might sway the battle in our favor.

I decided to go back to my roots and summoned a fireball into my hand. The burning red eyes of Naztasha could do with a bit more orange and so I threw it out. My new goal was to see if I could affect the boss's vision.

I started to throw fireball after fireball at its face: as close to its eyes as possible. Eventually my aim was spot on and one of them connected: the explosion sent burning sparks into Naztasha's left eye.

Naztasha let out an angry growl and even paused its attacks to swat its face momentary. The left eyelid twitched and a bit of liquid poured out. It wasn't considerable damage but the hit definitely annoyed it. Even Troy noticed the lull in attacks.

"Aim for its eyes!" he yelled. And suddenly we were focusing every bit of firepower on its face.

The melee, who after dealing with the Shroud Walkers had been patiently waiting, now joined the fray as well and were doing their best to find a route of attack. It was scary contending with paws as big as your body but they managed. I caught a glimpse of Kimmi behind the front-left paw.

We were all looking to claim those small victories. Even Kimmi had opted for less fatal damage and was trying to destroy a tendon or any bit of muscle to hinder its mobility. For a moment things were going well.

Naztasha was constantly jerking her head away in pain as explosions happened all over her face. Her attacks grew incredibly varied as the majority of time a paw rested over her snout. Growls escaped her mouth.

"Keep it up!" Troy yelled, and that was when things went bad. Naztasha kept her face covered and then all three of her tails suddenly rose. They looked like snakes about to strike as shadow spears formed at their tip.

I was under the impression the skill was only used when she was out of range of a melee attack, it seemed from their shouts of dismay that others had felt the same. The spears were like black beams as they shot out.

If it was just the three it would have been okay; but it wasn't. She continuously formed spears and shot them out. Her target was all the ranged DPS. No one had the time to cast and our formation went to shit.

A tail tilted towards our direction and it launched out a spear like a missile. I didn't hesitate to shove Aaron and move out of the way. It hit the grass next to us and caused a miniature explosion of dirt.

Not everyone was as lucky as us. I witnessed at least three people take a spear directly to the upper body. One person even had a spear go right through their neck. Worst of all, one of them was a healer.

Our attacks abated and Naztasha eventually uncovered her face. The tails lowered and she resumed biting and scratching at Troy. Her eyes were clearly injured as blood seeped into the fur around them.

The melee had made it a goal to attack her left paw incessantly and they did considerable damage. The entire time she was supporting herself on it they hacked and slashed. Bone and ligaments could be seen beneath.

She leaned to one side and put most of her weight on her good leg. Despite that, we were now down a healer and the damage we'd inflicted didn't seem anything but superficial. Everyone was terrified of attacking Naztasha's eyes now.

No one wanted to go back into that bullet time hell. I turned all my attention to the wounded left leg and casted Cremation. The fire rose from hell and the visible anguish was apparent on Naztasha's face.

It seemed her fur provided a great resistance, but her exposed skin and flesh was heavily susceptible to the fire. Almost immediately after casting the spell, I saw her jerk and hobble to the side. That reaction only made me want to cast Cremation repeatedly.

The situation had moved into a sort of lull with each side trading blows. That stability was superficially good, compared to the barrage of spears, but in reality it was terrible for us. The MP of each healer was already disastrously low. A war of attrition was not in our favor.

Almost immediately after I had that thought, the situation got even worse. Naztasha bit out and somehow managed to grasp onto Troy. Time seemed to stop as I watched her clench her teeth hard and tear off his sword arm.

The ease at which Naztasha dismembered him was like ripping apart a doll. Blood and gore flew through the air. Troy let out a cry of agony as he fell to the floor and started to push himself backward.

Our morale as a raid was fully broken. I was of a mind to retreat when the unexpected happened: Steven rushed forward and taunted Naztasha off Troy. There was no leaving now, unfortunately.

Naztasha swiped out with immense force and Steven managed to raise his shield in response. I was expecting something similar to when Troy blocked, but that wasn't what happened. Instead, Steven was sent flying through the air and tumbled like a beach ball.

I didn't know why the outcome was so different. Troy was definitely a better tank, but that wasn't just an issue of technique. Naztasha simply overpowered Steven by so much, which meant Troy was much higher level than I had expected.

Everyone who witnessed that collapse of the off tank must have fallen even further into despair. Not a single person available could take a single swipe from the boss. There was no tank and that put everyone on the menu. None of the other tanks even dared to step up.

In reaction to that, Naztasha raised all three tails and started to form shadow spears. They were half created when something miraculous happened. Every inch of Naztasha's pitch black fur turned pearl white.

Chains of gold rushed from below the earth and wrapped around the entire body of Naztasha. They tightened with such force her body squeezed and bulged before being pinned directly to the ground.

Naztasha let out repeated whimpers but couldn't struggle free. My eyes immediately darted around every direction before spotting a group rushing onto the farm. There was a female wearing a priest's gown leading the front.

She held a pure gold star symbol as large as her own body. It glowed like the moon and was no doubt the source of this magnificent spell. The four behind her rushed into action and started to bombard Naztasha who was helplessly strapped down.

I couldn't believe what I was seeing at all. This boss that we were completely helpless against, that was moments away from slaughtering everyone here, was at the mercy of just these five individuals.

The fight seemed to be coming to an end when I heard the voice of a god in the night sky above. *"Gloria Dominae."* Those two words echoed throughout the entire farm, sounding like a choir had sung them.

A holy symbol spawned hundreds of meters in the sky above Naztasha. It was pure silver and looked absolutely beautiful with the four moons as its backdrop. It swirled and spun as it dropped, before landing directly on Naztasha's back.

The impact shattered Naztasha's back and a crack louder than I'd ever heard rocked my eardrums. Blood immediately spurted from within Naztasha's throat. Her back was bent in the shape of a U. She let out one final whimper before dying.

The priestess looked around as if to take in the damage. Her face filled with sorrow when she saw the three corpses suspended on shadow spears. "I was late...," she said. "I'm sorry." I didn't know who she was apologizing too.

Her words had a soothing effect. Even Troy, who was frantically screaming in pain, stopped his howling. She walked over to him before healing him. I was almost expecting his arm to re-appear, but that wasn't what happened.

She did however manage to heal him fully. There was now a clean stump where his arm used to be. It wasn't even discolored in the slightest. His screaming abated but his face was still filled with pain. It was like George had said: circumstances out of your control. There was no doubt Troy would stop being an Adventurer after tonight.

The priestess slowly moved through the crowds before arriving at her party. They were grouped around Naztasha sorting through the loot. The sight made me feel incredibly sour even though I knew it was the way things were in this world.

They had killed Naztasha. We wouldn't have killed her without them. Therefore, the loot should go to them. Yet words came out of her mouth that I wasn't expecting at all: "This isn't right, just take the gem and leave the gear to split among the four parties."

Those words were like music to my ears, as well as everyone else's. We all rushed over and took part in the negotiations. In the end, we received a single item. It was a shield upgrade for Steven that he badly needed.

> ### THE IRON DOOR: STR +5 VIT +10
> ### A STURDY IRON DOOR. IT has a CONSIDERABLE WEIGHT.

I was almost sure if we put the shield in a doorframe it would fit. Regardless, it was a massive upgrade and definitely covered more of his body than the pathetic looking plate he had before. A Rainbow Faucet gem that Naztasha had dropped was taken by the unknown party, no one complained.

"Sorry everyone, I came as soon as my barrier broke. You all can return. We'll take it from here."

So this priestess was the person who had erected the barrier in the first place. What kind of magical power was this anyway?

The seventeen of us remaining walked off slowly and everyone started talking. I felt utterly confused, as the others were star-struck by the priestess, but I didn't know anything about her at all. "Who was that?" I asked wizard-type from another group.

"That was High Priestess Rhea! She's the guild leader of Valkyrie! How could you not know that?"

I didn't have an answer. *How could I not know that?* "What's special about her?"

"That's the main party of Valkyries. She's one of the highest levels in all of Yetera. Rumor has it she's in her level seventies."

Now that was something I could appreciate. The amount of EXP needed to get to level 70 was mind-boggling. It was no wonder the priestess had no issue restraining Naztasha. She was probably around twice the mob's level.

I remembered as well the map of Arturii. By the size of their hall, Valkyrie was definitely a top five guild. This was the first time I'd witnessed someone with such strength. It was strength above the level of super-human. She was a priest but I had no doubt she could wipe the floor with our entire party with her melee attacks alone.

Tomorrow would be our last day here and I felt relief. This mission had proven more than we had bargained for. I had jokingly said this was like a vacation, I couldn't have been more wrong. Once back at our farmhouse, I went to bed and faded in and out of sleep all night.

To my surprise, High Priestess Rhea was still there when we woke. The farmer gathered us up for a meeting to which Rhea gave a speech. "I am here to let everyone know that Arturii has upgraded this mission rank. If you already signed up before that, you are free to leave now." She waited for any reactions.

"If you choose to stay, you need to know that situations like last night will become more frequent. Something major has happened on the west side of the continent and is forcing a large majority of monsters eastward.

"I can safely say there won't be another boss encounter, but the number of predators seeking to snatch cattle will drastically increase."

"Your barrier broke last night though? Why won't it break again? How can you be sure?" someone asked.

"The barrier from last night is something I placed when I was only level sixty. That was five years ago," she answered, "my strength is much higher now and I've put in a considerable amount more effort to ensure it doesn't happen again."

Those who had recently arrived seemed to relax a bit. No one wanted to come out and fight bosses 10 levels higher than them. In all respects, we were all new Adventurers, at least in the context of North Maledith.

"As for those of you who are departing because your mission is up: the cattle which died during the attacks from Naztasha will not be counted against you. You should receive your full seventy-five thousand Zeny." This was very welcome news.

Two nights previously, six cattle had been snatched up. Every animal lost should have incurred a 5k penalty. That alone would have nearly halved our reward. Our time would have been better spent doing menial jobs.

The priestess looked over everyone and then gave advice that didn't seem to pertain to this mission or any mission in particular: "Times are changing quickly. Everyone here should seek to grow stronger or find shelter alongside strong individuals while you grow. That's all I have to say." Rhea nodded at the farmer.

"Alright, everyone who finishes their mission today come and see me for your slips. Those that are here for the next week should find their housing and rest up. It will be another long night."

How should I interpret the news from Rhea? Back on our trip to Tanyros, I felt I had plenty of time to grow stronger. My frenzied desire to level had abated and there was a bit of balance and peace in my life.

If even F missions were going to be this difficult, we were falling behind and fast. How long did we even have? My goal of starting a guild was drifting even further away.

"Let's get our slip and go," Aaron said.

It felt like every mission we undertook exposed more flaws in our party. We had a lot of work to do, and an even longer journey ahead of us.

"Maybe we should buy some new skills…" I suggested.

The words didn't come out easily. The idea ran directly against my desire to save towards the establishment of a guild. It had to be said though.

It was clearer than ever our group was severely lacking in defensive abilities. Isabelle needed at least one skill to protect her in the case of an emergency. Any single one of us could have been impaled on those shadow spears.

Chapter 26: Shopping for Skills

The walk back to Arturii was a quiet one. Probably every single one of us was thinking about how to increase our power. My original thought that the waves and tides of change would miss our small party, was completely off.

Our 75K reward was passed to us directly from behind the Adventurers' hall's counter. It was our first successful mission and despite the fact we had needed help, it was marked as a flawless completion. There was a bit of hesitation when the clerk asked if we wanted to accept another mission.

"Shall we see if there are any skills to buy?" Aaron asked. My suggestion hadn't fallen on deaf ears.

Even Isabelle, who was extremely protective of her Zeny, didn't dislike the idea, "Let's look."

We ended up visiting a shop near the city center, which turned out to be a complete mistake. The traffic was heavy and the goods over-priced.

Aaron asked around for something smaller and cozier, and so we traveled even further away. It was during that trek I discovered just how vast the world of Yetera was. Like any game would have, there were professions.

Professions were a part of the world that I had neglected: I hadn't even thought about them. Yet we could all learn a trade that could increase our effectiveness, especially if we balanced our professions as a group. As well as the obviously useful blacksmiths or alchemists there were many more, as was clear from the part of town that we were in.

The signs hanging over the shop doors offered reliable Magicsmiths, Gemcutters, Runecrafters, and Enchanters. It was a fascinating sight and I stared at the windows and street displays with a hunger to learn more.

We stepped into a Magicsmith shop and I started to observe the wares. There were wands and gowns, coronets and crowns, staves and all manner of magical equipment. "Excuse me." I asked the man behind the counter. "Is it possible you can explain what a Magicsmith does?"

I was looked at with confusion at first, and then he held out his hand. He wanted compensation for the information.

"How much?" I asked him.

"A thousand Zeny." I had at least that much to spare, and so I paid it.

"Where to start…" He pondered. "You know what a Blacksmith is yeah?"

"I do."

"Right, so a Magicsmith is similar except our wares focus more on endowing magic. A blacksmith is more of a physical profession. High quality goods ensure a great weapon, or shield or armor— mostly for melee and physical type classes."

"What ensures high quality magical gear isn't only the materials, but also the quality of the mana and the elemental affinity of the crafter. Our goods are crafted with magic. We can also take an item that has already been crafted and upgrade it; only the best of the best can do that, though." It was a simple explanation that made sense.

I didn't feel guilty about not buying anything at all. The goods were all incredibly expensive and I'd already paid for my information. We moved on to the next shop.

What we learned about each profession was fairly general and not too informative, only the Gemcutting profession was self-explanatory. Gemcutters shaped and cut gems in such a way to provide the biggest benefit for the user. It was a well-respected profession.

The most obscure professions were Runecrafters and Enchanters. Runes were symbols imbued into weapons or armor. They needed to be carved with precision by powerful magic. Once done, a rune provided a special effect: maybe your weapon now gave you the ability to cast fireball; maybe it had arching electricity over its blade; maybe it was cold as ice. The amount of runes that could be crafted per item varied greatly.

The first requirements for this upgrade, of course, were good weapons or armor. If the weapon or item wasn't a high enough quality then the rune would be useless. This was because the abilities granted by runes needed MP as a catalyst and if the weapon was cheap, MP wouldn't be able to flow through the material. Your rune would do nothing. The requirements were quite high as the stress on the weapon was considerable.

You can imagine what a rune that lit your weapon on fire would do. Not many materials could withstand being at such a heat for extended periods of time. That made Runecrafting an option for the elite, mostly.

Enchanting was the profession I found most interesting. The reason for that was its considerable access to all levels. There was no requirement on the weapon or armor. As long as you had the material you could enchant it.

This was also the reason we had made such a killing in Tanyros. The valuable gems and minerals we recovered were all enchanting materials. Forging or re-forging a weapon or armor with certain combinations granted special effects.

The effects weren't as exaggerated as new skills or special abilities. They were more linear in their benefits, increases to stats, HP, MP movement speed, and etc. There were also contingent buff effects.

Gain X effect on attack, gain X effect on cast, chance to gain X effect on X: the amount of possibilities were incredibly varied. It was clear the clerk was incredibly passionate as he explained, "There's so many combinations we have yet to figure out all the possible buffs!" or so he said.

The downside to this profession was its cost of entry. Obtaining enchanted equipment was difficult in that the materials required for Enchanter effects were tremendously expensive. Some even required Orichalcum, a 750k Zeny material. That was reserved for only the richest of the rich: the most powerful Adventurers.

As well as the costs of the material, if one of us was to become an Enchanter, they would have to learn the many possible combinations of gemstones, inscribing patterns, and runic symbols. Apparently, it took years to progress as an Enchanter, not to mention hundreds of thousands of Zeny to purchase that information.

After our detour around the stores, we ended up outside a cozy little shop, one that didn't even have a particular name; it was simply registered as a general goods store. We opened the door and a little bell chimed to let them know they had potential customers.

A man walked out from the back room, "Can I help you all?"

"We're looking for skills. Do you have any?"

"I have some." He walked from behind the counter and over to a chest in the corner. It was old and dilapidated. A chain and metal lock kept it tightly sealed. He shuffled through his robe before finding an inside pocket, pulling out a key and turning the lock. The chain slid and coiled on the floor.

"Go on and take a look. The descriptions are all on the front." Steven popped the trunk and I could see it was lined from side to side and from bottom to top with skill books. Every single one was forcefully sealed shut with a locking mechanism.

This was something I had neglected to even think about. What was to stop someone from flipping a book cover and learning the skill right then and there without paying? It seemed this contraption was the answer.

Aaron knelt down and started to select book after book, passing out the ones he thought we would want to browse through. There really was a wide selection.

BOOK OF SHRAPNEL SHOT LV. 1
MP COST: 17
SPLIT YOUR ARROW INTO MANY DIFFERENT PROJECTILES.

A ranged ability for bow users.

BOOK OF CHAIN LIGHTNING LV. 1
CAST TIME: 5 SECONDS
MP COST: 35
DISTANCE: 5 METERS
SHOOT OUT AN ARCH OF ELECTRICITY THAT JUMPS FROM ONE ENEMY TO THE NEXT.

A spell caster's dream, I was interested in it but my pockets were nearly empty.

```
BOOK OF PRAYER LV. 1
CAST TIME: 3 SECONDS
MP COST: 75
DISTANCE: 4 METERS
HEAL ALL PARTY MEMBERS AROUND YOU.
```

A group heal sounded good on paper, but it was definitely very situational. So far during our adventures it would have been useful just once, during the Marsh Pond exploration.

The books didn't seem to be sorted in any way shape or form. They were simply thrown into the chest randomly. Looking through them all was quite the pain and we quickly had an entire pile of unwanted skills at our feet.

Fortunately, our persistence eventually paid off. There was at least one usable skill for Isabelle in the bunch.

```
BOOK OF DIVINE SHIELD LV. 1
CAST TIME: 0.5 SECONDS
MP COST: 60
DISTANCE: 5 METERS
PROTECT THE TARGET WITH A DIVINE SHIELD, ABSORBS 500
DMG.
```

This wasn't a full stop like Barrier was, but it added a 500 HP buffer. That counted for a great deal. We quickly agreed that if the price was reasonable, then we should buy it.

There was also something for Aaron.

```
BOOK OF SHARPSHOOTING LV. 1
CAST TIME: 1 SECONDS
MP COST: 25
FIRE AN EXTREMELY ACCURATE ARROW WITH DEVASTATING
PIERCING POWER. CAN HIT MULTIPLE TARGETS.
```

And even something for Kimmi.

```
BOOK OF FLOWSTEP LV. 1
CAST TIME: INSTANT
MP COST: 25
DURATION: 30 SECONDS.
COOL DOWN: 2 MINUTES.
ENCHANT YOUR BODY WITH THE POWER OF WIND, INCREASING
YOUR NIMBLENESS AND SPEED FOR A SHORT DURATION.
```

There were a few interesting skills for me as well, but I was still broke. I didn't even have 30k Zeny to my name.

"How much for these three?" Aaron asked, while placing the skill books on the counter.

The old man looked with unconcerned eyes, as if completely clueless as to the importance of the skills. "Fifty k for Divine Shield, thirty for Sharpshooting, sixty for Flowstep." That was disappointing. These were good skills and probably the prices weren't far off their worth to our group, but I had hoped we had come to a place where we could have found a bargain.

I didn't bother to voice my dissatisfaction with the prices. Aaron would deal with this properly.

"That's a bit steep don't you think?" He started to peel at the well-worn edges. "These look like they've been sitting in that trunk for years now…" He suddenly turned his head towards the door.

"We're the only customers to have walked through the door in the past thirty minutes. Business must be rough lately."

And although the man knew what Aaron was doing, he couldn't help but nod in his in annoyance, "It's not my fault I can't compete with the new fancy stores. Even though they charge less on a few popular items, they charge more on the other skills, and you pay it, having been drawn in." This was a regular occurrence, even on Earth.

All that mattered were trends and the trend was to purchase from well-known stores with high visibility, which seemed to be the best places to visit, rather than dingy and remote shops with poor displays. That was to our advantage. "The way I see it, a sale is better than no sale," Aaron said. "Why don't we take the prices down a half? We're buying three items after all, a bulk sale if you would."

"Half? Too much."

If we went by his original pricing the entire lot would be 140k Zeny. That was incredibly steep, even if it was only fair. Fortunately, circumstances weren't fair. Money now might be more important to this man than money later.

"Let's do a bulk sale, seventy k for everything."

"I said I can't do half." The shop owner was stern and unyielding in his decision.

It was time for Aaron's special ability: indecision. My friend stood there in silence rubbing his chin without making as much as a counter-offer. He was acting like it was truly the most difficult and important decision in the world. The seller started to look anxious, as though realizing he might lose this sale.

Probably, 70k was a decent amount of Zeny for a shop like this. How much did it cost to rent a store in Arturii? A busy city like this wouldn't be cheap, even in a backstreet. I guessed we were offering enough for him to live off and pay store costs for two or three months.

"Alright, what's the best you can do?" Aaron asked at last.

And by now, fear was already visible in the store owner. Clearly, his business wasn't doing well. Looking around, I didn't see much of value other than the skills and even they hadn't been examined for weeks, to judge by the rectangle of dust at the base of the chest which became visible when we moved it.

The seriousness on Aaron's face suggested to the shopkeeper that one wrong move and the deal would be over. "Ninety... No, eighty k," he said.

"Alright, we can do eighty. That's a fair deal." Aaron collected the Zeny from Isabelle and Kimmi before handing it over. This was a great result for us despite Aaron's reluctant demeanor. The other stores wouldn't even let you barter. There was no shortage of suckers willing to overpay.

The clerk unlocked each book and the three of them learned their new skills on the spot. This was the first step of many towards creating a stronger party. The second was the simplest: level up.

Furthermore, I had always suspected that there would be specialist class options at some point. I would not be just a mage forever, Aaron wouldn't be an archer, Isabelle an acolyte. These were the generic classes and there was an opportunity to make another choice within them. After listening to High Priestess Rhea, I'd asked about this and learned that the new classes didn't unlock at a particular level, like 50, but there was a random aspect to it.

A secondary option might appear to an Adventurer as early as level 35 and as late as level 50. There was no guarantee at what level it would present itself to you. Those with more skills and better stats would receive a class change quest earlier than the less well prepared. It was widely recognized that skills played an important role in this.

When becoming a mage, I had gained increased HP and MP values, as well as scaling benefits per level and stat, I had also learned Energy Shield. I didn't know my options for my next class, as they varied, but the benefits should be considerable.

Even a repeat of the same—more scaling, new skills, higher HP and MP—that would be an upgrade across all fronts. The biggest strength increase we could obtain in the near future would be from unlocking our class changes. Leveling now was more important than ever.

Professions could also vastly increase our power, too. Unfortunately, they cost money, an ever-growing amount as you climbed higher. We were lacking in time, and, especially in my case, we were lacking in money.

It was a hard decision, but I realized I had to bury my ambition of creating a guild, for the foreseeable future at least. On Eastrath I had felt like a big shot. Only after coming to Arturii did I realize just how small and insignificant I was.

This was only the starting line for us as a party. Heck, back on Eastrath a person of my skill would be respected even by a royal family. 'A' rank missions would be handed to me like candy, but on North Maledith? I barely made the cut to watch over some cattle. It was eye opening.

"Should we find another mission?" Aaron asked.

"Can we scratch the missions for now?" I said, "I think we should forgo profit and prioritize EXP. Everyone heard what Rhea said. We need to grow stronger now or submit ourselves to a guild." I didn't want to join a guild as fodder if I could help it.

"We can still take missions. Let's just prioritize those that are located in better EXP areas, regardless of the pay," suggested Steven. It was the perfect middle ground.

Aaron nodded. "We can just ask the clerk, I'm sure we aren't the first party to consider it."

And that's what we ended up doing.

"You want missions but only in the best leveling areas?"

"Right."

"And you aren't part of a guild?"

"No."

"That could be difficult to find. Typically, the best leveling areas are controlled by the top guilds. There are a few… but instead of receiving a mission you'll have to sign a contract with the guild to operate in their territory."

"Any catch?"

"No catch, you sign a contract and buy the right to level in their area."

"Can you suggest what would be best?"

"At your level… there's only one place: the Hidden Jungle. As of now it's controlled by the Valkyrie guild, located just east of Arturii." The Valkyrie guild again, I suddenly felt like we would be hearing more about them as we continued our journey. I never forgot about the lesson I received in Egester of how important a guild was.

"If its hidden then how should we find it?"

"Ah, the name is a bit peculiar. The jungle itself is easy to find, the hidden part is more a description of those who enter. If, for some reason, you get lost, there's not much of a chance anyone will ever find you: you're the 'hidden' part of the jungle."

"Can I see a contract please?" Aaron asked. The clerk handed him a slip of paper over the counter and our spokesman read it aloud. "Five k Zeny per person, grants access for one month?" Aaron hesitated a moment.

"If you're thinking that's expensive you're mistaken." The clerk looked around with an expression of caution before whispering to us. "As far as I'm concerned that's on the cheap end. The other top tier guilds charge upward of two or three times as much."

"Why is it so cheap then?" I asked. Typically, if deals were cheap like this, there was always a catch.

"It's just how the Valkyrie guild operates. They like to give back to the people more than they take away. Of course, that doesn't come without its problems. It's not visible on the surface but several other top guilds are displeased with them."

"They are smothering all the competition with their low prices?" Aaron asked.

"Exactly! The other guilds don't want to devalue their leveling areas so they refuse to lower the price. It doesn't help that the Hidden Jungle is by far above the best place to level when in your low 30's. Anyway, lines are getting kind of long. Interested?"

Aaron looked back at us and we all nodded. The clerk behind the counter definitely did a solid job in selling us. I wondered if he even got a cut for getting us to sign the contracts...

"We'll do it."

"Great, fill these out over there and bring them back when you're done. I need to keep the line moving."

It didn't take us longer than two minutes to do the paperwork and we weaseled our way back towards the counter.

"Alright, you're all set. Next pickup is tomorrow morning at the east gate." He stamped each of our contracts before handing them back to us.

I was hyped up thinking about this new challenge. The way he described the region made it sound like a god's gift for EXP on Yetera: a one-stop shop straight to unlocking my second class.

It was hard to fall asleep that night due to a mixture of nervousness, excitement, and a bit of added fear that we'd somehow oversleep and miss the escort. Fortunately, that didn't turn out to be the case.

Chapter 27: The Hidden Jungle

The inner east gate was packed when we arrived. There were parties strewn about pretty much everywhere. I started to count and simply gave up after my tally reached 25 parties.

We waited for around thirty minutes till someone arrived, a female scout or ranger type, to judge from her leather armor. "Hi everyone, I'm a guide for the Valkyrie guild. If you're registered and here for the Hidden Jungle escort please move to the right side. Line up single file in front of me."

To my surprise, the entire area immediately moved. Almost every party in this space was going to the Hidden Jungle. It was no doubt as popular as the clerk made it out to be.

The line flowed smoothly. Eventually it was our turn, and she took each of our contracts and looked them over before giving them another stamp. It was a black stamp, unlike the red one we got from the clerk.

After that she shuffled us off to the side and had us wait till everyone was accounted for. Once that was done we departed as a group on foot, our guide first standing on a barrel and shouting: "Everyone should try and stay close. It's not hard to find the Hidden Jungle, but I can't guarantee your safety if you run off on your own."

I looked behind me and saw a cleric in another group, "What is she guarding us from?"

"Bandits. The other guilds will never admit it, but they have rogues and thieves setup all along this route."

"For what?"

"To steal some Zeny and to deter people who are on the fence about paying to visit the Hidden Jungle." This made sense, but was definitely an underhand tactic and worked against the spirit of co-operation that High Priestess Rhea had urged. Looking around at the swarms of people moving in this group, it was also ineffective.

The area around us slowly changed from a cultivated landscape to a wild, living and breathing jungle. Farms grew fewer and fewer, with more rough land between them. And the temperature rose distinctly. There was such a difference in the environment that I suddenly found myself peeling the clothes from my back.

The day was as humid as hell. There was dew on the surrounding branches and trees despite it not having rained at all recently. The flora was growing rich and verdant, as if being fed the strongest of fertilizers.

Trees grew dozens of times larger and thicker than I was used to. The light grew darker from the lack of sunlight able to shine through the thick upper canopy of these giants. Vines of all shapes and sizes dangled from above. Critters dangled from the algae-covered bark of the trees and stared curiously.

Calling it a jungle was no understatement. The guide ahead pulled out a weapon and started to slash and cut at the underbrush. There was no doubt this path was used regularly, and yet she needed to prune back the overgrowth. The growth speed of this jungle was mind boggling.

"Alright, here we are." She stopped and turned back to us. There was a single dark path behind her to travel through. "I'll need to check all your paperwork once more."

I was confused at first why she would need to do so, but after checking about thirty people she caught a rat red handed. It was either someone from a rival guild intent on stealing or someone who had tried to sneak in along the way and avoid the 5k Fee.

The captured rogue didn't even try to resist his detention, that or they couldn't. The guide in front of us was considerably higher level than us. Almost immediately after she caught the first culprit, a few other snakes rushed out of the group and into the wilderness. They didn't dare to try to get past her into the Hidden Jungle, but instead opted to give up.

Party after party walked inside and disappeared from view. The jungle was so lush with vegetation that an elephant just ten or twelve feet in front of you would be completely obscured.

Not only was visibility terrible. It was hard to hear anything as well. The jungle insects buzzed and chirped, while the birds constantly cawed. Every rustle of wind stirred up a storm of shaking leaves and battering trees.

It was no exaggeration to say you wouldn't be found if you became lost here. We were in the middle of the pack but didn't see any party that had set out ahead of us. I couldn't be sure if it was just a testament to how large the jungle was, or if foul play was afoot.

It quickly became clear that everything around you was always moving, whether it was the wind or a lurking monster. Fortunately or unfortunately, we didn't encounter anything on the outskirts of our camp.

The speed at which we moved was slow but steady. Steven remained in the front and did his best to chop any shrubs and vines in our path. Kimmi was right there to assist him as well. We were burrowing our own little path through the jungle.

No doubt in a few days the path we had carved would be swallowed up and another group would have the displeasure of carving a new one. We came across a sudden dip that descended quickly downward towards a flowing riverbed. It was there we encountered our first monster.

SLITHEREEN ANOMALY	**LEVEL: 34**	**BEAST**
	WATER	
HP: 8416		MP: 45
	STR: 30	
	AGI: 30	
	DEX: 25	
	VIT: 50	
	INT: 10	
DISTANT RELATIVES OF NAGA THAT HAVE DEVELOPED LEGS AND LUNGS TO SURVIVE ON LAND.		

The monster did resemble a Naga quite a lot actually. There were fins coming from its ears and head as well as sharp spikes jutting from its elbow. The entire body was slimy and sleek like a salamander. And the impression that it was better suited to water than land was topped off by its frog-like feet.

The Slithereen was just a few feet down the riverbed scavenging for whatever it could eat. There was a large spear strapped to its back made from bamboo and carved rock. It noticed our intrusion and jerked its head up before a gurgling sound came from its throat.

Steven immediately cast Charge and the two clashed. The bamboo spear looked flimsy from a distance but didn't budge in the slightest at Steven's attack. Kimmi appeared directly behind the Slithereen and dug her daggers into its back.

There was a moment in which surprise appeared on the monster's face, before it turned around and kicked out. Kimmi barely managed to dodge the lightning-fast leg sweep. Unfortunately for the frog-man, it wasn't able to contend with a full party on its own.

As our melee classes landed more and more blows, I felt Steven and Kimmi would be dispatching our enemy momentarily. At least that's what I expected. Instead, it turned tail and started to run. "Don't let it get away!" Kimmi yelled. She could already smell the blood in the water.

We started to chase after the Slithereen but were no match for its nimble movements. Its body was designed to survive in this habitat and we quickly lost it through the rustling underbrush. We chased for what felt like three minutes before finally giving up.

"Guys…" Aaron suddenly said. I was panting hard as I got our bearings. There wasn't the slightest indication the Slithereen Anomaly had even came through here. My attention turned to Aaron who was instead looking up towards the canopy, his finger outstretched pointing.

"What in the world…?" The entire canopy was littered with huts attached to trees. There were wooden bridges connecting them that disappeared into the distance. There was an entire little civilization here made of twigs and branches just floating there.

Only after looking up did we spot our culprit darting across a wooden bridge. There were two dagger wounds leaking blood on his back. None of his brethren paid him any heed. I felt my eyes widen as I realized there must be hundreds of potential EXP bags, err, monsters to face here.

"How do we get up?" Kimmi was the first to ask. We scanned the surroundings and realized there was no other way but to ascend the vines dangling from above. The Slithereen Anomaly had frog feet that seemed to help them suction to the trees and climb.

"Who's going first?" Isabelle asked. I was of the thought that it should be Steven… but I wasn't sure he would be able to climb up himself without a bit of help.

"I'll do it," I said. This was a good time to put my new physique to the test. I grasped the nearest dangling vine and dug in hard with my feet against the trunk of a tree. There was a thick patch of half-damp moss coating the entire thing.

Water started to leak onto my hand as I raised one arm over the other and walked up the tree. This was something I'd never have been able to do before, and now I was doing it with ease. The jungle floor got farther and farther away until I found myself grasping a wooden plank and pulling myself atop a rickety wooden bridge.

There was no rope, or even nails to hold the platform together. It was a mess of vines twisted and interlocked through the boards in a clever way to keep it from falling apart. I had to admit the intelligence of these creatures was impressive.

Isabelle went up next and Kimmi was right below her assisting. Steven was just below Kimmi and was grinning ear to ear. I knew exactly why he was smiling and I wanted to give him a smack. Aaron was unfortunate enough to be just below Steven. His face constantly grimaced in displeasure.

I did my best to help pull everyone up as they reached out. It became clear that getting used to combat up in the trees like this would be difficult. The bridge swayed side to side and even dipped irregularly. I felt like I was walking on a trampoline.

As a mage the difficult terrain didn't affect me nearly as much as Steven or Kimmi, they had to maneuver through this. The good news though, was the sheer amount of potential EXP in the area. Huts and bridges dotted our view as far as we could see.

The first encounter was three Slithereen Anomaly just in front of us at the other end of the bridge we had climbed up. Steven didn't even dare charge in fear of falling off and we decided to take it slow. Even as we discussed our plan, they started to gurgle in displeasure, having spotted him.

Aaron was the first to attack this time and shot out two Ensnaring Arrows in quick succession. It seemed like these arrows were born to thrive in this jungle and the nearby vines wrapped up two of the Slithereen Anomaly and sealed any chance of escape for the trio.

They were all water creatures, which worked out perfectly for me. Despite it being so incredibly moist, casting Fireball or cremation or any fire skill didn't sit right with me. I started to cast Ball Lightning and suddenly realized not buying Chain Lightning from that shop was a mistake.

Lightning damage was super effective against water monsters like this: the ones that had liquid slime coating their body. Their entire outer body was covered with a slick slimy goop that conducted electricity perfectly. One cast fried them through and through.

An added bonus came from the landscape, at least for me. The majority of real-estate up here in the canopy were bridges that at most could allow two people to walk side by side. It was nearly impossible to not get the most out of ball lightning.

"Should we just live up here?" Aaron asked. The huts didn't look too bad to sleep in. It was better than the jungle floor no doubt. We were safe off the ground from most predators. As long as we killed the Slithereen Anomaly nearby our nights would be safe.

"I think so." I agreed.

So we made it our goal to slaughter everything in sight. My suspicion that the Hidden Jungle was over-exaggerated in terms of EXP was shut down quickly. Not only did every Slithereen Anomaly give 650 EXP, there was almost no end to them in sight. Better yet, their aggro radius did not seem all that high. Instead of dozens of them rushing us, we only had to fight those very close to us.

Every hut across every bridge had at least two of the Naga-types, we even ran into patrols along the bridge. As of now we didn't know what would happen if we let them run away, but Aaron always managed to land Ensnaring arrow right from the get-go.

Our tactics were so effective that apart from the first one, which had led us here, none of them could escape. My Ball Lightning paired with Kimmi's accurate assassinations, the fights were quick and clean and the EXP was climbing fast.

```
CURRENT EXP: 35560/67000      LEVEL: 28
           MAGE           FORMIDABLE
       HP: 2002/2002  MP: 288/712
                STR: 21
                AGI: 21
                DEX: 35
                VIT: 30 +2
                INT: 54 +14
              AVAILABLE: 0
```

In the short time we'd been up here I gained around 30,000 EXP: a mind-boggling gain, only matched by how fast our MP was depleting as a group. The fighting was non-stop and Aaron was already dangerously low, despite only using Ensnaring Arrow once per fight.

"Should we rest a bit?" I asked.

Everyone else looked at the endless supply of EXP dotting the distance. There was longing and desire on each of our faces, "Let's keep going…" Isabelle said.

"I'm sure it will be fine," Kimmi agreed.

And so we continued onward regardless of Aaron's lack of MP. Every encounter was a mad dash to finish off the enemies before they fled into the distance. Things were going smoothly and EXP was still flowing. We were now playing with fire though.

It was only a matter of time until things didn't go as planned. Merely ten minutes after Aaron had stopped using Ensnaring arrow and we had our first jailbreak. A wounded Slithereen Anomaly managed to dart past Kimmi and down a bridge.

If it only pulled three monsters that would be fine, but it didn't stop there, it kept going. It ran across three bridges and trained four huts of monsters onto us. A total of twelve Slithereen Anomaly came rushing in our direction.

Isabelle immediately drank a MP potion and started to cast Divine Shield on each of us. Kimmi used Flowstep and rushed head first into the incoming mobs. Steven had to shove a Slithereen Anomaly off of him and rush to chase after her.

Aaron and I were left to contend with the remaining two Slithereen Anomaly in front of us while Steven and Kimmi did their best to hold back the incoming mobs. Their divine shields constantly chipped and cracked until there was nothing left of them.

I tossed Aaron a mana potion which he chugged immediately and then I threw out a Ball Lightning. My old friend opted for a classic and used Powershot. The combined power allowed us to defeat the two monsters in front of us, blasting them from the platform to the forest floor below. We rushed to the hut and were directly behind Steven and Kimmi.

"Move out of the way!" Aaron said. He started to cast Sharp-shooting and the air around his entire body suddenly shifted and changed. It was like all air resistance was being converted to vacuum so his arrow could fly freely.

Steven managed to twist to the side and Kimmi flipped back and dangled off the edge of the vine bridge. The arrow loosed from Aaron's bow thundered like a sonic boom before ripping directly through the chests of six of the incoming monsters.

The impact sent the front half into a panic, the survivors turning around to rush backwards and away. Unfortunately for them, the other six mobs were still rushing towards us hungrily. The collision between the two halves of their unit caused two of our enemies to fall off the bridge and splatter on the jungle floor below. The good news was we gained EXP from those kills.

Kimmi swung herself back up and started to hack and stab at the Slithereen Anomaly trying to run in fear. It was a total mess. Aaron shot a single Ensnaring Arrow to the back of the bridge, completely sealing any route of escape for them.

The dozen Anomaly on the bridge were now completely trapped in a figurative blender. Steven and Kimmi constantly cut across their slimy backs and dug their sword and daggers into their flesh. It only caused more havoc.

A spear jammed through the mess of bodies and struck directly into Steven's shoulder. "Fuck!" It just made him angrier. He thrust his sword directly into the throat of the monster that had dared to stab him.

My Ball Lightning was floating just above the mobs while all this was happening and it zapped to a crisp several of them. In just forty-five seconds of battle, we had a pile of Slithereen Anomalies completely blocking our path.

"Gah, this is disgusting." Steven had no choice but to grab them by their limbs and toss them off the bridge to clear a path. Their bodies landed with a thud every time. They were long dead by now, though.

When all was said and done, we were several thousand EXP closer to our next level and two items richer.

HUNTING SPEAR: STR +5, DEX +3
A SPEAR USED FOR HUNTING IN THE JUNGLE.

This was similar to the spear the Slithereen wore on their back. A bamboo shaft with a rock carved tip.

BARK SKIRT: VIT +2, STR +2, AGI +1
A SKIRT MADE FROM THE DRIED BARK OF A JUNGLE TREE. IT OFFERS DECENT PROTECTION FROM THE WEATHER.

"Can you wear that over your leggings?" I looked at Steven. He picked it up the skirt and eyed it with a bit of dissatisfaction.

Suddenly, there was now a skirt of worn and dried brown bark reaching towards his knees. "I guess so…"

Unfortunately, no one here could make use of the Hunting Spear so Steven stored it away for a potential sale.

"Let's break for now," said Aaron.

"Everyone's MP should be pretty low." I knew mine was. So we ended up sitting for a solid hour and a half before continuing forward and pulling small groups of Slithereen Anomalies, grinding through them efficiently.

> **CONGRATULATIONS! YOU HAVE REACHED LEVEL 29. AS A REWARD FOR LEVELING UP, YOU HAVE BEEN GRANTED THREE STAT POINTS!**
>
> CURRENT EXP: 460/69000 LEVEL: 29
> MAGE   FORMIDABLE
> HP: 2032/2032   MP: 588/719
> STR: 21
> AGI: 21
> DEX: 35
> VIT: 30 +2
> INT: 54 +14
> AVAILABLE: 3

I had managed to level just before sundown!

Delighted with my progress, I felt happy as we picked a hut to use as our camp. Our beds in it were arguably better than most we had experienced. The little huts, safe off the jungle floor, had bark beds. As I lay back in one, it seemed to me that the entire jungle was singing a lullaby. It was a beautiful night and I left my stat allocation for the morning.

The following day was more of the same. We had grown used to the antics of these mobs. Steven started blocking their path of retreat instead of needing Aaron to cast Ensnaring Arrow. Sometimes we let them go on purpose to gather more mobs, but only when our MP was high.

I had almost forgotten we were in a jungle while walking along these bridges. There was no brush to cut, no moist dirty ground to walk on and no scratching and scraping from the endless underbrush around you.

As we moved forward, continuously grinding EXP, I grew complacent. My best hopes for this region weren't any better than this. And yet the Hidden Jungle had something else to offer, as we worked our way to a view beyond the tree village, I was completely blown away.

These wooden bridges and huts, they led somewhere: somewhere magnificent and beautiful. We followed the walkways to the end and the end was a city. It wasn't a city of wood and bark and jungle, but a city made of stone.

It was ancient, maybe even something the Slithereen Anomaly did not build themselves, but chanced upon. Marcus, inside of me, was from such a city, it was very likely this was once from the same culture, only buried in time by jungle, to be used by the monsters as their new home.

Chapter 28: The Lost City

Why have you been so quiet lately? Seeing the city in front of us I was expecting a reaction from Marcus now more than ever.

"Just taking in the scenery." And yet I felt there was something more to it. Marcus was talking less and less ever since our return from death in the Marsh Ponds. While I missed his knowledge, I felt that his declining presence in my mind could also be considered a good thing.

He spoke to me again, "I heard that."

"Look there." Steven pointed. I followed his arm to see a Slithereen Anomaly, but one that was a bit different than normal. It was maybe a head taller than the others and had some colored inscribing on its clothing. There was something special about it, that much was obvious from a glance.

It wasn't only just the one though. The entire city section we could see had Slithereen Anomaly of similar size and attire. Was this city filled with elite Slithereen Anomaly? There must have been fifty or sixty moving about in the section we could see.

That didn't sound like much in the grand scheme of things, but we were only seeing a small portion of this stone city. It stretched an unknown distance into the jungle where it disappeared from sight.

"Let's be careful about this." Aaron suggested. "And try to find a single pull to test their strength." He was right of course. Fighting a dozen Slithereen Anomaly was possible, but the same couldn't be said with confidence about a dozen elites. We didn't know anything about these new monsters, only that they looked to be in the same family.

We were still high up in the jungle canopy and looking down. There were no more bridges or huts ahead of us. It was as if we were in the slums located just outside the inner city. Ahead of us was where the wealthy, fortunate, and powerful lived.

It was time to get down from our home of the past two days. Vines dangled from a nearby hut and we took turns descending as carefully as possible. Stepping on the moist—yet solid—ground felt completely foreign.

"How should we do this?" I asked.

"Let's just walk around the outskirts and see what we can find." Aaron answered, and that's what we did. We needed to find an opening into this city anyway. There were low stone walls surrounding it on all sides. We could throw some vines over and climb, but after that, getting out in an emergency would be risky.

I couldn't help but realize just how crazy this jungle was. From the canopy we could see the stone city clear as day, but down here? Down here the city was almost completely obscured from view.

We were maybe twenty or thirty feet away from the wall, only some jungle brush separating us, and yet we could see nothing. If I hadn't witnessed it before, I would have found it hard to convince someone such a massive city was nearby.

Steven cut a path right up to the wall and eventually we were walking just beside it. This was the safest way to not get lost in such a mess. There was also something unique about the terrain here: the jungle didn't grow on the wall. Nor did it fill the city as one would expect.

This was obviously very different to the rest of the jungle and its ravenous appetite for growth. Clearly, there was something special about the stone city, waiting to be discovered.

We walked and walked for what felt like an hour before coming upon an opening. It was interesting though, there were no guards. Surely, there should be guards stationed here to keep out intruders?

The reason why there were no soldiers at the gate became obvious a moment later, after we walked under an arch in the wall. There was someone else, some other party here, besides us: the bodies of Slithereen Anomaly were strewn about randomly.

"Should we leave?" I wondered aloud. This was the jungle and we were arguably on the lower end of the level spectrum. If the Adventurers ahead of us had bad intentions… we might not make it out in one piece. The EXP in front of us was so tempting though.

"Let's just… take it slow. Maybe they'll be friendly." Kimmi was thinking along the same lines as me it seemed.

"First sign of trouble we bounce," Isabelle said. She was keeping her Zeny closely hidden. Everyone had taken more precautions with their savings after learning that I was robbed. There were bad people on Yetera as much as back on Earth.

We followed the trail of bodies up a stone staircase and one block into the city. That was when we heard voices. They weren't at all calm; we could hear several people arguing.

"What are you saying? You can't just decide that!" This was a woman's voice.

A man answered, "We were here first. Those are just the facts."

"It doesn't matter. You don't own the Hidden Jungle." Another, different, voice chimed in.

"Power decides who owns it!" declared the man with a note of triumph.

We inched closer and closer to take a look.

"Who's there?" someone called out and I knew we'd been spotted almost immediately.

"Hello." Aaron walked forward, "We didn't mean to spy."

There were two parties in front of us. They were clearly in opposition of each other. Weapons were drawn and they were butting heads.

One side was clearly happy to see us while from the other was nothing but scowls of annoyance. "You're not going to tell them they also can't be here?" The woman who had previously spoke asked. She was an archer.

"Tch, suit yourself." The leader of the scowling group didn't bother to continue to argue and instead took his party and disappeared down another block.

"I hope we didn't cause you any trouble," Aaron said.

"Nope, you actually saved us there," she said. "Rachel." She held out her hand.

"Aaron." They shook hands, "what was that about?"

"That was just the Tyrant guild being their normal selves. They want to monopolize this city." It seemed their guild name portrayed their actions quite well.

"Why though?" I asked, "it's quite big isn't it? There's enough space for everyone here."

"That's true... but..." Rachel paused, "Can you give us a moment?" And her entire party walked away to talk amongst each other.

"There's something special about this place," I said.

Aaron nodded. "Definitely, there's no reason to argue over territory with how big it is."

"Treasure..." Isabelle mumbled.

It seemed their group was having a heated discussion and were quite conflicted. In the end three of them came back with confident smiles while two seemed uneasy. Rachel continued to speak for them. "Sorry about that, it was sensitive information."

"No problem."

"First off, I'd like to introduce ourselves formally. We're all from the Perseverance guild. This is Donivan, Roderick, Joshua and Laura."

Roderick was the main tank of their group, Donivan was their healer, Laura was a mage and Joshua was a swordsman. He didn't have heavy armor though, like Roderick, instead he wore chainmail and wielded two swords.

"Ah, we're un-guilded." Aaron did the introductions. "This is Joseph, Steven, Kimmi and Isabelle."

Rachel made eye contact with each of us and gave a nod. "We're now in the same boat so I'll cut right to it. This isn't our first time here at this city. This is actually our second trip. When we discovered it the first time, we left empty-handed and came back after doing a lot of research.

"At the very least, there's something special about this place, and we have some information that I can't yet share, that there may be some sort of treasure or special artifact here." We listened without interrupting while Rachel continued to explain. "The Tyrant group you just saw also seem to have the same or similar information they are acting on.

"They want to monopolize the discovery for themselves completely and that's why you saw us arguing with them. They're unruly and wave the power of the Tyrant guild around. Normally, we would have just worked out an agreement between the two of us, but frankly they can't be trusted.

"That's when you guys came along, and honestly, the timing couldn't have been better. We now outnumber them ten versus five and it's unlikely they'll cause any problems for us. Are you interested in working with us?"

"We should discuss the conditions first," Aaron suggested.

"Right, that's what we were talking about earlier. Based on the fact that we've researched thoroughly and gathered extensive information, I suggest a seventy-thirty split," Rachel offered.

"Can we think about it?" Aaron asked. We all ended up walking off to the side, "What does everyone think?"

"I think it can only be a benefit. We seemed to have angered that Tyrant group anyway, even if we stay out of their feud it doesn't guarantee they won't come after us." Isabelle said.

"I think so too," I agreed.

"If we can stay and grind here, I think it's worth the risk," Steven said.

"Besides that, has anyone heard of the Perseverance guild?" Aaron asked.

"I have," Kimmi said. "It would be on the generous side to consider them a top ten guild. They're right around the cusp though."

"And what about the Tyrant guild?"

"A contender for rank one," I said. It wasn't my first time hearing about their guild. The Tyrant guild hall was also massive. Possibly even the largest in Arturii.

"Alright," said Aaron, "let's see how it goes. Worst case we call this all off and get out of here."

"Right." Everyone agreed and we walked back to Rachel's group.

"Before you say anything I want to clarify something: you might think our offer is unfair, but the information we have is reliable.

Without it you'll only be spending your time killing mobs here and have no chance of anything else," Rachel said.

"I understand the basics of the situation. Realistically the only reason we're needed is protection against the Tyrant party, right?" Aaron said.

"Uhh…" Rachel scratched her head, "Yeah…"

"The risk to us should be relatively low then."

"Yes."

"Let's talk hypothetically for a moment. What if the Tyrant party manages to recruit a party of their own? The risk to us would increase drastically would it not?"

"It would, but there's a reason this place is called the Hidden Jungle. It could be they haven't even informed their guild of this discovery let alone another party. This is not the sort of discovery anyone wants to share. And even if they wanted to recruit help they would be hard pressed to find another party."

"Alright, that's fair. We can accept seventy-thirty as long as you're willing to change that split in the case something happens: if that Tyrant group somehow manage to recruit help. You can agree our role would be more crucial and we would be more deserving."

"Alright, if for some reason they manage to recruit help then we can split sixty, forty."

"Fifty-five, forty-five," Aaron responded.

"Fine, fifty-five, forty-five." And just like that, we were now in a partnership.

"How should we go about this?" asked Steve. "Am I second tank?"

Rachel shook her head. "It's a really big place and it will take us around three days to reach the city center. For now, let's stay in close contact but fight in our separate parties. Once we reach the city center we can form a raid and plan our set up from there."

"Alright, that works. Is there anything special we should know about?"

"Not particularly. These are elites though, and they don't flee as the regular Slithereen Anomaly do."

And so at a distance of about one block from one another our two groups began our advance through the city. We were close enough to easily hear it if anyone from either group called out. I could even hear the sounds of battle from the other group.

According to them, our destination was inward towards the city center. For now though, all I could see was just a few blocks ahead and then the lush canopy above. It was incredibly peculiar.

Nothing grew from the ground here but the canopy warped above and covered the city like a dome. It was an amazing sight to see, the vines literally stretching from one side of the city to the other with simply nothing supporting them from below.

We started to make our journey inward and as we did so, we had to battle constantly with elites.

SLITHEREEN CITIZEN*	LEVEL: 34	BEAST
	WATER	
HP: 29999		MP: 60
	STR: 45	
	AGI: 30	
	DEX: 25	
	VIT: 65	
	INT: 20	
AN UPPER-CLASS ELITE OF THE SLITHEREEN FAMILY.		

One of the surprising differences between the elite and the standard Slithereen was the fact they could speak. As soon as we drew aggro they would shout, "Human, die!" There was also something else we found incredibly odd: their skills varied greatly.

Some of them used no skills at all and yet others had a large variety of them. Every Slithereen was unique in a way, similar to humans. It was less like they were monsters and more like an entire intelligent civilization.

It was clear they could speak to each other, all had even mastered enough of human language to shout their anger at us. There were signs in odd script all over the city. The shops had signboards and there were maps for directions.

I even noticed strange drawings on some pillars. They were old and fading, but depicted scenes like Egyptian hieroglyphs. "What do you make of this?" I asked. It was a scene fading into the stones.

There was a man and his family depicted holding hands, they seemed happy. Suddenly, there was a storm and rain and thunder poured down on their heads. The stone depiction was chipped for several panels, and then it showed what appeared to be several Slithereen Anomaly.

"I'm not sure. Just looks like a kid's drawing."

"Maybe." There wasn't any proof it held significance at all but my intuition was that the story was related to the secret Rachel was keeping.

The varied skills of our opponents made getting into a good flow difficult. Those that used no skills or simply focused on melee combat were by far the easiest. A few were casters though.

The casters were the most dangerous, mainly because they didn't always choose to cast on Steven. We were complacent in our encounters because things were going so smoothly. That was obviously a mistake.

A Slithereen Citizen jumped back several feet and separated himself from Steven and Kimmi. He was covered in bloody wounds and gasping for breath. His defeat was imminent, and yet he raised his hands and chanted something in an odd language.

There was no sign of anything, no warning at all. A lightning bolt descended from the sky and through the canopy and zapped Aaron directly on the head. It nearly barbecued him where he stood. Isabelle managed to heal him, but he didn't have a full head of hair anymore.

Only after that did we start giving these elites our full respect. We also made sure to never pull more than one. Progress was steady for both us and the Perseverance party. It was mid-day when we regrouped to take a short break.

"How's it going on your end?" Rachel asked. She was the most talkative of their group by far. The others were still a bit reserved around us. This was something I was still learning: to be cautious of everyone. "Wait, what happened to your hair?"

"Ah…" Aaron rubbed his head where his red hair was now just stubble, "was an accident."

"Right, you probably didn't know about their skill usage. Sorry, maybe I should have mentioned that."

"No problem, I needed a haircut anyway."

"Well, I'll say that this is the farthest we've come, so everything beyond this street is completely foreign to us as well." That was not welcome news. She originally estimated a three-day journey and yet we had been moving for half a day.

"So, two-and-a-half days of unknown travel ahead of us?" I asked.

"Yeah… two solid days if we're lucky."

"Any signs of the Tyrant group?"

"None, either they fucked off on their own or they're taking a different route. Either way it'll be a race to who gets there first. If they beat us I have no intention of causing any problems." Rachel said.

"That's the way it should be."

"Agreed."

The road ahead of us was an obvious divide. It was the difference between the outer city and inner city. The buildings grew more grand and even the roads became a solid cobblestone instead of just dirt.

Everything gained a level of sophistication. The buildings were cut more cleanly and designed in an aesthetically pleasing way. The fading stones were maintained at least somewhat. It was clear this area received much more care and support.

SLITHEREEN ARISTOCRAT** LEVEL: 35 BEAST
WATER
HP: 67825   MP: 10
STR: 45
AGI: 30
DEX: 30
VIT: 60
INT: 20
AN UPPER CLASS SLITHEREEN.

We still had at least two days of travel remaining and had already encountered a two-star elite. Added to the fact their skill usage varied greatly, the fights ahead could be incredibly treacherous.

"Careful." Aaron warned. "Steven approach alone, Kimmi you just observe. Divine Shield yourself and me." We had discussed it earlier, but my HP pool was already quite high. Unless it was guaranteed I'd be taking damage then it wasn't worth using the mana to Divine Shield me.

The aristocrat wasn't a unique, but we treated it as if encountering a boss. We spread out to avoid any unnecessary AOE overlap. There was a Divine Shield on Isabelle and Aaron while Kimmi waited patiently to the side.

Steven started the battle off with a charge and the two began exchanging blows. The aristocrat wielded a spear; it was of higher quality than was normal for these mobs and completely metal. Not only that, the way the Slithereen wielded the spear was refined.

Even the stances the Aristocrat took and the blows exchanged were measured and practiced. It looked as if the Aristocrat knew martial arts of some kind. Steven always struggled tremendously with agile enemies and this was another perfect example.

The Aristocrat deflected or dodged every sword strike Steven launched at him. That wasn't the end either. It used its first skill. "Is that... Flowstep?" Kimmi asked. It looked like it was. The air around the aristocrat started to move in mysterious ways, as if to help move his limbs and body.

Steven was outmatched with the sudden transformation. It took everything he had to keep the blows from connecting with him. "Just focus on using your shield!" I yelled. He had been prioritizing attacking over his main role: defense.

The kicks and spear stabs and pole swipes were raining down on him repeatedly. Steven was constantly backing away and couldn't even attack anymore. "The shield is also a weapon!" I yelled again.

That seemed to have gotten through to him. Steven was a big guy and the shield even bigger. He stopped deflecting and trying to stab or slash out, and instead just rammed into the Aristocrat. The resulting impact was as expected.

The Aristocrat went flying backwards to the ground before flipping back up. A realization struck Steven, something so simple he should have known earlier. The shield was just as much a weapon as the sword was.

It didn't matter how agile the enemy was if all he needed to do was deflect their attacks. When the situation presented itself, he didn't try to stab out but instead pushed with his shield or charged if the opportunity arose. It was hard to miss with such a big weapon.

The exchange lasted around thirty seconds before we were confident that we could defeat the Aristocrat. It excelled in melee combat and speed, something Kimmi also excelled in. Aaron made the call to take him down, "Let's go!" He yelled.

Kimmi activated Flowstep and then blended in with the surroundings. The two together were a deadly combination that left almost any enemy surprised. No matter how fast, there was always a moment the enemy would be vulnerable. Kimmi grasped that timing perfectly.

She appeared just behind the Aristocrat after Steven sent it off balance with a sudden charge. Her daggers dug directly into the two back legs and ripped down, rending muscle and flesh. Its mobility was stripped from it.

I had opted to cast Glacial Spike at the same time. The icy pillar rose from beneath the two feet of the mob and stabbed directly towards the crotch area. It managed to penetrate a few inches into flesh. The Aristocrat let out a horrible scream.

Something more miraculous was how effective the freezing was. The chill turned the goopy slime into ice at record pace and very quickly the entire bottom half of our opponent was entombed. It couldn't move at all.

Aaron channeled sharpshooting and aimed perfectly. The bow twanged and a gust of wind raced past my face accompanied by a little explosion. The head of the aristocrat popped like a melon. The fight was over just like that.

This... this was a real encounter. This was how I wanted fights to be. Every action was measured and important and most of all, the EXP was great. The single aristocrat gave 5,000 EXP total. It was an absolutely absurd amount.

Steven seemed to learn a valuable lesson as well. He had known he was the tank from the moment he joined the party, but not in the literal sense of the word. Deep down Steven considered himself a damage dealer that could also tank.

Seeing how easily the foe went down without so much as a single stab or slash on his part really gave him the confidence needed to accept holding aggro was the only job he needed to accomplish. There was also the added fact of being in less pain if he focused more on defense.

```
CURRENT EXP: 17560/69000        LEVEL: 29
         MAGE          FORMIDABLE
     HP: 2032/2032  MP: 588/719
              STR: 21
              AGI: 21
              DEX: 35
             VIT: 30 +2
             INT: 54 +14
           AVAILABLE: 3
```

A single Aristocrat provided the same EXP as five elite versions of the Slithereen Anomaly. It was a staggering amount. Another ten kills and I would nearly be level 30. My blood was racing thinking about my class change.

We managed to make it one more block and battled one more Aristocrat before night rolled around. The Perseverance party regrouped with us and we sheltered inside an abandoned shop. Steven prepared dinner just outside the front door.

It seemed Steven was about to wow another party with his cooking skills. The moldy and moist smell that pervaded the city was replaced by a buttery garlic scent. Whatever he was frying up caused everyone's mouth to water.

"Ahem," Rachel came over. "What's for dinner?"

"Oh, did you guys not prepare meals beforehand?" Isabelle asked jokingly.

"We did… but, wouldn't it be a shame if we didn't share? It'll be a good way to promote trust between our parties." Rachel said.

I couldn't help but start laughing. You would think Steven had put some sort of drug in his meals to get this sort of reaction. It was more that Adventurers didn't have the time and leisure to eat meals like this.

"Let's share then." Aaron said. A simple gesture like this won over their favor completely. Everyone fell asleep with a full and satisfied stomach that night.

Chapter 29: Timing is Everything

I woke the next morning with Steven cuddled up against me. Except this time it wasn't just to find Aaron laughing at me. Rachel was standing right next to him laughing along. I was at a complete loss as to how this scenario ended up happening every time there was company.

It was the type of embarrassment that I couldn't reprimand him for. Steven didn't even realize he was doing it and I didn't want to make him aware of the issue. I just forgot about it, while pulling out my arm from under his body.

The morning was cool and a fog hovered over the cobble stone roadways. It was especially dark in the morning; what little sun there was in the sky was blocked by the dense canopy. I stretched while moving my legs outside.

There was another pillar here with hieroglyphs on it. This one was in much better shape than the others and I studied it carefully. The scene was similar as before.

The images showed a happily family enjoying their lives together. There was vivid color and obvious cheer in the scenes. Suddenly, the panels grew dark and a new figure was added.

A tall human was shrouded in darkness and presented a stark contrast to the colorful depiction of the family. The scenery grew stormy and tumultuous; the figure was depicted ominously. Over the course of several scenes, the happy family grew sad.

The dark figure took center stage with his hands raised. There was a staff drawn in his hands. He was speaking to the sky and yet I didn't understand the words written there. It was a spell he was chanting.

Suddenly the happy family was no more and instead they had been replaced by creatures looking exactly like the Slithereen Anomaly. Eventually, the depictions were just of the Slithereen Anomaly in the city. None of the remaining depictions were cheerful and instead all were dreary and dark.

"Find something interesting?" A voice asked from behind. I turned around and could see it was a member of the Perseverance party. It was Roderick, their tank.

"Ah, I'm not sure. Do you know anything about this?" I asked.

"We did see these on our first trip, but none were as detailed as this one." He started to look over it carefully.

"What is this place?"

"The information we could find was not easy to come by, but we can safely say it's an ancient city, near a thousand years old at least."

"What about the Hidden Jungle?" I asked.

"Records show the Hidden Jungle came about in the last one thousand years or so. But there are older manuscripts in which it never gets mentioned."

"Any word of what happened to the people living here?"

"That's the interesting part. There were no records of what happened to them. They just disappeared. Slithereen Anomaly sightings go as far back as eight-hundred-and-fifty years."

This was starting to sound eerily similar to Marcus's experience. I was leaning towards the theory that a world-changing event took place around a thousand years ago. One crucial question had to be: who was the man depicted wielding a staff?

"Roderick, we're heading out," Rachel said.

"Ah, I gotta go. Nice talking with you."

"Ditto." I turned my attention back towards the pillar and continued to look over every panel and drawing. No matter how I looked I couldn't see the staff-wielding man as anything other than the villain. At the very least he wasn't viewed favorably by the people who made this pillar.

It wasn't even five minutes later that my own party walked out. We were in for a long day ahead of us. I couldn't help but glance back at the pillar one more time before we left. There was some secret buried here.

Every encounter was fresh and new and that made it incredibly exciting. My blood was coursing through me each time we encountered an Aristocrat. It really gave me an appreciation of the diversity of skills and their strengths and weaknesses.

There were skills of all kinds and sorts, ones that I couldn't have imagined in my wildest dreams. They weren't common, and that made them especially interesting.

For example, one Aristocrat we encountered had the ability to enlarge objects. His spear grew longer, grew thicker, even his limbs stretched and enlarged in odd ways. It was absolutely fascinating.

Another seemed to have some control over space. It was able to stab his spear in empty space and the tip would vanish into the void only to stab out from a random location. The variety of spells they cast was uncountable and some of them left me green with envy.

All the tricky and confusing spells we saw paled in comparison to the most dangerous one we encountered. It was mid-day and I was about two Aristocrats away from my next level.

The Aristocrat ahead of us didn't look anything out of the ordinary at all. We engaged carefully as normal and Steven tested the waters. At first it seemed like it was a skill-less Aristocrat. While rare, we had encountered one just like it already.

Everyone went in for their respective attacks. We had developed a pattern over many encounters. Kimmi would always strike from the shadows after Steven mounted the pressure. Aaron and I would follow up with Disable and then finish the fight at a huge advantage.

This time, Kimmi came in for her attack and the most insane thing happened. My perspective suddenly shifted completely. Steven was somehow standing in front of me and then I felt a stabbing pain in my back.

Energy Shield flickered but it wasn't enough to stop Kimmi's two daggers digging into my flesh.

> **YOU HAVE BEEN AFFECTED BY POISON.**

"What?" Steven couldn't believe what he was seeing. I was also incredibly confused.

"I'm sorry… I didn't mean it." Kimmi seemed to lose her composure as she pulled the daggers from my now bleeding back.

I was in utter shock, so much that the pain in my back didn't bother me as much as it might have. The Aristocrat, however, was smirking like a devil and was conveniently standing exactly where I had been before…

It had switched places with me instantly. That wasn't the biggest problem though. The biggest problem was how incredibly close it was to Isabelle. Luckily, Isabelle reacted fast enough and cast Divine Shield on herself.

Still, the Aristocrat's spear lunged out and first cracked the barrier before stabbing directly into her gut. She fell a few feet back and Aaron managed to catch her. It took her longer than usual to heal herself.

Kimmi's hadn't been messing around at all when she had attacked. At 832 HP from 2032, I had lost 1200 HP so far and my total was constantly dropping every time the poison ticked. That huge amount of damage had been inflicted even after Energy Shield had absorbed a large chunk of it.

We didn't have any poison cleansing ability and I took out an expensive Panacea before consuming it. To be honest, I was still in shock. That transfer had been instantaneous, I had felt nothing. My viewpoint had suddenly changed and that was it.

Aaron dragged Isabelle away and she managed to heal her own wound. Her face was contorted in pain and covered in sweat. A heal for me came a bit later. In the meantime, Steven had rushed to stand in front of the Aristocrat and block its path to the rest of us.

"What should we do?" Steven called out. He sounded very unsure of himself, perhaps he was afraid of stabbing his sword out only to see Aaron, or Isabelle, or Kimmi, or me on the point of it instead of the mob.

In the same way, her arms at her side, Kimmi's body language showed that the battle hunger she normally felt was dampened as well. We were at a standstill. "I... don't know." Aaron said. "It must have a cool down of some kind though, or a requirement to cast the ability."

"It probably needs to see its target to swap positions with it," I shouted. "Can we blind it?"

"I think I can do it..." Kimmi mumbled. She cast Flowstep and then blended away into the surroundings. A moment later she leapt with her daggers out from behind the Aristocrat. The split second before she would connect with its head, she stopped her piercing motion and pulled her punch regardless. It was just as well that she trusted her intuition. Aaron appeared where the Aristocrat was standing as the two swapped positions, but he wasn't even touched by Kimmi's blades.

Perhaps having anticipated the swap, Isabelle succeeded in casting another Divine Shield and barely managed to dodge the impending spear strike.

Kimmi evidently didn't want to let this moment go to waste and rushed towards the enemy. I was hesitant to cast any ability at all and instead counted in my head. If the swapping ability was its only card, this encounter would be manageable.

The Aristocrat in front of us seemed to be well-versed in melee combat and managed to deflect every dagger attack thrown its way. Suddenly it swapped again and the victim was Steven this time. This happened right after I finished counting to 7.

"The cool down on the ability might be seven seconds," I called out. I took the gamble and cast Glacial Spike directly below the Aristocrat's feet. The ice jutted from the floor and barely scraped the side of its leg as it sprang to the side. The Aristocrat's awareness was amazing. It seemed nothing in the battle escaped his eyes.

I paid even more attention for the next swap and realized it was specially targeting Isabelle. Perhaps it had recognized she was the healer and aimed to eliminate her first? That was the smartest choice if it wanted to survive at all.

The only way to be sure about how it was targeting was to test it myself, so I rushed to Isabelle's side. Kimmi and Steven were going all out in the seven second window cool down and had managed to deal a small amount of damage.

There was a fresh gash on the arm of the Aristocrat, nothing serious though. The fight would be long and arduous if I couldn't figure out a way of interrupting these displacements. I looked across at the mob to see a facial expression that was anything but worried: instead it had a shit-eating grin across its face. "Stupid humans," it seemed to say.

A moment later I found myself swapped out with the Aristocrat. Kimmi managed to pull her daggers back in time but Steven couldn't do the same with his shield. It slammed directly into me and sent me rolling backwards. Once again, the Aristocrat stabbed at Isabelle.

I was counting from the moment the swap happened. "Isabelle come to me!" I yelled. And she rushed to my side in a heartbeat. Steven and Kimmi once again had the monster pinned in place.

"Be ready to heal me just in case…" I said. This would hurt like a bitch if it didn't work out. In fact, it was suicidal.

"Right." She didn't ask questions and put a Divine Shield on me. That made me feel a bit better.

Four… five… six… just as my count hit 6 I began casting Glacial Spike. Not at the Aristocrat, but instead directly at my feet. The channel had never felt so long and I feared for my private parts. If this didn't work I might be sterile my entire life.

Seven, almost immediately on my count, the Aristocrat looked in my direction. Glacial Spike was released at my feet and I knew the sharp ice was about to come jutting through the floor. My vision changed and our positions swapped.

A Glacial Spike burst from below the Aristocrat and stabbed him right in the ass. It wasn't the penetrating power I was looking for, but the special effect. The frost from Glacial Spike charged up its body and towards its waist. The entire bottom half of its torso was entombed in ice.

"Kill it now!" I yelled. And no one missed a beat. Aaron casted Sharpshooting and Kimmi used Penetrate. An Arrow cut through the air before tearing a gaping hole through the Aristocrat's cheeks. Kimmi's two daggers sliced horizontally and chopped the head off for good measure.

"Did… you cast Glacial Spike under yourself?" Isabelle asked. She hadn't been sure what I had planned but put it together quite quickly.

"Yeah…" I wiped the sweat from my brow. My body was drenched.

"What would have happened if that failed?" Steven asked.

"I really don't want to think about it." I confessed. My precious parts would have been split in half and frozen to ice cubes.

Isabelle suddenly fell to the ground and we all rushed over to her. Her cheeks were red and she was sweating profusely, "Is it the poison?" I asked. She had been the focus of all the Aristocrats attacks and had been stabbed by it.

"No… it's just that wasn't fun at all," she confessed. Normally she was safe in the back and spent time healing others. Being wounded wasn't part of her job description. Despite understanding that, I felt the fight had been an intense challenge, one I relished.

It was hard to get that adrenaline rush, that thrill, without being pushed to the edge. There was a point during the fight where I had been on the cusp of disaster, but seeing the outcome… I didn't regret the fight at all. I'm not sure I would have regretted it if my Glacial Spike had gone wrong even. Grinding mobs and working out strategies to cope with new challenges was addictive.

"Careful!" Rachel yelled. It was now the third day and we were working well together, although for the last twenty-four hours the two groups had been forced to form a raid to continue. The monsters in the inner section of the city were more dangerous than we had expected.

SLITHEREEN BARON***	LEVEL: 37	BEAST
	WATER	
HP: 119634		MP: 225
	STR: 54	
	AGI: 30	
	DEX: 37	
	VIT: 75	
	INT: 25	
A LORD AMONG THE SLITHEREEN. IT HOLDS CONSIDERABLE WEALTH AND POWER.		

The problem wasn't the high stats on the Slithereen: if they had been standard three-star elites, then our group could perhaps have managed unaided. The same issue came back time and time again. The wide variety of skill usage we encountered made each of them volatile and mysterious.

It was possible to continue in separate groups, but the risk wasn't worth the reward at all. We never knew when we might come upon a Slithereen that had a lethal one-shot ability. That risk was compounded even further as their level went up drastically.

This was truly not a place for us to be leveling at currently. The EXP was astonishing though, even in a ten-person raid. I had gained a level the previous day and was already halfway through to 31. We were leveling at record pace.

It was the morning of the third day and we could now see a towering castle in the distance that was no doubt the city center. "It should be there, whatever we're looking for." Rachel said.

The entire Perseverance party was nearly 35; if they were surprised to see our lower levels they didn't hold them against us. We were only now hitting level 30 and barely on the cusp of level 31. In the grand scheme of things, 31 wasn't a lot, but if several of us could achieve that next goal, it would account for a bit right now.

Rachel took the head as leader of the raid and Roderick was the main tank, with Steven as backup.

I now had six stat points waiting to be spent, but still couldn't decide on where to put them. There was no struggle in any particular area for me. The main achievements I was lacking were more skills.

```
CURRENT EXP: 54745/99000        LEVEL: 30
              MAGE          FORMIDABLE
        HP: 2062/2062  MP: 575/728
                    STR: 21
                    AGI: 21
                    DEX: 35
                   VIT: 30 +2
                   INT: 54 +14
                 AVAILABLE: 6
```

The EXP required for my next level had jumped considerably. It seemed that every tenth level was a milestone. The levels from 31-40 would be around the same, but once you needed to go from 40 to 41 it would spike up again. It wasn't quite a 50% increase in EXP requirement, but it was close.

We were fortunate that Rachel and her party were so reliable. They had a solution for every situation we encountered and they never lost their composure. Not only that, their healer, Donivan, knew the skill *Barrier*. It added an extra layer of protection that made us casters feel that much safer.

"At the rate we're going we shouldn't be more than half a day from the center," Rachel said.

"Is there any information on a boss or anything of the sort?"

"There's nothing written anywhere, but we should assume there's a boss waiting for us."

This made sense as the elites were gradually gaining ranks and stars as we got closer. Would we be fighting a monarch at the end?

"Still no sign of the Tyrant group," observed Aaron.

"Maybe they gave up," I suggested hopefully.

Rachel looked serious. "No, they definitely didn't give up. I didn't say this before but they're not in the Tyrant guild for no reason. Their skills are very real, we need to be careful."

And suddenly I felt we needed to be more concerned with them stabbing us in the back than any future monster encounter.

Despite it being a 70-30 split. Rachel was incredibly fair with the loot that dropped. We went 50/50 on items obtained on the way and I finally managed to replace my original staff. It was almost hard to put it away and I looked over the stats and remembered how powerful they had once seemed:

STAFF OF RECHARGE: INT +1, RECOVER 2 MP EVERY 15 MINUTES.

The *Staff of Recharge* had served me well since my first week in this mess. It definitely wasn't anything spectacular any more. I had a soft spot for it none the less. I put it into my inventory where it would always stay as a memento. The replacement rod was far better:

> ### Mana Pulsing Rod***: INT +10, VIT +3, DEX +5
> An ordinary looking rod filled with an extraordinary amount of Mana. You can feel it pulsing in your hand.

Any regret I had about taking the Lunar Brooch instead of the Moonlit Staff from the Lunar Ape disappeared immediately. While the *Mana Pulsing Rod* didn't have any MP regeneration, the stats were insane. Laura eyed it greedily but didn't put up a fuss when it came my way. My INT was now 77 and my MP 612.

The description of the rod was accurate. Despite having incredible stats, it didn't look like anything out of the ordinary. It was just a rod with two red stripes wrapped around it at the top. Without holding it you couldn't tell it was anything more than an ordinary stick. I was thankful for this as I didn't want to stand out any more than I needed to.

"After we get out of here, I want to learn Gemcutting," Isabelle suddenly announced.

"Why Gemcutting?" wondered Steven and I was thinking the same.

"It's the cheapest to start off with and it pays well." Everything always led back to Zeny.

"I think I'll try my hand at Alchemy." Steven had obviously been thinking of getting a trade skill too. "The mixing of materials reminds me of cooking."

"Good, you can make me some sick potions then," I chimed in. I hadn't really thought about what I would train myself in. Enchanting was definitely the most logical for my class and you could learn the basics for cheap as well. The issue was the scaling price climbed rapidly. Without a guild to support you it was unlikely you could accumulate the wealth to go very far with that skill.

"You know if you guys are looking to join a guild, the Perseverance guild is recruiting. I can put in a good word for you," Rachel had been listening in.

"Actually, this one here wants to start a guild," Aaron suddenly placed a hand on my shoulder.

"How ambitious of you." Rachel teased, "It's quite expensive these days and definitely isn't getting any cheaper. If you change your minds you're always welcome with Perseverance."

Our enemies grew stronger but the amount of them thinned. We were finding ourselves with a lot of free time in between battles. Although the three-star elites were dangerous, they couldn't hold up to a ten-person raid. As soon as we discovered their particular skill and found an answer to it, we dissected them completely.

Looking at Roderick calmly walking ahead and alerting us of any danger made me think of Bryan and Lady Briele all those many months ago. When we were just level twenty, they felt a world apart from us, an insurmountable gap. Now we were raiding with people just a few levels below them.

I had no doubt Bryan and Lady Briele had been continuously leveling up since then. I also regretted not finding out more about them. They were surely in a guild? I just never got the name. If we had never met them would we be here right now? Or still back on Eastrath slaying goblins and sewer rats?

"There's nothing here," Rachel said. We had been walking several blocks without seeing any more Slithereen Barons. Instead, there was nothing but empty streets. We were so incredibly close to the city-center at this point.

We picked up the pace immediately. The prospect that we could reach our destination several hours faster than I had anticipated because of the lack of monsters was exciting.

The entire party was jogging through the streets and cutting through alleys. Eventually we came upon the base of the tall building that had dominated the horizon for so long. For some reason it reminded me greatly of Egester. The heart of the city was a sole, tall building surrounded by smaller shops and residences.

The biggest difference with Egester was the lack of people moving about. This was a ghost town without even a single Slithereen in sight. I scanned around cautiously and didn't dare move forward.

The center building was as tall as a castle and could definitely hold a large number of people. A certain royal majesty exuded from it. It wasn't only remarkable because it appeared to be at the dead center of the town, the craftsmanship was a level above everything we'd seen so far.

"This should be it... right?" wondered Aaron.

"Let's see if we can get inside," Rachel said. There were no guards waiting outside for us. There was nothing indicating it was unsafe besides our own intuition. We walked forward one step at a time and up those steps until the doors were directly in front of us.

Roderick pushed the door open and was the first inside. He made sure there was nothing waiting to pop out and attack us before allowing us entry. "Come in," he said at last.

The inside of this castle was actually maintained to a livable state. The floors were polished and a beautiful red rug lay on the floor and stretched into the distance. There were many side doors in the hallway, but the obvious path was straight ahead.

Whatever we were looking for was through the double doors down the hall. There were paintings on the walls on both sides: depicting landscapes, indoor scenes, and portraits of kings.

The last several dozen paintings were all Slithereen. Funnily enough, the Slithereen looked almost exactly the same. There were fifteen pictures of 'different' Slithereen, although I couldn't tell the difference between any of them.

Eventually those pictures turned to human paintings. "I recognize that man," Marcus suddenly spoke inside my head. It was the first painting just after the Slithereen.

"He visited Andino once before. I'm sure of it." That was interesting. The events of Marcus's time were about a thousand years ago, which perhaps was the same time something happened to the Slithereen civilization.

"Isn't this kind of creepy?" Laura asked.

"Yeah…" I wondered whether to say anything more, but what did I really understand?

"So, would that be the throne room just in front of us?" Steven asked. He was walking just behind Roderick, ready as the backup tank. They stood before a large double door with golden door handles. There had to be something extraordinary located behind it.

"Is everyone ready?" Roderick asked. There was no way to know what would happen once the doors opened. Could it be a trap? A boss fight? Nothing? We didn't know.

"I'm ready," Aaron said and we all followed suit.

Rachel nodded. "Open it."

And so Roderick pushed with both hands and opened the majestic doors.

The room inside was a long and open hall with pillars lining each side. There were banners hanging off every pillar and beautiful stained-glass windows between the pillars. The sun shone in and covered the entire room in a rainbow hue.

We followed the red carpet with our eyes to the far end. A throne above a set of steps rested there. Two menacing statues of Slithereen waited on either side of the seat, as if guards protecting their king. The entire room felt magnificent.

The scene would have been perfect, except for one thing. The Slithereen sitting on the throne ruined the entire picture for me. He looked just like an ugly frog perched there waiting. There was no difference between his expression and that of the dozen kings in the portraits outside and he blinked. He was alive.

"Take it slow," Roderick warned. We spread out and started walking forward. The entire hall was empty and only the sound of our footsteps made any noise. The king resting on his chair watched us curiously.

Was it possible he wasn't hostile? I couldn't be sure. None of us could be sure. We only knew from what Rachel said that something waited for us here: a treasure, an artifact, something worth our time and effort.

We were merely twenty feet away from the throne when the Slithereen stood up. There was a staff in his hand and majesty in his eyes. He had the air of a ruler in his motion and pose. I started to wonder how each Slithereen king was chosen, was it by inheritance? Or simply by being the strongest of them?

Roderick stopped and we halted in our tracks. The king in front of us slowly raised his staff off the ground. A smile covered his face. It was mischievous and taunting, like a child looking at fun toys to play with.

The staff started to slowly fall to the floor. Was it slow? I actually couldn't tell. My body grew heavy just as it landed. Before I knew it, I was kneeling.

The pressure on my entire body forcing me down was so strong I was on my knees, my head pressed against the ground. It took everything I had to turn my head and see the others were in the same situation as me.

Every single one of us was being forcefully pushed to the ground: prostrate in front of the king of this ancient city. This was levels above what the Lunar Ape was capable of. It was night and day.

A look of utter despair spread across Isabelle's face. I felt the same. I felt as if I was going to go crazy from fear and anxiety, but that wasn't all. In the back of my mind, deep in my chest, my heart was pounding.

Something was welling up inside of me. I felt hopeless and yet my heart was racing. My adrenaline was pumping. My skin was tingling in excitement. I felt high. This was what it meant to be alive.

The pressure abated as swiftly as it came. Despite that, the short moment in a helpless condition had shocked everyone. Even Rachel's face was drenched with sweat and uncertainty.

"Do we retreat?" I wondered aloud.

Could we retreat?

I had seen the expression on the king's face once before, that day we ran from the Forest Troll; I remembered it very clearly. It was the face a cat had while playing with a mouse.

"No, it doesn't make sense for him to be this strong! I refuse to believe he can maintain that pressure for long," Rachel said.

"Was it a bluff then!?" Steven asked.

"I can't be sure," Rachel said.

"So, you're just guessing!" Isabelle wasn't having any of it. There was a decision to be made. Rachel had originally thought they could handle this encounter on their own. Her confidence had dwindled. Everyone's confidence must have.

It looked like we were on the cusp of backing out. I couldn't blame anyone here. That feeling from before... we were fish on a chopping block. Just tilting my head to look around had been almost impossible. Our deaths had felt certain at that moment.

"Fifty-fifty!" Rachel suddenly yelled. "Don't leave... fight with us. We'll split the loot fifty-fifty." She had made the decision to make that offer quite quickly. The fact the other group weren't running gave me a measure of confidence. In their eyes the battle wasn't impossible.

Each of us looked to Aaron to make the decision. In times like these he was always the most logical. He shrugged, "If not this time... then when? We can't always run away. Let's push ourselves to the limit, and past that."

He wasn't wrong. Lady Briele had told me once before... the injuries in Egester were light for a boss encounter. Heck, three people died back on the Arturii farms. Death was a regular occurrence on Yetera. If we didn't fight now to grow stronger, then when would we?

"Wait," I said. I looked at the king standing there and cast *Inspect*.

```
KING SLITHEREEN XVII***    LEVEL: 38         BEAST
                    WATER
    HP: 603111                    MP: 999
                    STR: 60
                    AGI: 30
                    DEX: 45
                    VIT: 99
                    INT: 40
    THE CURRENT RULER OF THE SLITHEREEN KINGDOM——A
              THRONE CLAIMED BY BLOODSHED.
```

I reported the king's level, hit points, and the alarming number of MP. All the same, "I think it's possible, if he can't keep forcing us down."

"Play your life!" Aaron yelled. It was a video game term that meant focus on surviving before anything else. Roderick charged in immediately after and the combat began. Funnily enough, he was a head taller than the Slithereen king.

The two exchanged dozens of blows in a matter of moments. The outcome of that clash wasn't good. It was clear at a glance the king's ability in melee combat was strong. He made it look effortless, and Roderick was no challenge for him at all.

It felt like the king was trying to prove a point to everyone here: that we were nothing but playthings in his eyes. There was an arrogance engrained in his bones. It was only after his next attack did he prove we were being toyed with.

Roderick suddenly stopped moving completely. His sword was half swung, his shield lightly lowered. His face was red and strained. I realized what it was: that terrifying pressure, that terrifying gravity. It locked him in place.

He was completely gripped in it and couldn't move a single finger. That wasn't all though. Roderick was lifted in the air and then flung into a nearby pillar like a beanbag. It was effortless and there was nothing Roderick could do at all to respond.

He collided with a crash and tumbling concrete. Collapsed stonework from the pillar now rained down over him. Roderick sat on his ass, with debris falling down his shoulders and chest. He was still conscious but definitely shaken up.

"He might be a king in one-on-one combat, but this is ten verses one!" Rachel suddenly yelled. There was some truth in her statement. It was the only thing keeping our morale from crumbling like the pillar. We all still had something to offer.

The king did something unexpected after flinging Roderick. He sat back down on his throne calmly and confidently. Suddenly, the two statues on either side of him stirred. This was more like what I had been expecting.

A king should have guards and these were those guards. The two statues fully separated from the wall and came to life. They each held a colossal sword that was nearly as tall as they were.

They stepped down from the throne platform and faced us. Their swords now hoisted over the shoulder and ready to chop in half any foe brave enough to come up.

Roderick scrambled to his feet and Steven rushed up as well. They needed to take care of one of these each. It was time for all of us to join in on the battle.

"Deal with Steven's first!" Roderick yelled.

All of our firepower was focused into the left statue. Even Steven, who was arguably the biggest among all of us here, looked like a dwarf in comparison to the statue. Every strike of its sword caused sparks to fly on his door-like shield.

I started off with *Cremation*, arguably my most damaging offensive ability in my arsenal. The pillar of fire rose through the throne room floor and engulfed the lower half of the statue's body. There was no reaction from the guard at all.

The stone simply grew discolored. It darkened as if being burnt but there was no other visible sign of damage. It didn't even become more brittle or weak under the heat. Aaron's arrows bounced off repeatedly.

I tried casting *Glacial Spike* next. It simply shattered on contact with the statue and while a bit of frost managed to travel up the left leg, it didn't make it past the knee. There was no real effect there either. The statues were just that big.

Not only were they large, they were also strong. Steven was constantly being pushed back with every attack. The sword came down like a sledgehammer, over and over.

It was such an overbearing assault that he couldn't do anything but defend with his shield. Both of his hands gripped the shield and held it out above him. One hand wouldn't be enough to deal with these raining blows.

Occasionally he countered with a bash towards the guard's thigh, but to no avail. The statues were sturdy and made of an unknown material. So far, I couldn't identify any weakness at all. They had no fear, no pain, nothing.

I tried to cast *Inspect* but received no prompt at all. Did that mean these were simply inanimate objects? They were being fully controlled by the king? If they were puppets then what would 'defeating' them accomplish?

The answer came quickly after my thought. Rachel nocked an arrow that burned bright hot. The tip looked almost like an explosive. Regardless, it was a spell I had never heard of or seen before. It took five seconds to charge and the room grew hot.

There was a flash of light as the arrow crossed my vision before connecting with the statue's upper arm. The entire arm from the elbow downwards exploded and that large sword collapsed to the ground with it. The clang of metal echoed through the room.

For a moment we saw hope, and then despair. The sword arm simply floated over to the sword and grasped it before reattaching itself to the body. The king was forcefully bringing the statue back together with this strange power.

"These aren't alive!" I shouted. "They're just puppets. He will reassemble them no matter how many times we defeat them." That much was obvious already. Our only solution was to attack the king directly.

The problem was what to do about these two powerful guards while we turned on the king? Neither Steven nor Roderick could deal with both at the same time. They didn't even have aggro. The king was just humoring us, which meant he could make his guardians attack whomever he pleased.

"We should focus on trying to control them." Aaron said. "How many CC abilities do you have?" He was addressing Rachel.

"We have three!" she said.

"Two here."

"Let's at least try then." And that's what we did. The only CC ability I truly had was *Shackle*. Something I had been neglecting for so long. That spell had seemed like a cheat ability when I first received it, but the requirements were harsh.

For this past while, I had felt that if I couldn't restrict an elite with *Shackle*, then what was the point of it? Normal monsters were a joke while in a five-person party, we never needed crowd control. But here... perhaps the statues were ranked as normal.

This was our only shot besides outright ignoring them and entering a free for all battle in which our tanks wouldn't last long. I looked at the left statue and started to cast *Shackle*. Aaron pulled back his bow and let an *Ensnaring Arrow* fly.

A moment later those spikes I hadn't seen in so long jutted from the floor. The golden chain quickly went from spike to spike and completely enclosed the statue. It didn't stop there as Aaron's arrow connected a moment later.

He shot another, and then another. Vines began pouring out from all over its body and tightened around its limbs. They went all the way to the floor. It wasn't just us though. Rachel, Laura, and Donivan all cast their own CC abilities as well.

Angels started to sing as they lowered themselves from the ceiling before dropping a Holy veil directly on top of the statue. The cloth fell to the floor and then squeezed tightly. The angels laughed mischievously like little children.

Golden arrows fell nonstop onto the statue and held it down to the ground with golden ropes. This was no doubt Rachel's ability. Finally, it was Laura's turn and the one I was most interested in.

I wasn't disappointed. A dark and angry cloud floated above the statue before shooting out bolts of lightning. It wasn't to attack but instead created a net of lightning that dropped on the statue and gripped it tightly.

All of our CC together proved considerable and the smirk on the king's face changed to one of anger. I could even see a bit of anxiety in his eyes. No doubt he was doing his best to move the statue but couldn't break it free. There was a limit to his strength: there was hope.

Regardless, he didn't like us raining on his parade. The statue Roderick was dealing with suddenly ignored him and instead rushed to the restrained statue. It swung down with all its might and crashed against the many barriers holding its partner in place.

My heart was in my chest. If everything we had just done had been for nothing it would be a considerable blow to our morale, and probably indicate how this encounter was going to end: with our deaths. Time seemed to slow as I waited for the end result.

The spells holding the statue in place shook as if battered by a heavy storm but held firm. They didn't break and the guard inside remained trapped in place. I decided to cast another *Shackle* for good measure and then turned my attention to the free statue.

"Steven get up there!" Roderick yelled. He was referring to the king. "Everyone focus on the king!" And it was the right choice.

Roderick managed to contend with that second statue for a moment before it stopped its assault on the stuck statue completely. The king needed to use it to lessen the pressure on himself, and so he sent the free statue out towards us, the casters.

The guard ignored Roderick and started to rush in my direction.

"We just have to deal with it!" I said. There was no aggro control we could use for the statue, it was going to do whatever the king pleased.

The king must have decided we were a considerable threat and that if he stopped us from casting, dealing with Steven, Kimmi and Joshua in melee range would prove that much easier. I could see Donivan hesitating, I knew what he was thinking already.

He wanted to cast *Barrier*, but that would be foolish. It would stand up to only one blow. "Don't waste it." I said. He hesitated and then nodded with a half-smile. It was the right choice. Unfortunately, the statue was already upon me.

Chapter 30: Endgame

"Call yourself a king? You're just an ugly ass frog!" I suddenly yelled, even though such an outburst wasn't my usual style. There was no other way I could think of to salvage this situation. The king was a prideful and arrogant being. My blatant disrespect was sure to be a provocation.

The statue didn't have any aggro, but if I pissed off the king enough? Well, I was sure he wanted to smash me to a pulp right now. That showed clearly with the statue rushing in my direction.

I made a split-second decision and used my 6 available stat points. I put every single one into STR bringing it up to 27.

Maybe this was foolish, but I truly didn't want to die. There was currently a sword twice the size of my body coming directly for my head. My hands gripped either side of the **Mana Pulsing Rod***** and prayed. *Please don't break in half...*

Part of the prayer was for the rod and part of it was for me. I raised the magic item above my head just as the sword came down and the two collided. Fortunately, this ordinary-looking rod proved to be anything but.

It didn't even bend at all, which definitely wasn't good for my arms. The impact of the blow caused my bones to crack. An electrifying shock of pain traveled through my body and all I could do was fall backwards.

I had managed to deflect the blow a fraction, but that was enough. It was all I needed to move out of the way and the sword came crashing down. Part of the floor exploded.

The king was definitely not pleased and could hardly believe his eyes. I was a mage. Where was the bloody pulpy body smeared on the floor?

Despite not having cut me at all, the blow took over 500 HP and 180 MP, leaving me on 1627 HP and 319 MP. That was just from the impact alone. In fact, it wasn't only the king who couldn't believe their eyes. Donivan appeared stunned in place. It took him a moment before he healed me.

I just needed to hold out a little longer. Once the pain had gone from my arms, I chugged an MP potion and started to run away. The king had it out for me now. He had a point to prove: he wanted my head.

The fact I had survived such a blow wasn't a surprise to the members of my party but must have been a shock to Rachel's. Little did they know I was like a clam. It was normal for me to take a hefty beating without kicking the bucket. "Just focus on the boss!" I yelled when I saw that both Rachel and Joshua turned as if to come assist me. "The best thing you can do for me is hurt the frog!" I shouted even more loudly, hoping it would be even more provocative.

Damn, he really didn't like being called a frog. Even while contesting with the constant blows, arrows and spells coming his way, the king Slithereen couldn't help but send evil glances in my direction. That giant statue pulled the sword embedded into the ground up and hoisted it back on his shoulder.

It was time to run for my life and run I did. I rushed behind a pillar just as the sword came swinging towards my back. The pillar exploded and debris shot everywhere. Half of the column was missing now, having crumbled to the floor.

The statue struggled to pull the sword out this time, "haha, d-u-m-b-a-s-s f-r-o-g king!" I yelled. Perhaps I sounded happy and carefree but the truth was I was terrified. One mistake and I'd be in two pieces.

I continued to run around the pillar fully expecting the statue to continue following. The statue didn't do that though, it didn't even pick up the sword that was now half embedded into the pillar. To my surprise, the statue was sitting there lifelessly, in the same pose as when we entered originally.

My attention shifted towards the throne and the king was still contending with our fervent melee assault and the occasional spell and arrow.

His staff twirled around and little froggy kicks and punches were sent out left and right. It would be hard to convince anyone at this moment he was losing. If he wasn't struggling then what was the reason for the statue's inactivity?

The only thing that had changed since the start of the battle was the statue's position. In its chase it had ended up behind a pillar: whether because it had moved too great a distance to be controlled, or whether it mattered that the king no longer had line of sight, something had brought it to a halt. Clearly, that was good news for us.

And yet there was a downside. The frog king started to push back the melee group. That was even with Roderick joining. Free from giving some of his attention to control the statue he had become that much more deadly.

Steven suddenly flew up into the air and rocketed into a wall. Kimmi crossed her arms defensively as a slimy frog foot kicked into

407

her chest and sent her tumbling back. Roderick managed to brace both hands on his shield and only slid a few inches back from a punch.

I realized after I moved from behind the pillar I had made a mistake. When a monster was this intelligent, trash talking was a form of aggro. The frog king suddenly hopped into the air and rushed directly in my direction.

For some reason I just couldn't keep my mouth shut, "What do you call that? Lily pad leap?" I managed to move slightly to the right and avoid the incoming foot. Just as I thought I had escaped a beating he spun in the air and kicked me with the other foot.

My staff was raised and stopped the blow from hitting me directly in the head. Regardless, the force was enough to send me hurling backwards, landing near the stained-glass windows. It was impossible to keep myself on my feet and I ended up on my back.

Unfortunately, he wasn't done with me. I could see him rushing in my direction. His froggy foot was coming down directly for my head. There was nothing I could to do but try and roll away.

Expecting a foot landing on the back of my head, I kept rolling until I could see why it had not. Kimmi had used blend and ended up directly behind the boss.

She had managed to stab both of her daggers deep into the king's back. Immediately after that she was sent flying with a kick. Her daggers still remained buried deep in his flesh. One of them was poisonous too. Every little bit of damage counted.

I didn't miss this opportunity and sent out a Ball Lightning from the floor. The frog king was definitely pissed off. He was dead set on sending me to hell and no amount of rolling would save me.

Time seemed to slow down. This was it; this was the end. At least that's what I thought. I couldn't be more grateful at this moment that Donivan had heeded my advice earlier. A barrier formed around me that stopped the foot from crushing me to a pulp.

It was a brief second of relief, but that was enough for Steven and Roderick to rush back over. Joshua joined in the dog pile and even Kimmi pulled out two inferior backup daggers. This was an absolute shit show of a fight.

I suddenly wanted to crack a joke but opted against it. Without that barrier to save me I would have smashed to death by the stamp of that powerful foot, no doubt. I scurried to my feet and increased the distance between me and the froggy.

This was a moment in which to catch my breath. I was so caught up in the fight I hadn't realized there was a lot of blood in my mouth. The rich taste of iron was everywhere. The impact of the statue's blow from earlier was more serious than I thought.

Even my legs and hands were shaking. My body was terrified, and yet I was aware of the fact that this battle made me feel more alive. This world made me a junkie for danger.

"Keep it up!" Roderick yelled. Our constant assault had put the Slithereen King in a bad position. The two daggers in his back had opened wounds that dripped blood all the way to his calves. The skin around the poisonous dagger had turned black.

There were gashes around the king's arms and legs. One of his eyes was closed: the work of Aaron and his sharpshooting ability. We had him completely surrounded in a circle.

Occasionally he would send someone flying into a pillar, but those successful blows were few and far between. It was taking all he had to just contend with the attacks coming his way. A far cry from the freedom and majesty he displayed before.

Eventually, the Slithereen king couldn't even resist the more obvious attacks coming directly at him. He rushed to move out of a Cremation pillar of flame only to be stabbed directly through the throat by Roderick's blade. Rachel nocked another explosive arrow and shot it directly into his chest.

We thought that would do it, but this frog motherfucker was resilient as hell. His entire body was dropping and there was now a gaping wound in his chest. Kimmi and Joshua went in for a dual attack: two swords, two daggers.

Both of the frog king's legs disappeared as his body plopped to the floor. He didn't even have two feet to stand on anymore. He suddenly reached out his hand and grasped at Steven's throat. A last-ditch effort.

Steven suddenly went stiff and I had a bad feeling. His face was turning red and he wasn't moving. "Stab out his remaining eye!" I yelled. Roderick didn't hesitate at all and dug the sword deep into his skull.

It was obvious when the pressure on Steven faded away and he sucked in a humungous breath of air. "My God, I thought he was gonna' squeeze me to death." Steven fell on his ass. Everyone was thoroughly exhausted and ceased to attack as the boss lay bleeding on the floor.

The frog king continued to struggle and twitch for several minutes before fully coming to a stop. He had no legs and no eyes that entire duration. There was no way for him to target anyone with his special ability.

Besides the loot appearing above his corpse, there was also something else. It was a ghost similar to the one from Specter Andino. It wasn't a frog but a human male. I felt Marcus stir suddenly.

"Thank you for saving us. This curse has lasted for far too long," he said. Those were his only words before the ghost disappeared. I noted that he had used the term 'us'.

The little bits of information I had gathered on our trip slowly melded together. The city people had disappeared because… they all turned to frog people. They were cursed nearly a 1000 years ago. The culprit? The staff-wielding villain in their depictions, whoever that was.

Rachel couldn't even wait to see what loot had dropped before rushing over to the throne looking for more rewards. Her hands darted across the walls pulling on every nook and cranny. She was about to give up when her foot stepped on an unsteady tile in the corner.

There was a click and then rumbling. There was a hidden doorway in the wall that slowly opened up for us. The loot wasn't going anywhere and we all excitedly rushed through the doorway.

It was a small room with scattered riches along the floor. There was a glass case in the center with a single item. It was a piece of rock, or maybe a gemstone of some kind? I couldn't tell at all what it was and Aaron just shrugged when I caught his eye.

The only indication that the quartz-like rock might be valuable was that it had been placed in this glass case dead center in the secret treasure room of the dungeon boss. The rest of the valuable gems and jewelry had nowhere to rest but the floor. Rachel and her party didn't hesitate to start scooping up the riches and storing them away.

Aaron looked wide-eyed for a moment in shock and I probably did too. Rachel seemed to realize how the entire situation looked to us. She couldn't find the words to hide her embarrassment.

"Ahem, we'll be splitting this all fifty-fifty as agreed. We have to have it appraised." She suddenly punched the glass and grabbed the stone from inside, "For now you can hold on this." She tossed it into the air.

The crystal flew right towards Aaron who caught it like a hot potato. He fumbled it in his hands a few times before tossing it to me. "You hold it."

"Why me?"

"You're as indestructible as a cockroach, so I think it's best in your hands." I couldn't think of a retort. He was right. So far at least, I had found a way out of trouble.

Once the room was fully swept of gems we returned to the corpse of the king to split the loot fairly.

> ### Assassin's Mask: AGI +5, STR +5, DEX +2
> #### A mask worn over the face. It does wonders for hiding your identity.

First up was an amazing item for either Kimmi or Aaron. Arguably, it was more benefit for Kimmi though. We left the decision up to the two of them. Aaron relinquished it and Kimmi gladly put it on.

> ### Cursed Brooch: All stats -1, MP Regeneration +10
> #### every fifteen minutes.
> #### A once-beautiful broach now swirling with cursed energy.

Isabelle was completely scared of donning a cursed item. It took a while before we convinced her to eventually accept the broach as being worth the trade off in the stat loss. She reluctantly put it on.

"What's next for you all?" Rachel asked when this was all dealt with.

Aaron shrugged. "Well, we wanted to at least hit thirty-five and try our hands at changing class."

"You'll be sticking around the Hidden Jungle then? We were planning to leave immediately after this," she said. "If that's your plan then you'll have to come to the Perseverance guild after you are done to collect your share." I hadn't known her for long but I trusted her words.

"We can travel together a ways," Aaron said. "Seems like we'll have to find a new leveling place though, our original plan was to head back into the canopy and slay more Slithereen." That was the sole downside to ending the curse. There probably weren't any Slithereen left.

"It's good we stick together for now anyway. The Tyrant party is still missing. I refuse to believe they just gave up," Rachel said. And so we started our trek back together.

I hadn't quite given up hope that the Slithereen people would still be around. They were an easy and accessible source of EXP, and lots of it. Unfortunately, even after spending the rest of the day walking back through the city, we didn't encounter a single one.

All of a sudden, I could suddenly feel Marcus acting funny. It was a weird emotion he was feeling, something like trepidation? *Spit it out.*

"Ahh, you're in a good mood after that victory right?"

Depends…

"Right. Well I just wanted to tell you that I recovered a bit of my power." And that instantly set me on alert. This son of a bitch was up to no good, that's why he was so quiet. "Don't get the wrong idea all the sudden."

413

I gave him a nasty little face in my mind. No doubt he could see it.

"This is exactly why I didn't want to say anything. I just need a favor from you."

First you need to explain yourself.

"You remember that miraculous fruit you ate? Well, long story short it seemed to really help me a lot as a spirit." That was a reasonable explanation and one which gave me some peace of mind. His recovery was a result of my actions and not a deceit on his part.

Fine, what do you want me to do?

"I just need you to find me a body I can possess." He said it like it was so simple. Like there were bodies just lying around everywhere waiting to be possessed.

That doesn't sound easy... or right. You're not trying to get me to kill anyone, are you?

He didn't respond for thirty seconds, which led me to believe that was his original goal. I didn't know how I felt about that at all. "You don't have to kill anyone. But if you come across someone that has died recently... maybe you'll think of me." He spoke sweetly. If that was all it took to free myself of this possession, I guessed it wasn't a bad compromise.

"Oh, come on. I'm not that bad," Marcus complained. I didn't bother to even retort.

Isabelle suddenly turned to me, "You know, I was thinking. When we go back to Arturii you can search for your brother... Ajax is a unique name... right?"

She had brought up a subject I had been neglecting, mostly out of fear. She wasn't wrong that my brother's name was unusual. My biggest fear in setting about a proper search was that I would not find anyone called Ajax. The changing circumstances had pushed

414

my priorities elsewhere. If my brother was still alive and somehow registered, then he was doing okay for himself. At least that's what I chose to believe.

"Yeah, maybe. What about you?"

"I think... I'll try as well." I realized that in part her response had depended upon my reaction.

"Great, then I'd be happy for us to do it together." That's what she wanted to hear, and I wasn't against the idea.

There was no obstacle ahead of us at all and our pace was stellar. We reached the city exit in record time. "Seems the Tyrant group really did give up," Aaron said. The relief was visible in everyone's body language.

We walked out into the jungle for maybe fifteen minutes when there was a commotion behind us. The sound of cracking branches and underbrush being pushed echoed through the jungle.

We all turned around to witness two members of the Tyrant party. Their faces were showing fear and something wasn't quite right.

"Careful!" Rachel yelled. We didn't know what they were up to at all.

I had the feeling that this wasn't an ambush, and I was right. They did their best to run around us and past us. We were totally stumped at their behavior. That was until we saw what stirred such a reaction.

It was a prehistoric looking creature: a giant bird with bright and colorful feathers. The size and color of the monster wasn't what caught my attention the most. It was the eyes, the two reptilian eyes that left me feeling chilled to the bone.

I couldn't even say anything before alarm bells were ringing inside of me. Marcus was going absolutely nuts. He was afraid, deathly afraid. So much so that he couldn't even speak the words to me.

The beast came rushing through the trees in a hurry, only to stop and stare at us curiously. It tilted its head to the side and then turned it an odd angle while sizing us up. I didn't know what the monster was at all.

No one was moving. I suddenly heard Rachel start to mumble, there were tears mixed in her voice, "Why… why is this here?" She hadn't reacted in such a way, even when facing the Slithereen King.

It seemed everyone in their party knew what it was. "Everyone should run…" Roderick said. His voice was calm, way calmer than it should be in this situation.

"Wait, what are you planning to do?"

"Isn't it obvious? Please just take care of my little brother." Only then did I realize he was resolved to die.

"Don't… we can all run together."

"We both know that's not possible…"

Is the situation really that bad? I still couldn't feel anything. Their reactions were creepier than the beast in front of us.

"Everyone should run on my charge… Get as far away as possible." My hands started to get clammy and I came to a sudden realization. This thing… this thing in front of us was the cause for all those disappearing parties and deaths in the region.

Roderick suddenly charged forward and everyone in their party started to run past me in the opposite direction with tears in their eyes. I almost felt disdain for their actions. How could they abandon a comrade like that so readily?

The thought didn't even finish in my brain when I understood why they ran. Roderick made it halfway towards the beast before its figure completely blurred. All that was left standing there were two legs. Roderick's upper torso was completely bitten off and swallowed up. The bite was so fast I couldn't see it.

Everyone started bolting like the wind. We ended up chasing after the Tyrant party in the distance. I could hear the galloping footsteps behind us. "Fuck! Why is it chasing us?" I yelled.

"Don't look back!" Aaron ordered. This was real life or death, even more serious than the Forest Troll. This thing behind us was clearly an anomaly. It shouldn't be here and it was strong enough to wipe out every group it encountered.

The fact that the highest level characters in the realm hadn't yet managed to killed this monster worried me to no end. Marcus who had been quiet up until this time suddenly spoke, "Joseph, I will give you a chance..." he said. "You can't miss that chance no matter what."

What are you going to do?

"I die if you die!" He was more aggravated than I'd ever heard. "So the only chance I have is if you survive. I don't know if I'll ever wake up again, but please, don't miss that chance." It felt like he was saying goodbye. That whatever he was about to do would silence him in my mind.

This was what I wanted right? Why did it feel so sour? Was it because we weren't parting on our own terms, but someone else's? This didn't sit right with me but I couldn't argue, not right now.

We had always made it out as a team before. As I pounded through the bushes with my friends either side of me I told myself: this would be no different, right? I kept repeating that thought in my head. We were going to be fine. I wanted to tell Marcus that as well, but the view in front distracted me.

It was the two Tyrant party members. They were just a ways ahead of us and constantly looking back. We were all running for our lives together. And yet they were despicable scum. One of them turned back and nocked an arrow.

It took my brain a second to realize he wasn't aiming at the beast behind us... he was aiming at us. He shot out without hesitation and I heard Steven let out a cry.

"Don't look back!" Aaron yelled again.

I heard a tumble and another groan from Steven before I heard a crunch. My hair stood on end and I didn't dare to look back. Tears were already coming out of my eyes. Hatred was burning in my heart.

The Tyrant member in front of us looked back again and loosed another arrow. This time it was Aaron who let out a cry in pain. His voice didn't falter at all, "Don't look back!" He yelled. "Keep going!"

The Tyrant member turned around again, "Don't you do it again you motherfucker!" I yelled. But there was nothing I could do. He didn't heed my yelling. I was yelling like a fool anyway. Snot was coming out of my nose and tears were pouring from my eyes.

My breathing was heavy and rough. The arrow was loosed and this time it hit Isabelle. She cried out and my heart ached. Aaron didn't call out this time... he wasn't there to call out. I wanted to turn around and fight, but I was afraid... *I'm a coward...*

There was another crunch and it was only mine and Kimmi's steps remaining. The Tyrant member turned around again and loosed another arrow, this time in Kimmi's direction. She managed to side step the arrow but tumbled in the process.

I couldn't bear to be the only one, and so I looked back. I immediately regretted it. The beast chasing us didn't give her a single glance… it just slammed its three clawed foot directly onto her body. That was the crunching I heard every time.

I wanted to vomit right then and there. Just like that, I was alone. "Keep running you idiot!" Marcus yelled. And so I did. I couldn't do anything if I died. One day I could get revenge… I turned that into my fuel.

The Tyrant guild? *One day I'll destroy you.* I started to repeat that in my head over and over again. They were the cause of everything. They dragged it here. They cut us down like weeds to slow its chase.

By now my legs felt like lead. They were heavy and hard to lift. My breathing was erratic and my throat burned hot. I couldn't swallow from the lack of liquid in my throat.

The Tyrant group in front had pulled ahead a decent distance, head down, the archer didn't bother nocking any more arrows in my direction.

I couldn't go on any longer. This was the end.

"Don't resist!" Marcus said. "Trust me and don't resist." I felt like I couldn't resist if I wanted to. My legs gave out and I stumbled to the floor. I managed to turn over and see the beast rushing at me.

I was expecting it to crush me like a twig, just like it had done with everyone else. Marcus's voice echoed in my head once again, "Don't resist…" There was an odd feeling that washed over me. Every ounce of MP in my body was expelled, along with something else.

There was a moment of confusion in those reptilian eyes. It was brief, but enough for it to miss my body. The monster stepped over me and as if it had forgotten my existence continued chasing that Tyrant party into the distance.

What did you do? There was no response. *Hey Marcus, what did you just do?* I asked again. He was really gone, and I was really alone. I was broken, and worst of all I couldn't move.

My body wouldn't move in the slightest, I didn't have an ounce of strength. That wasn't the problem though. I literally couldn't move at all. Whatever Marcus had done had left me completely immobilized.

I lay there with nothing but my own tortured thoughts. I suddenly missed Marcus dearly. At least I would have had someone to talk to. Hours passed like years and I could feel the jungle life crawling over my body.

There were suddenly voices, "Here's another one!" someone yelled. I realized they were talking about me, and yet I couldn't even respond. I sensed several people gathered around me and looked me over. They started to fumble around me, "Why can't we loot this one?" They asked.

One of them suddenly gave me a kick and then smacked my face, "Well he's definitely dead."

"Whatever, let's get out of here before someone blames us for it." And they walked off just like that.

I didn't know what time it was when I could finally move my body. It was deep in the night. I barely managed to stand and light a fireball. The pathway of carnage was clear in my view.

If I just walk this way... Then I would end up seeing sights I definitely didn't want to see. My mind drifted back to that first journey from Elesham. That wagon of bodies we burned to keep the insects from devouring them.

I knew what my friends would have wanted, but could my heart take it? I truly felt dead inside, and so I started to walk. Kimmi was the last to fall and the first I found. She was face down in the jungle mud. There was a pool of blood around her.

I was scared to turn her over and look at what I'd see. I couldn't bring myself to do it. Instead I placed my hand on her shoulder. Her body was cold, there wasn't the least bit of warmth. The jungle insects were already crawling around her body. Within a day there wouldn't be anything left.

Once again, I didn't have anything to dig a grave, nor did I have the strength to move a body. I cast Cremation, my eyes glazed over as I looked through the flame towards nothingness.

It was Isabelle I came upon next. This time I couldn't stand the sight. My stomach erupted and I vomited until there was nothing but acid left. The arrow was embedded into her chest. Her entire upper body was smashed from the beast's claw. I cast Cremation and for the first time in my life I said a prayer.

Seeing Aaron resolved me even further. One day, no matter how long it took. I would destroy the Tyrant's guild. The arrow was embedded above his collar bone, and yet he had been strong enough to tell us to keep going.

Worst of all, the beast claw had only smashed one of his legs. The claw coming down on him didn't kill him. It was the arrow wound. That Tyrant member had murdered him.

"You know…I considered you as my brother." I started to ramble. "Isn't that weird? You were a good person and I know your mom would be proud of you." I couldn't hold the tears back. "What am I supposed to do without you? It's not the same anymore. I thought leveling and getting stronger was enough to make me happy… Fuck," I blew my nose hard. "I was wrong." I sat there in silence for several minutes before I worked up the courage to cast Cremation.

By the time I reached Steven I was angry at the world. How could something so unfair, so utterly bullshit happen like this? That sadness I was holding turned to hatred. For the first time in my life I felt scared of my own actions. If the person who shot those arrows was in front of me right now… I would kill him no question.

> **CONGRATULATIONS! YOU QUALIFY FOR YOUR CLASS ADVANCEMENT.**

Is this some sort of sick joke? I wanted to scream at the top of my lungs. This is what I wanted, wasn't it? It didn't mean shit to me right now. I started to walk and didn't look back.

Level Up publishing specializes in LitRPG and GameLit books. If you have enjoyed *The RPG Apocalypse 2* you might be interested in our other titles, which can be found at www.levelup.pub/books

To join our mailing list for news about forthcoming books and opportunities to be an ARC reader, just fill in the form on that page.

You can also find us on:
Facebook @LUPublishing
Twitter @LevelUpPub

… and by searching for Level Up WhatsApp group

A big thanks to all our Beta readers who read this book and particularly Len M. for his thoughtful and precise feedback.